Next of Kin

JOHN BOYNE

BLACK SWAN

TRANSWORLD PUBLISHERS
61–63 Uxbridge Road, London W5 5SA
A Random House Group Company
www.transworldbooks.co.uk

NEXT OF KIN
A BLACK SWAN BOOK: 9780552777407

First published in Great Britain in 2006 by Penguin Books Ltd
Black Swan edition published 2012

A CIP catalogue record for this book is available from the British Library.

Addresses for Random House Group Ltd companies outside the UK can be found at: www.randomhouse.co.uk

The Random House Group Ltd Reg. No. 954009

The Random House Group Limited supports the Forest Stewardship Council (FSC®), the leading international forest-certification organization. Our books carrying the FSC label are printed on FSC® paper. FSC is the only forest-certification scheme endorsed by the leading environmental organizations, including Greenpeace. Our paper-procurement policy can be found at www.randomhouse.co.uk/environment

Typeset in 11/14.5pt Giovanni Book by Falcon Oast Graphic Art Ltd.
Printed and bound by Clays Ltd, Elcograf S.p.A.

4 6 8 10 9 7 5

For Con

Acknowledgements

For all their suggestions and comments during the writing of this book, many thanks to my agent Simon Trewin and my editor, Beverley Cousins. Thanks also to Claire Gill and Zoe Pagnamenta at PFD, and all the team at Penguin.

By John Boyne

NOVELS
The Thief of Time
The Congress of Rough Riders
Crippen
Next of Kin
Mutiny on the Bounty
The House of Special Purpose
The Absolutist
This House Is Haunted
A History of Loneliness
The Heart's Invisible Furies
A Ladder to the Sky

NOVELS FOR YOUNGER READERS
The Boy in the Striped Pyjamas
Noah Barleywater Runs Away
The Terrible Thing That Happened to Barnaby Brocket
Stay Where You Are and then Leave
The Boy at the Top of the Mountain

SHORT STORIES
Beneath the Earth

Chapter 1

1

MANY YEARS EARLIER, when he was a lieutenant in the army stationed just outside Paris, Charles Richards had come across a young recruit, a boy of about eighteen years of age, sitting alone on his bunk in the mess with his head held in his hands, weeping silently. After a brief interrogation it turned out that the boy missed his family and home and had never wanted to join the army in the first place but had been forced into it by his ex-serviceman father. The thought of another early morning call, followed by a twenty-mile march over rough terrain, all the time ducking enemy fire, had reduced him to an emotional wreck.

'Stand up,' said Richards, gesturing the boy to his feet with his finger as he took off the heavy leather gloves he was wearing. The boy stood. 'What's your name, boy?' he asked.

'William Lacey, sir' he replied, wiping his eyes

and unable to look the officer directly in the face. 'Bill.'

Richard had then gripped his glove tightly by the fingers and slapped the boy about the face with it twice, once on the left cheek and once on the right, leaving a sudden explosion of red bursting out on his otherwise pale skin. 'Soldiers,' he said to the stunned conscript, 'do not cry. Ever.'

It was a matter of some astonishment to him then that sitting here in the eighth row of a private chapel in Westminster Abbey on a bright June morning in 1936, he discovered a spring of tears itching to break forth from behind his own eyes as Owen Montignac reached the conclusion of the eulogy for his late uncle, Peter, a man who Richards had never particularly liked, a fellow he in fact considered to be little more than a rogue and a charlatan. He had attended many funerals in his life and now, at his advanced age, he was depressed to note how the intervals between them were becoming shorter and shorter. Still, he had never heard a son express his feelings for a departed pater, let alone listened to a nephew convey his sorrow for a lost uncle, in quite so eloquent and moving terms as Owen Montignac just had.

'Damn fine,' he muttered under his breath as Montignac returned to the front pew where Richards could still make out the shock of his extraordinary white hair in the distance. He casually pressed the tip of an index finger to the corner of his eyes to stem any approaching tide. 'Damn fine speech.'

Later, with the scent of freshly turned soil assaulting his senses, he stood only a few feet away from the open grave as the pallbearers walked slowly towards its hungry mouth and found his eyes searching the crowd of gathered mourners for Montignac's face, an unexpected urge overcoming him that he would like to attract the younger man's attention and offer silent support.

It was only as the coffin was lowered down into the ground that he realized that his quarry was acting as a pallbearer himself. The sight of the handsome young man easing his uncle's body into the damp earth was almost too much for him and he had to swallow hard and cough to maintain his composure. He reached out to his right and took his wife's hand in his own. The surprise of her husband's rare touch, coupled with the shock of the gentle, deliberate affectionate squeeze, was almost too much for Katherine Richards, who steadied herself before turning to smile at him.

Fifteen feet away and always prone to emotional displays, Margaret Richmond held a handkerchief to her face and allowed the contents of her streaming eyes to pour into it, her body shaking with grief as her employer of twenty-eight years was laid to rest. Beside her, Peter's daughter Stella stood erect and tranquil, her pale face unstreaked by tears. She seemed pinched, however, as if the effort that she was making not to cry was almost enough to make her faint instead.

It was to the side of these two women, his former

nanny and his cousin, that Owen Montignac automatically stepped while the priest delivered the final benediction, and it was Stella's arm that he took when it was over and that moment arrived when the mourners began to shuffle awkwardly away, wondering whether they should return to their cars or stand in the graveyard until the immediate family had left, staring at the names and dates on the gravestones and looking out for those who died tragically young or ruthlessly old.

The rain which had held off from the moment they had entered the church appeared suddenly and thunderously now and within a few minutes the graveyard was empty, save for the two groundskeepers who appeared as if by magic from behind some nearby trees and began to fill in the grave while they chatted to each other about the weekend's football results and smoked hand-rolled cigarettes.

The air in the drawing room had begun to grow thick with cigar smoke.

About sixty people had been invited back to Leyville, the main Montignac residence where Owen, Stella and Andrew had grown up together, and they were steadily working their way around the ground floor of the formal east wing, which was the designated area for the wake. Although the family had not been so crass as to place a velvet rope across the staircase, or to lock the door which opened on to the corridor towards the more convivial west wing where the dining room and the china were kept and where Peter Montignac had sat in his ancient armchair night after night straining to listen to the wireless, it was understood by all that there were only a few rooms into which it was appropriate to wander.

Almost all the guests had homes like this and almost all had buried parents or spouses and were able to recognize the etiquette of the moment.

A group of five dark-suited men, three of whom wore extravagant and competitive moustaches, stood underneath the portrait of a dead Montignac who had lived two hundred and fifty years earlier, the same one who had begun the purchase of land around London which had led to his family's almost incomparable wealth. By coincidence their five wives were gathered on a small settee and two armchairs on the other side of the room, beside the portrait of the dead Montignac's wife, of whom little was known and even less was cared. The family, after all, traced their lineage through the male line, the Williams, the Henrys and the Edmunds, and concerned themselves little with that helpful breed of mothers who assisted their regeneration.

The servants glided through the room, their presence felt but their persons ignored; young girls bringing tea to the ladies, their male counterparts refreshing whiskies for the men. Wine was introduced.

'I'm not saying it wasn't moving,' muttered one guest to another as they stood by the fireplace. 'I just don't care for it as a new fad, that's all.'

'Well I'm not so sure it is a fad,' replied his

companion. 'It's been happening for thousands of years. Think of Mark Antony extolling the virtues of Caesar on the steps of the Capitol.'

'Yes, but hadn't he just murdered him?'

'No, Mark Antony wasn't one of the conspirators. He came to collect the body on the steps of the Senate after the deed was done. You recall, *Mark Antony who, though he had no hand in his death, shall receive the benefit of his dying*. Somewhat appropriate under the circumstances, don't you think?'

A third joined them, a Mrs Peters who always enjoyed creating controversy by strolling up to groups of men and insisted on taking part in their conversation. (Her husband had died some years earlier and her brother lived in India so there was no one to control her; besides, she had money.) 'What are you men gossiping about?' she asked, liberating a glass of whisky from a tray as a young servant glided past her.

'Alfie says it's a fad,' said the second man. 'I say not.'

'What's a fad?'

'This new business. At funerals.'

'Well what do you mean?' asked Mrs Peters. 'I'm not following you.'

'You know,' said the man. 'Eulogies and the like. Pretty speeches. Children lamenting their parents and what not.'

'Or uncles,' said Mrs Peters. 'If it's Owen's speech you're referring to.'

'Or uncles,' admitted Alfie. 'The whole emotional mess of it. I'm against it, that's all.'

'Oh for heaven's sake,' said Mrs Peters, frustrated at the idiocy of men, how they had no problem fighting wars but baulked at the idea of fighting back a few tears. 'It's a funeral after all. If a boy can't show a little emotion at his father's funeral, well when can he?'

'Yes, but Peter wasn't Owen's father, was he?' pointed out Alfie.

'No, but he was the closest thing he had to one.'

'Perfectly understandable, if you ask me,' said the second man.

'I'm not criticizing him,' said Alfie quickly, anxious not to be seen to be immune to the grief of a wealthy young man such as Owen Montignac who, after all, had just inherited one of the largest estates in England and was therefore not a man to alienate oneself from. 'I feel for the fellow, I really do. I just don't see why he needs to put on such a show for the whole world to see, that's all. Keep it inside, that's for the best. Nobody likes to see such a naked parade of emotions on display.'

'What a miserable childhood you must have had,' said Mrs Peters with a smile.

'Well I fail to see what relevance that has to anything,' said Alfie, standing to his full height, suspecting an insult.

'Isn't it outrageous the way the servants automatically hand tea to the ladies and whisky to the men?' asked Mrs Peters, already bored by the conversation and desiring a change of subject to something a little more risqué. 'I intend to leave strict instructions in my will that everyone must get merry at my funeral and do embarrassing things, boys and girls alike. If they don't, then I'll come back to haunt them and see how they like that.'

2

The journey from Tavistock Square to the Old Bailey normally took no more than an hour on foot and throughout his career Mr Justice Roderick Bentley KC had always preferred to leave his Rolls Royce at home if it was a pleasant morning. The walk offered him a chance to think about the case he was working on at the time, to deliberate privately without the interference of barristers, solicitors, bailiffs or defendants; the exercise was good for him too, he reasoned, as a man of fifty-two could take no chances with his health. His own father had died of a heart attack at that exact age and with that in mind Roderick had approached his most recent birthday with fatalistic dread.

Today there was a distinct chill in the air and there had been rain a little earlier in the morning but even if the sun had been splitting the trees and the sky had been a perfect blue there was no question in his mind that he would have asked Leonard to bring the car around. Those damned newspaper men had been camped on his doorstep since Thursday evening after he had brought proceedings to a close and he had felt like a prisoner in his own home throughout Friday, Saturday and Sunday.

He had woken up early that morning, around half past four, and had lain in bed for another half-hour or so, willing sleep to return and allow him a little more respite before the trials of the day began but as daylight started to break through the curtains he knew it was pointless. Quietly, so as not to disturb his sleeping wife, Jane, he slipped out of bed and padded downstairs to the kitchen to make a pot of tea. It was too early for the post to be delivered yet but he noticed that yesterday's edition of *The Sunday Times* was still sitting on the table. He reached for it eagerly but Jane had already completed the crosswords – both simple and cryptic – so he set it aside again with a sigh.

Typically, he had avoided the newspapers throughout the weekend. From his earliest days as a pupil at the chambers of Sir Max Rice KC, through to his years as a junior barrister scrapping for cases around the various law courts of London and the outer circuit, where he was permitted only to sit in the second row of the courtroom, whispering advice into the ear of his learned leader, and subsequently with his famous work as an advocate before he had taken silk, Roderick had avoided reading newspaper articles which referred to cases he was working on at the time. Since his appointment as a high court judge, presiding over some of the most infamous crimes of the day, this policy had become a matter of honour to him.

And considering the extraordinary amount of attention his current trial had received, he didn't dare turn from the crossword to the front page for he knew how the headline would read; he declined to scan the editorials for he could not allow his decision to be influenced by public opinion or editors' points of view or, worse still, readers' letters. Instead, he threw the paper in the bin and made for his bath.

An hour or so later, shortly before six-thirty in the morning, he sat in his study rereading the opinion he had written over the weekend, the cause of this morning's sleeplessness, which he would be delivering at eleven o'clock precisely to an assembled court and representatives of the fourth estate. He read it thoroughly, checked and double-checked a few points of law against his impressive legal library for fear of error, and then sat back with a sigh, contemplating the fact that he was forced to make this decision at all.

To be a judge, he decided, was an odd profession. To have it within one's gift to grant liberty or deny it was a curious authority; to allow a man to continue his life or pronounce that it should be ended, a humbling power.

There were sounds of stirring in the house now and he guessed that Sophie, the downstairs maid, and Nell, the cook, would be up soon. His wife, Jane, never rose before nine o'clock and generally preferred to take breakfast in bed and he had an urge to deliver it to her himself that morning. She had been particularly thoughtful over the course of this difficult weekend, suggesting a quick overnight break to a hotel in the Lake District for Saturday night in order to take his mind off his worries. It would offer him a peaceful environment in which to write his opinions, she reasoned, but he'd declined the offer, imagining how it would look to the newspapers if he was holidaying in Wordsworth country while a man's life was at stake.

'Who cares what they say?' she'd asked him, noticing how much greyer her husband had grown over recent months since this terrible trial had begun. 'Who cares what they write about you anyway?'

'I care,' Roderick had replied with a sad smile and a shrug. 'If they criticise me, they criticize the judiciary as a whole and I can't allow myself to be responsible for that. Perhaps we'll go away next weekend, when this dreadful business is behind us. Anyway, they'd only follow us up there and we'd have no fun at all.'

There were footsteps on the stairs now and he could hear the voices of Sophie and Nell as they descended together from the small flat they shared in the attic of the house. They were keeping their conversation low as they assumed that both the master and the mistress were still asleep upstairs and he felt an uncommon urge to follow them into the kitchen and join in whatever trivial conversation they might be having, but of course it was out of the question. They would think he'd lost his reason entirely and if that got into the hands of the reporters, well it was anyone's guess how the whole business would resolve itself then. There were spies everywhere and no one except his wife could be trusted; he'd learned that over recent months.

Two framed photographs sat on either side of his desk and he looked at them tenderly. The first was of Jane, taken two years earlier on the occasion of her fortieth birthday party. She had barely changed in all the years he'd known her and even in that picture she could have passed for a woman ten or twelve years her junior. She was as strikingly beautiful – and difficult – as she had been when they had first met, when he was a barrister in his late twenties and she a debutante ten years his junior, the daughter of an ageing colleague on the lookout for a potential husband and a comfortable lifestyle.

The second was of their son, Gareth, a picture taken the summer before when he'd gone sailing with a friend of his from Cambridge, a boy who'd been the cox in the boat race if Roderick remembered correctly, when they'd won by about four lengths. Gareth was grinning madly in the photograph, his arm wrapped around the other man's shoulders, his hair too long for a boy, his attitude too carefree for someone who had yet to settle down and find suitable employment. He'd been considerate over the previous few months, however, knowing the pressure that his father had been under. He'd made the odd supportive comment whenever he'd been around but that was a rare enough thing these days. Roderick found that he could go almost a full week at a time now without laying eyes on his son, who kept unusual and antisocial hours with his set, a group that seemed bent on achieving nothing else from their twenties other than the pursuit of hedonism and gaiety. Roderick knew that the boy kept out of his way so that they wouldn't have to finally engage in the conversation which would lead to his finding work; he had been neglectful as a father in this respect in recent times. That too would have to change after today.

It was all so different from when he had been that age. He'd always wanted to study the law but hadn't come from a particularly wealthy family so it was a struggle to see his studies through to their conclusion. Certainly, once he began to practice he had quickly made a name for himself as one of the brightest of the new men at the Bar, but then every day of his twenties had been put into building his reputation, achieving success in a variety of trials and impressing Sir Max, who hinted that he might head chambers himself one day in the distant future, long after Sir Max was dead of course, if he kept up his volume of cases and didn't allow distractions to enter his life. And publish of course. Publish or perish.

And distractions had been few and far between until the arrival of Jane, who had made him realize there was more to life than work; how it all meant nothing really, without love.

Now, all these years later, he was indeed head of

chambers and a wealthy and celebrated man; wealthy enough, it seemed to him, for his own son to assume that he was under no obligation to find a life or a career of his own when his father's bank account could support him forever. A twenty-three-year-old man needed a career, though, Roderick was sure of that. And weekly mentions in the social pages could not be considered as an alternative.

But what right had he, he thought, to debate how a young man should live his life? For after all, at the same moment that he sat there in his elegant home surrounded by luxury and symbols of his own success, debating the merits of how his son frittered away his time, another twenty-three-year-old man was no doubt awake in his prison cell, nervous and frightened at what the morning might bring, for in a few hours' time Mr Justice Roderick Bentley KC would be taking his seat in the courtroom and informing him whether he was to serve at His Majesty's pleasure in prison for the rest of his natural life or whether he would be taken away to another place until a time could be fixed for his execution, when he would hang from the neck until dead.

Had Roderick broken his cardinal rule and read *The Times* that morning he would have found that both twenty-three-year-old men were indeed mentioned, one on the front page, and one in an indirect fashion on the seventh page where matters of society and parties and engagements and social events were gossiped over and dissected with languid humour and tedious puns. Fortunately for his blood pressure, however, he would never see either.

The kettle began to whistle in the kitchen and Roderick snapped out of his thoughts and headed in that direction. He wanted tea, he wanted a very strong cup of tea.

3

'The problem is that one runs out of things to say. It seems so insincere to offer the same old condolences over and over.' This now from Mrs Sharon Rice, a widow who lived three miles east of Leyville with her son, a successful banker whose wife had left him in a scandal.

'But the alternative, my dear, is simply to ignore him and pretend that this is just another party,' replied Mrs Marjorie Redmond, looking around at the gathered guests in their dark and sombre attire and wondering what was the significance of wearing black to a funeral. It only succeeded in making people feel even more depressed than they already were.

'I very much doubt that Owen Montignac will be hosting any parties for a long time. I don't expect to see the inside of Leyville again this side of Christmas.'

'No, the young people never hold on to the old customs,' said Mrs Rice with the offended sniff of one who knew that her most vicious days were behind her.

'Of course he won't remember the parties that used to be held here. Back in the day, I mean.'

'But do we know that it is actually his?' asked Mrs Redmond, looking around cautiously and lowering her voice. 'After all, he was only the nephew. By rights everything should have gone to Andrew but it's always possible that Stella will be the beneficiary.'

'The Montignacs have always let their money inherit by the male lines,' replied Mrs Rice. 'And Peter Montignac was a stickler for tradition. Stella will be taken care of, I have no doubt about that, but no, I imagine Owen will be a very wealthy man when the will has been read.'

'Do you think that's what accounts for the eulogy?'

'My dear, I wanted to applaud him. There are far too many people who bottle their feelings up, if you ask me. And after all that Peter did for that boy, taking him in as he did despite what his father had done, of course he needed to say what he felt. I rather admire him, to tell you the truth.'

The men at the billiard table debated a separate issue back and forth, trusting that they would not be disturbed by anyone as they competed against each other. One of their number, a young man named Alexander Keys who had been to Eton with Montignac, had wanted to ask permission of their host before playing as he felt it might be considered inappropriate during a day of mourning, but their host was nowhere to be found and so they had begun anyway and agreed on only a small wager, just to keep things interesting.

'Keep that door closed,' suggested one.

'So we're agreed then?' asked Thomas Handel, lining up a shot. 'The man should be allowed to do as he pleases?'

Alexander snorted. 'I don't see that we are in agreement. You believe that it's no one's business but his own. I don't. There's such a thing as duty, you know.'

'Glad to hear you say that,' said an older man, leaning on his cue for support. 'Too many of you young fellows don't believe in it. Think you can do whatever you want and hang the consequences. Duty's exactly what it's all about. I'm with you, sir.'

'Nothing will come of it anyway,' said Thomas. 'You mark my words. There was that other woman, a year or two ago. What was her name again?'

'We believed in duty once,' said the older man, drifting off into contemplation and blurred memories.

'Seven-day wonder, she was. And yet the society gossips would have had us believe that an announcement was imminent.'

'If you ask me,' boomed the oldest man in the room, a retired Home Secretary whose voice carried more weight than anyone else's present and for whom everyone remained silent; even the shot on the black was held up for his pearl of wisdom. 'The whole thing is a lot of stuff and nonsense dreamed up by chaps like Beaverbrook for public titillation. He should simply do what his ancestors have been doing for years. Take a wife and keep a mistress, like any decent man would. An honest to goodness whore.'

'She's no oil painting, though, is she, sir?' asked Alexander, the whisper of a smile breaking out around the corners of his mouth.

'I am led to believe,' said the old man in a perfectly serious tone of voice, 'that love is blind.' He arched an eyebrow for this was a statement that he considered to be humorous and one that might outlive him and be replayed at his own funeral one day. 'And if that's true, then one can only assume that the king is in need of eyeglasses.'

'A seven-day wonder,' repeated another young man, shaking his head and laughing. 'I say, I rather like that.'

'Well that's what it will be, you mark my words. Next week it'll be some other floozy. Another man's wife, another man's daughter, another divorcée.'

'Where's the damn girl with the damn brandies?' asked the former Home Secretary, whose alcohol level was becoming dangerously low.

'I'm here, sir,' said the damn girl, all of nineteen years old, who had been standing right beside him, holding the damn tray all along.

Sir Denis Tandy stood alone in the library and ran his fingers appreciatively across the spines of a leather-bound collection of the complete Dickens. The room was in astonishing order, mahogany bookcases lining the walls, each one a dozen shelves high with ladders positioned to run along a top rail to help the ambitious reader stretch ever higher in their pursuit of knowledge and entertainment. The books were separated around the room into categories, with histories of London occupying almost six shelves of their own on a left-hand wall. In the centre of the room stood a heavy oak reading table with a couple of lamps at either end. Bound folio editions of maps were gathered underneath, some of which contained references to the many plots of land, whole streets at a time in fact, that were owned by the Montignac estate, their value enormous, their annual income difficult to calculate with any accuracy.

He had known Peter Montignac for almost forty years and had slowly moved from the position of lawyer to close friend and confidant in midlife, before returning to the role of functionary and employee during Peter's final years as the old man grew grouchy and despondent. It was the death of his only son, Andrew, that had brought this on; anyone with even a slight acquaintance with the older Montignac knew that he had never quite got over the tragedy. The boy's death in a shooting accident at the age of eighteen had never been explained to the father's satisfaction; Andrew had been an experienced marksman after all, Peter pointed out whenever the subject came up. And he knew how to clean a rifle. It was too ridiculous to suggest that he would have made such a fatal error.

The relationship between lawyer and client had been

fractious at times over the years but he knew that he would miss him nonetheless, his unpredictability and charm, the bursts of anger and venom he reserved for his enemies. Peter Montignac had been a man of extremes, capable of the fiercest loyalty to his friends but also willing to exact bitter revenge against those who had betrayed that friendship over the years. Sir Denis knew him well enough to feel pleased that he had managed, for the most part, to stay on the right side of him.

He had spent a half-hour since returning to Leyville from the funeral trying to locate Owen Montignac in order to arrange a suitable time for the reading of the will, but Peter's young nephew was nowhere to be found. He had certainly come back with the party – that unmistakable shock of white hair had been visible emerging from the first car to arrive back at the house – but he had failed to put in an appearance since then, which Sir Denis found to be in poor taste. Mourning was not allowed to surface when there was a house full of guests. And as for that eulogy he'd delivered; well, he could just imagine Peter turning in his grave at the thought of such stark emotion.

Sir Denis wanted to arrange the reading for as soon as possible and planned to fortify himself with several stiff brandies before it began as he could not imagine the interview having a happy conclusion. He glanced at his watch; if Montignac did not appear within the next half-hour, he decided he would speak to Stella instead; she had also kept a low profile throughout the day but was managing to contain her grief with a lot more dignity than her cousin had displayed. And this despite the fact that she was the man's natural child.

It was in this house that Peter and Sir Denis had drafted his original will many years before, leaving all his money and interests to his now late wife, Ann; it was here that it had been amended in favour of his son, Andrew, within hours of the boy's birth. It was here that allowances for Stella and his nephew, Owen, had been added as a codicil and here that the entire thing had had to be changed again after Andrew's death.

He didn't relish the idea of the reading, wondering how the relatives would react when they heard the news. Perhaps it wouldn't be unexpected, despite the Montignacs' sense of tradition; perhaps they might have predicted one final outburst of spontaneity from their late patriarch. It was difficult to know. Sir Denis couldn't even guess at their reaction for they were a strange family, given to unpredictability and capriciousness.

4

Roderick Bentley held the breakfast tray gingerly in his hands as he opened the door to the bedroom, trying his best not to surrender the carefully balanced contents to the carpet beneath him as he stepped inside. Jane was already awake but dozing and sat up in bed with a sleepy smile when she saw her husband appear.

'Darling,' she said. 'What a perfect servant you are.'

He smiled and stood before her like a well-trained butler while she arranged the pillows behind her back, and then settled the tray on her lap carefully.

'Breakfast, madam,' he announced in an affected voice and she smiled and took the lid off the plate to reveal a selection of scrambled eggs, bacon and sausages.

'Scrambled,' she said with a frown. 'I'll have to speak to Nell about that. They're very twenties, don't you think? But she refuses to poach for some unfathomable reason.'

'I'm afraid I'm not up to date with the current fashions in eggs,' said Roderick, settling himself in an armchair by the window as his wife buttered a slice of toast.

'You should have brought up another cup,' said Jane, pouring herself some tea. 'There's enough in the pot for two.'

'No, I've had enough tea,' he said, shaking his head. 'I've been up since five o'clock drinking the stuff and I'd better stop or I'll have to keep excusing myself from the bench this morning.'

'Five o'clock?' she asked, turning to look at him in surprise. 'Why on earth—?'

'I couldn't sleep,' he said. 'I'll be all right once today's over.'

'You do look tired,' said Jane after a pause, a suitably

sympathetic look crossing her face. 'Poor Roderick. It's really taken it out of you, hasn't it?'

A loud commotion muffled its way up to the window from the street below and Roderick stood up and parted the curtains slightly to see what was happening out there.

'Oh for heaven's sake,' he said in an exasperated tone.

'What?' asked Jane. 'What's going on?'

'It looks like two reporters are getting into a fight over who has the better position on the pavement and the others are cheering them on,' he said, closing the curtains again. 'Probably taking bets on it too, the bloody parasites. Perhaps they'll knock each other out.'

'The neighbours won't be sorry when this is all over,' said Jane. 'Catherine Jones called me yesterday to ask when you would be passing sentence.'

'And what did you tell her?'

'I said you never discuss your cases at home. That there's such a thing as judicial integrity. Well, I didn't put it in quite such stark terms, but I think she got the idea.'

'Good girl,' said Bentley, nodding his head in approval. 'You did right.'

'Roderick?'

'Yes?'

'You will be passing sentence today, though, won't you?'

Roderick thought about it and bit his upper lip,

breathing heavily through his nose as he did so. Jane had been right about one thing; he never did discuss his cases at home. But then he had been a judge for almost fifteen years and he had never presided over a case with quite so much notoriety and public interest as was attached to this one. Nor had he sat on the bench for one which had caused this level of difficulty and media intrusiveness for his family. Or his neighbours. He decided that on this occasion, and on this occasion alone, it would not damage his integrity too much if he bent one of his rules a little.

'Yes,' he said finally. 'Yes, it will be over today. You can be sure of that.'

'And what will it be?' asked Jane in as casual a manner as possible, not looking in his direction now but scooping a little of the offending scrambled eggs on to a slice of toast in order to imply her lack of interest in the answer. 'Life or death?'

'Now, Jane,' said Roderick, smiling slightly at the wiles which his wife employed to trick him into answering; he had grown familiar with her tricks over the years and rarely found himself trapped. 'You know I can't tell you that.'

'Oh for heaven's sake, Roderick,' she said, as if it was a trivial matter and hardly worth her time anyway. 'You'll be telling the whole world in a couple of hours. You can tell me now, can't you? If I promise not to say anything to anyone in the meantime?'

There was a polite tap on the bedroom door and Jane

frowned and called for the visitor waiting outside to enter. It was Sophie, the maid-of-all-work, with the morning edition of *The Times* which had just been delivered.

'Oh thank you, Sophie,' said Jane. 'Just lay it on the bed there, would you? And could you run my bath for me too please? I'll be getting up in a few minutes.'

'Already, ma'am?' asked Sophie, surprised, for her mistress normally liked to luxuriate in bed for a little while longer before rising to face an inferior world.

'Yes. I'll be accompanying the judge to the Old Bailey this morning so it's rush-rush and all hands to the pumps.'

'Yes, ma'am,' said Sophie, leaving the room quickly and heading in the direction of the bathroom.

'You're coming to court?' asked Roderick when she had left. 'You're attending the sentencing?'

'I decided last night,' said Jane. 'You don't think I'd miss it, do you? I want to show you some support. To let you know that you're not alone in that chilly courtroom. And besides, everyone will be there.'

'*Everyone* won't get in,' said Roderick irritably. 'There's not enough room for *everyone*.'

'Well there'll be room for the judge's wife, I expect,' she said, setting her tray aside, the food only half eaten. 'What time is it now anyway?'

'Ten past nine,' he said, unsure whether he should be flattered or nervous about his wife's presence in court. She always attracted the attention of the reporters and seemed to thrive on batting their questions aside like a skilled cricketer.

'Oh my,' she said. 'Well then, I better hurry. What time are you leaving at, around ten?'

'Yes.'

'Well *don't*,' she said, stressing the word, 'leave without me.'

Roderick nodded and watched as his wife got out of bed and went to the wardrobe for her robe. Even now, even after all these years, he could barely take his eyes off her. It wasn't that he had been inexperienced with women when they had first met and it wasn't just that she'd given him the kind of sensual life over two and a half decades that he had never previously imagined would be part of his destiny. It was also the fact that she was the type of woman who grew more and more attractive with age and every day brought fresh delights. To be by her side, to enter the Old Bailey with her on his arm, made him feel like a young man in the throes of his first romance again. Everything about her energized him; he loved her.

As a young woman Jane's hair had been a pretty shade of blonde and now that she was in her forties the brightness of it had faded a little but that only made her seem even more knowing, more complex, more attractive. And she had cut it shoulder length recently too, a brave move that had worked wonders. Jane Bentley was not a woman who had any intentions of pretending to be anything other than her years and knew that her forties could be just as sensual as her twenties or thirties, even more so, if she allowed them to be. She didn't suffer fools and had an aristocratic bearing that had taken her years to perfect.

'What?' she asked, turning around and noticing her husband staring at her. 'What is it?'

'Nothing,' said Roderick, shaking his head. 'You're a beautiful woman, Jane. Do you realize that?'

She opened her mouth to make a joke but saw that he was being serious. She felt a rush of warmth for him, a gushing wave of appreciation. She had chosen well all those years ago, there was no question of that. Marriage to a kind and decent man who she didn't love, or the creeping misery of remaining a spinster daughter in a family whose wealthy days were long behind them; there had been no real difficulty in making her decision. His comment required no reply; it was an honest compliment and she decided to take it as such.

Passing by the bed she picked up *The Times* for a moment and glanced at the headline, turning it around to face her husband for a moment, who looked away, closing his eyes.

'Tomorrow's fish wrappers,' he said.

'*Royal sentence expected today*,' she announced, reading it aloud. '*Bentley expected to be lenient*.'

'Don't,' said Roderick, shaking his head.

'Royal sentence indeed,' said Jane. 'The boy is a third cousin of the king's. It's not as if he was in the direct succession. We're all probably royal if those are the requirements.'

'Well that's the newspapers for you,' said Roderick, harking back to his favourite theme. 'They will exaggerate. That's how they've sold so many papers off the back of this case. I should be on some sort of percentage commission.'

'Nevertheless,' she said. 'Oh look, there's a rather good picture of him here too. That's unusual. Not a bad-looking boy I suppose, if you see him in the right light, although I've never been a fan of that Hanovarian jawline. None of them has a chin, it seems to me.

'He was on trial for the murder of a police officer, Jane,' said Bentley. 'Not for the aesthetic charm of his appearance.'

'It's sad, though, isn't it?' she asked. 'He's only the same age as Gareth. To have the rest of your life . . .' She looked at her husband who was giving nothing away. 'Well whatever happens to him, whatever the sentence, it's unfortunate. I can't imagine how his mother must feel, how *I* would feel if our son was in such a situation. I know it's a terrible cliché but it's impossible not to blame the parents in such a case, isn't it? They must have set him a dreadful example.'

'Our son would never find himself in such difficulties,' insisted Roderick. 'But it doesn't matter who the defendant is, the law is the law. Whether you're a third cousin of the king's or the youngest and most illegitimate son of a fish trader from Cockfosters. The law is the law,' he repeated.

Jane nodded and threw the paper back on the bed. 'I'll read it in the car,' she said. 'I'd better go and have my bath. And you can't be the most illegitimate,' she added for she was a stickler for grammar. 'There are no superlatives. One is either a bastard or one is not.'

Roderick shrugged it off and continued to watch her as she left the room although he stayed seated until he heard her footsteps padding up the stairs to the bathroom on the third floor. Only then did he walk across to the bed and – against his better judgement – pick up the newspaper and look at it. It wasn't the article he wanted to read, there was nothing that the reporters could tell him about this case that he didn't already know; rather, he wanted to see the picture.

For almost six months now that young man had sat across from him in the dock, his expression changing from arrogant dismissal at the start to terrified anguish at the end and running the gamut of the emotional spectrum in the time in between. Caught by a photographer for the paper, however, being bundled into a Black Maria handcuffed to a middle-aged policeman, he looked startled, as if he couldn't believe that this whole drama was actually drawing to a close and the curtain was about to descend on what, until now, he had viewed as little more than a disagreeable diversion. That he had been found guilty of murder and that he would either be spending the rest of his life in prison or be put to death. He appeared younger than his twenty-three years, almost like a little boy caught doing something he shouldn't; he looked terrified.

Roderick threw the paper on the bed in exasperation at his own lack of judgement in looking at it in the first place.

'One rule for all,' he muttered fiercely between his teeth. 'Paupers or kings. One rule for all.'

5

Margaret Richmond went into the kitchen to check on the servants. A lot of things had changed during the nearly thirty years she had worked for the Montignacs but this was one of the rare occasions now when there was a full complement of staff on hand, although most had been hired especially for the day. When Andrew, Stella and Owen had been children there had been a full-time staff employed at Leyville: a butler, two footmen, a gardener, a cook, an upstairs girl, a downstairs girl and an in-between. And of course Margaret herself who looked after the children and supervised the girls. She had always rubbed along quite well with the butler, who managed the gardener, and the footmen, who came and went like the seasons.

But times had changed. After Ann Montignac's death six years earlier, Peter had let half of them go.

'We don't need all these people hovering around,' he

had insisted. 'I can look after myself, and Stella and Owen aren't children any more either. Let them take care of themselves for a change. You can stop nannying them too, Margaret.'

Now there was just a part-time cook, one girl and no butler or footmen at all, and a couple of local girls who came in to clean and dust every day. Her own role was unspecified. She lived in hope that either Stella or Owen would marry and stay on at Leyville as she would then be the natural choice for nanny when the time came for them to have children. After all, she reasoned, she had only just turned sixty and had a lot left to offer yet. But there didn't seem to be any sign of that happening. Stella had been seeing Raymond Davis for over a year and they had declared an engagement a few months earlier but there seemed no sign of them allowing that engagement to develop into a marriage. She suspected it would be one of those long-drawn-out affairs, beloved by the young these days, ending not in the purchase of a hat but in a separation. While Owen's private life, of course, was a complete mystery to her. And so she just ran the household as best she could in the meantime. For the funeral she had hired a group of girls and young men from the local village and both Stella and Owen had seemed content for her to do so.

'You might want to check on the guests,' she stated firmly as she saw three of her charges standing in a corner of the kitchen, chatting to each other and smoking cigarettes. 'Rather than standing around in here.' They stared at her and frowned, slowly putting their cigarettes out, and walked back out towards the groups of mourners. Margaret was relieved. The last thing she wanted was an argument. Not on a day like this. But girls had to be watched, there were no two ways about that. She'd taken her eyes off one once and look at all the trouble that had caused.

She stepped out into the hallway again and considered joining the group in the drawing room but knew that she would only feel out of place among the gentry. She felt misplaced, the unwelcome drawing room to her left, the hostile kitchen to her right, and so stood perfectly still instead, wringing her hands nervously.

She tried not to think of Peter Montignac because if she did she would only think of Ann, who had not just been her employer but had been her best friend as well, and if she thought of Ann she would think of Andrew, who she had loved as if he was her own. There was too much death there, she thought, and she didn't want their pictures in her mind any more. To summon them up would only produce tears and she wanted no more tears until the guests had left. Instead she walked upstairs and paused outside the door of Owen's room, leaning closer in to hear whether he was inside or not. She had seen him come through the front door a little earlier but he had gone straight upstairs, taking the steps two at a time as he went, and no one had laid eyes on him since. She tapped lightly on his door.

'Owen,' she said in a low voice. 'Owen, are you in there?'

There was no answer.

'Owen? Are you all right?'

A muffled sound, a cough from within. Then the word drifting out quietly, like a trail of smoke through the keyhole: 'Fine.'

'Do you want to come downstairs?' she asked. 'The guests . . .' She trailed off, not knowing what to say about the guests. They were all perfectly content, drinking and eating, even the men who were forgetting themselves and playing billiards during a wake. After all, everyone – she knew – enjoyed a funeral.

'Thank you, Margaret,' came the voice from within.

The acknowledgement was also a dismissal and she nodded and went back downstairs, pausing halfway to rearrange a bouquet of flowers on the window sill, the better to give her more time to know what to do or where to go when she got there. She had been proud of her Owen that day, more proud than she had been of him in ten years when her love for him had changed so suddenly. What he had said in the church had moved and surprised her. Was there ever a boy who loved his uncle so? *This boy that I raised,* she thought. *As much mine as theirs. This boy who I saved.* She stood stock still, her eyes focused on nothing but the past, the childhoods, the finger paintings, the hugs, her babies.

A lady whose husband was the former Home Secretary emerged from the drawing room and touched her arm with the tip of a velvet-gloved finger, as if a servant was potentially riddled with disease and should be approached with caution.

'It's Miss Richmond, isn't it?' she asked.

'Yes, ma'am.'

'I wonder would it be too much trouble to ask for some more tea? I asked one of those young girls but really, she looked right through me as if I was trouble personified.'

'Right away, ma'am,' said Margaret, happy to have a task again, happy to be of use. 'Sorry, ma'am. I'll see to it immediately.'

In the small parlour to the right of the kitchen Annie the cook was relaxing. Most of the food had been prepared the night before and the fresh sandwiches had been made that morning; there was little for her to do now but wait for the guests to leave and instruct the hired help about the cleaning arrangements afterwards, although she knew that Margaret Richmond would likely look after that too. Annie's niece, a local girl called Millie, brought her a cup of tea. Millie was one of the girls who had been hired for the day but was hoping for a more permanent residency.

'Precious little chance of that now, my girl,' said Annie, shaking her head. 'I can't see me lasting here very much longer myself if I'm honest.'

'But you've been here for years,' said Millie.

'Only eight years. That's just a blow-in to an old family like this. And with just the two of them left now, what need do they have of a cook? That Owen hardly spends any time here as it is, he's always gadding about in London, getting up to Lord knows what. And as for Stella . . .' She rolled her eyes for she had disapproved of modern girls ever since her arms had turned flabby and her waistline had disappeared. 'She's no better then she ought to be. No, I wouldn't be surprised if I got my marching orders soon enough too.'

Millie frowned. She would have to look elsewhere for employment then, and there were precious few opportunities to be found anywhere. 'What was he like anyway?' she asked, settling on a chair beside her aunt.

'Who?'

'Mr Montignac. Him as was buried today.'

Annie shrugged. 'He was all right, I suppose,' she said. 'I've known worse. Not very friendly but not deliberately rude either. They say he was a lot different in the old days, before his first son died. His only son, I should say, as that Owen's not his. But I didn't know him well to tell you the truth. It was a shock, though, him going like he did.'

'Really?'

'Well he never seemed like he was on death's door,' said Annie. 'Oh he had his problems of course. Heart problems. Stomach problems. Every kind of ailment known to mankind it seemed sometimes. Kept that doctor busy over the last few years and no mistake. But he ate like it was going out of style and always had his meat cooked so rare that any half-decent vet could have brought it back to life. And then suddenly, just out of the blue, that was it.' She clicked her fingers together dramatically. 'Gone.'

'It seems a shame to have such a big house for only two people,' said Millie, imagining for a moment what it would be like to be mistress of it; Owen Montignac had caught her eye earlier in the day when he had returned from the funeral and she'd stared at him, transfixed, as he ran up to his room, her heart beating faster inside her chest as she saw what appeared to be a pained expression on his extraordinarily handsome face. She had never seen a young man with such white hair before, nor with eyes of such a piercing blue.

'His father was the same,' said Annie. 'Married a Frenchwoman, if you please.'

'He's very handsome,' said Millie, lost in thought.

'I wouldn't set much store by that.'

'Not like most of the others round here.'

'Everything's changing,' complained Annie. 'People don't live in houses like these any more. They can't afford to, most of them. Costs run too high. They all live up in London in townhouses and fancy flats and keep their country retreats locked up all year round. They're just for show now, most of them.'

'Is that what Mr Montignac is planning on doing?'

'Well I don't know, do I?' said Annie, laughing as she took a long drag on her cigarette. 'He doesn't let the likes of me into his thoughts. He's like his father that way. His uncle, I mean. Doesn't have much time for anyone on the staff, except maybe Margaret Richmond.

But then she practically brought him up from the day he came here.'

At that moment the lady in question walked through the door and Millie stumbled to her feet quickly while Annie remained unmoved, refusing to acknowledge the older lady's authority.

'I'm getting questions about the tea, Annie,' said Margaret in a tired voice.

'The tea?'

'The lack of it.'

Annie shuffled in her chair and dragged herself up as if she was carrying a ton weight and the effort was almost too much for her. She stepped past Margaret without acknowledging her and went into the kitchen to issue short, sharp orders.

'And . . . Mildred, is it?' asked Margaret.

'Millie, ma'am.'

'Millie, yes. Perhaps you would go and check on the gentlemen in the billiard room. I don't hold with the playing of games on a day like today but they will insist.'

'Yes, ma'am,' said Millie, blushing scarlet as she was spoken to and leaving the room.

Margaret glanced around the parlour irritably when it was empty, annoyed that everything was left to her. If only Stella or Owen could circulate a little bit, she thought, thank the guests for coming, then everything would be so much easier.

6

Leonard brought the car around to the front door of the house on Tavistock Square, driving slowly so as not to knock over any of the reporters who were loitering outside, despite his desire to do that very thing. A couple of them tapped on the window, throwing a few random questions at him through the glass, but these came only from the most inexperienced journalists; the rest knew that the chauffeur would neither say anything to them nor have anything interesting to say.

'Ready?' said Roderick, as his wife checked her appearance one final time in the hallway mirror. It was a quarter past ten already and he was anxious to leave.

'Ready,' she said, nodding her head.

'And remember – not a word to any of them,' he reminded her as he opened the door and they stepped out on to the street to be greeted by more than a dozen newspapermen, pencils poised in anticipation above their notebooks as they peppered him with questions.

'Will you be passing sentence today, Your Honour?'

'Have you spoken to the palace, sir?'

'Will it be life or death, Judge? Life or death? Will he be treated the same as everyone else?'

Roderick kept his head down and marched determinedly towards the car, whose back door Leonard had opened and was standing beside protectively. Jane, as requested, kept her mouth shut, but her head held high and she smiled at the gathered throng, disappointed that there were no photographers present. There were sure to be some at the Old Bailey, though, she knew that much. She was wearing a new hat for the occasion.

'Drive on, Leonard,' said Roderick once they were safely inside with the doors closed again. 'And quick as you like.'

'Yes, sir,' came the reply from the front seat as the car shifted into gear and they turned out of the square en route to the Palace of Justice.

'I don't think I can take much more of these damn busybodies,' said Roderick, feeling a little more relaxed now that they were on the move. 'What kind of a job is that anyway?'

'People are interested, Roderick,' said Jane, shrugging her shoulders as if it was the most natural thing in the world. 'You can't blame them for that. It's human nature. It's also their job.'

Bentley grunted and looked out the window. Summer had started to make its arrival felt. The trees along Southampton Row had sprung into life and he noticed one or two brave souls who had changed their winter jackets for lighter ones. It was an uncommonly warm June morning.

'Roderick?' said Jane after a moment. 'Have you heard from them at all?'

A question from one of the reporters had stuck in her head, something she'd never thought of herself over the previous few months, and it made her wonder.

'Heard from whom?' he asked, turning back to look at his wife.

'From the palace,' she said. 'The king. He hasn't been in touch, has he?'

Roderick laughed. 'Of course not,' he said. 'You don't seriously think that the king would try to influence a court case out of personal interest, do you?'

'Well, I wouldn't like to think so,' admitted Jane. 'But I wouldn't be too sure either. He's hardly the man his father was, now is he?'

'That's neither here nor there,' said Roderick.

'Do you realize that since the succession we haven't been invited to Buckingham Palace once?'

'My dear, it's hardly as if we were regular visitors in the past!'

'Not regular, no,' admitted Jane, 'but we were invited to the garden party in thirty-two, don't you remember? When Queen Mary said such nice things to me about my hat.'

'Yes,' said Roderick, who remembered the event but not the compliments and certainly not the pulchritudinous hat.

'And then there was the dinner party after you received your knighthood. And Ramsay MacDonald was there too, you remember,' she added.

'Twice,' said Bentley. 'Twice in all these years does not make us intimates of the royal family.'

'No, of course not,' said Jane. 'But I do think it would be nice to be invited to more functions, don't you? After all, the new king is of the same generation as us. He might enjoy our company.'

'The same generation as you, perhaps,' said Roderick with a laugh. 'I'm a good ten years older than him.'

'Well a few years here or there hardly makes a difference. We should try to get an invitation to the next state dinner perhaps. How would one go about such a thing anyway?'

'I have no idea,' he replied, not caring much either way, for social events like that didn't interest him enormously.

'At the very least we should be regulars at the garden party,' she added. 'If we got friendly with him there's always a chance we could be invited to the coronation too next summer. Perhaps if I invited the Simpson woman to tea some afternoon. Would that be all right, do you think, or are we supposed to snub her until told otherwise?'

The car came to a sudden halt and the Bentleys, husband and wife, fell forwards abruptly.

'Sorry, Your Honour,' said Leonard, turning around and shaking his head. 'Boy selling papers,' he added as a small child with a sandwich board and an armful of papers disappeared out of sight before Leonard could jump out after him. The sandwich board bore the legend: *Royal Cousin Sentence Imminent*.

'I can't get away from them,' said Roderick irritably.

'Of course,' said Jane, settling back into her seat and removing her compact from her bag to check her hat was still in place after the incident. 'We could be off the guest list at the moment because of the trial. The king mightn't want to be seen to be influencing you in any way.'

'I should think that's a very reasonable assumption,' said Roderick.

'But he doesn't know you, does he? He doesn't know how incorruptible you are. How disgustingly honest,' she added with only a touch of sarcasm. 'Your famous integrity and ethics. The incorruptibility of the judicial system. He doesn't know about any of that, does he?'

'Well I would like to think that my reputation precedes me,' he replied, trying to maintain his humility. 'I have been a high court judge for fifteen years now after all, and I think I've achieved a certain level of respect.'

'What do you think he thinks about it all anyway?'

'The king?'

'Yes.'

'About what?'

'About the case, Roderick,' she said irritably. 'Don't be obtuse. About Henry Domson. His cousin.'

'His third cousin,' he replied, correcting her. 'Henry Domson has been convicted by a jury of his peers of killing a policeman in cold blood. A policeman whose ultimate responsibility is to the monarch. I imagine he thinks that the sentence should fit the crime.'

'But his own cousin,' said Jane.

'His *third* cousin,' insisted Roderick.

They remained silent for a few moments. It was clear

to both of them that there was something Jane was anxious to say but was unsure how to express it. Only once in their married lives had she actively tried to influence her husband on a decision regarding a case and he had taken it very badly at the time and they had had one of their very rare fights, which had resulted in her promising that she would never interfere in one of his trials again. But still, there was too much at stake here. Social position, invitations to garden parties at Buckingham Palace, a seat at the coronation . . . it was all there for the taking. The kinetic energy of the moment sat between them as they passed along Holborn.

'Roderick,' she burst out finally.

'Jane, don't,' he said sharply.

'Roderick, let me just say this—'

'I don't want you to say anything. I have made my decision and I won't change my mind—'

'Just hear me out, please,' she said. 'Just let me say one thing and then I promise I won't say another word on the matter.' She hesitated for a moment. 'Please, Roderick,' she repeated. 'You have my word.'

'Spit it out then,' he said, unwilling to debate the issue. 'But I warn you, no matter what your plea is, you'll be wasting your time. I've made up my mind.'

'Fine,' she said. 'Then let me say just one thing. Two things actually.'

'Ha!' said Roderick.

'The first is that, no matter what this young man has supposedly done—'

'There's no supposedly about it,' said Bentley, growing angry now. 'He's been convicted. We live with a jury system and when a fellow's convicted—'

'Whatever this young man *has* done,' she said, interrupting him, not wishing to get involved in a semantics debate. 'I think it would be a very great disgrace for the nation for a cousin of the monarch, a *third* cousin,' she added before he could say it, 'for a third cousin of the monarch to be sentenced to death. I mean, what does that say about our society? The boy went to Eton for heaven's sake. And I imagine the king would be very grateful to a judge who recognized the fact and let the boy off.'

'I'm saying nothing,' said Roderick. 'Are you finished now?'

'No, I have one more thing to add,' she said, lowering her voice now. 'This boy, this Henry Domson, what age is he again?'

'Twenty-three,' said Roderick, who could have recited any fact about the boy's life without a moment's hesitation after so many months spent learning about him.

'Twenty-three years old,' said Jane, shaking her head sadly. 'Just a child. The same age as Gareth. Now imagine if the situation was reversed, would you want your son to meet such a fate?'

'That would never happen,' said Bentley. 'As I told you earlier, Gareth may be a lot of things but he would never do the kind of things that Domson has done.'

'You stepped in for him once before,' said Jane. 'Don't you remember?'

He threw her a look; it was an incident he preferred to forget.

'You put your ethics aside on that occasion to save him from expulsion, don't you recall?'

'Of course I do,' said Roderick. 'But that was a schoolboy stunt. It's not the same thing at all.'

'It was a violent act.'

'It was a prank gone wrong.'

'Well you're a father, Roderick, just remember that. And this boy is just a boy.'

'He's twenty-three years old!' he cried in protest. 'He's hardly a boy.'

'Well I've said all I'm going to say on the subject,' said Jane, as the Old Bailey appeared before them. 'I'll leave it to your conscience. I think you know what the right thing to do is.'

'I believe I do,' sniffed Roderick as the car pulled up and the newspapermen, a fresh pride, rushed towards them again. 'Oh bloody hell. There's reporters everywhere. Just keep your head down, hold my hand, and don't speak to anyone until we're inside the court, do you understand?'

An hour from now, he thought to himself this will all be over and life can return to normal. The judge stepped into the melee and fought his way through to the steps beyond and the comparative peace and safety of his beloved courtroom.

7

'That eulogy you gave . . .' said Stella Montignac, sitting in an armchair in the corner of her cousin's room while tossing a tennis ball between her palms. 'Well I never thought you had such poetry inside you.'

'That surprises me,' said Montignac, seated at the desk. 'I'm not made of steel, you know.'

'I know that,' replied Stella quickly. 'I didn't mean . . .' She trailed off and shook her head, sighing a little. 'Don't let's fight,' she said finally. 'Not today.'

'I'm not,' said Montignac quietly. He looked across at Stella and was a little surprised to see how much trouble she had put into her appearance for the funeral. She wasn't normally given to elaborate outfits or a surfeit of make-up but she had put in an extra effort for her father's burial. The dress was the same shade of black as her hair and she had applied a little mascara too, which had stayed intact as she hadn't shed any tears throughout the internment.

'It was a very nice service too, all things considered,' she continued. 'Everything he would have wanted. Beautiful hymns, lovely flowers . . .'

He looked down at the piece of paper on the desk in front of him and reread it quickly before signing it and putting it in an envelope. When Stella had come in a few minutes earlier he had been engaged in writing a letter to Nicholas Delfy, the owner of a small casino in the East End of London, to whom he owed a considerable sum of money. The amount had been outstanding and accruing interest for quite some time and hints, rather than outright threats, had started to come his way. He had been trying to find the right blend of words to employ in the letter, something between offhand humour which might imply what a trivial matter this was to a Montignac and bland sincerity, which might convince Delfy that he meant to pay him what he owed him, and soon. Within the next few days, in fact.

'Actually, when I was a little girl he used to enjoy hymns and he took an interest in the gardens,' insisted Stella. 'But I suppose you're right. They weren't exactly his passions in life.'

'Perhaps it was before I knew him then,' said Montignac.

'Perhaps,' she acknowledged. 'You are all right, Owen, aren't you? You're not too upset?'

He put his fountain pen down with a sigh and placed the letter in the top drawer of the bureau, which he promptly locked, placing the key in the pocket of his waistcoat. He turned around and looked at his cousin and found himself able to identify the sadness beneath her tough exterior. He began to feel something perilously close to affection for her. Whatever unexpected emotion it was, however, he quickly dismissed it.

'They're all still down there I expect,' he said.

'Quite a few. We really should go down. It's very bad form for the pair of us to be sitting up here on our own like this.'

'You go.'

'They'll expect to see you too. If it's too upsetting—'

'Oh, Stella, stop being such a martyr, would you please?' he asked, growing irritable now and brushing a hand across his eyes. 'He was your father, not mine. If anyone has a right to be upset it should be you, not me. And I think I have the strength of character to be able to sweep around a few nosy houseguests without breaking down in tears.'

'He was as much your father as mine, you know that,' insisted Stella.

'He was my uncle.'

'But he thought of you like a son. Don't deny that, not today.'

Montignac nodded and remained silent for a moment. 'I know,' he muttered finally. 'I know what he thought of me.'

'Then we're in it together and we'll go down together,' she continued. 'Anyway, we should support each other at a time like this. That's what families are for after all. You know some of the men are playing billiards down there,' she added after a moment.

'Billiards?' he asked.

'Yes. Or so Margaret told me anyway. She doesn't think it's right.'

'It's not,' replied Montignac, considering the etiquette of the matter. 'I'll go down and set them straight.'

'But not with a scene.'

'No. Perhaps not.'

'And another thing,' she said. 'Denis Tandy came to speak to me earlier. About the will. He wants to set up the reading for as soon as possible.'

'You're not serious,' said Montignac, appalled by the man's insensitivity. 'He came to you with that today? And why didn't he speak to me about it anyway?'

'Well he'd been looking for you but—'

'He couldn't have looked very hard then, and I do think he might have waited before burdening you with it. It's not as if there are going to be any great surprises in there. You're not worried about it, are you?'

'No, no,' she said, shaking her head. 'It was explained to me a thousand times how I would never be able to inherit for the extraordinary fact of my being a girl. The Montignacs always inherit on the male line,' she chanted, looking away with a sneer. 'Very modern of them, I don't think.'

'You have nothing to worry about, Stella,' said Montignac, stepping forwards and taking her hand in his. 'You don't think for a moment that I'd let anything happen to you, do you? What I have . . .' He didn't go quite so far as to suggest that what he had, she had too, and she noticed this and let the sentence hang in mid-air between them.

Stella looked down and noticed the way his fingers slotted in perfectly between her own and welcomed the touch, the first time he had held her hand like that in many years now. Her eyes lifted and met his and he held them there for a moment before releasing her and turning away.

'Anyway, I told him tomorrow morning would be fine,' she said to his retreating back. 'He'll be here around eleven. I don't suppose it will take very long.

'Fine,' said Montignac, whose mind was elsewhere, lost in bitter memories. 'I'd better go downstairs anyway.'

The two cousins stood and walked towards the door together. 'I've never understood why we have to have wakes anyway,' said Stella. 'Everyone gets so upset at a funeral that it seems like a pointless prolonging of the pain to invite people over for the next best thing to a party.'

'I wouldn't have bothered if it had been down to me,' he said. 'But form's form. People come over automatically. It's not as if we specifically sent out invitations.'

'No.'

'We should have lunch together tomorrow,' he suggested. 'Just the two of us. After the reading of the will, I mean. To discuss plans. For the house and so on.'

'Yes,' said Stella, nodding her head. 'I think some of the staff are worried. Margaret overheard Annie complaining that she was going to lose her job.'

'She would have lost it years ago if I'd had my way,' he said quickly. 'She drinks more than anyone else in the house and smokes like a chimney. But we'll talk about it tomorrow, it's not important right now. We should go downstairs and start trying to get rid of some of these bastards or they'll never leave.'

Stella blinked in surprise. She almost never heard her cousin use language such as that – he prided himself on his elegance and gentlemanly behaviour – and it seemed particularly inappropriate for a moment like this, when they were almost close, when they were almost talking again like they did when they were teenagers. There was violence to the sound of the word, an anger that reminded her of things she preferred to forget.

She stared at him now as he examined himself in the full-length mirror, pulling his jacket down to displace the creases. She remembered when he had first been brought to the house at the age of five, short for his age, slightly grubby, with freckles, buck teeth and a French accent. And that hair, of course, that unmistakable shock of snow-white hair upon his head that had made her mouth drop open in surprise when she'd first laid eyes on him. The way his blue eyes had seemed to pierce right through her. And now here he was twenty years later, master-designate of the Montignac estate, six feet tall, his naturally pale skin coloured slightly by regular exercise and healthy eating. He was as handsome now as he had been charmless then. He had changed in so many ways in the two decades in between that she could barely count their number. But she had welcomed him then, she and Andrew had both welcomed him, and had never made him feel like an outsider despite his insistence on placing himself in that very position time and again.

'I wanted to tell you,' she said as they walked out on to the landing. He stopped short and looked at her expectantly. 'I was very proud of you today. I don't think I could have got through it without you. I found myself missing Andrew terribly – the whole thing brought back such bad memories – but having you by my side, well it was a comfort. Of sorts.'

Montignac placed his tongue in the corner of his mouth and bulged it out slightly as he considered this, taking the compliment with a slight nod before stepping briskly down the stairs and leaving her alone at the top.

8

Jane Bentley made her way directly to the gallery of Court number one at the Old Bailey, where she spotted her friend Eleanor Tandy sitting in the front row and took a seat beside her. Beneath them the phalanx of court reporters, solicitors, barristers and policemen were moving into position like the actors in a play before curtain-up and the crowds of interested spectators – the ones lucky enough to have secured a seat by arriving early – were settling into the stalls out front. The only things missing were an usherette patrolling the aisles with ices and the sounds of the string section being tuned up.

'I was starting to worry about you,' said Eleanor,

taking her bag off the adjacent chair and placing it on the floor beside her feet. 'I wasn't sure how much longer I could hold on to your seat but I knew you wouldn't miss this for the world.'

'How could I?' asked Jane. 'It's like I said to Roderick earlier, simply everyone is going to be here today.'

'Not everyone,' replied Eleanor with a knowing smile. 'After all there are those who are conspicuous by their absence.'

Jane nodded. 'The king, you mean? The Duke of York?'

'Among others. They're staying well out of it, aren't they?'

'Well do you blame them?' asked Jane. 'The poor man's only been on the throne a few months, there's all this talk of the American woman he's going about with and now this. A killer in the family. All in all it's not a very auspicious start to his reign. It makes you wonder what the next forty years hold.'

'They have strange blood, if you ask me,' said Eleanor.

'The Windsors?'

'Of course. You know they say that Queen Victoria's grandson might have been Jack the Ripper. And he was the present king's uncle.'

'Oh that's just conjecture,' said Jane with a laugh, who didn't enjoy mystery novels quite as much as her friend. 'Quite unlikely, I think.'

'There is a difference, I suppose. The Ripper chose tarts as his victims. The new king chooses one as his mistress.'

'Eleanor, really,' said Jane, stifling a laugh. 'Someone will overhear you.'

'All the same,' said Eleanor. 'It's hard to know who to trust, isn't it? This one, though, this Domson boy, he has the look of the late king, don't you think? Around the eyes, I think.'

Jane shrugged. 'I haven't seen him up close,' she admitted. 'Only in photographs.'

'I've come every day,' said Eleanor. 'Haven't missed a word. I practically gave up my life over these past few months to attend court. And Roderick's been awfully good.' Jane smiled and inclined her head a little at the compliment. 'I don't suppose you can tell me in advance what he's going to say, can you?'

'I don't think so, sorry,' said Jane.

'But he'll be announcing it in a few minutes. There's no one I can tell.'

'I'm sorry, no. There are certain secrets between a husband and a wife that must stay secret,' she said, despite the fact that she too had no idea whether her husband would be sentencing the boy to a lifetime in Brixton prison or a trip to the scaffold. 'And what kind of a wife would I be if I divulged them?'

The case of Rex vs Henry Domson had begun six months earlier when the police had foiled a warehouse robbery near a jewel factory beside London Bridge. Domson had been the brains of the operation and had they been successful they would have succeeded in stealing almost two hundred thousand pounds' worth of diamonds and other precious stones. However, one of the gang had been too loose with his tongue and the police had received a tip-off on the night of the incident. They arrested his three accomplices but Domson himself escaped and was chased along the docks until he was cornered by two policemen near a container lorry. When they moved in to arrest him, Domson pulled a gun from his jacket pocket and then shot the first officer – PC Peter Milburn, aged fifty-two – in cold blood. He would have shot the second too had his gun not stalled and he'd been overpowered in the ensuing struggle.

The newspapers had not made too much of the incident at first – crimes like this were two a penny after all – until it was discovered that Domson was a second cousin of King George V, and a third cousin to the Prince of Wales who, just after the trial began, had succeeded to the throne. Buckingham Palace had been conspicuously silent on the topic, refusing to comment except to say that no members of the royal family were either acquainted with Mr Domson or had ever even met him but the connection was enough for the case to constitute a scandal.

Throughout the trial several of the daily participants had become celebrated figures; the chief prosecutor, Mr Justice Harkman, his learned colleague for the defence, Mr Justice McAlpine, and of course the trial judge, His Honour Sir Roderick Bentley KC, in whose hands the case now lay.

Although it seemed like something of an open-and-shut case, Domson had pleaded not guilty and the trial had dragged on until the beginning of June when the jury had finally delivered a guilty verdict on the Thursday of the previous week. Domson had looked stricken in the dock when the announcement was made and there were those close to him who imagined he would disgrace his noble lineage even further by breaking down in tears but somehow he managed to keep control of his emotions, merely gripping the handrail in front of him for support.

The newspapers had been debating the matter back and forth ever since. Murder was a capital crime, often punishable by death. The murder of a policeman, killed in the line of duty, was even more heinous and there had never been a conviction in such a case leading to anything other than the death penalty. However, there had also never been a trial quite like this one before either. The majority of the newspapers believed that Judge Bentley would suspend the death penalty and sentence Domson to a life of hard labour on account of his royal connections. Indeed, such a given was it that editorials had started to be written about the injustice of such a sentence and how the class structure was as relevant to crime as it was to normal, everyday life. Unbeknown to anyone in the courtroom, *The Times* had already prepared a leader for the following day's edition attacking Roderick and calling for his removal from the bench, questioning whether the sentence would have been as lenient had the murderer been a poor, unemployed lad from Walthamstow rather than an ex-Etonian with dubious connections to higher powers.

'Where's Denis?' asked Jane, looking around for her friend's husband. 'I would have thought he'd be here, considering he's a solicitor himself.'

'He's at a funeral today,' explained Eleanor. 'Peter Montignac's. Did you know him?'

Jane narrowed her eyes and tried to remember when they had last met. 'A little,' she said. 'Not at all well. I used to know his wife, Ann, socially but we were hardly friends. Just people who sometimes got invited to the same functions.'

'Ann was a dear woman,' said Eleanor. 'Very witty. An excellent mimic.'

'Really?'

'Yes. Quite the girl to have at a party in her younger days. Lost a little of her sense of humour after her son was killed, of course.'

'Well that's to be expected,' said Jane, trying to stifle a laugh.

'Oh I know, but she dragged it on a little too long if you ask me,' said Eleanor. 'Grief's grief but it doesn't do to dwell on it. It only embarrasses other people. Anyway, he died last week and Denis was his solicitor so he's attending the funeral.'

'I see,' said Jane.

'He's staying down there overnight for the reading of the will in the morning so remind me to telephone him when we leave here to let him know the sentence. He's been following the trial too and is distraught that he's gong to miss the climax. It's like sitting through an entire murder mystery play and then being summoned away because the children are sick just as the curtain rises for the final act and all the characters have been gathered together in the living room to unmask the killer.'

Jane smiled; Eleanor Tandy was nothing if not colourful.

'I presume you'll be glad when this is all over,' said Eleanor after a lengthy pause.

'Roderick will, that's for sure,' said Jane. 'We're all sick of the reporters camped outside. And I'm sure that one of our neighbours, Catherine Jones, is preparing a complaint for the police.'

'And you?'

'Well,' said Jane, considering it. 'It's taken its toll on Roderick, that's for sure. I'd like him to take a holiday, if I'm honest. It would be nice if we could spend a little more time together now that the trial is behind us.'

'He should have sentenced him immediately after the verdict came through. I do think it was wrong of him to wait this long. It was all I could think about over the weekend.'

After the verdict had been declared by the jury the previous Thursday, Roderick had announced that he would delay sentencing until Monday morning to give him time to consider his decision. Most commentators had agreed that he had been seeking advice on the legality of commuting the standard sentence to something less harsh and were poised to condemn him; but not only had he given himself a few days to think about it, he'd given his critics time to prepare their assaults too.

'He was only doing what he thought right,' said Jane, who was often critical of her husband in private but would be damned if she'd allow anyone else to be. 'After all, a boy's life hangs in the balance.'

'I doubt it,' said Eleanor. 'It would take enormous courage to hang him.'

Jane opened her mouth to take issue with the implication but as she did so the clerk of the court called for silence and a hush fell around the courtroom while Henry Domson was led into the dock for the last time.

9

'It's a good job the old man's dead,' said Charles Malroy, chalking his cue and squinting with his bad eye to get a better view of the black. 'Although I imagine he'd be turning in his grave if he knew what was going on.'

'What is it with these Americans anyway?' asked Samuel Levison. 'One minute they want nothing to do with us, insist on running their damn country themselves, and the next they want to steal the bloody throne. Watch out or they'll become even more imperialist than we ever were.'

Charles opened his mouth to reply but closed it again as Montignac stepped through the door of the billiard room and stood staring at them with an angry look on his face. Samuel started in a surprise and mishit the white; it bounced clear off the table and rolled along the floor, stopping precisely in front of their host's feet. Montignac looked down at it for a moment, as if unsure what a billiard ball could possibly be doing there, before reaching down and picking it up. He held on to it tightly, unwilling to replace it on the table.

'Gentlemen,' he said quietly.

The others, old and young alike, were unable to look him in the eye and had the good grace to appear a little ashamed of themselves.

'Bad business,' said one.

'Terrible loss,' muttered another into his beard.

'I wanted to thank you all for coming,' said Montignac quickly, in a voice which implied he wanted to do nothing of the sort. 'Very good of you. My uncle would have been touched.'

'He was a fine man, Montignac,' said the retired Home Secretary, waddling over and slapping him on the shoulder. 'One of the finest I ever had the good fortune to know. And I've known them all.'

'Yes,' replied Montignac in a non-committal voice. 'Is everyone all right for drinks?' They muttered that they were. 'Because they're serving tea and whiskies in the drawing room if you'd like to join them.'

A five-second silence, a quick glance at the retained white ball in Montignac's hand, and the men took the hint and replaced their cues in the rack on the wall, shuffling past their host, unable to look him in the eye. Only Alexander Keys remained, his oldest friend, and Montignac glanced at him, not particularly wanting a conversation.

'All right, old man?' asked Alexander.

'All right,' replied Montignac quietly.

'Want me to stick around later? We could have a few quiet drinks.'

'Maybe,' he said. 'I'm tired. We'll see.'

They remained silent for a while and Montignac replaced the white ball on the billiard table, lining it up so that he had a direct view of the black and the left-hand corner pocket.

'Sorry about all this,' said Alexander, nodding at the table. 'We couldn't think of anything to do and just sort of drifted in here. We'd already started when we realized it mightn't be quite the thing.'

'Forget it,' Montignac said, shaking his head as if the matter was no longer of any interest to him. 'What time do you think these people will leave anyway?'

'Soon enough, I imagine.'

'God, I hate them,' he added with a sigh.

'Hate them?' asked Alexander, laughing nervously. 'That's a bit strong, isn't it?'

Montignac said nothing for a moment but slammed

the white ball down the table with his hand, where it hit the black, sending it crashing into the corner pocket. The white bounced back, ricocheted off the cushion and crossed the table where its trajectory began to slow down as it approached the side pocket; it teetered there for a few moments on the edge before falling in. He frowned and shook his head.

'Want me to drop a few hints out there?' asked Alexander. 'Get them to put a shake on?'

'Be grateful if you would.'

'Consider it done,' said his friend, passing him by and leaving the room, tapping his arm for comfort as he went. 'And if you want me to stick around later, you only have to ask. You know that. How's Stella holding up, by the way?'

'She'll be fine,' said Montignac. 'I'll see to that.'

'Right. Good,' said Alexander. 'I noticed that Raymond fellow mooching around outside in the garden. You'd think he'd be taking care of her today rather than playing with the flowers.'

'I can take care of her,' said Montignac in a tone which made it clear to his friend that his presence was no longer required. After a few moments he heard the door close behind him and he turned around with a sigh, allowing his body to relax for a moment, glad to be left alone. In the corner he noticed a suit jacket that one of the men had left behind and stared at it, narrowing his eyes as he identified a bulge in the inner pocket. He walked over at a steady pace to where it lay, reached inside and withdrew a wallet. Opening it he saw a clutch of twenty-pound notes and selected five, placing them in the heel of his shoe, before returning the wallet to the jacket and leaving the room, closing and locking the door behind him.

Raymond Davis stood in the grounds of Leyville, examining the different breeds of roses that were planted outside the living-room bay windows. His parents had been keen gardeners and had passed their passion for all things horticultural down to him, and he had been growing new strains of roses in the grounds of his own home a few miles to the east of Leyville for several years. One particular variety, a deep pink, yellow-striped Cabana Hybrid Tea with ovoid buds, had taken him the best part of four summers to perfect but it was doing excellently now and a cutting from it, planted in the flower beds here, had taken root and was beginning to prosper. He touched the petals of the flower, stroking them tenderly as he might a sleeping cat, and recalled how Stella had decided to plant the cutting close to the house so that their scent might rise up when the roses had grown sufficiently and infiltrate the atmosphere of her father's bedroom, which was situated just above. Remembering this made him step back a little and he wandered down the steps into the garden proper. He didn't want to seem macabre but his eyes plotted a trajectory of their own and he found himself staring at the large bay windows of Peter

Montignac's room some twenty feet above. They were locked now and the curtains were closed; they had remained so since his death.

Turning away he checked his watch and wondered why Stella had avoided him so completely today when he had hoped to be a source of comfort and support to her but she had spent most of her time with her cousin Owen instead, whom Raymond only vaguely knew. They had been together for just over a year and he was keen for them to take the next step towards marriage but whenever the subject came up she dismissed it quickly and said they would talk of it another time. Their engagement had already been announced but Stella seemed to view that as something of no great importance. They had shared intimacies, however, and in a moment of weakness she had confided in him that she had been hurt before and that he should forgive her if she seemed difficult to grow close to.

It had been his intention recently to take Stella out to dinner and make a more formal proposal, setting a date in their diaries for the nuptials; in fact he had gone to Peter Montignac only a week earlier and asked for his approval, which he had grudgingly given. However, events had seen to it that the proposal could not take place for the moment and he wondered about the etiquette of such a thing, how long one was supposed to wait after the death of a prospective bride's parent before asking for her hand.

He turned to step back inside and looked up again

towards the bedroom window where he saw the curtains twitch and suddenly open, followed by the windows themselves, and a shadow stepping away. He shivered, the unmistakable feeling of being watched.

The guests had left now and Owen had declined Alexander's offer to stay overnight. 'Better if it's just the two of us,' he said. 'Stella might want to talk in private. But thanks anyway.'

'When are you coming up to London? We could go together. Make a time of it.'

'Later this week, I expect. Lots to do. Lawyers and so on. Sick of it already and it's only just begun.'

'I could come with you, Owen.'

'Yes, do,' he said. 'I'll speak to you tomorrow and we'll arrange things.'

The house seemed empty now as he made his way upstairs, although he could hear the servants moving between the kitchen and the drawing room, cleaning up and chatting away without a care in the world. He noticed his reflection in the stairway and discovered he had a smile on his face and immediately wiped it away. Stella had gone to her room and he could hear her gramophone playing quietly in the distance, a tune he didn't recognize and didn't much care for either.

Passing by his own door, he found his feet steering him along the corridor and up the small flight of stairs towards the room that had been his late uncle's. The door was closed but unlocked and he turned the handle, stepping back slightly as he did so, as if he was afraid of what he might find inside. But as he looked around he found that everything was exactly as he remembered it. He looked from left to right and walked across the room towards the windows which had been closed since his uncle's death a few days earlier; the atmosphere in the room was stuffy on account of it. He stood close to them and placed his hand on the latch, holding it there for a moment before pushing it open, and a rush of air came in, followed by the scent of roses.

Looking below he saw that fool Raymond Davis stepping back inside the house and frowned. He thought everyone had left by now and he particularly despised Raymond. A mutual friend had told him how Stella and he had taken a suite at the Savoy two weeks before and stayed there together overnight, something she had never told him herself, and he felt a stab of pain and jealousy at the thought of it. If Raymond was any kind of man it wouldn't be so bad, he thought, but he was a simpleton. A lover of flowers. Beneath Owen and unworthy of Stella. Undeserving of her intimacies. Exactly the kind of emasculated fool that Montignac could hardly look at without feeling a violent contempt. Why was he still here anyway? Couldn't he just leave like everyone else?

He stepped back from the windows and his eyes moved to the bed where Peter Montignac had been on the last occasion that his nephew had seen him.

He looked at the pillows that had surrounded his

weakened uncle on the bed and felt a slight twitch of unhappiness as he blocked the memory of that afternoon from his mind. Something he had eaten earlier made his stomach feel uncertain and he stepped quickly from the room, closing the doors behind him, and resolved not to enter again until the estate had been settled and was finally his.

With the death of his uncle there was no doubt in Owen Montignac's mind that he was about to become a very wealthy man; the one thing he could not afford, however, or so he told himself, was a conscience.

10

Henry Domson entered the dock with a look of remorse and humility on his face; however, had his expression mirrored how he felt inside there would have been a wide smirk plastered across his youthful features.

It had been almost six months since the evening when he, along with three friends, had broken into the Schulberg Jewel Warehouse beside London Bridge and almost nine since he had first drawn up the plans for the heist. It had all seemed remarkably simple to begin with. Through some of his more dubious underworld connections he had managed to get a schematic of the warehouse itself along with a timetable of the different guards who were on duty each night. They had simply forced the lock and overpowered two of the guards before filling their bags with millions of pounds' worth of jewellery and beginning their escape.

Everything had gone according to plan until they turned to leave the warehouse, when they were surprised to see a group of policemen enter, shouting at them to drop the bags. When a chase ensued and he had found himself cornered by two of them, he had felt no hesitation in shooting the first and only regretted that his gun had stalled or he would almost certainly have made a clean escape.

When he first met his barrister, Mr Justice McAlpine, and the instructing solicitor, they had looked at him contemptuously and informed him that this was something of an open-and-shut case and the best he could hope for was to admit the offence, throw himself on the mercy of the judge and pray for a custodial sentence. More and more murderers, they told him, were seeing their death sentences commuted to life imprisonment if they appealed for clemency but the murder of a police officer, well that was different. There was really very little hope.

'It's encouraging to see that you throw in the towel so easily,' Domson said to McAlpine with a sarcastic laugh. 'Do you have much of a record of winning your cases or are you generally too frightened to fight them?'

'I can fight a case if there are merits on which to fight it,' said McAlpine in a gravelly tone, for he was far too old and experienced to allow himself to be spoken down to by a young man who had thought nothing of taking a life in cold blood. 'But it's very difficult in a case like this to make out grounds for leniency.'

'Perhaps I should tell you a little bit about my background then,' said Domson with a smile. 'Maybe I can help you out.'

And so the business of Domson's birth and genealogy was brought to the surface. At first neither Mr Justice McAlpine nor his solicitor believed what Domson was saying – that his great-grandmother had been the youngest child of a daughter of King George III. They made a few notes on a piece of paper and tried to calculate what the relationship would be.

'What does that mean then?' asked McAlpine. 'That would make you a first cousin once removed to the king, would it?'

'A third cousin once removed actually,' said Domson, referring to George V, who was enjoying the dying months of his reign. 'Queen Victoria was my first cousin three times removed.'

'Then you would claim a position within the succession,' asked McAlpine dubiously.

'Very distantly,' said Domson. 'I believe I'm number ninety-seven at the moment. Although some years ago I reached as high as eighty. Until they started breeding,' he added with disdain.

McAlpine smiled and nodded his head; he was accustomed to prisoners making up the most outrageous stories in order to help their case but he generally offered them very little credence. This, however, was the most audacious suggestion he had heard in a long time.

'Well I'll have to investigate this,' he said. 'I'll be back in to see you tomorrow morning and we'll talk again then.'

Later that day McAlpine set one of his pupils the task of investigating the ancestry of young Mr Domson and, to his surprise, he was informed that everything he had been told was in fact true.

'This puts the case into an entirely new light,' he told his client the following morning. 'I think it's safe to say that we will be able to avoid the death penalty.'

'I thought as much,' said Domson dismissively.

'But it will be important for you to show remorse and ask for mercy,' said the barrister. 'You do understand that, don't you?'

'I'm not pleading guilty,' he replied.

'I'm sorry?'

'I said I'm not pleading guilty,' said Domson with as nonchalant an air as if he was simply deciding between the soup or the melon starter. 'If I plead guilty I'll automatically be sentenced. They won't hear my case.'

'Well . . . yes,' said McAlpine.

'Then I want to plead not guilty,' explained Domson.

'If you do that, young man, the chances of the judge showing you any mercy in the event of your conviction diminish tenfold.'

'In the event of my conviction perhaps,' said Domson. 'But that won't happen. I am an old Etonian, Mr McAlpine. I am twenty-seventh in line to the throne of England and a second cousin to the king. Do you really think that a dozen fishmongers and schoolteachers and cobblers are going to take it on to their consciences to send me to the gallows? There's enough of a mystique about my extended family among the plebs and the riff-raff to ensure that I'll be let off. Just give them enough reasons to be unsure about the safety of a conviction and I guarantee they'll jump at the chance.'

'I'm not so sure about that,' said McAlpine, who had been practising at the Bar for almost thirty years and had never come across a client so convinced of his own ability to persuade the jurors while yet being so obviously guilty.

'Trust me,' said Domson. 'In any event, those are my instructions.'

And so Henry Domson had pleaded not guilty to the capital crime and over the course of the previous six months the evidence had mounted up against him. George V had died, to be replaced by Edward VIII, and suddenly he was twenty-sixth in line to the throne, albeit reverting from a second cousin of the monarch to a third. Throughout it all, as McAlpine tried to convince him to change his plea mid-trial, he had refused, continuing to maintain that his social standing would, at the end of the day, save his neck.

Then, on the Thursday of the previous week, the foreman of the jury had stood up in the dock and announced that after only twenty-three minutes of deliberations they had voted, twelve to zero, to find Henry Domson guilty as accused.

'And that wiped the smile off the bugger's face,' McAlpine told his wife when he returned home that evening.

He had spoken to his client only once in the time between the reading of the verdict and this morning, when the sentence was to be passed, and his self-confidence had certainly taken a beating in the intervening days; however, his arrogance was still such that he refused to believe that the judge would give him anything other than the most lenient of sentences.

'He seems like a decent old fellow,' said Domson, who had observed him throughout the trial, noting the expression on his face when the more unsavoury aspects of the night in question were brought up in court. 'Where did he go to school anyway?'

'Where he went to school is of no more concern to this case than how he likes his eggs cooked in the morning,' said Mr Justice McAlpine abruptly. 'Really, Henry, at some point you are going to have to start taking these proceedings seriously. Your life is at stake here.'

But Domson didn't care. No judge at a British court, he insisted, would ever sentence a man of his standing to such an extreme punishment. He would be given a few years at an easy prison and, following an appeal, would be quietly released after six months and allowed to return to his former life with a slap on the wrist and a promise to go forth and sin no more.

'I have every faith in the victory of British snobbery

over British justice,' he said as he adjusted his tie in the mirror.

However, as he was not entirely stupid, he tried to appear remorseful as he stood in the dock while Mr Justice Roderick Bentley KC entered the courtroom and took his seat on the bench, rearranging a few books and papers around him and pouring a tall glass of water as he waited for the assembled throng to settle down. The judge looked around and felt slightly irritated by how many people were there, as if the decision regarding a man's life and death was nothing more than a spectator sport. Throwing his eyes up to the gallery he saw his wife, Jane, sitting beside their old friend, Eleanor Tandy, and she inclined her head a little to him when their eyes met. He was glad that after today there would be no more conversations between them regarding what he should do for the best in this case, what he should do for *their* best. Because justice, he had decided within minutes of the verdict coming through the previous Thursday, had to be blind to all matters, including those of class and social standing.

Under instruction from the bailiff, Henry Domson stood up and the entire courtroom went silent, collectively holding their breath as Roderick cleared his throat and began to speak.

'Henry Domson,' he began. 'You have been found guilty of the murder of Police Constable Peter Milburn who, at the time of the offence, was acting in accordance with his duties. Murder, of course, is a capital crime and the murder of a police officer is a particularly heinous one.'

He continued for some minutes in this vein, citing precedent and incident which he had considered during his deliberations and Domson tried not to yawn in boredom while the spectators tried not to shout *Hurry up!*

'The court is aware,' said Roderick finally, 'of Mr Domson's previous good character, his educational achievements at Eton.' He said the school's name with a contemptuous sigh as he himself was an old Harrovian. 'And his relationship, albeit distant, with certain celebrated figures in the hierarchy of our country. However, the scales of justice are weighted by one who is oblivious to matters such as these, by one who is blind to both circumstances and title. They are merely side notes by which one can feel shock and disappointment that a fellow with so much to offer the world chose to turn his back on it.'

He opened his mouth to pass the final sentence and as he did so a vision of his son, Gareth, who at twenty-three was the same age as Henry Domson, came into his head. What if things were different, he thought? What if it was Gareth standing in the dock while another silk made such a decision? What would he think of this then? It was obvious, he decided. He would take his punishment like a man. The law was the law and had to be upheld; these were the foundations upon which he had built his life and nothing could make him turn his back on them. He blinked and dismissed the image from his head; he had a job to finish.

'And so I direct that you, Henry Domson, be taken from this place to await execution for the murder of Peter Milburn. I sentence you to be hanged from the neck until dead and may God have mercy on your soul.'

The court let out a collective gasp, Domson looked dumbstruck for the first time since the police had charged through the warehouse doors, and Lady Jane Bentley – her mind on invitations to garden parties at the palace and the outfit that she would wear to the coronation – sat in the front row of the upstairs gallery, closed her eyes slowly and shook her head with a sigh. *Oh Roderick,* she thought with as much sorrow as anger. *What have you done?*

Chapter 2

1

WHILE LESS CONFIDENT or successful men may have developed a chip on their shoulder regarding their lack of stature, Nicholas Delfy, the owner of the Unicorn Ballrooms, never allowed such a trivial and superficial matter to be of any concern to him. Standing at no more than five feet and four inches in height, Delfy had a small frame and glided around his club with the elegance and grace of a ballet dancer. A stickler for grooming and personal appearance, he had his thick, dark hair trimmed by his personal barber first thing every Monday morning while a manicurist simultaneously attended to his nails. He wore dark Savile Row suits with black shirts and ties and, with his youthful and clean-shaven complexion, he more closely resembled a teenaged boy smartly dressed for a funeral than a thirty-eight-year-old man who controlled an underground business empire around London, catering for the needs of those who were unable to find satisfaction elsewhere.

There was a quick two-rap knock on the door and he looked up to see Jimmy Henderson, also dark-suited and dark-tied but considerably taller and bulkier of build than his employer, stepping inside. Henderson was in his early forties and had the bald-headed, bull-nosed look of a former boxer who had come off the worst in most of his bouts.

'Boss,' said Henderson, hovering awkwardly in front of him for a moment until Delfy nodded towards the chair on the other side of the desk and he lowered himself into it gingerly; it was not a chair designed for a man of his build.

'Is it busy out there?' asked Delfy.

'It's getting going,' said Henderson, glancing up at the clock as he did so. 'It's only nine o'clock. It'll pick up.'

'Anyone in?'

'No one special.'

Delfy nodded. He only asked out of form. The Unicorn Ballrooms – not a ballroom at all, of course, but the elaborate title pushing the gambling tables closer to respectability – was one of the busiest and most profitable concerns of its type operating in London and Delfy one of its most successful entrepreneurs. Stretched around five thousand square feet of underground rooms and passages beneath a laundry, a homeopathy store and a tobacconist's it made its money from gambling and drinking, and those who visited found themselves lost in such an atmosphere of luxury and hedonism that they never wanted to leave. There was no natural lighting but the furnishings were of a high standard and formal dress was mandatory. As an employer, Delfy was well known for valuing his loyal staff highly – his wage bill was almost fifteen per cent higher than that of his nearest rivals – and they responded by making sure that every client was pampered and groomed and, most importantly, came back for another visit. He knew that it was money well spent.

He tapped his fingers on the desk nervously, needing to ask but not wanting to appear weak in front of his henchmen. There was no way around it but he looked at his papers while asking the question so as to appear disinterested in the answer, hating the fact that he couldn't hide his vulnerability.

'Well?' he asked eventually. 'How did it go? Is everything sorted?'

'It went fine,' said Henderson with a shrug. 'You can put her out of your mind now.'

Delfy nodded; a girl called Alice who had worked for him, a girl he had come close to liking, had been discovered stealing from the club and he hadn't been left with any choice.

'I don't . . .' began Delfy, trying to find the correct words but stumbling over them. 'I don't want her mentioned around here again, is that understood?'

'Sure, boss.'

'Let the others know, all right?'

'Will do.'

'And keep those new ones away from me too,' he added irritably, referring to the half-dozen girls who had recently been recruited to the Unicorn and who were coming to the end of their first week of employment there. 'They come down here asking whether I want a drink or a cigarette all the time and it's starting to annoy me. I'm their employer, not their friend, all right?'

'I know, boss. I'll tell them.'

'I don't want to make this corridor out of bounds but if I have to . . .'

'Don't worry about it, boss. I'll take care of it.'

'It just makes me . . . bloody angry,' he continued, his voice rising despite the fact that Henderson was agreeing with him. 'You need to keep them in line, you understand me?'

'I understand, boss. I'll see to it,' he replied, keeping his voice quiet and steady, the only way he knew to control his employer when he began a tirade like this.

'Well start seeing to it then,' said Delfy, practically shouting now. 'Because if another one of them turns up at my door claiming they've gone down the wrong corridor again they'll be sorry they did it.'

'Yes, boss.'

'I'm trying to run a business here.'

'I understand, boss.'

'I shouldn't even have to tell you.'

Henderson nodded; he could see that his employer

was getting that twitchy, irritated air about him that always hit when a situation arose that he didn't feel in control of.

'I won't be out there tonight,' said Delfy, who felt incredibly tired now and didn't want to face people. 'So just let me know if there are any problems or anyone comes in I should speak to.'

Henderson nodded. On most evenings, Delfy liked to parade around the club like a peacock for a couple of hours, talking to the clients, observing the games of roulette or blackjack that were being played at various tables, monitoring his employees from a distance to ensure that they were treating the clients in an acceptable fashion. He brought complimentary drinks to his more established patrons, or those who were losing incessantly but still had a bulge in their wallets.

There was also the matter of face-spotting. On an average night he could wander through his club and know the names, occupations and annual incomes of most of the people out there but from time to time there were a few strangers present too, men who had heard about the club through word of mouth or a personal recommendation. Some of these were clients who needed to be cultivated, some just wanted to be left alone to satisfy whatever vice they were indulging, and some needed to be turned out before they gave the place a bad name.

'Well if there's nothing else . . .' said Delfy eventually, looking across at Henderson with a strained smile on his face and indicating a mass of paperwork before him.

Henderson stood up. 'Benson will be bringing him in shortly,' he said, before turning away.

'Him?' asked Delfry, frowning. 'Him who?'

'Montignac,' said Henderson. 'You told us you wanted to speak to him, remember?'

Delfy sighed. 'Is that tonight?' he asked, frustrated.

'You said it was urgent.'

'I did, I know,' he said. 'All right. When? Within the hour?'

'Give or take.'

'Well show him in once he gets here, and you better wait outside then. Make sure he's clean too; I've never trusted that boy.'

'You don't need to worry about that,' said Henderson. 'What do you want us to do with him? Afterwards, I mean,' he added.

Delfy opened his mouth to reply but hesitated for a moment. 'I'm not sure yet,' he said. 'I'll see what he has to say for himself first. I'm very disappointed in our young Mr Montignac. After all the promises he made me. I don't like to be let down by people. I think it's time we showed him the error of his ways.'

Henderson nodded and took that as his cue to leave, closing the door quietly behind him.

Delfy remained seated behind his desk. He craved a drink and he missed Alice. But one would be ruinous to his health and the other . . . the other was beyond his reach now.

2

Gareth Bentley arrived at the Unicorn Ballrooms shortly before ten p.m. with two friends, Jasper Conway and Alexander Keys. They had enjoyed a large meal, supplemented by many bottles of wine, at a new restaurant in Covent Garden and were in high spirits but not drunk enough to be turned away by the doorman. Two of them had been there before. Conway was a regular visitor who was slowly working his way through his trust fund at the roulette tables while Keys preferred blackjack, although he never brought more money than he could afford to lose and was exactly the type of customer that Nicholas Delfy could have done without: the type who pocketed their winnings when they were ahead and left without throwing it away again.

Gareth, on the other hand, was a novice at the Unicorn, although he wasn't a stranger to similar types of establishment and he knew enough to pull his jacket down and appear as non-threatening as possible as they stood on the filthy London street being scrutinized by the doorman.

'Mr Conway,' he said, trained to remember names as he nodded his head politely at them. 'And Mr Keys. How are you gentlemen tonight?'

'Very well, Dempsey,' said Alexander, slipping a couple of shillings from his wallet and preparing to hand them over.

'You've brought a guest, I see,' said Dempsey looking

Gareth up and down for any signs of potential trouble.

'This is Mr Gareth Bentley,' said Conway with a swagger, draping his arm around his friend's shoulders. 'A particular friend of mine. Needs a bit of a treat, you see. It's his birthday. Twenty-four today. Very depressed about it.'

'Right you are,' said Dempsey, not caring about such things but stepping aside to allow them to enter. 'Have a pleasant evening, gentlemen,' he said as the coins slipped from Alexander's hand into his own and from there into his pocket. It was well known that the doormen at clubs such as this were among their highest earners; the power of entry and exit was a highly marketable one.

The three young men stepped through the doors and into the dark and narrow corridor beyond, surrendering their overcoats at the cloakroom. They wore tuxedos, for their birthday celebrations had been a formal affair, and had gone from the restaurant to bottles of champagne at a more legitimate club where standards of dress were encouraged. While there, they had made the decision to end their evening at the Unicorn and had loosened their bow ties only a little as they sat in the taxicab, assuming an air of louche disarray, the type that young gentlemen of their position and wealth liked to affect.

'I can't believe you've never been here before,' said Conway as they continued down the corridor towards the place where two more silent doormen stood on either side of a set of silver doors and opened them dramatically to reveal the club within. 'It's really one of the best of its sort.'

They stepped inside and Gareth blinked his eyes to adjust them to the surprising darkness on the other side. There was nothing particularly unexpected to be seen. A series of enclosed booths, all filled with well-dressed men of his own age and older, laughing and talking in small sets, and before them a wide bar where a group of attractive young women in a paucity of clothes were filling out orders and bringing trays to the tables. At the far side of the room there were a couple of billiard tables and beyond them, through another corridor, he could see and hear the sounds of the gaming rooms.

'Let's get a seat,' said Alexander, moving in the direction of an empty booth and glancing around a little nervously as he did so to see whether there was anyone he knew at any of the booths that surrounded them. He wasn't embarrassed about being seen in such a place – after all most of his acquaintances and friends attended them regularly – but he had a particular image of his own persona in his head and felt less than proud of the secret vices which threatened its unstable foundations. Alexander had taken a first in English and French literature at Cambridge and was employed as a book reviewer and literary correspondent for *The Times*, a position which he felt gave him a certain superiority in society. In his private time he was working on a novel in the tradition of Henry Fielding which he was so far afraid to show anyone in case they judged it crass and old-fashioned, a judgement which could only compromise his position and carefully nurtured view of himself.

'Champagne, I think,' said Jasper Conway when the girl arrived and he looked her up and down appreciatively while she smiled in return, attempting to appear pleasant but not encouraging. 'Your best champagne and four glasses, my dear.'

'Four glasses?' asked the waitress, looking around the table. 'Will you be having a friend join you then?'

'I thought you might like to sit with us for a while,' he replied jovially. 'It's my friend here's birthday today. Wouldn't you like to wish him well?'

'Happy birthday, sir,' said the waitress, smiling across at him. 'But unfortunately I can't join you, I'm on duty until closing time.'

'Not even for a quick snifter?' asked Jasper in disappointment. 'No one will mind, surely?'

The waitress shook her head but smiled and Jasper accepted defeat gracefully. He knew the rules of a place like this. The girls who worked in the bar section were attractive and pleasant but untouchable; they weren't tarts. The girls who worked in the gaming room beyond were less attractive and all business and you wouldn't want to touch them anyway; they kept track of everyone's hands at cards and their focus was unbreakable.

Of course it was entirely acceptable to try to lure one of the waitresses into your group but bad form to push them when they declined.

'Three glasses then, said Jasper, a little disappointed but not overly concerned. 'We'll drink alone.'

The waitress vanished, leaving the three men together in their booth.

'Actually, I don't think I should drink any more,' said Gareth. 'I should probably just get some water.'

'Not drink any more?' asked Jasper in an appalled tone, as if he had just made some lascivious comment about his mother. 'What on earth are you talking about?'

'I've already had a couple of glasses of wine. You know that it's bad for me.'

'Oh don't be ridiculous,' he replied. 'It's your birthday after all.'

Gareth threw a look across the table at Alexander, hoping that he'd back him up. It was difficult to maintain his sobriety without some support.

'If he doesn't want to, don't make him,' said Alexander. 'You still worry about it then? I wondered when I saw you drinking at dinner,' he added, looking across at Gareth.

'I had a glass of champagne because, as Jasper says, it's my birthday. But other than that, I never do any more. It's too risky.'

'Don't worry, we'll keep an eye on you,' said Jasper, who was damned if he was going to allow him to stop drinking now. 'Have you cheered up yet anyway?' he asked, looking across at Gareth who gave a small laugh and nodded.

'I'm all right,' he said. 'I was being ridiculous.'

'Of course you were. Twenty-four's nothing. I'm twenty-nine for heaven's sake. Nearly thirty. I'll be an old man come next September.'

'It's not the fact of turning twenty-four that's bothering me,' said Gareth, who had spent much of the early evening bemoaning the fact that another birthday had come along to attack him. 'It's the fact that I don't seem to have much of a life going on for a chap of my age.'

'Not much of a life?' asked Jasper in surprise. 'For heaven's sake, man, you lead a charmed life.'

'As you see it.'

'As any sensible person would see it,' he said. 'Do you know I have to get up every weekday morning at eight o'clock, I have to present myself for work to the bank by nine – nine in the morning, mind you, regardless of where I've been or what I've been doing the night before – I have to work flat out until lunchtime when I'm lucky if I get more than an hour or two for myself, and then it's back to the slog until four. That's my life, Gareth. You should try working in a bank if you want to know the meaning of hard work.'

'Jasper, your father owns the bank,' remarked Alexander with a smile. 'You're a board member. Your working days consist of long lunches with clients and making sure that all your assistants do your work for you. It's not as if you're sitting behind a counter all day, filling out lodgement and withdrawal slips.'

'Well I don't see how that's relevant,' sniffed Jasper, a little offended. 'It's still work. I mean granted it's not as demanding as sitting around reading novels all day long and typing a few hundred words of praise or damnation but all the same.'

Alexander laughed and shook his head. 'I'm not having this debate again,' he said, for the subject of working in a bank versus the literary lifestyle was one they had contested many times. He glanced around as the waitress brought their drinks and noticed an enormous burly man – the type that was always present in places such as this to undertake the less than savoury aspects of their employer's business – disappearing down a corridor with another man being led before him like a prisoner on his way to the firing squad. He narrowed his eyes to try to see the fellow's face, as the sudden shock of white hair was more than familiar to him, but the two men had disappeared out of sight now and he dismissed it as a trick of the light and turned back to his friends.

'I think I need a job,' Gareth announced as they clinked glasses.

'Steady on,' said Jasper. 'That's just the drink talking.'

'And that's exactly why this has to be my last one. Anything that will get me out of the house would do,' he continued. 'Something to keep me busy. Father won't stop harassing me about it until I start something.'

'You don't want to come to work at the bank, do you?' asked Jasper, secretly hoping that his friend might say yes.

'No,' said Gareth firmly. 'Not that.'

'What does your father want you to do?'

'He wants me to join him in chambers,' he said. 'He says it's absolutely insane for a young man to have studied law and passed all his exams and then not want to practise at the Bar.'

'It does seem a little pointless,' admitted Alexander.

'I suppose so. But I'm not like him,' said Gareth, who had enjoyed his studies at Cambridge but was frustrated by the fact that he had a great desire to rebel against his father, the eminent judge Mr Justice Roderick Bentley KC, but could not find a subject of sufficient disagreement between them. 'He loved being a barrister, he absolutely adored getting people off on some technicality that he'd thought up or getting them sent down when he knew they were guilty, and being a judge is what his whole life has led to. But he's always been uncommonly kind to those guilty bastards that have come before him, that's what bothers me. I'm not sure I have that generosity of spirit within me.'

'He's not always kind,' pointed out Jasper. 'He let that fellow swing a couple of months ago, didn't he? What was his name . . . the chap who was the king's nephew or some such thing.'

'His third cousin,' Gareth corrected him. 'Yes, he did, I'll give you that. But that's because he said that justice was blind or some such rot and that if anyone else had been standing before him convicted of the same offence then he would have sentenced him the exact same way.'

'Still, it seemed a bit strong,' said Jasper. 'All things considered.'

'Rubbish,' said Alexander whose literary pretensions had turned him into something of an anti-establishmentarian, although he still couldn't quite decide whether he wanted to tear down the palace or become the poet laureate. 'Your father did the right thing. He didn't allow himself to be swayed by powerful and mysterious forces.'

'Well anyway,' said Gareth. 'That's what he wants. For me to take my pupillage in his chambers and then practice alongside him.'

'And are you going to do it?' asked Jasper, who sensed in his friend a desire to be told that to do such a thing, to work for a living, was not really so awful.

'It doesn't look as if I'm going to have much choice,' said Gareth. 'It's either that or he says he's going to cut off my allowance. I'm afraid that the days of Gareth Bentley playing the carefree bachelor are behind me. Good God, he'll want me to get married next,' he added with a shudder.

'If I was you I'd play for time,' said Jasper quietly after a brief silence when they had all taken a moment to consider the horrors of taking a wife. 'I wouldn't give him an answer quite yet. You'll find that he'll be slow to cut you off if he feels you're actively searching for something and not just lying around.'

'Do you think so?' asked Gareth hopefully, for his relaxed and untroubled lifestyle was exactly the sort of existence he wanted to lead; he was not ambitious at all for anything more challenging.

'Of course,' said Jasper. 'You just string him along for as long as you can and sooner or later something will turn up. Something always does.'

Gareth looked across at his friend and nodded hopefully as Jasper lifted his glass and drained it before pouring another round for everyone from the magnum and ordering a second bottle.

3

Owen Montignac stood outside the door to Nicholas Delfy's office, hesitating for a moment as he tried to organize his thoughts.

The last few hours had been particularly disagreeable. First there had been a fractious dinner with his cousin Stella at Claridge's – she had phoned him earlier in the week, worried because she hadn't heard from him in days and he wasn't returning any of her calls, but he'd happened to answer the phone when she phoned that time and he couldn't avoid the conversation any longer – and now this further unpleasantness.

'Are you all right?' Stella asked when she finally tracked him down. 'Why haven't you called me back?'

'I'm fine,' he told her. 'Absolutely fine. Sorry, I've just been very busy, that's all. Up to my eyes in it actually.'

Stella hesitated before replying. 'I hope that is the only reason,' she said finally.

'Well what else could it be?' he asked her, able to hear

the note of bitterness in his voice himself even as he said it.

'What else indeed,' she muttered. 'Look, I'll be in London tomorrow evening. Let's have dinner together.'

'Tomorrow evening,' he said, thinking about it. 'Tomorrow evening might be tricky.'

'Why might it be tricky?' she demanded.

'I may have other plans,' he said.

'And do you?' she asked. 'Do you have other plans?'

Montignac sighed. It was useless. It didn't matter how many times he tried to put her off, he knew that she'd only keep coming back at him until he finally gave in. And besides, there was a part of him that missed her. He hadn't seen her since the morning Sir Denis Tandy had gathered them together for the reading of the will, and she was in his thoughts a lot.

'I suppose I could cancel them,' he muttered.

'I'd be very grateful if you would,' she said. 'How about seven o'clock? At Claridge's?'

'I'll see you there,' he said, ringing off before she could question him further.

The dinner had lasted for a little over an hour and had been a difficult encounter, made even more unpleasant for him by the fact that she'd decided to bring her fool of a boyfriend, Raymond Davis, with her. When Montignac made his excuses for leaving just before half past eight Stella sighed loudly, looking thoroughly exhausted with him.

'You can't go, Owen,' she said. 'We haven't finished discussing things yet. We've barely begun.'

'I'm sorry, but we'll have to pick it up another time,' he said. 'I have important business to attend to.'

'More important than this?'

'Stella,' he said quietly, equally tired with their on-going battle. 'The world doesn't run to your timetable, you know.'

'I don't expect it to,' she said, insulted. 'But I wish I could just pin you down for five minutes and talk about what happens next. You seem so angry with me. The way you're behaving anyone would think that I'd planned all of this.'

'Would they?' he asked in a matter-of-fact voice, looking her directly in the eye. 'What an absurd idea.'

'Look here, old fellow,' said Raymond, using that phoney Englishman-in-Africa syntax that he'd picked up from the most recent Waugh. 'All the old girl's trying to say is—'

'Drop round to the gallery tomorrow,' Montignac said to his cousin. 'Around lunchtime. We can talk then. Just the two of us.' He ignored both Raymond's interruption and his presence as if he was nothing more than a hovering maître d', waiting to find out whether they wanted teas or coffees to finish.

'Well you'd better be there,' said Stella as he stood up. 'If I arrive and you've gone off somewhere for the day—'

'I'll be there,' he promised, attempting a smile, trying to avoid noticing how magnificent she looked in her new gown – an expensive, dark-red taffeta dress that she had bought earlier in the day. 'And we'll talk then. Alone,' he repeated for emphasis.

Leaving Claridge's at breakneck speed, he stood outside on the street for a few minutes, trying to recover his composure, counting to ten to prevent himself from going back inside and dragging Raymond Davis out on to the street with him, or down some back alley to show him what happened to fools who thought they could come between him and Stella. A light drizzle began to threaten and he made his way along Brook Street, looking for a quiet bar where he might settle his nerves.

A few minutes later he was relaxing in the Duck and Dog with a large whisky, quietly watching a game of feathers being played by two middle-aged men opposite. The bar was half empty and he noticed a large man, tall and heavy in a dark suit, enter and look around before smiling at him for a moment and walking over towards the bar. He glanced around again, checking to see what Montignac was drinking, said something to the barman, and a moment later started to walk towards him with a glass in each hand.

'Whisky's your drink, I'm told,' he said. 'Here's a top-up,' he added, handing one across and keeping one for himself.

Montignac's eyes narrowed. He looked across at the door and wondered whether he should just stand up and leave. Whether he would even be allowed. He didn't touch the drink.

'I'm sorry,' he said. 'Do I know you?'

'You've met me before.'

'I have?' Montignac tried to recall; he was sure he would remember such a mountain of a man. 'I'm sorry, I don't—'

'I work for Nicholas Delfy,' said the man. 'He was hoping that you might be able to pay him a visit this evening.'

Montignac felt his stomach sink a little. 'Nicholas,' he said quietly, considering it, pretending that it was difficult for him to remember who Nicholas Delfy actually was, his life being so full of important and powerful people that a few were always likely to slip through the cracks. 'Yes of course, Nicholas. I haven't spoken to him in quite some time.'

'I believe that's what he's concerned about,' said the man. 'Perhaps he misses your company.'

Montignac smiled, although it wasn't comforting that the man had a sense of humour. 'Well you can tell him that he's on my list,' said Montignac hopefully. 'I have a busy couple of days coming up but I'll try to make it in to see him on Friday if that's convenient.'

'Friday,' said the man in a neutral tone.

'Yes.'

'Morning or afternoon?' he asked.

'Oh, let's say afternoon,' said Montignac, finishing his own drink but ignoring the one the man had bought for him. 'About three o'clock?'

He stood up and the man stood too, his face relaxing into a mocking smile.

'Mr Delfy would like to see you tonight,' he said in a tone which suggested that he wasn't going to take no for an answer.

Montignac nodded, recognizing the futility of trying to escape. 'Fine,' he said, reaching down and finishing the second drink in one mouthful. 'Shall we go then?'

Twenty minutes later they pulled up outside the front doors of the Unicorn Ballrooms and marched straight past the doorman with only a quick exchange of nods between the two employees. In the dimly lit corridor beyond, Montignac caught sight of his own reflection in one of the mirrors and the burst of white hair on his head stood out like a beacon in the darkness.

He had been to the club on many, many occasions in the past but had been deliberately avoiding it over the previous five or six weeks. Even at night, when he had the urge to drink or gamble, or the sudden thirsting need for a woman, he had stayed away. He'd written a letter to Delfy on the morning of his uncle's funeral the previous month and that had been the only communication between the two during that time and, although he hardly dared to believe it, he had started to think that Delfy might have forgotten about him entirely and the matter would be dropped. It was a foolish thought, however – the debt was far too large to be simply written off. In fact, he had been waiting for just such a visit as the large man had made to the bar tonight – he must have been observing him from earlier in the evening and he was grateful that he hadn't made his presence felt at Claridge's – and knew that the inevitable could be put off no longer.

He didn't look around as they went down the stairs to the bar area but could hear from the sounds of conversation and laughter around him that most of the booths were full. He could make out the distinctive whirring of the roulette tables in the distance, a sound that was like an addictive music to him, and remembered the first night he had ever come here, almost two years earlier, when he had entered the casino with just over a hundred pounds in his pocket and left having increased it fivefold. He'd gone home that night, enraptured by his success, and even started to make calculations of just how much money he could make at the tables if he devoted himself to them for a few hours every night, a wealth that could accumulate over five or six years into a figure that could rival even that of his uncle's bank account.

Of course, that first night was the last time he had left as a winner.

Montignac felt like a prisoner being led to the scaffold as they reached the end of the corridor. The man who had escorted him to the Unicorn Ballrooms moved him slightly out of the way, rapped on the door of the office and opened it, pushing his charge inside before closing the door again and taking up his position outside.

'Owen,' said Nicholas Delfy, looking up from his

paperwork. 'I thought we'd have to send out the cavalry to track you down.'

4

Stella Montignac and Raymond Davis returned to her suite on the top floor of Claridge's having said little to each other along the way. During the walk from the table to the lobby, and again on the stairs and corridors that led to her room, Raymond had been expecting her to turn to him and give him the signal that it was time for him to depart to his own flat in Chelsea; he was unsure now whether she hadn't suggested it because she desired him or simply because she was too exhausted by the events of the evening to even remember that he was there, trailing behind her like an attentive puppy dog.

'Pour me a drink, Raymond, would you?' Stella asked as he closed the door of the suite behind them. He nodded and walked over to the bar while she collapsed on the sofa for a moment before standing up again and pacing the floor like an expectant father. She let out a sigh of frustration. 'That bloody boy,' she added after a moment.

'A glass of wine, darling?' asked Raymond

'Vodka and tonic,' she said. 'Plenty of vodka. Light on the tonic.'

He nodded and poured the drink. He'd felt all along that it was a mistake for him to join the cousins for dinner that evening but Stella had insisted and any opportunity to spend time with her was something he was only too happy to go along with. The look on Montignac's face when he had walked in and seen him sitting there, however, had told a different story.

'I don't know what to do,' said Stella as he handed her the glass. 'I simply don't know what to do for the best.'

'He is a tricky customer,' replied Raymond, unwilling to criticize him outright for he had learned before that only Stella claimed the right to do that.

'He's more than tricky, Raymond,' said Stella irritably. 'He's downright difficult.'

'Well you must remember the whole thing has come as an enormous shock to him. I wouldn't say he was looking forward to profiting from your father's death exactly—'

'Raymond, don't!'

'No, I don't mean profit,' he said, correcting himself quickly. 'But he may have had certain plans laid out for his future. Things that he was hoping to do. I mean when the contents of the will were read, it had to have come as a most unexpected blow.'

Stella gave a brief laugh. 'You have no idea,' she said. 'You should have been in the room with us. His face went even whiter than his hair.'

Raymond poured himself a drink and sat down opposite her. They had known each other for almost a year and a half now, having met through mutual friends on Ladies' Day at Ascot. Raymond had fallen for her immediately; on any day she was a stunning girl but dressed to the nines with a hat that was the envy of most of the crowd, he had been unable to take his eyes off her. It had become something of a joke between them that he had missed most of the races that afternoon, and even the fact that he had had a 16/1 winner and filled a four-horse accumulator, because he was too busy staring at her.

For her part Stella liked to play along and tell him that she had liked him immediately too but for the life of her, and she tried very hard, she couldn't remember that first introduction. She recalled being at the races, of course, and she remembered her friends introducing her to some new people, but then that happened all the time and really, as she told herself, how could she possibly hope to keep them all straight in her head?

But Raymond had done a most extraordinary thing, out of character for him and totally unexpected for her. He had called on her at Leyville a few days later, claiming to have been in the area, and offered to take her to lunch.

'It's Raymond Davis,' he said extending his hand, quick to give her his name in order to avoid the embarrassment of her having to ask for it. 'We met at Ascot, don't you remember?'

'Of course I remember,' she lied. 'It was a lovely day and you were perfectly charming.'

'We said we should have lunch some day. If I was ever

down here. And here I am. Down here,' he added nervously.

'Well then, we should have lunch,' she said, for he seemed a personable enough chap and a girl had to eat after all. 'Let me just get my coat.'

They had taken a stroll down to the local village and dined in the restaurant where Raymond had told her all about his own background. His father was retired from the navy, where he had been an admiral, and his two older brothers held various ranks there now. One of them was currently stationed somewhere in the Caribbean, near an island whose name he could never remember.

'You didn't want to join up?' asked Stella.

'I don't like the water,' said Raymond apologetically, which made her laugh. 'I can't even swim. So it seemed a little pointless.'

'I bet that went down well with the family,' she said with a smile. Raymond had found in the past that most girls lost interest in him when he admitted to failings like this but Stella, always contrary to most girls, seemed to think it a point in his favour.

'Not very well,' he admitted. 'I am something of the black sheep.'

Her smile faded a little and she looked out the window to where some noisy children were being allowed to run wild. 'Every family has one of them,' she said. 'Or creates one for themselves anyway.'

'I don't mind too much,' he said, sounding like a man who minded rather a lot.

'So what do you do then?' she asked.

'I studied for a degree in botany,' he told her. 'And I'm currently working at the Royal Horticultural Society in London, researching and propagating some new species of roses. Hybrid Teas, mostly. Some floribundas and climbers. It's tremendously interesting.'

'Flowers,' she said, simplifying things rather.

'Well . . . yes,' he admitted with a nod. 'I mean there's rather more to it than that, of course, but I suppose at its most basic level . . . it's flowers, yes.'

Stella leaned forward and took his hand for a moment, squeezing it tightly, and he opened his eyes wide, surprised and thrilled by the intimacy. 'I think that must have been a very brave choice,' she said, as if he had just admitted to a perversion he was hoping to conquer, before releasing him and leaning back in her chair.

'Do you . . . do you do anything?' he asked after a few moments, once he had managed to compose himself again. 'For a living, I mean.'

'Good Lord, no,' she said, laughing a little at the thought of it. 'Nothing at all. There was talk a year or two ago of me getting a career but in the end it came to nothing. Nothing appealed to me, you see. I try to keep busy by doing some charity work of course. I ran a tombola last summer at Leyville to help provide medicine to the children of miners in the North-East and it was a tremendous success. And earlier this year I raised almost three thousand pounds for the local hospital by organizing a village fête. My father's very wealthy, of course.'

'Yes, I know,' said Raymond, instantly regretting the way that sentence had come out; it made him sound like a gold-digger. 'Mine is pretty well off too,' he added then in order to atone for it, and then worried that he was coming across as competitive. 'And you have brothers, I suppose?'

Stella shook her head. 'I had one brother,' she told him. 'Andrew. But he died when he was eighteen. A shooting accident.'

'I'm sorry,' said Raymond.

She shrugged her shoulders and looked away for a moment. She had become immune to people saying that whenever the subject came up.

'So there's just you?' he asked.

'Well no,' she told him. 'I have a cousin, Owen, who lives with us. He's a few months younger than me. I suppose he's more of a brother in a way. He came to us when he was five, just after his parents died and he's been with us ever since. We were all very close as children, actually.'

'And what does he do?' asked Raymond.

'He studied history of art at Cambridge,' said Stella. 'He took a first and then got his master's in record time. And now he's working at an art gallery in London. I've been there. It's very contemporary, and Father says it's all rot of course. They don't allow anything in that was produced before nineteen hundred.'

'Really?' asked Raymond in surprise. 'And has there been any decent art produced over the last thirty years?'

'None whatsoever,' said Stella, breaking into a laugh. 'But it's awfully good fun looking at the rubbish that gets put on show there all the same. Everyone's afraid to criticize it because no one wants to appear old-fashioned. So they sell these dreadful canvasses for huge amounts of money and Cousin Owen pockets a fairly decent commission, I imagine. Not that he's in it for the money of course. Nothing as vulgar as that. I think he quite enjoys his job. He seems committed to it anyway.'

'Well, we all need money,' said Raymond with a smile.

'Not Owen. He stands to inherit the entire Montignac fortune. The Montignacs always inherit on the male line,' she explained. 'Right through our ancestry. They've never let a girl take over the estate, the sexist swine. It should have gone to Andrew, of course, but since he died . . . well Owen's stood as heir ever since. His father was my father's elder brother. He was cut off in a scandal years before I was born but then he died during the war and there was nothing else my father could do but take the boy in. And he's very fond of him.'

Raymond nodded; he wasn't particularly interested in the financial operations of the Montignac family but he enjoyed watching her talk about them because it gave him an excuse to stare directly at her. As usual she was wearing very little make-up and her porcelain-like skin made him want to reach across and touch her, like one might have the urge to stroke a sheet of satin in a fabric shop. Stella turned away from the window and looked across at him, narrowing her eyes for a moment as if she was deciding something for herself.

'I suppose we might start seeing more of each other from now on then,' she said decisively and he nodded quickly and that was that.

In the eighteen months since then, they had officially established themselves as a couple. They spent much of their time in London where Stella lived the charmed life of a lady of leisure during the day and by night they went to plays and restaurants with their friends. From time to time – and Raymond could never predict when – Stella would invite him to stay in her suite with her and they would make love so passionately that he couldn't quite understand why he was so quickly dismissed again the following morning. She wasn't the only girl he had ever been with but he couldn't imagine another any more, despite the fact that there remained something of an emotional distance between them, a wall that she wouldn't allow him to climb over.

'I don't like talking about love affairs,' she told him once. 'I did it once, a long time ago, and it was very nearly the death of me. Quite literally.'

He tried to press her on this former romance but she was close-mouthed about it and he had since stopped trying.

He dreaded the rare occasions when he was invited to Leyville for the weekend; Peter Montignac was polite enough, for form's sake, but seemed completely disinterested in his entire existence. Raymond tried to engage him on any number of topics but it was pointless; the man simply didn't want to know. And while Owen Montignac had warmed a little from the iceberg frostiness of their initial relationship, it was obvious to Raymond that he didn't think him good enough for his cousin. He sought every possible opportunity to mock Raymond's profession, while ignoring the fact that he was hardly an army serviceman himself, and Raymond felt intimidated whenever they were together. But Stella had insisted that he join them for dinner that evening and he had dutifully gone.

'You may as well stay tonight,' she said, kicking her shoes off now and finishing her drink. Raymond beamed and found that he could relax at last.

'All right,' he said. 'If you like.'

'I do like,' she said quickly. 'Now tell me,' she added, leaning forwards. 'The truth now. Be completely honest. Do you think that Owen believes I had anything to do with Father changing his will?'

5

'I've been meaning to come to see you,' said Owen Montignac, standing with his back to the door but not edging any further forwards for the moment; he tried to speak in as casual a fashion as possible, as if the whole thing was terribly trivial and unworthy of his attention. 'Everything's just been so busy at the gallery recently that it slipped my mind.'

'Perfectly understandable,' said Nicholas Delfy, extending his hands wide in a show of magnanimity. 'We're both busy men after all.'

'Indeed.'

'Have a seat, Owen.'

There was no hint of a request here; it was a simple order and Montignac obeyed it. There were very few men in the world who had ever scared him but Delfy was one. It wasn't that he himself was physically intimidating; in fact, with his short stature and angelic face he could hardly have been less threatening. And it wasn't concern about the henchmen and bodyguards that surrounded him and could injure a man without a second thought that made Montignac wish he was anywhere but in his office right at that moment. It was Delfy's reputation that made him nervous, for he was not known as a man who went so far as to kill his enemies. He was crueller than that. He found ways to hurt them through the people they cared about or, if there was no one of sufficient importance in the victim's life to harm, he inflicted only enough damage to cause endless misery to his target. He had been known to paralyse people, leaving them in wheelchairs or hospitals for the rest of their lives, or blind them by ripping the eyes from the sockets. From time to time, he liked to remove a vital organ. He didn't believe in giving anyone the easy escape of death.

'I was sorry to hear about your uncle,' said Delfy. 'Were you close to him?'

'I lived with him from the time I was five years old.'

Delfy smiled. 'That's not what I asked,' he said.

'I was close to him,' he said hesitantly. 'Up to a point.'

'I had an uncle myself once,' said Delfy. 'I don't remember him well, except that he was very kind to me as a child. Always brought me presents when he came to visit and played chess with me too, as I recall. Although he wasn't very good and I could beat him by the time I was seven. I seem to remember that he never minded when I won. If anything he was proud of me for it. But then he was killed in the Great War.'

'My father died in the war too,' said Montignac, biting his lip as he said this because he didn't like to talk about his parents much and certainly wouldn't have chosen to discuss them with someone like Nicholas Delfy. He had only a vague recollection of his mother and father and knew that people had been discouraged from mentioning their names at Leyville while he was growing up.

'Really?' asked Delfy, interested now. 'How did he die?'

'He was at the battle of the Somme,' he replied. 'His platoon was hit by a shell from a German artillery tank. He was only thirty-four at the time.'

'Is that so,' said Delfy quietly, nodding his head out of respect. 'I didn't know that.'

'Why would you?' asked Montignac.

'True, true. And was your father a gambler, Owen?'

Montignac sighed; he didn't want to discuss his father

as a metaphor for his own behaviour. 'I'd hardly label myself as a gambler,' he said.

'Wouldn't you?' asked Delfy as if he was truly surprised by the answer. 'How extraordinary.' He reached across the desk to his ledger and started to flick through it until he came to a page about a third of the way from the end. He examined it silently for a moment before looking across at Montignac. 'It says here,' he began, 'that you are in debt to me for a very large amount of money.'

'Reasonably large, yes.'

'Fifty thousand pounds,' said Delfy with a whistle. 'And change.'

'I don't think it can be quite that much.'

'Would you like to see the figures?' asked Delfy, the smile fading from his face. 'I think you'll find it's perfectly accurate.'

'No,' said Montignac, shaking his head. (In fact he thought the figure had been slightly over sixty thousand so, up to a point, he was pleased.)

'And then, of course, you wrote me a letter,' said Delfy, lifting an envelope from the page and carefully removing the piece of paper within, as if it was an important piece of evidence that had to be handled with caution. 'Quite an extraordinary piece of prose, if I may say so.'

'The thing about that letter—'

'Dear Nicholas,' said Delfy, scanning it and reading selected passages. 'Nothing too important to begin with

. . . sorry I haven't been in touch . . . Well we were all sorry about that, Owen,' he said, looking up and smiling again as if the whole thing was an enormous joke. 'I could hardly sleep out of concern for you. I thought perhaps you'd done a runner.'

'I wouldn't do that, Nicholas—'

'*However I believe I will be in a position to start repaying you the money I owe you very shortly. My uncle has just passed away and once the estate has been settled I will be able to send you a cheque for* . . . very sad when a beloved family member passes away, Owen. You must have been distraught.'

'If you would just allow me to explain,' said Montignac, fighting to control his temper now.

'Fine,' said Delfy, leaning back in his chair and willing to let him dig his own grave. 'Explain. Thrill me with stories of anticipation and disappointment.'

'I was led to believe, I was *always* led to believe, that upon my uncle's death the Montignac estate would pass to me.'

'And let me guess, Owen,' said Delfy with a smile. 'Things didn't quite go according to plan.'

Montignac shook his head. 'No,' he said. 'No they didn't. But I can set them right. You'll get your money. You don't have to worry about that.'

Delfy nodded slowly and considered things. He waited so long before speaking again that Montignac wondered whether he should say something himself, only he didn't feel that would be a sensible idea.

'What worries me,' Delfy said finally, 'is that two months ago, shortly before your uncle's untimely passing, I asked you to come to see me to discuss the outstanding amount which, at the time, was some three thousand pounds less than it is now. What with the exorbitant amount of interest I'm forced to charge in order to meet my overheads. You do remember that meeting, don't you?'

'I remember it,' said Montignac.

'And you told me this story about being set to inherit the Montignac estate which, if I recall correctly, you stated to be worth in excess of two million pounds.'

'The capital is,' interjected Montignac. 'But most of that is landholdings which are untouchable. It's the interest and the rents that form the basis of my income. Would have formed the basis of it, that is.'

'Indeed. And I asked you what condition your uncle's health was in and you told me that it was passable but that he wasn't getting any younger and that could change any day.'

'Yes,' said Montignac.

'And I had no choice but to tell you of some of the things that I might be forced to do to you if you didn't start to pay me back the money you owed me.'

'Yes,' said Montignac.

'And then some weeks later I was reading the newspaper and what do I find? Only a front-page story informing me that Peter Montignac has passed away in his sleep at his country home. Quite suddenly. And quite unexpectedly. Well you can imagine my surprise.'

'I could try,' said Montignac.

Delfy narrowed his eyes; sarcasm was only permitted on his side of the desk. 'I'm not playing a game with you, Owen,' he said.

'No. Of course not.'

'It seems that there was an uncommon stroke of good luck in your uncle's death which was countered by an unfortunate twist of fate when it was discovered that you were not to inherit after all. That must have been disappointing for you.'

'It was . . . very surprising,' admitted Montignac.

'Semantics,' said Delfy quickly. 'And which I am to be then?' Disappointed or surprised?'

'No one was more shocked than I was when—'

'All in all it leaves me wondering how long I am going to have to wait for my money.'

Montignac shuffled nervously and leaned forwards. 'Nicholas, don't think I'm—'

'I think it's better,' said Delfy sharply, holding up a hand to halt him. 'If we revert to the formalities. I only allow my friends to call me by my given name. Not those who are trying to steal from me.'

'I'm not trying to steal from you, Nich—, Mr Delfy. I just need a little more time, that's all.'

'It's an enormous amount of money, Owen. How much time are you talking about?'

'Six months,' said Montignac, plucking the figure out of thin air.

'Six months?' asked Delfy, laughing. 'You can't be serious.'

'The figure currently stands at just over fifty, right?' asked Montignac. Delfy nodded. 'If I can clear off the ten thousand in four weeks' time, as a show of good faith, will you give me five months after that to come up with the balance? Say until Christmas?'

Delfy breathed heavily through his nose and leaned back in his chair, a slight smile crossing his lips. If nothing else, he admired the boy's courage.

'Ten thousand in four weeks, you say?'

'It's either that or you do your worst now and there'll be no chance of me being able to get any of it. Trust me and if I haven't delivered in a month's time then what you do next will be for you to decide. But if I manage to fulfil my part of the deal then you give me till Christmas Day to find the rest.'

Delfy considered it, Montignac was quite right. If he did anything to damage the boy now it would be a beating that would cost him fifty thousand pounds. This way at least there was a chance.

'I suppose I wonder how committed you would be to finding the money,' he said finally in a thoughtful voice.

'I understand the consequences if I don't.'

'Indeed,' said Delfy, leaning back in his chair. 'And tell me this. How far would you go to spare yourself?'

Montignac frowned. 'As far as I had to,' he said.

'That's good to hear. Because there would be some who would have moral objections to doing anything a little . . . unpleasant.'

'I would suppress any such instincts,' said Montignac, as if it was a point of honour. 'You can rely on that.'

'Some would draw the line at stealing, for example.'

'Some might,' said Montignac.

'Others would hesitate before hurting someone.'

'I can imagine,' he replied.

'And there are those who would never consider the gains that could be made from killing a man.'

Montignac opened his mouth for a moment but hesitated, unwilling to respond.

'All right,' said Delfy, smiling slightly, gratified to know that there was probably nothing he wouldn't do if asked. 'We'll give your little scheme a go. Four weeks from today. Not a minute longer, though.'

Montignac sighed in relief and stood up before Delfy could change his mind. 'You can trust me,' he said.

'That's neither here nor there,' said Delfy with a shrug. 'I'll look forward to seeing you here four weeks from tonight. And I will be extremely disappointed if you don't show up.'

'I won't let you down,' said Montignac, opening the door and stepping back out on to the corridor quickly.

Delfy sat still for a few moments as the door closed and smiled, shaking his head as he wondered whether the boy would be able to manage it or not. It was an awful lot of money to find in such a short space of time but somehow he didn't put it past him. And it was useful to know that there was something that Montignac might be able to do for him to help them both out. He reached for the phone and dialled a Westminster number.

6

Despite having very little money of his own in his wallet, Jasper Conway insisted on taking Gareth and Alexander into the casino where, he told them, they could end the night with a bang.

'Of course there are other ways to enjoy oneself in a place like this,' he told his friends. 'But this might be the best option for tonight.'

Alexander was happy to join him but Gareth wasn't quite so sure; having never gambled before he was nervous of showing himself up among his more experienced friends.

'Don't be such a drip, Gareth,' said Alexander. 'It's your birthday after all. If you can't have a little luck about you on your birthday, well when can you?'

Gareth shrugged. 'Won't the other card players get angry if I have to keep asking for the rules, though?' he asked.

'We could play roulette,' suggested Jasper. 'It's perfectly simple, you'll pick it up in a flash. How much money do you have on you anyway?'

Gareth took out his wallet and looked inside. 'About thirty pounds,' he said.

'That's plenty,' said Jasper. 'Hand it over.'

'Hand it over?'

'Yes.'

'Why, for heaven's sake?'

'Because I have to cash it in for chips,' explained Jasper, looking across at Alexander and shaking his head at the boy's naivety. 'Don't you know anything? Now come on. Don't look so scared, old man! You could triple or quadruple your money inside an hour if luck's on your side.'

Gareth frowned but took the money from his wallet and gave it to Jasper anyway, who smiled broadly and leaped away from the table with another ten pounds belonging to Alexander and told them he'd be back shortly with their markers.

'Were you serious about what you were saying earlier?' asked Alexander while they were waiting for him to return.

'About having to get a job? Perfectly serious. It's rotten luck.'

'You never know. You might enjoy it.'

Gareth shrugged and an idea came to him. 'I don't suppose there's anything going in your place, is there? Reviewing books perhaps? Seems like a cushy number.'

'Eh, no,' said Alexander quickly, for the number of books which could be reviewed for the newspaper was finite and he already tried to grab as many of them as possible for they paid by the word. 'No, I don't think that would work out. But working for your father does seem a bit extreme. How have you managed till now anyway?'

'Well until now I've officially been studying, haven't I?' explained Gareth. 'I only graduated last summer. I've been able to get away with the excuse that I'm taking some time off since then but there's only so much the old man can take. I may have pushed him to the limit.'

'I'm just surprised it's taken him this long,' said Alexander, who had met Roderick Bentley once or twice over the course of his friendship with Gareth and had been struck by his gravity and strong convictions regarding his own career; he found it hard to imagine that he would be at all happy with his twenty-four-year-old son lurking around the house idly for too long.

'He didn't really notice me for months at a time,' explained Gareth. 'With the Domson trial and everything. He spent all his time working on it. It's only now that it's over and done with and the newspaper interest has died away that he's starting to focus on other things again. Mother wants to take him on a long holiday to recover from the strain of the case but he says he can't yet, that he doesn't want it to look like he's running away from the storm over Domson's execution.'

'Is there a storm?' asked Alexander. 'I thought everyone agreed that he should swing.'

'Well, most people did. But Father still thinks he needs to let it all die down before taking time off. I think he's worried that if he should take any leave at all then it'll be an excuse for the Lord Chancellor to retire him behind his back.'

'Like when those African tyrants skip off to Paris for a

few days' R&R and come back to find there's been a *coup d'état* in their absence and they're out of a job,' said Alexander with a smile.

'Exactly. Anyway, I think I'm his new project.'

'Well then, my dear Gareth,' said Alexander, lifting his champagne glass and clinking it against the side of his friend's. 'Then I think you simply have to bite the bullet and let him have his way. Or find something else to do that he will approve of.'

'The only question is, what?' said Gareth. 'Keep your ears open, though, will you? I'll do absolutely anything if it means I can steer clear of the law.'

'Leave it with me,' said Alexander with a wink. 'I'll let you know if I hear of anything.'

Jasper Conway returned at that moment with handfuls of chips and separated them into two uneven piles; five-sevenths for Gareth and two-sevenths for Alexander.

'What about you?' asked Gareth. 'Aren't you playing too?'

'I'll guide you,' said Jasper with a smile. 'I'll play the informal role of mentor. And you can cut me in for thirty per cent of your winnings, how does that sound?'

Gareth frowned but allowed himself to be led into the casino silently where they stood around the roulette table and laid their chips out on the baize.

'The trick is to play the odds,' said Jasper quietly, placing an arm protectively across Gareth's shoulder. 'With a one-number bet there's less than a three per cent chance of striking. You need to try more than that. Perhaps a four- or five-number bet. Then your odds go up to somewhere between ten and thirteen per cent.'

Gareth frowned. 'How do you know all this?' he asked.

'It's not my first time,' said Jasper with a smile, who was bereft of money for that very reason. 'Of course you can't lay all your chips down in one go, though, or you risk losing them all. Perhaps you should start off with something easy. Try for the colours.'

Gareth nodded and looked down at the pile in front of him. He selected a red chip – three pound's worth – and waited for the other players to start laying theirs at different points around the table before placing it in the centre of the black square.

The croupier placed the silver ball at the side of the wheel and sent it spinning anticlockwise around the rim while turning the wheel itself in the opposite direction. Gareth watched, transfixed, as it started to slow down, the ball gradually slipping down into the silver cups and skimming from red twenty-one to black two to red twenty-five to black seventeen before finally settling in red thirty-four.

'Oh bad luck,' said Jasper, shaking his head. 'But you can try again. It's fifty-fifty with the colours.'

'Well obviously,' muttered Gareth, a little irritated that he was already three pounds down; he wondered whether Jasper would cover thirty per cent of his losses as well.

'Try black again,' suggested Alexander, who laid one of his own chips in the black square in a show of solidarity. Gareth nodded and put another red chip on the square and just as the croupier spun the wheel he added to it with two more.

'Steady on,' said Alexander. 'You don't want to blow it all too quickly.'

'He does right,' said Jasper confidently. 'Win back his losses in a single spin.'

They watched and this time as the ball slowed down it hovered teasingly over black twenty-four before slipping backwards and coming to rest in red fourteen.

'Bad luck again,' said Jasper, frowning. 'But never mind. Third time's the charm.'

Gareth looked at him and shrugged off the arm that his friend still had around his shoulders. Twelve pounds down already. His mother, Jane Bentley, had given him the thirty pounds as a birthday present earlier in the day and he had hoped it would last him a few weeks yet. Although he was from a wealthy family, his father had shrivelled his allowance down to a pittance in recent times with the promise that it would increase again when he found suitable employment, preferably alongside him in chambers. Throughout this evening his friends had paid for the dinner and the drinks – well, Alexander had for the most part – as it was his birthday but now he was starting to haemorrhage money that he could ill afford to lose.

'It'll never go red three times in a row,' said Jasper. 'Try again. Seriously, Gareth, there's nothing to be afraid of.'

He felt a strong desire to cut his losses and head for home with the remaining eighteen pounds intact but something about the way that Jasper was speaking to him had started to irritate him. It was the patronizing air of the man who had nothing to lose but his friend's money. In a show of defiance he reached down and picked up all his remaining chips and placed them on the red square.

'No, black,' insisted Jasper quickly.

'Red,' said Gareth.

'No more bets,' called the croupier as the ball started to slow down in its trajectory.

'You'll get it this time for sure,' said Alexander as all three friends pinned their eyes to the wheel. Gareth's hands bunched into fists and his head started to bob back and forth, urging it into the red pocket.

'Well that's rotten luck,' said Jasper a few moments later. 'But I did say put it on the black.'

They walked back into the bar, Gareth feeling a little shell-shocked that he had thrown away so much money in the space of a few minutes. The loss of this final piece of financial security made it feel like the weight of the horsehair wig was being placed firmly on his head while the gown was being secured around his shoulders.

'You will keep your ears open for any suitable job, won't you?' he asked in a pleading voice of Alexander as they returned to their booth, but on this occasion his friend was barely listening because he could see the familiar shock of white hair emerging from an office on the opposite side of the room and making its own way towards the bar area.

'I *thought* it was him,' Alexander muttered to himself as he walked over to greet his closest friend, Owen Montignac.

7

Stella Montignac emerged from the bathroom wearing a white cotton towelling robe and went straight to the side table to pour herself another drink. Her dark hair hung lank and wet around her shoulders as she sat down and ran a brush through it in front of the dressing-table mirror.

'Feeling any better?' asked Raymond, who had taken off his jacket and tie and shoes and rolled up the sleeves of his shirt; the more relaxed he appeared, he believed, the less chance there was of Stella changing her mind and sending him on his way.

'A little,' said Stella. 'I just need some sleep really. Especially if I have to deal with him again at lunchtime tomorrow.'

'Then let's go to bed,' he said, standing up and stretching his arms wide. He walked across to his fiancée and took the drink from her hand and placed it on the counter, leaning forwards then and kissing her lightly on the back of the neck. She turned and responded in kind for a moment but then edged back and smiled at him, shaking her head.

'I'm going to finish my drink first,' she said. 'And dry my hair a bit. You go to bed. I'll be there in a minute.'

He smiled and nodded, moving away from her as he started to undress. 'You know what the real problem was,' he said as he took his trousers off and folded them neatly on a chair for the morning, smoothing out the creases with his hand as he did so. 'He was so disgusted that I was there at all that he was determined to make things as awkward as possible. I told you that was a mistake. I shouldn't have come.'

'Of course you should,' said Stella. 'You're my . . . well you're with me, aren't you?' she asked. Stella never liked to use words such as 'boyfriend' or 'fiancé'; she found such terms a little ridiculous, phrases directly from the romance novels she despised.

'He doesn't like me,' insisted Raymond.

'Oh how could anyone not like you?' she asked, watching him in the mirror as he changed. For someone who spent so much of his time propagating new species of Hybrid Teas in a glasshouse, she never failed to be impressed by the muscular definition of his body. At moments like this he was a joy to watch; it was one of the things she liked most about him. 'You're perfectly adorable.'

'Thank you,' said Raymond with a self-conscious laugh. 'But I don't think your cousin thinks so.'

'Oh he's just a little jealous, that's all,' she said.

'Of me? But why?'

She bit her lip. She hadn't meant to say that and was keen to change the emphasis. 'He sees the two of us together, happy in each other's company, and I suppose he wishes that he too could find a girl to be happy with. I'd be jealous in his shoes.'

Raymond nodded. 'Well I suppose that makes sense,' he said. 'But why doesn't he then? There must be plenty of girls out there who'd fall for him. He's a handsome chap, after all. The waitresses at Claridge's couldn't keep their eyes off him.'

'Yes, he does rather attract attention in that way,' admitted Stella quietly.

'He's a little intense, of course,' he continued. 'And not exactly a barrel of laughs, but I'm sure there must be some girl out there who could break through his defences if she had a mind to. Has there been anyone?'

Stella shrugged and looked away. 'There was someone once,' she told him, 'but it was a long time ago. He was quite a bit younger. I think they were very much in love, actually.'

'And what happened to her?'

'It's hard to say. It was around the time that my brother was killed. I think the affair, or whatever it was, was at its peak then. But then Andrew died and the whole family was thrown into turmoil. By the time I was thinking clearly enough again to wonder what had become of their relationship, it already seemed to be over.'

Raymond climbed into bed and settled some pillows behind his head, sitting up straight and watching her. 'He was only eighteen when he died, wasn't he?' he asked

'Yes,' said Stella after a moment's hesitation, not to remember the age but to remember the boy.

'So Owen was—'

'Fifteen. It was a shooting accident. The two boys, well they loved to shoot rabbits on the opposite side of the estate, near where the gamekeeper's hut is.'

'You've never really told me what happened,' said Raymond. 'If you don't want to discuss it, of course, that's perfectly fine.'

'No, it's all right,' said Stella. 'I suppose I should have told you long before now anyway. Andrew had just had a birthday, in fact, and father and mother had given him a new gun. He came down to breakfast one morning and asked Owen would he like to go shooting with him later in the day and they arranged it for the afternoon. When Owen went looking for him before lunchtime it turned out that he'd already gone, without a word to anyone, which was most unusual because Andrew would always go searching the house or screaming for one of us at the top of his voice if we had plans.'

'Perhaps he couldn't wait,' suggested Raymond. 'I know that when I first got a gun—'

'Yes, perhaps,' interrupted Stella, who was telling her brother's story and didn't necessarily want it complemented by Raymond's. 'Well I remember that I was up in my bedroom and Owen was there too and then he asked me what time it was and when I told him he became terribly anxious and jumped up and ran off. The whole thing seemed a little unsettling at the time actually, he went in such a dreadful rush. The funny thing was that he left in such a hurry that he forgot his own gun and when I saw him making his way down the driveway without it, I shouted at him from the window but he couldn't hear me. I thought of following too but I wasn't dressed, as I recall, so I stayed where I was. I'm glad now that I didn't go too.'

Raymond sank down a little on the bed. He could feel a distinct chill around his body and wished that Stella would climb in beside him so that he could hold her while she told this tale. But she wasn't even looking at him now; in fact she had an expression on her face that suggested she was barely aware of his presence in the room at all.

'Well, I didn't really think much more about it after that,' she continued. 'I remember I went to take a bath, and then got dressed, and was on my way downstairs when I ran into Margaret, our old nanny, who started complaining to me that I spent far too much time in bed and that when she was a girl of my age she wouldn't have been allowed to sleep past eight. The usual things that people say, I suppose. Anyway I wasn't in the mood for it at the time and we started an argument, although I didn't think that either of our hearts was fully in it. She's always felt she has to be a mother figure to me, but at the same time she knew that I was hardly going off the rails. And I loved her too much really to be angry with her. But anyway, we were going at it hammer and tongs when suddenly the front door burst open and Owen came running in, his face pale, his hair standing on end and . . .' She hesitated before going on, her voice catching in her throat as she remembered the worst part. 'And there was blood on his jacket. A lot of blood, I mean, really ridiculous amounts, Raymond, as if he'd just spilled a bucket of red paint all over himself. Needless to say, Margaret and I stopped whatever it was we were arguing about and turned to look at him, open-mouthed.

'"What on earth's happened to you?" Margaret asked and I remember I could feel the blood draining from my face as I looked at him. At first I thought *he'd* had an accident, I thought the blood was his own but there was so much of it and it wasn't as if he was collapsing at our feet in agony so I couldn't understand it.

'"It's Andrew," he said then. "He's hurt himself."

'A lot of things were probably said then but I don't remember them all. What I do remember is sitting down on the staircase and clinging on to the railing while Margaret ran for the telephone to call a doctor and then her running out of the house on her way to find Andrew herself.'

Stella burst out into a bitter laugh and shook her head, surprising Raymond who could feel a sting of tears behind his eyes at the thought of the tragedy.

'And you'll never believe what she did before she went,' she said.

'What?' asked Raymond.

'She collected a first-aid box from the kitchen. You know the type, a few plasters and a bottle of iodine, and went racing off to the woods to find my brother as if this was going to be of any use to him. He'd lost all that blood and she thought a few plasters would make him better.'

'People don't know what to do when things like that happen. I remember my cousin Charlie's appendix exploded one afternoon and—'

'It was the gun, you see,' said Stella quietly, ignoring the story about Cousin Charlie. 'It was the first time he'd used it and he hadn't taken the time to get to know it properly. Of course that was Andrew all over. Impetuous to the end. Never stopped and thought. Burst into rooms without knocking, spoke without thinking, and rather than sitting down for an hour and examining the gun and getting comfortable with it, he just loaded it up and took a shot at the first rabbit he saw. And it exploded back on him, the pellet going right through his face.'

Raymond winced.

'He was almost unrecognizable,' said Stella quietly. 'Not that I saw him of course. But that's what Owen told me. It was horrible.' She hesitated and thought about it before offering the valediction. 'It was the beginning of the most horrible time of my life and afterwards I thought that if I could get through that, then I could get through anything. And I have.'

She put her glass down then turned off the main light, leaving only the bedside lamp beside Raymond switched on. Without a trace of self-consciousness she slipped her robe off her shoulders and left it on the chair and stepped naked towards the bed, pulling back the sheets and climbing in beside him, lying down immediately and wrapping herself around him for comfort.

Raymond decided not to offer any sympathies for her dead brother. He knew how fake it would sound. She had told him the story and that was all he needed to know.

'And Owen's romance ended at the same time?' he asked.

'Almost immediately. It wasn't mentioned for a long time afterwards anyway. I know that much for sure. I mean obviously he was very young too. She was his first love. But she seems to have damaged him somehow.'

'He must have loved her very much if he's closed down all his emotional faculties since then,' said Raymond. 'I mean he was only fifteen.'

'Don't let's talk about it,' said Stella, closing her eyes. 'It's all so long ago. I don't like to remember those days.'

'I imagine that Owen's been very protective of you since then,' he said.

'Yes.'

'Perhaps I should make more of an effort to get to

know him,' he suggested. 'Show him I'm not such a bad chap after all.'

'I'm not sure,' she said. 'He's not easily swayed by words. Let me speak to him tomorrow. I'll see if I can't get some things straightened out on my own.'

She rotated in the bed then, turning her back to him as he moved closer and started to kiss her neck, his hands reaching further down under the sheets to appreciate her warmth and suppleness. She allowed him to continue and began to respond but she was pleased that he had switched off the light because it meant that he was unable to see the sorrow and regret in her eyes and the pain that always threatened to overwhelm her at any moment if she permitted it.

8

His first instinct was to leave the Unicorn Ballrooms as quickly as possible but his pride took over instead. He looked around and noticed that Delfy's security men were watching his every move and he didn't want to give them the satisfaction of thinking that he was too scared to stay so, rather than making his way towards the stairs and the exit, he strolled over to the bar instead and ordered a drink. Alone, there was no point in sitting down at a booth and besides, he knew they would all be full at this time of night as the minds of young men turned towards drink, money and women. He considered moving into the casino but he had so little cash left in his wallet that he knew it would be a waste of time; what little he had left was better spent on drowning his sorrows.

He sat at the corner of the bar and kept his head down, wondering how he got himself into this situation and how he would get himself out of it again. The gambling had been a mistake, he knew that now. He had always had an addictive personality and the moment he started with something like that the more difficult it became for him to give it up. And the less he wanted to. It always felt to him that with just one more turn of the roulette wheel or one more hand of cards his luck could change. And the moment it did he would just keep on winning. But that moment had never appeared and so his debts had mounted to the ridiculous level they were at now.

He thought about what Delfy had said. Whether he would steal to repay the money, whether he would hurt someone. Whether he would kill. It almost made him laugh aloud. The casino owner, he realized, had no idea at all of the things he would do for self-preservation.

Gambling had made him happy for a time and he couldn't remember feeling happy very often in his life. Perhaps as a small child, before he came to Leyville. Before his parents were killed. Perhaps during that single year before Andrew's death, when he had been in love. Perhaps that was happiness. No, he decided, gambling *didn't* make him happy, it just gave him some peace. It allowed him to forget the things he'd done and the things that had been done to him.

A young girl passed him by and the scent of her perfume made him lift his head a little and he watched her as she spoke to the barman. She was a few years younger than him, perhaps in her late teens or early twenties, and might have been attractive if she hadn't been wearing so much make-up and a tacky dress. She felt his eyes on her and turned her head slowly to look at him. He held her gaze there for a moment before turning away, not knowing why he was watching her in the first place.

Montignac checked his watch; it was nearly midnight and he was feeling desperately tired now. It had been a strenuous evening, from the dinner with Stella and Raymond through to his virtual kidnapping by Delfy's henchman and then ultimately the interview with the club owner himself. He stifled a yawn and wondered whether he should just finish his drink and get a taxi on the street back to his flat in Bedford Place but his legs felt heavy beneath him and he couldn't face standing up just yet. He remembered that he had arranged to have lunch with Stella the following day – alone, he had insisted – and considered for a moment the idea of discussing his financial problems with her then, before dismissing it out of hand. He couldn't ask her for the money, his pride was too strong for that. Besides, he knew full well that the provision of his uncle's will would make it difficult for her to cover the debt. She would be required to sell something but most of the landownings were held in trust for her own heirs. Peter Montignac had made it clear that he was reluctant to break the family tradition by passing down his wealth to his daughter but ensured that, since he was faced with no other choice, she would have access only to the bank accounts, the interest and the rents. Her children would have the freedom to do whatever they wanted when their time came but traditions would be observed for this generation. He obviously didn't trust his daughter, his only surviving child. But he trusted her more than he had trusted his nephew.

'You looking for company?' asked the girl from the bar, moving closer to him now and lowering herself on to a stool. She leaned forwards, her head resting on one hand, as she tried to get a better look at his face. He recognised her immediately as one of the girls Delfy employed to keep the wealthy young men coming back for more.

'Not really,' said Montignac.

'Here, I know you, don't I?' she asked, remembering the startling white hair that distinguished Montignac from most of the other regulars.

'I've been here before, yes.'

'Aren't you going to buy me a drink then?'

He turned and looked at her, blinking his eyes for a moment at her presumption, and shook his head. 'No,' he said. 'No, I'm not. But I'll have another whisky if you're offering.'

'I'm not offering nothing,' she said, offended. 'What kind of gentleman refuses to buy a lady a drink anyway?'

'I didn't,' he said.

'You just did.'

'You're not a lady.'

The girl narrowed her eyes and stared at him angrily. She felt the urge to launch a stream of abuse at him but perhaps her evening had been just as strenuous as his own and instead she simply shook her head and stood up again, nonplussed by his attitude.

'Suit yourself,' she said in a tired voice. 'Stay on your own then.'

He nodded and she drifted away. There were moments, of course, when he wanted a woman and nights when he found one, just to satisfy his needs. The idea of finding someone more permanent never crossed his mind; the idea of letting someone in again, allowing himself to be as badly scarred as he was the last time, was something he couldn't countenance. He lifted his empty glass and nodded at the barman who poured him another drink and he paid for it now in loose change without embarrassment.

Out of the corner of his eye he could see the figure of the large man who had escorted him here earlier in the evening stepping into Delfy's office. He was precisely the kind of character who was always employed in clubs like this and who usually ended up working for men like Nicholas Delfy. Quiet, polite, softly spoken, all traits in marked contrast to his enormous size and vast body weight. The type that would have a pleasant conversation with you about the football results or the price of cigarettes while he brought you to a deserted wasteland somewhere outside of London and released your arms from their sockets. The sort that would slice off your ear and then pass you a handful of handkerchiefs to stem the bleeding. It meant nothing to him; it was only a job. A way to pay off his own debts, buy his own women. He could only imagine the man's disappointment when his employer told him that he had given the young white-haired man a second chance. *Four weeks to raise ten thousand,* Delfy would have told him by now. *Otherwise, he's all yours.*

From the casino to his right he could hear the sounds of people playing, voices raised in excitement around the tables, the sharp calls of the croupiers as they extended their rakes to collect the scattered chips on the baize, their eyes moving from player to player as each lost more and more money and tried to look ever more unflappable to their friends, as if there was plenty more where that came from. He knew that no one ever looked as pleased with himself as the man who was losing his shirt. Despite the fact that his insides would be churning in tension and self-loathing for coming back here again and again and again when he knew there was never a chance of victory. Everyone would save so much time, he thought, if they simply deposited all their money in a bag when they came in to the club and then just turned around and went home again. Cut out the middle man of the tables entirely. There was no such thing as a winner, he knew that only too well. Even the players who had lucky nights returned to pour it all back to the croupiers only twenty-four hours later, and then some. People like Nicholas Delfy were in business because the house always won.

He was faced with only a couple of real choices, he realized. Fight back or buckle under.

The tension and concern for his future health lifted for a moment and he had a moment of clarity. He wondered why he allowed himself to feel so depressed. If he continued to act like this there was no way that he would ever raise the money and save his own skin. He was Owen Montignac, after all. He had faced worse obstacles than this one. He thought of his past, of his parents, of Andrew, of Stella, of his uncle, Peter; he considered what they had done to him, what they had tried to do, and what he had done in return. Then he pictured himself, sitting alone on a bar stool, crying into his whisky. This was not the man he was born to be. He was better than this.

He stood up, drained the remains of his glass, and was about to walk away when a hand clasped him on the arm. He spun around, suddenly afraid that Delfy had changed his mind about the grace period and was demanding payment after all, but it wasn't him or any of his henchmen standing there. It was his oldest friend, Alexander Keys, who stood before him with a wide smile on his face.

'Owen,' he said. 'I thought you'd sworn off this place for life.'

9

Leaving the Unicorn Ballrooms five weeks earlier, only a few days before the death of his uncle, Owen Montignac had sworn to Alexander Keys that he was finished with gambling for good. He'd wasted enough of his time in places like this, he'd told him, laughing it off and pretending that he'd cost himself another thirty or forty pounds over the course of the evening when in truth his accumulated debt stood at about twelve hundred times that figure. Not that he could have let Alexander know the truth; the trick to remaining solvent when almost bankrupt was never to allow others to recognize your financial difficulties. In fact, if ever there was a time to appear generous towards one's friends, it was at the moment when one could least afford it. That night, as they had left the club, Montignac had insisted on bringing his friend to an expensive restaurant and paying for dinner for them both.

'Alexander,' said Montignac as he turned around, surprised and not entirely happy to see him standing there. 'What are you doing here?'

'Well I'm here with a few friends,' said Alexander. 'Jasper Conway for one. You know him, don't you?'

'A little,' said Montignac, who didn't care for him and

could never understand why his friend associated with such a leech.

'And Gareth Bentley. It's Gareth's birthday so we've been out celebrating. Have you met him?'

Montignac shook his head. 'No,' he said. 'No, I don't believe I know him.'

'Well you must come over and say hello then,' said Alexander. 'What are you drinking anyway?'

'Actually, I was just about to leave,' said Montignac, glancing hopefully in the direction of the doors. 'It's getting late.'

'Oh nonsense,' Alexander replied, dragging his friend back to the bar. 'We're having champagne. You'll join us in a glass, won't you?'

Montignac shrugged; there seemed little chance of getting out of it. 'Well all right,' he said. 'But I can't stay long. I'm tired and I have a long day ahead of me tomorrow.'

'No one ever should refuse champagne,' said Alexander cheerfully. 'It's terribly rude.'

'If I wake up with a hangover, it's you I'll blame,' replied Montignac with a smile.

'Anyway, you still haven't answered my question,' he continued. 'The last time you and I left here you promised me that you wouldn't be caught dead in one of these places again.'

'That's almost exactly how I was caught tonight, replied Montignac ruefully.

'Hmm? What's that?'

'Oh nothing,' said Montignac. 'Let's just say I had a moment of weakness.'

'At the bar or at the casino?'

'Only at the bar, I'm pleased to report.'

'Well that's something, I suppose,' said Alexander. 'It's not the worse vice of the two.'

'No.'

The barman came over and Alexander ordered another magnum of champagne and four glasses.

'So,' he said finally. 'I'm sorry I haven't called in to the gallery to see you recently. It's been on my to-do list but I've just been very busy at work.'

'Yes, reading all those novels must tire one out so,' said Montignac. 'All those hours spent trying to decipher metaphor from actual plot.'

'Don't be ridiculous, Owen, I'm a book reviewer,' said Alexander sternly. 'Reading the blasted things would prejudice one enormously.'

'I suppose it would. Actually I read something recently that you recommended in *The Times* a few weeks back. You said it was a masterpiece.'

'Really? And was it any good?'

'Perfectly dreadful.'

'Oh I am sorry,' he said cheerfully. 'Well never mind. I'll be recommending something equally appalling next week no doubt.'

'No doubt,' said Montignac.

'The problem is that one reads these books and they don't make any sense at all but one never knows when

Kenneth Tynan or Bunny Wilson will suddenly turn around and proclaim it to be a masterpiece. The last thing one wants is to be on the wrong side of a literary phenomenon.'

'What a simple life you lead, Alexander,' said Montignac.

'Well you must see it in the gallery too, surely? All that dreadful rubbish you sell.'

'That dreadful rubbish, as you put it, goes for enormous amounts of money.'

'To people who wouldn't understand a piece of art if it came up to them in the street and deconstructed itself in broad daylight. When was the last time you had anything of any actual merit in your gallery?'

'Only last week we sold a small sculpture by Tony Shefley for eight thousand pounds.'

'The last piece of any *artistic* value,' asked Alexander.

'Oh God, don't be ridiculous,' said Montignac with a laugh. 'I can't remember the last time we even had one in stock, let alone sold one. You know a fellow came in a few days ago – just off the street – with one of his own paintings and asked to have it valued.'

'And how was it?'

'It was magnificent. A landscape. An unusual use of colour, almost contemporary *sfumato*. Brushstrokes that would have made Van Gogh proud. Really, something quite extraordinary.'

'And you sent the fellow away with a flea in his ear, I presume.'

'Well naturally. There's no chance at all that we could sell something so obviously good. Our customers would look down their noses at it. No, I sent him next door to the Clarion. Under any other circumstances I might have made an offer on the thing myself.'

Alexander stopped smiling and he leaned forward slightly, making sure that no one could overhear him when there weren't any more *mots justes* to be thrown around. 'How are you doing now anyway?' he asked. 'Have you come to terms with what happened?'

'With what exactly?' asked Montignac innocently.

'Well you know. Your uncle's death. And the . . . unpleasantness afterwards.'

Montignac nodded. 'If you're referring to the fact that I was entirely cut out of his will, then yes, let's just say I've managed to get the fact of it straight in my head. I'm learning to accept that for the time being I am a young man without any prospects. In fact, I rather think my uncle meant to teach me a lesson. To show me that, despite all the effort I've put in over the years, he has left me exactly as he found me.'

'How do you mean?' asked Alexander.

'As the poor relation,' said Montignac, the bitterness coming through clearly in his voice. 'It turns out he wasn't such a traditionalist after all and that blood, real blood, turned out to be thicker than water.'

'And how's Stella?' asked Alexander after a pause, unsure how to respond to the tone of bitterness.

'Basking in glory.'

'I see.'

'Oh come on, Alexander, don't mind me,' said Montignac, slapping his friend on the shoulder in an attempt at jollity. 'It's hardly the end of the world. What is it they say? I still have my health.' For the moment anyway, he thought.

The champagne and glasses came and they took them over to the table where Jasper and Gareth were engaged in an animated debate about whose responsibility the cab ride home should be. Each felt it should be the other's.

'Montignac,' said Jasper in delight as he sat down at the booth. 'Where the devil did you spring from?'

'I found him alone and palely loitering at the bar,' explained Alexander. 'And told him he should come and drown his sorrows with us. This is Gareth Bentley, an old friend of mine,' he said to Montignac, introducing the boy on the other side of the table who was rooting through his wallet to see how much money he had left. 'And Gareth, this is my oldest friend in the world, Owen Montignac. We went to school together.'

Gareth looked up and opened his mouth to say hello but words of greeting caught in the back of his throat, as if his breath had been stolen from him for a moment. Forcing his eyes up a little higher he was so struck by the young man's startling white hair that he felt an unexpected urge to reach across and stroke it.

'I believe it's your birthday,' said Montignac.

'Yes. Yes, it is,' he replied quietly.

Montignac nodded and no one spoke while they waited for him to offer his congratulations but after a moment it became clear that none were to be forthcoming and an uneasy silence descended.

'We've been leading Gareth down the road to rack and ruin at the roulette table,' said Jasper, interrupting it. 'He cost me thirty pounds, would you believe.'

'It was *my* thirty pounds,' protested Gareth. 'My mother gave it to me this morning.'

'Oh really, Gareth,' said Jasper with the air of a frustrated mentor. 'If you can't afford to lose it, then you really shouldn't bring it with you.'

'Three turns at the wheel,' said Gareth in a glum tone, appealing to Montignac's sense of right and wrong. 'That was all it took. Three turns at the wheel and every penny was gone. Isn't that awful?'

'If I was you I wouldn't allow myself to get led astray,' said Montignac who would have loved to have been able to return to the days when the loss of thirty pounds would have been a matter worth shedding tears over.

'Don't worry, I've learned my lesson.'

Oh come on,' said Jasper irritably. 'You can't give up just because of one bad night. That's hardly the action of a good loser, is it?'

'Well I'd rather not be any kind of loser, thank you very much,' said Gareth, quite sensibly. I'll stick to my other vices from now on.'

'And what vices would they be?' asked Montignac, pricking up his ears.

'Sloth and covetousness,' replied Gareth with a smile.

Montignac laughed. 'The sloth I can understand,' he said. 'But what exactly is it that you covet?'

'The ability of the idle rich not to have to get a job,' he replied quickly.

'You don't want to say that,' said Jasper. 'Old Montignac here *is* one of the idle rich. He's worth millions.'

'Sadly not,' said Montignac.

'Really, Jasper,' interrupted Alexander, looking suitably embarrassed. 'I hardly think that's a suitable subject for conversation.'

'Quite right, quite right,' said Jasper apologetically, his face starting to redden now as all the alcohol he had consumed over the course of the evening began to take effect. 'I never did get round to offering my condolences by the way, Owen. Over your uncle, I mean. I'd intended to write but it went clean out of my head. Anyway, I was sorry to hear the news.'

'Thank you,' said Montignac, staring at the table.

'Owen's uncle died recently,' Jasper explained to Gareth, beginning to slur his words so badly now that Alexander considered relieving him of his champagne glass. 'One of the wealthiest landowners in England he was too. Left the whole stack to our friend here.'

'Jasper, that's enough,' said Alexander sharply.

'He disinherited me, Jasper,' said Montignac without a trace of embarrassment. 'He left it all to my cousin.'

'To Stella?'

'Yes.'

'Good God.'

'Indeed.'

'So that means you're—'

'Stony broke and up to my eyeballs in debt,' he replied cheerfully, lifting his champagne flute and draining it in one mouthful.

'I wouldn't have believed it,' said Jasper, shaking his head in surprise.

'Well, there you are,' replied Montignac in a disinterested tone.

'And is she still seeing that flower fellow or is she on the market?'

Montignac turned to face him and his lip curled slightly. He could feel a twinge of temper burning at the back of his brain and fought to control it. Jasper swallowed nervously, aware that he had caused offence.

'Perhaps that didn't come out quite right,' he began but Montignac interrupted him by standing up and making a polite bow to the assembled group.

'Gentlemen, it's very late and I'm very tired. I'm afraid I have to take my leave of you,' he announced.

'Oh you're not going already, are you?' asked Gareth, who felt a peculiar desire for him to stay and for the others to leave instead. The manner in which he had answered Jasper back was exactly how he would have liked to have behaved at the roulette table earlier and he wanted to learn a little about it.

'I'm afraid so. Nice to have met you, Mr Bentley.

Alexander,' he added, with a nod to his friend. 'Come and see me soon.'

And with that he turned on his heel and marched away, determined this time to escape the club without further assault.

10

The rain had started, only a light drizzle at first but threatening more, and Montignac buttoned his overcoat and reached inside his pockets for his gloves but they weren't there; he frowned, wondering whether they had fallen out at Claridge's earlier, in his haste to get away from Stella and Raymond, in the pub from which he had been whisked away against his will or whether they had slipped out in the cloakroom of the Unicorn Ballrooms. They had been quite an expensive pair of leather gloves and he was sorry for the loss of them.

He glanced up the street for a taxicab but there was nothing coming yet. He looked at his watch and sighed in exhaustion; it was already half past midnight. Although only twenty-five years old, Montignac had never been one for late nights and the thought of rising at seven-thirty after only a few hours' sleep to spend another day in the gallery, worrying about money, filled him with misery.

'Mr Montignac!'

A voice called out from behind him and he looked around, unsure which of the many people from inside might have followed him out and for what reason, and was surprised to see his new acquaintance, Gareth Bentley, bounding towards him like a hound pursuing a rabbit, a broad smile plastered across his eager young face.

'Mr Bentley,' he said. 'Hello again.'

'Please, call me Gareth,' he replied. 'Alexander said you live in Bedford Place.'

'That's right, yes.'

'Are you getting a taxicab?'

'Yes, do you want to share?'

'If you don't mind.'

'I don't mind at all,' said Montignac with a shrug of the shoulders, pleased to share the expense even if it would be just a trifling amount. He considered in his head for a moment the fact that there could be no such thing as trifling amounts for him any more; every shilling needed to be accounted for. 'But were you finished with your party?'

'Oh I'd had enough of that,' said Gareth dismissively as if the whole evening had been nothing important and merely a prelude to getting home again.

'Didn't they mind you leaving so suddenly?' Montignac asked, considering the speed with which he had followed him out of the club.

'They'll barely even notice,' he replied, anxious to change the subject. 'Anyway, I was tired. It was time to go home.'

'Indeed,' said Montignac. 'So are you for Bedford Place too then?'

'Tavistock Square,' he said. 'But we can drop you off and I'll take it the rest of the way. If that's convenient for you, I mean.'

Montignac shrugged and pointed down the street. 'Well we should probably start walking this way then,' he said. 'I think we'll find it easier to pick one up on the main road. They don't often come down here.'

Gareth nodded and they began to walk along together as the rain continued to drizzle down on them. The street seemed surprisingly empty of people and the traffic was light.

'I was glad of the opportunity to leave actually,' confided Gareth. 'I'm not much good at long nights out.'

'Not even on your birthday?'

'Especially not on my birthday. It reminds me how old I am.'

'And how old is that?' asked Montignac, guessing that he was no more than twenty or twenty-one years old for he had a very youthful countenance to him, clear of skin and full of good health. His personality seemed childlike too, as if he had never known the difficulty of life as an adult; his stride along the street betrayed a happy-go-lucky, entirely carefree young man.

'Twenty-four,' said Gareth sadly. 'Ancient.'

Montignac laughed. 'Well I'm twenty-five,' he said. 'We're not exactly on the scrap heap yet, you know.'

'I feel like I am.'

Montignac sighed; he didn't really have the energy for vanity such as this. If all the boy had to worry about in his life was the trauma of entering his twenty-fifth year, then he wasn't doing too badly for himself. After all, he himself was wondering whether he would even see the end of his.

'My cousin died when he was eighteen,' said Montignac, wondering whether it was entirely hypocritical of him to mention this.' I think he'd have given rather a lot to get to our age.'

Gareth nodded but didn't offer any condolences as Montignac had failed to congratulate him on his birthday earlier. It seemed ridiculous to him to offer sympathy to a man he didn't know over the death of a boy he never would.

Montignac whistled suddenly as a cab approached and it slowed down and they got inside. 'Bedford Place,' he said, pleased to be out of the rain at last. 'And then on to Tavistock Square.'

'Right you are, sir,' said the driver as he pulled out again.

'So how do you know Alexander?' asked Montignac after a moment. 'I haven't heard him mention you before.'

'We met at my club,' explained Gareth. 'Well my father's club, actually. White's, in St James's. Do you know it?'

'Yes, I'm a member, although I rarely have the time to go there.'

'Well then you know that it's Alexander's too. I go there sometimes to read the newspapers in the late afternoon and he's often to be found sitting there, engrossed in a book.'

'Yes, apparently he calls that work,' said Montignac.

'He told me that. It seems like rather a good job if you ask me.'

Montignac shrugged. 'And Jasper Conway,' he asked. 'He's a particular friend of yours?'

'Not really,' he replied, shaking his head. 'He's more friends with Alexander than with me. I don't like him enormously, if you want to know the truth.'

'Really?' asked Montignac, who didn't care for Jasper either. 'Why not?'

'He's terribly vain and arrogant and never pays for anything. And he cost me thirty pounds tonight which I could scarcely afford to lose and he seemed to take great delight in doing so. To be honest I left because I knew he'd end up insisting that I pay for his trip home too. That and the fact that he kept forcing me to drink.

Montignac looked across at him. 'How do you mean?' he asked.

'It's a silly thing,' said Gareth, shaking his head. 'I'm not really supposed to take too much. It can affect me quite badly. I did very well tonight, though; I only had a couple of glasses.'

'And did he force you to bet on the roulette too?' asked Montignac.

'Well no, but—'

'Then it seems a little harsh to blame him for your own mistakes, don't you think? Although I agree with you entirely in your judgement of him. He's a leech. And a spineless coward too. I could tell you stories about that one that would make you avoid him like the plague.'

Gareth nodded but didn't ask for further details; he watched through the windows as the streets rolled by and wished that the traffic was heavier and their conversation could continue for longer yet. Staring at his reflection in the dark mirror his eyes drifted again towards his companion's bright white hair which stood out in stark contrast to his own dark, unruly thatch. He had found Montignac's dismissal of Conway enormously refreshing. He suddenly felt tired and let out a tremendous and unexpected yawn.

'What time do you have to be up at in the morning?' asked Montignac, trying to make conversation as they continued their journey along Oxford Street and towards Bloomsbury.

'Whenever I feel like it,' said Gareth. 'I don't have any work to go to.'

'Really? And there you were coveting the lifestyle of the idle rich earlier. It sounds to me like you're one of their number.'

'Well I'd like to be,' laughed Gareth. 'If my father would allow it. But I rather think my days of wine and roses are drawing to a close. I'm about to be sucked into the family business.'

'Which is . . . ?'

'The law. My father's a barrister. Well he's a judge, actually. He's the head of the Rice Chambers.'

Montignac nodded and searched his memory for the name; there was a flicker of recall there somewhere and he chanced across it. 'Roderick Bentley,' he said. 'The judge who sentenced Domson to death. He's your father.'

'Guilty as charged.'

'I see,' said Montignac thoughtfully.

'He refuses to support me any more unless I get a job and I can't find one to suit me so I've decided to bite the bullet. Tonight might have been my last night as a free man. Perhaps I should have got drunk after all.'

Montignac nodded as the cab turned the corner from Russell Street into Bedford Place and he gave the driver the number of his flat.

'Do I take it you mean that you'd rather not be heading for a career in the law yourself?' he asked.

'Of course not. It makes me feel like my whole life is being taken away from me.'

'And do you have any preference for what you'd like to do instead?'

'Not really,' said Gareth, shaking his head. 'It's ridiculous really to get to this age and never to have given any thought to the subject. I feel like I've wasted my youth, Mr Montignac.'

'Well it's not over yet.'

'No, but I'm not sure I'm built for work. It's like we

were saying earlier. I'd like to be one of the idle rich.'

Montignac smiled. 'In order to join that class, one needs a sizeable inheritance or a lack of scruples.'

'I'm not sure I have any scruples,' said Gareth.

'Really?'

'Well I suppose I've never really been tested,' he added with more caution.

'They're unnecessary things,' said Montignac, staring straight ahead and lowering his voice. 'Anyone has the choice about committing certain acts in order to improve the condition of one's life. It's whether or not one is willing to proceed with those impulses or not that counts.

'Anything to keep me away from the Rice Chambers,' replied Gareth flippantly.

'Whether one would lie, for example,' continued Montignac.

'Everybody lies.'

'Or steal.'

'Depends who it was from, I suppose.'

'Or even kill.'

Gareth turned and stared at his companion, who immediately broke into a forced smile and patted him on the arm. 'Don't look so appalled,' he said quickly. 'It's just idle chatter.'

The cab pulled up and Montignac hesitated before saying anything else, aware that the young man hadn't replied to the last suggestion.

'Listen, Gareth,' he said, reaching into his pocket and taking out his card. 'I think I know a little bit about the predicament you're in and I might be able to help you. My details are all down here. Why don't you call on me over the next few days and we'll meet again and discuss it?'

Gareth took the card and stared across at this relative stranger, almost unable to believe his luck. 'Do you mean you might have a job for me?' he asked.

'Not exactly,' he replied. He looked out the window towards his flat and opened the cab door quickly, unwilling to discuss it further tonight. 'Just call on me,' he said, stepping out on to the street. 'You might find that it's to your advantage.'

Gareth nodded and put the card in his overcoat pocket as Montignac closed the door and waved them off. Young men with connections, such as Gareth Bentley was, were always young men worth getting to know.

The young man in question was driving across Woburn towards Tavistock Square when he realized that Montignac had done to him exactly what Jasper Conway had been planning on doing: leaving him to pay the full cost of the taxi. And yet somehow he didn't seem to mind so much any more.

He put his hand to his pocket several times in order to make sure that the card was still there, just in case it had mysteriously disintegrated or vanished into thin air over the previous few minutes.

Before arriving home he checked for it three more times before deciding to hold it in his hands for safe keeping. The last thing he wanted was to leave it behind in the taxicab.

Chapter 3

1

The Threadbare Art Gallery opened its doors for the first time in 1930, specializing in the presentation and sale of contemporary art. The owner, Mrs Rachel Conliffe, was a middle-aged lady of independent means who believed that the young painters and sculptors of London were being shamefully overlooked by their local gallery owners, most of whom were stuck in an artistic time warp. To counter this she made it a rule that nothing produced before the death of Queen Victoria could be put on display in her gallery; Edwardian was fine, Georgian even better. The critics mocked at first; it seemed to stand out as an anachronism in the row of commercial galleries along Cork Street, which were notorious for their neglect of younger artists, but it slowly began to develop a reputation for eccentricity and the art-buying public drifted curiously towards it. Within a couple of years a purchase from the

Threadbare had become something of a status symbol, a whisper to the world that one was of a fashionable mind and not stuck wallowing in the dull traditions of the past.

Mrs Conliffe maintained a hands-off approach to the business, showing up once every few weeks to cast an eye over the new displays, but she made a comfortable living from a distance and preferred not to involve herself in the daily operations. For that she had hired Owen Montignac, a talented and personable young Cambridge graduate, after her original manager had left for a position in the Tate; Montignac's appointment came under the recommendation of his late uncle, who had been a business acquaintance of Mrs Conliffe's husband for many years.

The morning after the meeting with Nicholas Delfy at the Unicorn Ballrooms, Montignac woke earlier than usual, at around six-thirty, and was unable to get back to sleep. He found that no matter what problems were weighing him down – financial concerns, worries about Stella's forthcoming marriage, the possibility of being ripped apart by Delfy's thugs – they tended to make their appearance only at night, like owls or vampires. And on this occasion, there was only one problem pressing on his mind: money.

He rose and washed, eating a light breakfast before leaving his flat an hour later. It was a fine summer's morning so he was able to walk to the gallery as usual. The time alone and fresh air might, he hoped, help to clear his head. His options were limited now. Four weeks to raise ten thousand pounds. The idea was absurd. And after that there would still be the matter of raising four times that amount before the end of the year, but he dismissed that from his mind for the moment as being beside the point. He had to concentrate on the initial payment first.

He considered how much money he had left in his savings – just under nine hundred pounds – and wondered whether it would be worthwhile taking that to a different casino later in the day and trying to win enough money to pay Delfy back what he owed him, but he quickly shrugged this idea off before he could even countenance it; it had been thinking like this that had got him into this mess in the first place.

The shocking thing, the thing that made him sick to his stomach whenever he thought of it, was how his uncle had cut him off. It was one thing for him to decide to leave his fortune to Stella – after all, she was his only surviving child and he could just about have understood this decision – but to leave him with nothing at all? It was beyond cruel.

They had gathered, Stella and he, in the library at Leyville the morning after the funeral and Sir Denis Tandy, Peter Montignac's lawyer, was waiting for them when they shuffled in. Stella looked pale and drawn, as if the events of the previous few days were beginning to take their toll on her, while Montignac himself felt energized and excited by what was to come. Finally, the stolen Montignac fortune would return to where it rightfully belonged. An injustice would be set right.

'Stella, Owen,' said Sir Denis, looking up from the reading desk and rising to greet them. 'How are you both feeling this morning?'

Stella shrugged and said nothing, lowering herself heavily into a wing-backed armchair, her eyes lingering for a moment on the sinister document laid out on the desk.

'We're both quite tired,' said Montignac. 'I don't think either of us has had much sleep over the last few days. It will be nice to get things back to normal.'

'Well they're not going to get back to normal, are they?' Stella pointed out irritably. 'I mean Father's not coming back so I don't see how normal is a possibility.'

Sir Denis opened his mouth but found that he had used up all his words of condolence already and could find no more. He was unimpressed with Stella's attitude. It was one thing to mourn and be upset during a funeral, that was perfectly understandable, but once it was over? Well then it was only good form to return to normal and pretend that nothing had ever happened. Showing emotions never did anyone any good. He didn't respond to her and moved around behind the desk as Montignac sat down opposite him.

There was a tap on the door and they looked around, surprised to be disturbed, but it was only Margaret Richmond, who arrived in the room carrying a tray with a pot of coffee and three cups balanced precariously alongside it.

'Sorry to disturb,' she whispered as she approached them, placing the tray on a side table. 'I thought you might like some coffee.'

'Margaret, you're a lifesaver,' said Stella gratefully, standing up and pouring three cups out and handing them around.

She stood there nervously, wringing her hands as she was wont to do, and looked at her two former charges.

'Everything all right, Margaret?' asked Montignac, noticing her still standing there.

'Fine,' she said. 'If there's anything you need, just call me.'

'Thank you, Miss Richmond,' said Sir Denis in a loud voice, dismissing her with a wave of his hand. 'I think we just need a little privacy if you don't mind.'

Margaret nodded and left the room quickly, closing the heavy doors behind her and Montignac turned back to the other two with the hint of a smile on his face.

'She seems a little frazzled this morning,' he said.

'She was a witness to the will,' explained Sir Denis. 'Perhaps it's a little unnerving for her to know it's about to be read out.'

Montignac shrugged, unsure why that would be the case, and went over to add a little cream to his coffee.

Only one of the other galleries on Cork Street had their lights switched on at this time of the morning and

Montignac glanced through the window as he passed by to see Arthur Hamilton, the manager of the superior Clarion Gallery next door, prising open some large wooden delivery containers with the help of some assistants. Hamilton saw him looking and raised a hand in greeting. Although considerably older than him – he had been working on Cork Street before some of Montignac's artists had even been born – the two neighbours got along very well and he made a mental note to visit later and see what new work was on display. They had enjoyed many long conversations about their favourite artists and Montignac felt at times that he had learned more from the gallery owner next door than he had from most of the ageing dons at Cambridge during the years he had spent there.

Montignac had studied history of art at the university and had originally hoped for a career in painting himself but he had no talent for it; a year's worth of unoriginal canvases had seen off that particular ambition. His passion was for the French artists of the nineteenth century – the urban preoccupations of Manet, the impressionist landscapes of Pissarro, the symbolism of Paul Gauguin – something he put down to the fact that he himself was French on his mother's side and had spent his first five years near Clermont-Ferrand before being claimed back for the English by his uncle, Peter Montignac.

Unlike many of his wealthy friends, however, he was not the sort who was happy to laze around all day, lunching and drinking and gossiping in their clubs, and was glad to have a job to go to, particularly as he was in charge of the gallery and could run it as he saw fit. It was an elegant life, the only negative being Mrs Conliffe's insistence on displaying only young artists, most of whom had barely a scrap of talent as far as he was concerned. In recent times he had started to make a particular point of buying the very worst canvases he could find – complicated pieces with no central theme, no unity of expression whatsoever, replete with bad brushwork and jarring colours – or the most perverse sculptures simply in order to see how gullible the wealthy art buyers of London actually were. And he had his answer: very.

He let himself into the Threadbare and switched on the lights. He liked the gallery at this time of the morning, before his assistant Jason had arrived. Before the customers started parading through with their bad taste on display for the whole world to see. Before the scruffy artists appeared sheepishly at his desk with their alleged masterpieces under their arms.

The design of the gallery was particularly pleasing to him, fifteen hundred square feet of space over two floors with a balcony on the mezzanine level from where one could see down to the ground floor and out through the windows along Cork Street, from the Burlington Arcade on one side to Clifford Street on the other.

'It was all one building originally,' Mrs Conliffe had

explained to him on his first day there as she showed him around. 'This, the Clarion next door, the Bellway to our left. Then of course it was sold as three separate units. They're all quite different now. Ours is by far the most modern,' she added with pride. 'Although the storerooms at the top of the buildings are not in the best condition. Hamilton next door transformed his beautifully. He uses it as a restoration room, of course, but we've never done that. Our work is too new to need restoring after all.'

He locked the door again and took off his coat, walking into the small kitchenette out the back to make some tea as he looked through the post and found, among other things, a note from Margaret Richmond asking him to call her as she had been unable to get in touch with him herself.

He had been very fond of Margaret when he was a child, but he resented the fact that she had known about his uncle's will before he did. He found it disloyal that she would not have warned him in advance and he had repaid this ever since by refusing to take her calls and ignoring her messages. He felt a pang of remorse for that now and left the note on top of the pile, considering a reply later in the day.

He could only imagine how she had felt, standing in the hallway of Leyville while Denis Tandy told them the news.

'Your uncle's will is a somewhat complicated affair,' he explained. 'As the wills of extremely wealthy men often are. But for the purposes of this meeting I think it's best if I just summarize it for you.'

'I don't imagine there are any great surprises in there,' said Stella, a little bitterly.

'As you know,' continued Sir Denis, ignoring her. 'Traditionally the Montignac fortune has been inherited through the male line. Under normal circumstances your grandfather would have left his estate to your father, Owen, but of course that proved . . . impossible.'

Montignac raised an eyebrow. His father had been cut off from the family after eloping to France with one of the housemaids; he wasn't sure he liked that crime being passed over so politely.

'And then, of course, your father was killed in the war anyway so the estate passed to your father, Stella.

'And now I imagine it's going back to where it originally should have been,' said Stella.

'Well no, actually,' said Sir Denis. 'Your father decided that on this occasion the tradition would be broken. The land-ownings, the house here at Leyville and the bulk of the capital are to be left intact, with you, Stella, as titular owner without, however, the right to sell or transfer any of the properties in your lifetime. The income from the various bank accounts and the rent from the properties will be paid directly to you every month.'

'Montignac and Stella both stared at him in surprise.

'What was that?' asked Stella, unsure whether she had heard him correctly.

'To put it simply, you have inherited your father's estate but only after your death will your own heirs be able to sell or transfer any of the assets. However, the income you will receive for the rest of your life will be enough for an extremely comfortable existence.'

Stella's mouth dropped open in surprise and she looked across at her cousin in shock.

'And what about me?' asked Montignac. 'What do I get?'

Sir Denis sighed; he couldn't bring himself to look the boy in the eye. 'I'm afraid Mr Montignac hasn't made any provision for you, Owen,' he said.

Montignac sat back in his chair, racking his brain for anything he might have done recently to displease his uncle but could think of nothing. He had been cut off, disinherited, just as his father had been before him. The poor relation. It had all been for nothing.

A tap on the door snapped Montignac out of his thoughts and he looked down to see his young assistant standing outside and went to let him in. He checked his watch – it was five minutes past eight – and without so much as a good morning he informed the boy that the next time he was late he might as well turn on his heels and walk back home as he would be out of a job.

2

Gareth Bentley woke to the sound of tapping on his bedroom door. He groaned to himself and crawled further underneath the covers, hoping that whoever was out there would simply go away, and soon enough, to his surprise, the tapping stopped only to be replaced by a voice speaking sharply to him from inside the room.

'Gareth,' said the voice. 'Gareth, wake up.'

He eased his head slowly out from underneath the blankets and prised his eyes open to find his mother, Jane Bentley, standing over him with a mug in her hands. She stared at him, her lips pressed tightly together, distinctly unimpressed.

'I've brought you some tea,' she said. 'I want you to drink it, then I want you to get up, have a bath and get dressed. You can't lie around in bed all day like some sort of invalid, you know.'

He groaned again and stuck his tongue out to dampen his dry lips. He could feel the suspicion of a hangover lurking sleepily behind his eyes and tried to make no sudden movements for fear of rousing the beast within.

'What time is it?' he asked.

'It's gone ten o'clock,' she said, placing the mug on the bedside table and looking down at the ground where he had strewn his clothes from the night before. 'Honestly, will you look at this mess? You could at least put your clothes in the laundry basket before you go to bed. What time did you get in last night anyway?'

'It was almost one I think,' he said. 'Not too bad, all things considered.'

'Not too bad? One o'clock in the morning?'

'It was my birthday, Mother,' he replied in a grumpy tone, sitting up and putting the pillows behind his back as he reached for the tea. 'Thanks for this,' he said, taking a hesitant sip as he checked the temperature.

'I know it was your birthday,' she replied, sitting down on the bed and pushing his legs over a little beneath the sheets. 'I hope you weren't drinking.'

'Mother, please.'

'*Were* you drinking?'

He shrugged his shoulders, feeling like a naughty teenager again. 'I may have had a few glasses of champagne,' he admitted. 'Just to celebrate, you know.'

'Oh, Gareth,' she sighed in exasperation. 'And how do you feel now?'

'Not too bad. Slight hangover.'

'You didn't do anything bad, did you?'

'Not that I can recall.'

'How do you mean?'

He shook his head to reassure her. 'It's all right,' he said. 'I remember everything from last night, I did have a couple of drinks but only in moderation and nothing untoward happened.'

'You shouldn't drink at all,' she said, only partly satisfied. 'You know that.'

'I know. And I don't. Normally.'

She nodded and reached across to sweep his messy fringe away from his eyes. 'Well all right,' she said. 'I suppose on your birthday it can't do any harm. Actually that's why I need to speak to you.'

He looked across at her warily; he hated lectures, particularly early in the morning.

'You're twenty-four years old now, Gareth,' she said. 'Have you thought about what comes next?'

'Twenty-five?' he asked.

'Don't be funny,' she snapped. 'It's unbecoming. You should think yourself lucky that it's me and not your father who's having this discussion with you. He'd be a damn sight less polite.'

'Perhaps we could talk about it later, Mother?' he asked. 'When I'm feeling a little better. And I look a little more presentable.'

'We're going to talk about it now,' insisted Jane. 'Its all I can do to keep your father from coming in here and dragging you into a suit of clothes and off to chambers with him, and I can't hold him off forever. Do you know, I ran into Eleanor Tandy yesterday in Harrods and she was telling me all about their Damien and how he's being promoted again in the Bank of England. They say he might be a director by the time he's thirty-five.'

'Damien Tandy and I are very different people, Mother,' said Gareth, who had gone to school with the Tandys' son and had always considered him to be an arrogant poseur, despite their once close friendship. 'Believe me, we have very different outlooks on our futures.'

'Yes, but at least he's actually carving out a future for himself. And what are you doing? Lying around in bed all day, that's what.'

'It's ten o'clock in the morning!' protested Gareth. 'It's hardly all day.'

'Ten o'clock on a Wednesday morning,' she corrected him. 'If it was the weekend perhaps I could understand. But a Wednesday? Your father's been up for hours and he isn't even sitting today.'

Gareth sighed. He had known that this conversation would have to be endured at some point during the week but he hadn't expected it to come quite so soon.

'Then why is he up?' asked Gareth. 'Why isn't he having a rest?'

'Because he's not one to let life pass him by, that's why. Because if he has some time to himself then he wants to make the most of it.'

'Well,' said Gareth in a grumpy tone. 'Father and I are very different people too. Perhaps he'd be happier if Damien Tandy was his son.'

'Oh don't behave like a petulant child,' said Jane in frustration before continuing in a more gossipy tone. 'By the way, while we're on the subject, the other piece of news I had from Eleanor is that Damien is getting married.'

'Married?' asked Gareth, bursting into a laugh and placing the cup down again in case he spilled its contents over the bedsheets. 'You can't be serious.'

'Well of course I'm serious,' she said, frowning. 'Why would I make a joke of such a thing?'

'No reason, I suppose. I'm just . . . very surprised, that's all.'

'Why, for heaven's sake?' asked Jane. 'Because he realizes he isn't a child any more and wants to put down roots? Very admirable, if you ask me.'

'No,' said Gareth firmly. 'I just didn't think he was the marrying kind, that's all.'

'Damien Tandy? He's a very handsome young man, isn't he?

'Oh yes,' admitted Gareth with a snort. 'I think that was generally agreed upon.'

'Well I don't know what that's supposed to mean,' she said dismissively. 'And I'm not sure I care to. All I know is that he's engaged to be married and about to set forth on a decent life and my son, *my* son, is doing nothing at all. Every time one of my friends asks me about you I don't know what to say. It's embarrassing. Gareth, don't you realize that?'

'Tell them I passed away. That'll make it easier. Tell them there was a freak accident involving a streetcar which resulted in the untimely passing of Bentley Minor.'

'Gareth! What a thing to say!' she cried, appalled by how easily the young people made light of such things.

'Sorry.'

'Don't be sorry. Just sort yourself out. I won't have you mooching around here any longer. It's time you earned your keep. Now, I've made an appointment for you at Ede and Ravenscroft for later this week for a fitting and

I don't want to hear any complaints about it, is that understood?'

Gareth raised an eyebrow and stared at her. 'A fitting?' he asked. 'What am I being measured for exactly? My coffin?'

'For a wig and gown, of course. You're to begin your pupillage at your father's chambers next Monday and you'll need something for your appearances in court. He's planning on asking Quentin Lawrence to take you on as his pupil. You can take a note for him at various appearances while you learn the ropes and then, hopefully, you can start to handle your own cases. You know, you could be head of chambers yourself one day if you would only apply yourself.'

Gareth's mouth dropped open in surprise. He knew that they wanted him to join the family firm but the fact that appointments for the prison uniform were being made on his behalf was too much. Why, at any moment, Alistair, his father's clerk, might burst into the bedroom brandishing a brief for him.

'I'm not sure if that's at all likely,' said Gareth. 'And besides, I certainly can't make time for a fitting this week.'

'And why not?' asked Jane Sternly. 'A good answer, please.'

He racked his brain for a moment trying to think of a suitable reason and then the memories of the previous evening began to return to him. His heart sank a little as he recalled the thirty pounds he'd gambled away at the roulette table but then he remembered the conversation he'd had with that friend of Alexander's, the one with the startling white hair, in the taxicab home and the things he had said to him as he was leaving. He'd claimed to be around the same age as him but he'd seemed a lot older; not in appearance, perhaps, but in confidence. Now, in the face of this latest assault from the enemy, he summoned the events back to his mind and began to put his faith in them.

'Because, Mother,' he said smugly. 'I may have a different job lined up.'

'Really?' she asked suspiciously. 'Doing what?'

He wasn't sure and didn't want to admit it. 'It's all a bit hush-hush for now,' he said. 'A fellow I was talking to last night runs his own business it seems and thinks there may be a position for me there.'

'Oh really, Gareth,' she said, frustrated. 'You can't be serious. You don't just accept jobs from random people you meet on the street.'

'He wasn't a random person,' he protested. 'He's a close friend of Alexander Keys.'

'Alexander is a book reviewer and not a very good one at that,' said Jane. 'Every time I buy something on his *Times* recommendation I end up regretting it enormously. And anyway, when was the last time I saw you reading a book? You don't even have one beside your bed.'

'It's not a job working with Alexander, it's something else entirely.'

Jane wasn't to be put off but was beginning to grow curious. 'Well who is this fellow anyway? What's his name?'

Gareth racked his brain; he knew that his whole argument might suffer a fatal blow if he couldn't even remember that much but then, fortunately for him, the dam of memory finally broke and it all came flooding back.

'Owen Montignac,' he said cheerfully. 'His name's Owen Montignac.'

'Owen Montignac?' asked Jane, equally surprised. 'You don't mean Peter Montignac's nephew do you?'

'Yes, I believe I do,' said Gareth.

'Well that puts a different perspective on things,' said Jane, breaking into a smile and standing up from the bed now. 'He's one of the wealthiest landowners in England.'

Gareth nodded, not wishing to dissuade her of that fact.

'And what job does he have for you exactly?'

'I'm not entirely sure,' admitted Gareth. 'But he gave me his card and told me to call on him later in the week and we'd discuss things then.'

'Well then I suggest you do,' she said. 'But are you sure you wouldn't prefer to go in for the law? It is what you studied for after all.'

'I think I'll just see what this Mr Montignac has to say first,' said Gareth. 'I can make a decision then. It can't do any harm to find out, can it?'

Jane nodded. 'I suppose not,' she said. 'But decide

soon. I can't keep your father from cutting off your allowance forever, you know. It's only because I worry about you – you know that, don't you?'

'Of course, Mother,' he said, grinning at her, aware of how easily he could wrap her around his little finger. She laughed and shook her head.

'Oh, Gareth,' she said, feeling a sudden rush of love for her only child. 'You'll be the death of me one of these days, you really will. And tidy this place up,' she added, looking around the room in disdain. 'It looks like a pigsty in here.'

She went out then, still smiling affectionately to herself, and closed the door while Gareth reached for his trousers which were lying on the floor beside the bed. Digging in the pockets he found the small card he had been given the night before. *Owen Montignac,* it read. *The Threadbare Art Gallery, Cork Street, W1*. Nothing else. Simple and to the point.

Gareth frowned. An art gallery. He didn't know much about art. Still, it was better than nothing, he reasoned, putting the empty mug back on the bedside table and returning to his former position underneath the blankets where he quickly fell asleep again.

3

Stella Montignac spent the morning shopping on Regent Street and it was only a short walk from there across Burlington Street and Savile Row to her cousin's art gallery. She had gone out with the intention of cheering herself up by spending a lot of money but had changed her mind halfway through, thinking it might be insensitive to turn up to meet Owen laden down with shopping bags. The autumn fashions would be in the shops in a few weeks' time, she knew, and she would plan a special trip up to London from Leyville then to purchase an entirely new wardrobe.

As she turned on to Clifford Street she saw a familiar figure walking along the pavement towards her, a woman of her own age, a face from her past. She knew instantly that it was a girl she had been at school with some years before but wondered whether she would recognize her in return, so her eyes flitted back and forth in semi-recognition until they finally met and both acknowledged the relationship.

'Stella Montignac,' said the girl, stopping first and breaking into a smile, her eyes darting immediately to Stella's hands to see whether she wore an engagement or wedding ring. 'It's Vicky Hartford. You remember me, don't you?'

'Of course I do,' said Stella. 'It's been a long time but you haven't changed a bit.'

'I hope that's not true,' said Vicky. 'What a coincidence our running into each other like this.'

'Yes it is, I suppose,' replied Stella who couldn't see why it was a coincidence at all. Unanticipated, perhaps, but not a coincidence.

They stood nodding at each other, both waiting for the other to play the opening gambit of the conversation and finally things became awkward and Stella gave in.

'I've spent the entire morning shopping,' she said in an exhausted tone. 'Couldn't find a thing I wanted.'

Vicky glanced at the three bags she was carrying and doubted that. 'I haven't seen you in such a long time but I'm actually very glad I ran into you,' she said in a hushed tone and Stella knew immediately what was coming next. 'I read about your father in the paper last month. I was very sorry to hear about it. I meant to write to you at the time but I've just been so busy.'

Stella nodded. 'Thank you,' she said.

'Was it very sudden?'

'Well, it was unexpected,' admitted Stella. 'He'd been sick on and off for years but no one expected him to go quite like that. In his sleep. Perhaps if there'd been some warning we would have been more prepared, but there we are. It was peaceful, I suppose.'

'I'm sure it's been terribly hard,' said Vicky. 'How are you coping?'

'Oh I'm fine,' said Stella in a dismissive tone, suddenly anxious to get away. It was coming back to her now how much she had disliked Vicky back in her school days. An insufferable gossip who was never happy unless she was discussing someone else's business, she had managed the remarkable feat during their years together of keeping on the right side of everyone. No matter which power group on the school happened to be in control at the time, she always found a way to ignore all the malicious things she had ever said about them behind their backs by pretending that she had never been friends with anyone but the person standing directly in front of her. As corrupt as a politician and as duplicitous as a schizophrenic, Vicky had been one of the people Stella had been happiest to get away from during her exile in Switzerland.

'My own father died a few years ago,' said Vicky. 'You probably heard about it.'

'No,' said Stella, shaking her head, unsurprised that suddenly it had all become about Vicky rather than her. 'No I'm sorry, I hadn't heard.'

'Well,' she said, looking a little offended. 'He did. It was terribly upsetting for everyone but we soldiered on and that's what you must do, Stella. You must soldier on.'

She lunged forwards and for a horrible moment Stella thought that she was going to take her face in her hands and kiss her but it turned out she had simply lost her footing on the pavement and slipped slightly.

'We really should go for lunch,' suggested Vicky. 'You won't have heard my news.'

'I can't, I'm afraid,' said Stella. 'I'm meeting my cousin.'

'Your cousin?' she asked, looking interested now. 'Not that terribly handsome boy who used to come to visit you in school all those years ago? The one who nearly got you thrown out?'

Stella felt her face pale a little. 'You knew about that?' she asked.

'A lot of people did. I saw you climbing out your window one night and the two of you heading down the driveway together. The year before you left us. It was his hair that I remembered the most. What was his name again – Oliver, wasn't it?'

'Owen.'

'Oh yes, that's right. Most unusual. We were all a little in love with him. And you're still in touch, isn't that lovely!'

'Well he is my cousin,' explained Stella with a smile. 'Of course we're in touch. He's all I have left now, in fact.'

Vicky nodded. 'Well you can rest assured that I never told anyone whatever pranks the two of you were up to. And compared to the things that happened in our final year, after you had left us of course, going off on midnight walks was neither here nor there.'

'I'm sorry I missed that,' said Stella, hoping that the strain of sarcasm in her voice would not go undetected.

'Oh you were better off. Living the high life at that finishing school in Paris.'

'Geneva,' she corrected her.

'Oh Geneva, was it? How lovely. I've never been to Austria.'

Stella smiled and opened her mouth to correct her

again, but thought better of it. That was another thing about Vicky that she had forgotten; her plain stupidity. But that final year of school when her education had been interrupted by her father's decision to send her to Geneva was not something she liked to remember at all. It had been Margaret Richmond who had arranged it all of course. It was Margaret she had to thank for nearly destroying her life. Or perhaps for saving it.

'Anyway, I must get on,' said Stella. 'Owen will be wondering what's keeping me.

'Oh but you haven't heard my news,' insisted Vicky, who was damned if she was going to allow her to go without imparting it. 'I'm engaged to be married.'

Stella smiled and nodded politely. 'Really,' she said. 'How lovely. Congratulations.'

'Thank you. You must forgive my excitement about it. I'm still getting accustomed to telling people. It's only been a few days.'

'Well,' said Stella. 'I hope you'll be very happy. When's the big day?'

'Not till next summer, I don't think,' said Vicky. 'Damien thinks we should have a long engagement so that we can afford a really expensive honeymoon. We're thinking about a safari in Africa. I've never been there before, have you?'

'No,' said Stella, shaking her head.

'Well that's what we're talking about, although we may end up doing a European tour instead. Also,

Damien's just received a promotion in the bank so he thinks he should devote himself to his work for a year or two before we settle down, which I think is for the best too, don't you?'

'I wouldn't know,' said Stella with a shrug. 'Whatever makes you happy, I suppose.

'And what about you?' asked Vicky, irritated by her friend's indifference and distinct lack of envy. 'Are you married yet?'

'No,' said Stella

'Engaged?'

'No,' said Stella, surprising herself by her unwillingness to admit that, in fact, she was.

'Oh, I'm so sorry,' said Vicky. 'But you're involved, of course?'

'No,' said Stella again. 'I'm neither married, engaged nor involved. I'm all on my own and happy to be so.'

Vicky's mouth dropped open and she stared at her as if she had just announced that she had a terminal illness and felt the better for it.

'Well. I'm very surprised to hear that,' she said.

'It's a mystery to me too,' said Stella, who had no idea why she was denying Raymond's existence but enjoying tremendously the look of triumph on her old friend's face, thinking she had one over on her.

'Do you know,' said Vicky, leaning forwards now. 'Damien knows a great many eligible young men at the bank. It wouldn't be very difficult for me to ask him to keep an eye out for a suitable beau. What if I take your number and try to arrange a dinner?'

'No thanks,' said Stella quickly, seeing her plan begin to backfire on her. 'No, I'm perfectly happy as I am, thank you.'

'Oh don't be ridiculous,' said Vicky with the pride of a spider who has already managed to snare her own fly in the web. 'How on earth can you possibly be happy without a husband? The idea's ludicrous. No, you leave it to me, I'll organise it. We'll have you engaged by Christmas.'

'No really, Vicky,' said Stella, feigning a look of humility. 'It's too soon after Father's death.'

'Oh,' said Vicky, visibly disappointed. 'Oh I see.'

'It wouldn't be proper.'

'I suppose not. Although he would want you to be getting on with your life.'

'I need more time first,' said Stella, feeling a little guilty at using the memory of her late father to get out of the social awkwardness.

'I understand perfectly,' said Vicky. 'Well not to worry. If I can find a husband, then anyone can.'

'Yes, I'd imagine that's true,' said Stella with a smile.

Vicky narrowed her eyes with the faintest feeling that she might have just been insulted. 'Where do you stay when you're in London anyway?' she asked.

'My father had an apartment in Kensington,' she said. 'So I'll be there in future. But I've been to Claridge's this week because the apartment needs a good clean-out. But mostly I'm down at Leyville.'

'Well give me the address,' insisted Vicky, pulling out a pad and paper and thrusting it into her hands. 'And I'll be in touch some day and we can have lunch.'

Faced with no choice, Stella wrote down the address and handed the pad back. The two ladies kissed and said their goodbyes and Stella continued on her way towards Cork Street, irritated that she hadn't crossed to the other side of the street when she saw Vicky coming. The insistence of her old school friends living their lives based around whether or not they had found a suitable husband riled her. Maybe that was why she liked being with Raymond so much. He was so clearly unsuitable, she was so obviously marrying beneath her, that their relationship could only shock people. So why then, she wondered, had she not admitted it when asked? Was it because she didn't love him? If so then that was a good thing for she had loved once and it had nearly been the end of her and she had sworn off it for life ever since.

She turned the corner on to Cork Street and recognized the figure of Jason Parsons, her cousin's assistant, leaving the gallery halfway down the street on his way to lunch and was pleased to see him go. She had timed her visit so that he wouldn't be there. She wanted to speak to Cousin Owen alone.

4

The letter arrived while Roderick and Jane Bentley were sitting down to brunch. Roderick had been presiding over a long but rather tedious trial which was entering its third week when one of the chief witnesses for the prosecution had been taken ill. He had granted an adjournment of two days and was enjoying the fact that he would have to spend a couple of days at home although, as he would have happily pointed out to his dormant son, he was not going to waste them lying around in bed. He had some reading to catch up on and planned to take the dogs for a long walk later in the day.

'I spoke to Gareth this morning,' said Jane, a little nervous at bringing up the topic but hoping that a pre-emptive strike might prevent her husband from going after the boy himself. 'He's agreed that he needs to start taking things a little more seriously.'

'A lot more seriously,' corrected Roderick.

'Yes, a lot more seriously,' said Jane. 'Well he's agreed to it anyway. He's accepted the fact that he's a young man now, not a boy—'

'My dear,' said Roderick in frustration. 'He's been a young man for three or four years. It's a little disconcerting that he's only picking up on the fact now.'

'Roderick, don't argue, please,' she said. 'You don't have to worry about him any more is what I'm saying.'

Roderick nodded and buttered another slice of toast, laying a thin layer of marmalade across the top. 'You made the appointment then?' he asked after a moment.

'The appointment?'

'At Ede and Ravenscroft.'

'Oh yes,' said Jane. 'Yes I did. He's perfectly well aware that he's expected for a fitting.'

Roderick laid down his knife and peered across the table at his wife, who smiled back at him nervously. After all these years together he knew immediately when she wasn't being completely honest with him; it was in her careful syntax, in the way she inclined her head a little to the left, deliberately not catching his eye.

'There's something you're not telling me,' he said.

'What's that?' she asked innocently.

'I said there's something you're not telling me,' he repeated. 'So why don't you just spit it out. He is going to the fitting, isn't he?'

Jane sighed and for a brief moment wished her son had more determination about his future – like Damien Tandy, who even had the decency to give his mother a wedding to prepare for – and wouldn't keep putting her in uncomfortable situations like this. 'Now, Roderick,' she began. 'You're not to get angry—'

'Oh bloody hell!' said Roderick, who rarely swore. 'What's the boy done now?'

'Nothing, he hasn't done anything at all,' said Jane, looking around nervously. 'And keep your voice down please. The servants will hear you.'

'I don't care who hears me. You told him that he was coming to chambers with me from Monday?'

'Yes.'

'And that he was to be a pupil for Quentin Lawrence?'

'I told him that, yes.'

'And that he was to attend Ede and Ravenscroft to get his wig and gown?'

'Roderick, I told him all of that,' insisted Jane. 'I told him everything you told me to tell him and a lot more besides. And he's perfectly happy to do all of that if his other plans don't work out. He's excited at the prospect of being a barrister . . . some day.'

Roderick narrowed his eyes. 'Some day,' he repeated.

'Yes.'

'But not next Monday?'

'I don't think so.'

'Well what are these other plans then?' he asked suspiciously. 'What's he got in mind?'

'Well,' said Jane, leaning forwards as if this was the most exciting news in the world and something of which they should both be extremely proud. 'He may have found himself a different position.'

'Where?' asked Roderick, who knew his son well enough to take pronouncements like this with a pinch of salt.

'Well I'm not exactly sure what the job is, and nor is he right now, but his potential employer—'

'Where?' insisted Roderick.

Jane sighed. She couldn't put it off any longer. 'It seems that Owen Montignac has offered him a job.'

'Owen Montignac?' he asked, unable to conceal his surprise. 'Peter Montignac's boy?'

'His nephew, yes. Not his son.'

'No, you're wrong there,' said Roderick, shaking his head. 'I used to know Peter many years ago. He did have a son.'

'Yes, but he was killed in some sort of accident, I think. Owen is his brother's boy. I read about it in the death notice last month.'

'Well what of it?' asked Roderick who didn't much like to be corrected, neither by defence counsel, prosecution barristers nor his wife. 'And what does this Montignac fellow do anyway?'

'I don't know,' said Jane.

'You don't know?'

'Well not exactly anyway. I imagine it's something to do with all the land he owns. He has properties all over London, you know. He's extremely wealthy.'

Roderick scowled. He felt unsure what his attitude to this new piece of intelligence should be. On the one hand he didn't much care for his son turning down the opportunity to come into chambers when there were more qualified men than him crying out for the spare desk, not to mention the pupillage of such an eminent man as Sir Quentin Lawrence. He himself had always loved the law and thrived in his career; he couldn't understand why a son of his would not feel the same way. And he was wasting so much time! By the time he was twenty-four, Roderick had already established quite a name for himself as an advocate. On the other hand, however, there was no doubting Owen Montignac's status in the world. If he was prepared to offer Gareth a position, then maybe it would be for the best. At least if he made a mess of it it wouldn't reflect on Roderick in the way it would in chambers. He grunted, dissatisfied but accepting, and returned to his breakfast silently.

'I didn't even know that he was friends with Montignac,' he said after a long pause during which Jane had begun to relax a little, thinking that he would allow this turn of events to continue unhindered for the time being.

'Oh yes,' she lied. 'They've known each other for ages. They're about the same age, of course. They probably run in the same set.'

'Well you know what I think of them.'

'I do, yes,' said Jane patiently. 'You've told me many times.'

'It's only because I worry about him,' he said defensively. 'Gareth is the sort who lands himself in trouble and then relies on me to get him out of it. You know that.'

'But he's not going to get in any trouble,' she said, defending her son as always. 'It'll be a perfectly respectable job and—'

'He was bloody lucky not to get sent down from Harrow, you remember. If I hadn't—'

'Oh, Roderick, that was eight years ago,' protested Jane, who didn't like to think about that awful incident and wished that everyone would just forget about it. 'You can't hold it against him for the rest of his life.'

Roderick frowned. He had a lot more to say on the subject but at that moment Sophie, their family maid, entered the room with a small silver tray which held a letter. He looked at it in surprise for the morning post had already been and gone.

'Another letter?' he said, picking it up and noting the formal calligraphy of the address.

'Just arrived, sir,' said Sophie. 'Hand delivered.'

'Thank you,' he replied, dismissing her and staring at the envelope for a moment. As a rule he didn't like unexpected correspondence like this; it tended to bring bad news.

'What is it?' asked Jane as he took a clean knife from the table and slit the top of the envelope open. He extracted a piece of vellum paper with very neat type on it and let out a sigh of frustration as he finished reading the contents. 'What is it, Roderick?' she repeated, hating to be left in the dark.

'It's from the Lord Chancellor's office,' he explained. 'He's invited three KCs to meet with him next week to discuss a most important matter.'

Jane had to stop herself from laughing at the pomposity of it and Roderick stared across at her.

'That's what it says here,' he said innocently. '*A most important matter*.'

'How extraordinary,' said Jane. 'Whatever can it be?'

'I have a pretty good idea,' said Roderick, placing the letter back inside the envelope.

'You do? What is it then?'

'It doesn't matter,' he said dismissively. 'I could be wrong.'

'Roderick, tell me for heaven's sake,' said Jane, who couldn't stand to be left out of anything, especially something as unusual as this. The last time her husband had been called to the Lord Chancellor's office it was to inform him that he was to be knighted. What further honour could he have earned since then? 'We don't have any secrets, do we?'

He shrugged, wondering whether the amount of secrets she probably kept from him were enough that a herd of stampeding buffalo couldn't knock them over.

'Well I've sort of been expecting it,' said Roderick quietly, looking around to make sure that Sophie and Nell hadn't slipped unnoticed into the room. 'Or dreading it, rather.'

'Dreading what?'

'I suspect the prime minister has asked the Lord Chancellor to take some initial soundings from senior judges.'

Jane frowned, trying to decipher what her husband might be talking about. A sudden idea came into her mind and she inclined her head, unsure whether this would be too ridiculous an idea to even suggest.

'It's not about . . .' she began, unsure whether even to

say it in case he laughed at her. 'It's not about the king, is it?' she asked.

Roderick gave her the faintest of nods. 'I believe it could be,' he said.

'The king and this woman? This American woman?'

Roderick nodded again.

'Well that's ridiculous,' said Jane, laughing it off. 'Nothing's ever going to come of that. It's just a piece of London gossip, that's all.'

'Perhaps,' said Roderick. 'But oftentimes, gossip has a way of becoming fact.'

'Oh I can't believe it,' said Jane. 'The man's not that stupid. And the prime minister wants to find out what you would all think about it?'

'I imagine so. Constitutional implications and so on.'

Jane shook her head as if the entire thing was utterly absurd. 'Well that seems an enormous waste of time,' she said. 'Four senior members of the judiciary talking about something that's never going to come to pass in a million years! Sooner or later a suitable wife will be found for him and there'll be no more talk of this woman, this Mrs Simpson or whatever her name is. Or she'll get bored and return to her husband.'

'I believe she's planning a divorce, my dear,' said Roderick.

'Well she'll return to America then. She's no better than she ought to be anyway,' Jane added with a sniff, standing up from the table and laying her napkin down and displaying the kind of resentment reserved for those intending to marry above their station from those who already had. 'Anyway I don't have time for this foolishness. I have to rush off,' she said. 'I have some shopping to do in town and then, for my sins, I'm meeting Eleanor Tandy who will no doubt spend the entire afternoon telling me what a wonderful son she has and what a charming daughter-in-law she's about to welcome into the fold.'

She came over and kissed Roderick on the cheek and he put an arm around her waist, grateful for any kindnesses she offered him.

'And don't worry about Gareth,' she said. 'He'll meet with Mr Montignac and all will be well.'

'I hope so,' he replied as she kissed him again and left the room

He sat there silently for a few more minutes, considering the matter, and read the letter he had received once more, praying that on this occasion his wife would be correct and the whole thing would come to nothing. The last thing he wanted was any further publicity, or more newspapermen camped out on the doorstep. The neighbours would lose their reason entirely.

5

He could sense her presence in the gallery before either laying eyes on her or hearing her voice; it was a skill he had developed over the previous two decades, a talent he wished he could shrug off.

There were only two or three other people browsing downstairs, each one cooing over some inane canvas as they made reckless attempts at deciphering it. At most times during their opening hours both he and Jason Parsons were present on the gallery floor but there was rarely any need for both of them. Security wasn't an issue as the canvases were tightly secured to the walls and most of the sculptures were too heavy to remove without being observed so he felt perfectly comfortable spending time on the upper floor without having to monitor what was taking place downstairs.

Montignac was standing on the mezzanine floor of the Threadbare, examining a light fitting that kept flickering on and off over an abstract painting when she stepped through the doors and looked around to locate her cousin; instinctively he moved back to a position from where he knew he would be invisible to anyone on the ground. He watched as she drifted around the front of the space, taking in some of the new pieces on display, and walked towards the desk where he could usually be found at this time, checking through some catalogues or finishing off *The Times* crossword while his assistant took care of more trivial matters such as assisting the customers or attending to matters of fixture upkeep like he was currently engaged in.

A small bell chimed from below; Stella had tapped on it and he made his way to the balcony and looked down on her. They both spoke at the same moment.

'Shop,' she said.

'Stella,' he called out. 'I'm up here.'

She turned her head upwards and grinned. 'Hiding away, are you?'

He smiled and shook his head. He noticed that she was carrying three bags of shopping and wondered how much of his stolen money she had already spent that morning and how much more would be delivered into the cash registers of Oxford Street, Regent Street and Covent Garden before the day was over.

'I'll be down in a few minutes,' he called out. 'Make yourself comfortable.'

'Thanks. I will.'

He watched as she deposited her bags behind his desk and took her coat off, laying it across his chair, and felt momentarily flattered and irritated by how much she could make herself at home in his place of business. He felt that this was one of her specialities; believing that the world existed purely for her comfort.

For a moment he cast his mind back to the first time he had laid eyes on his cousin. He was five years old at the time and had recently been delivered off a boat from Calais to Dover where his uncle, Peter Montignac, had collected him and driven him back to Leyville.

'This is to be your home from now on,' Peter explained to him as they drove along. 'You're to live with my wife and me and our two children. Are you happy about that?' He spoke with enormous pride, as if he was God himself who, in an act of charity, was welcoming an unrepentant sinner through the gates of Paradise.

Montignac stared at the stranger, afraid to answer.

'What's the matter? Peter asked. 'Cat got your tongue?'

He replied in faltering English and said he was glad to be there. He had never spoken anything but French during those first five years with his parents and was nervous of it now. His father, Henry, had taught him English but they had rarely employed it in day-to-day conversation; he found that he was uneasy about using the language now, scared that he might appear foolish or ignorant among his newly discovered relatives.

'We'll have to do something about that accent of yours,' Peter said irritably. 'Can't have you talking like that around here. You'll frighten the locals.'

Andrew was eight and Stella had just turned six when Montignac arrived to live with them. Their mother, Ann, explained to them that he was their cousin, that he'd lost both his parents and had no one else to look after him but them and they must treat him like a brother.

'Why have we never heard of him before?' Andrew asked suspiciously. 'Why hasn't he been here to play or come to any of my birthday parties?'

'Well, because he's been living in France,' she explained. 'It's much too far away for someone to come just for a party.'

'You've never even spoken of him before,' Andrew said, nervous at the prospect of having another boy in the house and his own carefully carved-out position being usurped.

'Of course I have. We've often told you about your cousin, Owen.'

'You've never mentioned his name once,' insisted Andrew quite correctly because the truth was that she never had. 'What happened to his parents anyway?'

Ann sat her two children down in the library and tried to explain it to them in a way that she hoped wouldn't scare them.

'Well,' she began. 'You understand that there's a war going on at the moment?'

The children nodded. Everyone knew about the war; it was all anyone ever talked about. Some of their friends' fathers were even fighting in it but their father didn't have to because he had important business to take care of in London.

'Well your uncle, Owen's father, was killed in a battle. And his wife—'

'Our aunt,' said Andrew.

'His wife,' repeated Ann. 'Well she died in an explosion at a factory. But she was French, of course,' she added, as if that meant she had probably brought it on herself. 'She lived here for a time some years ago but that was before any of this.'

'She lived here?' asked Andrew, wide-eyed.

'Long before you were born,' said Ann. 'I never met her myself. She was a maid when your grandfather was still alive.'

Andrew considered it and couldn't quite understand how that could possibly be. 'You're saying that our uncle married one of our maids?' he asked, unable to believe it for a moment.

'It was all a very long time ago,' repeated Ann, sorry that she'd begun this at all. 'And it's neither here nor there any more. The important thing is that we welcome their little boy into our home because he has nowhere else to go and if you can't rely on family at times like this, well then who can you rely on?'

'I'll make him welcome,' said Stella quietly, who had remained silent throughout all of this.

A little later that afternoon the children stood nervously at the door while their father's motor car made its way up the driveway towards them.

'Well?' asked Peter of his young charge. 'What do you think of it then?' This is where your father grew up, you know. Magnificent, isn't it? Perhaps he spoke about it from time to time?'

Montignac could hardly believe it. The house they had lived in in Clermont-Ferrand was perfectly pleasant but it was small, cosy enough to fit just the three of them. This house, on the other hand, was a mansion. It was like one of the castles that he had seen when his parents had taken him on a holiday to Versailles. He thought such places were just there for visiting or for housing museums; they could hardly have been places in which people actually lived. His mouth dropped open in amazement and he found it hard to accept that he was actually going to be staying there.

'And standing at the door over there are your aunt and your cousins,' he said, bringing the car to a halt. 'They'll make you feel at home.'

Although he had been a little scared of his uncle ever since arriving in England, he clung close to him now as the introductions were made. He was accustomed to being around other children in France but these two who called themselves Andrew and Stella seemed like an entirely different breed altogether. For one thing they were extremely clean and well dressed, unlike his old friends who were generally scruffy and bathed only once or twice a week. They both extended their hands politely for him to shake and said, 'How do you do?' and when he nodded politely and said, *'Bonjour,'* they twisted their faces up in surprise and looked at their father for reassurance.

'Now, now, Owen,' said Peter. 'Remember what I told you on the way here. We speak English in this country. There's no need for any more of that.'

'Oui, mais j'ai oublié le mot pour—'

'Owen, you're doing it again.'

'Sorry,' he said.

When he looked up again he saw Stella staring at him, not quite at his face but a little higher, and he knew that she was looking at his hair, surprised by how white it was.

'It's quite extraordinary, isn't it?' said Peter, following his daughter's gaze. 'At least we know we won't lose him in the dark, eh? He's like a torch. Well come on, old fellow,' he said cheerfully then, putting his arm around the boy's shoulders. 'Let's get you inside. You must be tired after your trip.'

And in they had gone, closing the large oak doors firmly behind them to begin his new life as the poor relation.

Montignac finished inserting a new tube bulb into the overhead fitting and switched it on. It worked perfectly. It was lighting up a large canvas, perhaps six feet by four, which contained a series of increasingly dark stripes, each one with a red circle drawn in the centre. The significance of the circles and the lines was beyond him but if he had been forced to choose the least reprehensible work in the gallery, this might have been it. It wasn't as hideously awful as some of the other pieces on display, which perhaps explained why it had languished there for almost three months without even a hint of a buyer.

'Owen.'

A voice from behind him made him jump; he had been lost in his thoughts and memories and hadn't heard her come up the stairs.

'Stella,' he said, breaking into an embarrassed smile. 'Sorry for jumping. You startled me.'

'When you're quite ready . . .' she said, smiling back at him and he noticed how even now, even after all these years, she could barely bring herself to look him in the eye. Instead her gaze was directed just a little north of his forehead as if it didn't matter how many years she spent looking at him, it was still impossible for her to believe that such a shade of white could exist on a human being.

He didn't know whether it was his hair that continued to fascinate her or whether she just couldn't hold his gaze; in truth he found it hard to look directly at her either after everything they had been through. If he could go back twenty years, he wondered, would he have jumped overboard as the ship passed through the English Channel or would he have come anyway and faced what was to come?

'I think we need to talk, Owen,' said Stella quietly and he nodded.

'Yes,' he said. 'Yes, I think we probably do.'

6

It was well past noon by the time that Gareth Bentley was washed and dressed and ready to present himself to the outside world. His hangover was pulsating slightly behind his eyes but had not developed as painfully as he had imagined it might earlier. Still, his whole body felt like it was in denial, skin pale and wan, hair lank, limbs uneager for movement. But he liked the house at this time of day. His father would be at work, his mother would be out having lunch with her friends or shopping, and Sophie and Nell, if they were around at all, would be hiding out in the basement or taking their early afternoon hours off.

He padded downstairs in his socks and made a pot of tea, leafing through the morning newspaper which was laid out on the breakfast table as usual, although there was nothing much of interest to be found there. He stretched out, yawning extravagantly, and was considering retiring to the living-room sofa for another snooze when the telephone rang and he drifted out to the hallway to answer it.

'Hello?' he said in a distracted tone but there was silence on the other end so he repeated himself. 'Hello?' he asked again.

'Hello, yes,' said a gruff voice immediately in reply. 'Who's this?'

'Who's this?' asked Gareth, half amused, half irritated. 'Who's *this*? You phoned me!'

'Yes, who is it?' said the voice.

'It's Gareth Bentley,' he said, not eager to continue with this line of questioning. 'Who are you looking for?'

'Ah yes, Gareth, you're the one I'm after. It's Quentin Lawrence here. I'm sure your father told you I'd be in touch.'

'Quentin Lawrence,' said Gareth to himself, trying to recall where he knew the name from. It rang a distant bell.

'Now I just needed to talk to you about Monday,' said Sir Quentin. 'I have a long fraud trial beginning in Newcastle so we'll be going up on the Sunday evening train. I'll need you to take a note for me during the proceedings, of course, but also to organize the luggage and the tickets. Can you come around here Sunday afternoon, say around four? I realize it's a bit in at the deep end but there's no harm in that.'

Gareth listened, unsure what the man was talking about. 'I'm sorry,' he said. 'I think you must have the wrong person.'

'Nonsense,' said Lawrence. 'You're Roderick's boy, aren't you?'

'Well yes, but—'

'You don't have a brother, do you?'

'No.'

'Then you're the one. You're my new pupil. Now come along, let's not waste time on all of this, I need to make sure that you—'

While Sir Quentin Lawrence twittered on about train timetables and four-star hotels, Gareth remembered where he had heard the name before. His mother had mentioned it earlier in the day when she'd been trying to rouse him from his bed. This was the fellow who was to be his mentor in chambers. For a moment or two he developed a new-found respect for his father for managing to put his plan into action without so much as consulting him. It was a good job, Gareth realized, that he had gone to the Unicorn Ballrooms the night before or he might well have had no choice but to accept.

'I'm sorry, Mr Lawrence,' began Gareth but he was quickly interrupted.

'It's Sir Quentin,' said the man on the other end of the phone proudly.

'I'm sorry, Sir Quentin,' he said, correcting himself. 'I think there's been some sort of misunderstanding.'

'Misunderstanding?' Sir Quentin asked irritably. 'I don't see how. Your father asked me as a particular favour to—'

'Yes, I'm aware of that, only my father didn't know that I've found another position in the meantime.'

There was an offended silence on the other end. 'You're going to another chambers?' Sir Quentin asked in appalled disbelief, as if he'd just announced his intention to vote Labour at the next general election.

'No, not to another chambers. To an entirely different career altogether.'

'A career outside the law?' he asked, even more dumbfounded.

'Yes, that's right.'

'Well don't be ridiculous, boy. You studied at Cambridge, didn't you? I did so myself and look at me now. Why on earth would you move to a different career? Nonsense. You stick with what you're good at, that's what I say, and you won't come undone. Now if you can just manage to get round here by four on Sunday then I can—'

'I'm sorry, Sir Quentin, said Gareth quite affably. 'I do appreciate the opportunity you're giving me but there's simply no way I can accept it. I've already given my word to my new employer.'

'To your new—?'

'But thank you anyway, I do appreciate the offer. And thanks for calling. Goodbye then,' he said, replacing the receiver on the cradle gently, and grimacing. He stood there tensely, waiting to see whether anything would happen, and sure enough it rang again within the minute and this time it sounded, if such a thing were possible, even angrier than before. He chose not to answer it, however, and simply stared at the device, willing it to stop and leave him in peace. Finally it did and it didn't ring again. He breathed a sigh of relief and returned to the kitchen.

A key was heard in the front door a few minutes later and his father appeared. The two men looked at each other warily along the corridor, knowing that they were currently in the middle of mediation talks but that the person organizing them – Roderick's wife, Gareth's mother – was not present to keep the peace. Wishing that the kitchen door had been closed so that he could have retired to the library without appearing rude, Roderick walked down the passageway and poured himself a cup of tea from the pot. They spoke without exchanging any opening pleasantries.

'Your mother tells me that you may have a new position organized already.'

'Yes,' said Gareth. 'Just last night, actually. I don't know all the details yet.'

'Well I'm pleased to hear that you're starting to take things seriously,' said Roderick, who didn't want a fight.

'It's about time you buckled down and started thinking about your responsibilities.'

'I don't have any responsibilities,' said Gareth, wondering whether he'd forgotten a stray wife or child somewhere who was pleading for his attentions.

'You have responsibilities to your mother and me,' said Roderick sharply. 'Who brought you up and fed you and clothed you and gave you a decent education that apparently is of no interest to you now.'

'Yes, well . . .' muttered Gareth, looking away, unable to catch his father's eye.' I suppose if you put it like that.'

'I do put it like that. Now this new job. It's with Owen Montignac, isn't it?'

'That's right, yes. Do you know him?'

Roderick shook his head. 'I knew his uncle a little,' he said. 'Just socially, of course. But I'm sure if he's a Montignac he's a good fellow, his uncle certainly was. What does he do anyway?'

'It's all land deals, I believe,' said Gareth, who had picked up that nugget of information from his mother and really didn't have any idea what Montignac did on a day-to-day basis. He had of course seen the business card with the details of the gallery on it but he couldn't imagine that there was a position there for him; after all he didn't know anything about art. But if this Montignac fellow really was a property magnate then there might well be something interesting that he could do for him. 'We haven't discussed the ins and outs of it yet. I'll be speaking to him soon.'

'And you're sure this is what you want to do?' asked Roderick.

'I think so, Father. I just don't think the law's for me. Sorry,' he added with becoming humility.

Roderick nodded and looked a little sad. 'Well I can't say I'm not a little disappointed,' he said. 'I would have enjoyed having you in the family chambers. But if your mind's made up . . .'

'It is, Father. I really think this is for the best.'

'Well there we are then. As long as you're happy.' Roderick attempted a half-smile, which Gareth appreciated because he knew it was difficult for him to accept this change of profession. 'I'll have to give old Quentin Lawrence a call, though,' he mused. 'He'll be expecting you next week. I called in a favour on that and he won't let me forget it, if I know him at all.'

Gareth nodded, unwilling to offer any further apologies, but chose not to mention the phone call of earlier.

'You're not sitting today?' he asked after a long silence.

'No,' said Roderick, shaking his head. 'A witness went down sick. We couldn't go on without him. I'll quite value the few days off if I'm honest.'

'Lucky you,' said Gareth, as if his whole life didn't consist of sitting around doing nothing.

'Just do one thing for me,' said Roderick before he would allow the conversation to end. 'Just find out a little more about this Montignac fellow before you commit yourself to anything.'

'But you said you knew him. You said he was a decent fellow.'

'I said his uncle was. And generally the apple doesn't fall far from the tree although . . .' He looked at his own son sceptically, as if he was proof that the axiom wasn't always true. 'Just do a little research, that's all I'm asking. It's always wise to know who you're getting yourself involved with.'

'All right,' said Gareth, eager to please his father now that the difficult task of persuading him that he shouldn't be a barrister had been completed successfully. 'I'll see what I can find out. He's a friend of Alexander Keys so I'll speak to him.'

'Good,' said Roderick. 'I'm probably being overly cautious but it does no harm to be sure.'

Gareth agreed and felt relieved when his father left the room, heading towards his study. As he followed him a few minutes later and began to walk down the corridor he heard the phone ring again. He slipped his shoes on by the front door and left the house quickly, closing the door behind him as quietly as possible while his father went to apologize to Sir Quentin Lawrence, now sadly left without a pupil for his difficult fraud case, due to begin the following Monday morning in Newcastle Crown Court.

7

'It's very quiet, isn't it?' asked Stella, looking around at the handful of browsers making asinine comments about shape and form as they examined some of the more preposterous pieces on display at the Threadbare Gallery. 'I wonder that you can make a living here at all.'

'It gets busier later in the afternoon,' explained Montignac. 'We only actually sell a couple of pieces a day but they're ridiculously expensive.'

'It's hard to see why.'

'If we sold them for what they were actually worth then we'd never get rid of any of them. The only way to shift them is to fool people into thinking that the price tag matches the artistic merit.'

'They're all very . . .' Stella bit her lip, trying to find the right word, not wanting to insult her cousin if she could help it. 'Very contemporary,' she settled on finally. 'Quite challenging.'

'Utter rubbish, you mean,' he said.

'Well yes. If you want to put it like that.'

'I'm well aware of how bad they are,' he said, lowering his voice so that none of the customers could hear him. 'This gallery is one of the greatest con-jobs on the London art scene. Still, if people want to waste their money here and pay my salary while they're at it, then who am I to stand in their way?'

Stella nodded. She watched her cousin as he settled down behind his desk, sifting through the mail and a couple of catalogues which had just arrived. There was a mass of papers threatening to spill over on to the floor and she had a rare urge to help him tidy up but resisted it, not wanting to make herself too familiar. He hadn't bothered to get a seat for her so she pulled one over from beside a window and sat down opposite him.

'So,' she began, wondering why she hadn't spent more time preparing for this conversation before actually embarking on it. 'Last night didn't go terribly well.'

'No,' he replied, shaking his head. 'No, I suppose not.'

'I didn't expect you to just leave like you did. Walking out like that before anything was settled. There are still so many things we need to talk about and—'

'Things that *we* need to talk about, yes,' said Montignac pointedly. 'You and I, Stella. Not the two of us and Raymond.'

'Raymond's my fiancé, Owen, you know that,' she said with a sigh. 'I can't just exclude him.'

He gave a small, slightly embittered laugh and looked away, shaking his head. 'Remind me to send a note to Margaret, will you?' he asked. 'She's been trying to contact me and I haven't returned her calls.'

'We've all been trying to contact you, Owen,' she said. 'You never answer your phone. You don't respond to letters—'

'I'm very busy, Stella,' he said, interrupting her. 'Some of us need to work for a living, you know. We don't just get things handed to us on a silver platter.'

She sighed and leaned back in the chair. 'Is that what this is all about?' she asked.

He shrugged his shoulders.

'Owen, I knew nothing about what Father was planning,' she said in a determined voice. 'Absolutely nothing.'

'Really.'

'Yes, really. And even if I did, which I didn't, but even if I did I'm not going to apologize to you for my own father singling me out in his will. The way the Montignacs have traditionally left their money . . . well it's outrageous when you think about it. Personally I feel quite proud of him that he took a more forward-thinking approach. I mean for heaven's sake, we've even got the vote now; inheriting the Montignac estate, in comparison, would seem rather minor.'

The bell over the door rang and two more customers came into the store and started examining a somewhat obscene sculpture that was too close to Montignac's desk for them to be able to continue the conversation comfortably where they sat. He nodded towards his cousin and they walked back upstairs towards the mezzanine floor which remained empty.

'What bothers me,' he said when they were alone again, 'is the way everyone keeps sympathizing with me on my loss. As if the only thing I was interested in was the money. Why should I care if your father chose to exclude me?'

'But you do care.'

'I haven't given it a second thought,' he said without conviction.

Stella stared at him. 'Why do you think he did it anyway?' She asked after a few moments. 'Could it have anything to do with Margaret?'

'What does it matter?'

'Well I just need to know whether you're going to continue ignoring me for the rest of my life because of something my father did, or whether I'm going to get my cousin back? Which is it to be?'

Montignac sighed. He could see the unhappiness in her eyes as she said this, the truth of how much she felt for him, and it made him sick now to remember how he had once felt the same thing for her. How easy it would be, he thought, simply to move towards her, lift her from the floor and send her over the balcony, crashing to the ground below. How many of his problems would be solved in a simple move. When they were children he used to play a game with her where they would stand facing each other silently for as long as possible and then he would stamp one foot forwards, lunging towards her without actually making contact, and she would always scream and fall backwards; they had played it over and over again for years and she'd never managed to prepare herself enough for the shock to remain still. The idea came into his head unbidden now and he realized that two of the customers downstairs had left and the others were out of sight. No one would ever know. No one would be able to prove anything and he was her only heir. He steadied his feet on the ground beneath him, keeping his mind blank to prevent himself from thinking about it and—

The ping of the bell over the door sounded again and he snapped out of it, looking down to see Jason Parsons returning with a couple of sandwiches for their lunch, waving one of the bags up towards him. Stella looked around too and turned back to him irritably.

'I thought we were having lunch together,' she said.

'I can't,' he told her, stepping back again, out of temptation's way. 'We have a delivery coming later this afternoon and we have to clear some space. I don't have time for anything but a sandwich at my desk I'm afraid.'

She sighed and turned away, moving towards the wall and looking at the paintings of the stripes and circles, the one whose overhead light Montignac had been repairing when she'd arrived.

'It's not too bad actually, is it?' she said.

'Yes, I quite like it too,' he replied. 'I don't know what I was thinking of taking it for here. It's far too good.'

'Who painted it?'

'A young artist from Hackney. Name of Hutton. He's done another few as well but they're pretty dreadful and have sold quite well for us. I can't get rid of this one at all.'

'I mean it's not wonderful,' she said, correcting herself. 'But it shows some promise.'

Montignac turned away. He wished she would just leave. Seeing her standing there in front of him brought up such a wealth of emotions that filled his head and made him want to scream in frustration. The memories of their childhood, the things he had done to please her, how remorselessly his cousin had betrayed him. No one could make him feel as twisted inside himself as she did. He was torn between wanting things to go back to the way they once were and wishing he had never known her at all. He had an urge now to hold her.

'You know you're going to have to try harder with Raymond,' she said, turning back to him. 'He's really a very decent fellow if you get to know him.'

'Decent,' he said with a sneer. 'Who wants decent? And Raymond is only interested in flowers, it seems to me. What kind of—'

'Oh for heaven's sake, Owen, you work in an art gallery. You're neither of you exactly mountaineers or Arctic explorers. You can't play the manly card when it comes to him so stop looking down your nose at him all the time.'

'I don't look down my nose at him, I just don't like him sticking his nose in places where it doesn't belong, that's all.'

'If it concerns me, it concerns him,' she said sharply. 'We are to be married and whatever happens from now on involves him.' She hesitated, unsure whether she should say the next line or not but felt an uncommon urge to hurt him. 'He loves me, after all,' she said.

The smile drifted away from Montignac's face. 'Now I

am starting to feel some sympathy for him,' he said bitterly.

'Owen—'

'Look, I really have to get on if you don't mind. I'm quite busy.'

'There's just one thing I wanted to ask you,' she said, not moving away. 'Something I was worried about. By your attitude last night, I mean.'

He raised an eyebrow and indicated that she could ask but he would not necessarily answer.

'You're not in any kind of trouble, are you?' she said.

'Trouble?'

'Yes. I mean you don't have any financial problems yourself? Anything I should know about?'

Montignac laughed and shook his head; he would never admit as much to her. 'Not at all,' he said. 'Nothing I can't handle anyway.'

'Because I could always help you out if you did,' she said. 'I mean obviously you know the terms of the will. I can't sell anything or touch the capital. But I have a healthy income. You only have to ask, you know.'

Montignac tried to control his temper. The temptation was so strong, to simply say yes, to throw himself on her mercy, to allow her to save him.

'I'm fine,' he said. 'I don't need your money.'

'That's what it's all about, isn't it?' she asked in frustration. 'The fact that it's *my* money. I don't know what Father was thinking of, changing things.'

'But aren't you glad he did?' he asked with a smile

and she didn't have an opportunity to answer because at that moment Jason Parsons came clambering up the stairs and informed his boss that the delivery men would be there within the hour and they had to make sure that one of the downstairs walls was cleared in time.

8

Like all right-thinking sons, Gareth Bentley thrived on spurning as many of the opportunities that his father had offered him in life as possible but he was sensible enough to hold on to those ones which might benefit him in some way. His rent-free home represented one such advantage. His free food and laundry service was another. And a third lay in the form of his membership to White's Club in St James's, an exclusive establishment for gentlemen and the sons of gentlemen, where the complimentary newspapers were all laid out on a side table every morning, the whisky was a touch on the expensive side but never less than a dozen years old and where they did a perfectly decent grilled salmon with baby potatoes, green beans and fresh herbs at lunchtime at a very reasonable price. Gareth had been coming here on and off since his twenty-first birthday three years earlier, when Roderick Bentley and another senior judge had sponsored him for membership and he found it a pleasant and relaxing way to while away a few idle hours while his bedlinen was being changed.

The gentlemen who attended White's were almost all professional men, barristers and solicitors, doctors and politicians, even the odd novelist and philosopher. They sat around in book-lined, oak-panelled drawing rooms in leather wing-backed chairs, smoking pipes and cigars, and discussing what was wrong with the world, the government, the French and the young, in that order. There were fifteen handsome bedrooms available on the third and fourth floor but they had to be booked well in advance as there was always great demand for them. It goes without saying that ladies were not to be entertained.

'Good afternoon, Mr Bentley,' said Kenneth Milton, the on-duty porter that afternoon as he arrived. 'Nice to see you again, sir.'

'Afternoon, Milton,' he replied, handing over his coat and hat. It had been almost a week since he'd last been there and he felt a sense of tranquillity as he looked into the parlours beyond, which were about one third full at this time of the day. He had spent many happy afternoons here since graduating from Cambridge with his lower second; it represented a pleasant respite from home and the answering of difficult questions regarding his future. 'I wonder,' he asked. 'Have you noticed Mr Keys arriving today? Alexander Keys?'

Milton looked down at his ledger and ran a finger along the list of names. 'Yes, you're in luck, sir,' he said. 'Mr Keys arrived about half an hour ago.'

'Oh, excellent,' said Gareth.

'He's probably in the lounge, sir, or perhaps upstairs in the large drawing room.'

Gareth nodded and made his way through the doors, scanning the faces and seeing one or two nodding acquaintances as he went along. He recognized a celebrated actor who had recently achieved an unexpected triumph in motion pictures in Hollywood and who was celebrating by divorcing his wife; he noticed a former prime minster, sitting alone in his dotage, having difficulty refuelling his pipe. Then, seated in the corner with a confused expression on his face, immersed in a thick novel, he spotted his friend Alexander Keys.

'Hello there,' he said as Alexander looked up at him.

'Oh hello, Gareth,' he replied. 'Didn't expect to see you here today. How's the head?'

'Not too bad, all things considered. I tried not to drink too much.'

'I noticed that,' said Alexander. 'I was very impressed by your willpower, despite old Jasper's best efforts. What brings you here anyway?'

'Escaping home,' he said, as the well-trained waiter brought him a pot of tea immediately. 'Hoped I might run into you actually. What's that you're reading?' he asked as he lowered himself into the chair opposite.

'It's a new novel I've got to plough my way through,' said Alexander. 'By a fellow from Sheffield, if you please. A coal miner's son. Still, takes all sorts, I suppose.'

'Oh yes? What's it about then?'

'Who knows,' replied Alexander with a shrug. 'Five hundred and fifty pages long, all written in one paragraph without punctuation or dialogue, just this sort of internal monologue going on in the mind of the narrator.'

'Sounds hideous,' said Gareth with a shiver.

'You have no idea,' said Alexander with a sigh. 'I've been stuck on page one hundred and forty-three for half an hour now and I can't for the life of me figure out what's going on. I read every sentence carefully, I try to place it in context with what's come before but I just can't comprehend a word of it. And I have to have five hundred words on it ready by tomorrow evening.'

'Painful work,' said Gareth. 'Will you pan it?'

'Oh good Lord no,' replied Alexander, shaking his head. 'They'll be teaching it in the universities in a few years' time I daresay. I better not say anything negative about it or they'll say there goes the fellow who criticized the genius du jour. It'll be a difficult one, though, especially since I don't understand a word of it. *This is a novel that defies simple explanation*, I shall say. *And to summarize such a fatuous concept as plot would be an insult to the art of the novelist*. Then I'll throw in a few things about metaphor and so on—'

'That internal monologue line was rather good,' suggested Gareth.

'Yes. I'll use that. I'll make it all sound terribly clever and everyone will be happy.'

'Except the poor slobs who spend their one and sixpence buying the masterpiece.'

'Well yes,' admitted Alexander. 'But that's no fault of mine, now is it? They should know better than to listen to me.'

Gareth nodded and smiled as he looked around the room. He could see a man he knew to be a retired Home Secretary snoozing in a corner with a cigar hanging out of his mouth and a thin line of drool tracing a path like a slowly creeping slug along his chin, and he looked away immediately in disgust. At another there were two men playing a game of cards which brought back bad memories of the previous night's misadventure. Alexander noticed where his gaze was and picked up on it.

'Bad luck on that thirty pounds of yours last night,' he said. 'Jasper's a swine for encouraging people to throw their money away. Never wastes any of his own, mind you.'

'Yes,' said Gareth. 'I could have done without it, that's for sure.'

'Well you live and learn. You'll know not to gamble with quite such high stakes next time. Never been much of a roulette man myself to be honest. It's all too based on chance. I prefer a good game of poker or whist. Something with a little skill attached to it.'

'I don't think I have the temperament to be a gambler,' said Gareth.

'Wouldn't look good for the newest member of the

Rice Chambers to be caught in such a place either, I imagine,' said Alexander with a laugh. 'Still, it was your birthday.'

'Well actually, Alexander, that's what I wanted to talk to you about,' said Gareth. 'You remember me telling you how unhappy I was about joining the family firm?'

'Yes.'

'Well after I left the Unicorn last night I was waiting for a taxicab and I ran into that other friend of yours, Montignac, and we got talking.'

'Ran into him?' asked Alexander. 'You fairly bounded out of the place after him, didn't you?'

'No,' said Gareth, frowning. 'It was time for me to leave anyway.'

There was only a slight hesitation on Alexander's part as he took this in; after a moment he nodded his head. 'Well he's a good fellow, Montignac,' he said.

'Certainly seems to be,' said Gareth. 'We shared a taxi back home. He's in Bedford Place and I'm in Tavistock Square so it was quite convenient.'

'Yes I know,' said Alexander. 'I've never been to his flat there but I've been to Leyville many times. That's his family seat, you know.'

'I heard. How well do you know him anyway?'

'Owen? Oh we go back a long way,' said Alexander, trying to recall. 'I think we met when we were . . . let me see . . . about seven years old. At Eton. We shared a room right through school. Became very close friends.'

'Oh, I didn't realize you knew him that well. I thought he was just an acquaintance.'

'Well the thing about Owen Montignac is that no one really knows him that well,' explained Alexander. 'He's always been something of a closed book. Used to get bullied mercilessly in the first few years of school. On account of his accent, I mean.'

'His accent?' asked Gareth. 'I didn't notice any accent.'

'That's because he learned to shake it off. He's French by birth, you see. Spent the first few years of his life there if I have it right. I think his uncle took him in when he was about five or six, after his parents died. But when he first came to school he still spoke with a sort of French twist and he got ribbed about it constantly by the other fellows. Name-calling and so on. There were one or two fights as I recall.' Alexander thought about it, trying not to recall certain incidents when he had perhaps let himself down in this respect. 'Of course, after a few years he grew tired of being bullied and started to fight back and then there was . . . well an incident of sorts, and it all stopped.'

'An incident?'

Alexander opened and closed his mouth nervously. He was not, by nature, a gossip and didn't like talking about people behind their backs. He particularly didn't like talking about Owen Montignac as he considered him his best friend and had always rather feared his volatility, that temper of his he had witnessed on only a few occasions.

'One of the boys went a little far with the name-calling,' said Alexander dismissively. 'And Owen rather saw red over the whole thing. It was all a long time ago of course. There was an altercation of sorts. Quite a bit of trouble. But old Peter Montignac made sure that he kept his place.'

Gareth frowned and considered this; it had echoes of his own misadventure at Harrow, an incident that had clouded his life for some years.

'Oh for heaven's sake don't look like that,' said Alexander, attempting a laugh. 'That was fifteen years ago. We were all just children. Owen's a magnificent character, you know. A good friend to have.'

'He gave me his card,' said Gareth, 'which said something about an art gallery on it. But my mother said the Montignacs are involved in land.'

'His uncle was. His grandfather too. And his father, I imagine, before he was sent away. But Owen doesn't have anything to do with that, I don't think. He probably would have expected to, of course, but like he told us last night, the old man left it all to Stella.'

'His cousin?'

'Yes. Also a fine girl. I should introduce you sometime.'

Gareth shrugged, as if that was neither her nor there. 'The thing is,' he explained. 'As we were driving home we talked a little about my . . . unwillingness to join my father in chambers and he suggested that he might have a position for me.'

'Really? At the gallery?'

'Well he didn't specify. He just said that I should come down and talk to him some day and he might have one or two ideas.'

Alexander hesitated for a moment but couldn't see any harm in it. 'Well I think that's splendid,' he said. 'I think you should take him up on his offer. Like I told you, he's a magnificent fellow. My very best friend.' He used the word 'best' rather than 'closest,' as it was difficult for him to imagine anyone being very close, emotionally speaking, to Owen Montignac.

'Right,' said Gareth, pleased with the result of this conversation. 'Well that's all right then. I just wanted to check him out really before throwing in my lot with him.'

'Well I wouldn't throw too much in with him if I was you,' said Alexander cautiously. 'I mean not under my recommendation at least. Just play it carefully.'

Gareth frowned. 'Carefully?' he asked. 'Why do you say that?'

'For the same reason that you should take any new opportunity carefully,' he replied, thinking that was quite a good reason for his hesitancy. 'Talk to him by all means. See what he has in mind. But think it through. You studied law for several years, you know, Gareth, it does seem rather foolish to—'

'Everyone says that,' insisted Gareth, his voice rising a little in frustration. 'But do you know, the thing I dread the most in the world, the thing that keeps me awake at night, is the idea that five years from now I'll be doing something I don't want to do, be with someone I don't want to be with, just because I'm too frightened to actually be the man I really am. If that happened, if I turned out like that . . .' He shook his head slowly at the idea. 'Well I'd rather die than have that happen to me.'

'Alexander bit his lip. 'I think you need to be careful then, Gareth,' he said. 'Don't expect too much from Owen.'

'I believe I'll talk to him,' he said quickly. 'He struck me as a very interesting character.'

'Oh he is that all right.'

'Thanks, Alexander,' he said, standing up. 'I'll let you get back to your book.'

'Do you have to?' he asked with a groan. 'I'm worried that the more I read the closer I'll come to having an aneurysm.'

Gareth smiled, patted him on the shoulder and walked back to retrieve his coat and hat. Alexander watched him for a few moments, wondering why Montignac would have offered a job to a complete stranger. It seemed quite out of character for him. And then, before returning to page one hundred and forty-three, he spent several minutes convincing himself that, unlike the novels he spent so much time reading and reviewing, everything would turn out fine in the end and that there was nothing for him to worry about at all.

9

'You make a start on it,' Montignac told Jason Parsons, who wanted help in clearing the paintings off one of the walls in order to prepare for the new delivery. 'That's what you're paid for, isn't it?'

'It's a two-man job,' he protested. 'Some of those pieces are too heavy to handle on my own.'

Montignac sighed and ran a hand across his eyes in frustration. 'Well just get going with the smaller ones for the moment then,' he said. 'And I'll be with you in a few minutes, all right?'

Jason stared at him irritably, wanting to protest but lacking the confidence to do so, and made his way back down the stairs, muttering as he went.

'I should probably go,' said Stella, who had been watching out the window at the street below while the two men talked, filled with the kind of tension she had hoped would never exist between her and her cousin again. 'I can see you're busy.'

'A little bit, but it's all right,' said Montignac. 'I am sorry about last night, you know,' he added in a neutral tone after a moment.

Stella stared at him, unsure whether he was being sincere or not. 'If you'd just give Raymond a chance,' she began hurriedly but he cut her off.

'If it makes you happy, then I'll try,' he said. 'Although I doubt that I'll be seeing all that much of him, will I?'

'Why not?'

'Well I'll have to spend most of my time in London, working. While you'll be down at Leyville. And I don't think that Raymond and I are going to be meeting up in town to go to the theatre together anytime soon.'

'Don't suddenly stop coming down, though,' said Stella. 'Leyville's your home too.'

'Is it?'

'You know it is. For pity's sake, Owen, haven't we always made you feel welcome there?'

Montignac stared at her, amazed that she could say something so insensitive. The thing that Stella seemed so keen to forget was that the house, by rights, should have come to his father and not hers, and thereafter to him. For after all, Henry had been the elder of the two boys.

Throughout their childhoods and adolescences, William Montignac had doted on both his sons but, like a monarch who has provided an heir and a spare, he concentrated most of his time and affection on Henry, who was the elder by two and a half years, and left Peter to the care of his mother.

Henry was taught to hunt and to manage the estates. He was encouraged to read all of William Montignac's favourite volumes from his library, to sit in on the meetings he had with his lawyers and estate manager while he was a teenager. The Montignac minions knew that they had to show deference to the heir presumptive, who showed an aptitude for his learning as well as a pleasant disposition and cheerful nature. William wanted him to be tough and harsh, but these were characteristics that were not part of the boy's character. He hoped that he would excel at sports but he turned out to be merely adequate and had no taste whatsoever for the hunt. As he reached his late teenage years William Montignac found himself increasingly disappointed that his son was not more like him. Even his looks disappointed him, for Henry didn't have the distinctive dark hair and eyes of the Montignacs, but rather the paler skin and blond hair of his maternal grandparents. Still, for all his disappointment, William believed in tradition and knew that his son was an honourable boy and would be a worthy heir when the time came.

However, events at Leyville were to overshadow that.

In the spring of 1906 a couple of young French housemaids were employed by Margaret Richmond's predecessor at Leyville and one of them – Nathalie Reims – caught the eye of Henry Montignac. Like him, she had thick blond hair and pale eyes but she was shy and found it difficult to make eye contact with any of her new English masters, particularly the handsome young man who seemed to be always watching her and would appear as if from nowhere whenever she went for walks around the estate.

Over the course of a year of illicit meetings and secret conversations the two fell in love and Henry informed his parents that they were to be married. For several months the house was thrown into chaos as the French maids were despatched back to their homes just south of Paris while Henry was placed under virtual house arrest. William Montignac refused to countenance the marriage and even locked his son into his room at one point for almost three weeks as he tried to make him see sense. When the dispute between them finally became violent, Henry was banished from Leyville and moved to France, where he married his paramour within a few days.

Naturally, he was quickly disinherited and Peter Montignac then found himself in the unexpected position of first son and heir. Had his grandfather not been so violently opposed to the marriage, however, not only would Owen Montignac's parents have lived, but they would have ended up as master and mistress of Leyville, and he would have been master in turn after his father's death.

The house and the fortune, therefore, rightly belonged to him.

'Haven't you always made me feel welcome there,' repeated Montignac in a quiet voice, as if he was trying out the words for himself just to hear how ridiculous and selfish they really were.

'Don't say we haven't,' said Stella defensively, who had no idea of what he was thinking. 'My father always made it clear to us that you had as much right to be there as any of us.'

'That was guilt, I imagine,' said Montignac.

Stella stared at him. 'Whatever happened between

your father and our grandfather is nothing to do with either of us,' she said, trying to keep calm. 'We shouldn't let it come between us after . . . after all that we've been through. And it's certainly not why Father didn't leave Leyville to you.'

'Isn't it?'

'Of course it isn't,' she said, raising her voice now. 'If he had any negative feelings towards you, then why would he have taken you in in the first place? Why would he have brought you up and given you a good education? He could have let you stay in France. He could have just let you fend for yourself.'

'I had family there too,' he pointed out. 'I'm sure I wouldn't have starved.'

'He offered you a better life.'

'I suppose so,' said Montignac, who suspected a lot more about his uncle's reasons for disinheriting him than she did.

'We were always told to treat you like a brother, and that's what we did,' she insisted, looking to be on the verge of tears now and with this line he could hold back no longer.

'Really, Stella?' he asked, dumbfounded by her ability to rewrite history. 'Just like a brother! Are you seriously saying that to me? After all this time? That you treated me just like a brother?'

Stella swallowed nervously and looked away. 'I'm not getting into all of that, Owen,' she said, brushing past him.

'No, I didn't think you'd want to.'

'You're obviously not in any mood to have a civilized conversation so perhaps I should just leave you alone for now.'

'Yes, I think you should,' he replied, watching as she picked up her coat and shopping bags.

'I just want to say this,' she said, turning back to him and he was surprised by how the appearance of tears in her eyes could still pull at his heartstrings. 'My home is your home. There is no distinction in my eyes. It should have been Andrew's, it might have been yours, it happens to be mine. And if you turn your back on your home, then it's like you're turning your back on me,' she added in a softer tone. 'And I don't want that. I don't want that at all.'

'I don't want it either,' he muttered, turning away so as not to have to look her in the eyes.

She reached across and touched his arm but she took him by surprise and he recoiled, as if he had just been struck by an electrical charge.

'After all we've been through, after all we've survived, Owen,' she said, laying a stress on the words, 'it would be ridiculous for us to fall out now.' She hesitated before adding, 'Just think how much worse things could have been. If it hadn't been for Margaret.'

Montignac breathed in heavily, wanting her to leave now; he didn't want any more part of this conversation.

'I have to get back to work,' he said. 'We'll speak soon, though.'

'Do you promise?'

'I promise.'

'And you'll make an effort with Raymond?'

'I'll make an effort with him,' said Montignac. 'For your sake, not for his.'

'That's all I ask. He's really a very nice chap when you get to know him.'

Montignac felt an irresistible urge to laugh but hid it carefully. There was nothing more to be said between them and Stella reached forwards and brushed her lips casually against his cheek, holding them there for a moment, breathing in the scent of him before turning around and leaving the shop without looking back.

'That your sister?' asked Jason Parsons, coming up beside him now and watching her disappear down the street.

'My cousin,' said Montignac, watching too.

Jason let out a low whistle of appreciation. 'She's a bit special, isn't she?' he said. 'No offence, like,' he added quickly, noticing the look of irritation on his employer's face.

'Don't we have a wall to clear?' asked Montignac, brushing past him before the urge to hit his assistant became too strong.

10

Montignac stayed in the gallery later than usual that night; the prospect of returning home to the empty flat in Bedford Place and trying to concoct a scheme to escape the clutches of Nicholas Delfy not being an attractive one. The work on the new additions had been completed successfully and he'd already managed to sell two pieces in the afternoon and interested a private collector over the phone in another, which meant that he wouldn't have to look at the hideous creation for any longer than necessary.

A few regular customers had been lingering later in the day and had tried to engage him in a conversation about an artist's exhibition that had just opened at a rival gallery along the street, but he was unusually taciturn.

'Have you seen it yet?' asked one lady, who had spent many thousands of pounds in the Threadbare Gallery and displayed no traces of discernment whatsoever.

'I dropped in yesterday morning,' said Montignac.

'I didn't care for it,' she said. 'I don't know what they're doing giving the artist so much space. I can't see any of it selling, can you? The things you bring in here are so much more interesting. So different. So challenging, don't you agree?'

'Absolutely,' Montignac said, although for him the only real challenge lay in resisting the urge to take a pair of scissors and destroy every one of them before they could decrease the aesthetic value of the world any further.

'Of course the exhibition I'm most excited by will be the Cézanne,' she continued.

'Yes, I've heard about that,' said Montignac; Arthur

Hamilton from the Clarion Gallery next door had already told him how a dozen or so paintings from the exhibition were coming to his gallery for some restoration work before joining the touring collection, and he hoped to get a private viewing.

After Jason Parsons left at six o'clock he locked the door from the inside and went back to his desk, pouring himself a glass of whisky from a bottle he kept locked away in the bottom drawer and began work on the ledger he kept, recording all transactions made during the month. His stomach started to rumble as he had barely eaten all day. Lunch had been disturbed by Stella's visit and by the time she left he had looked at the sandwich that his assistant had brought for him and found that his appetite was gone; he regretted having thrown it away now as the thought of drinking on an empty stomach only increased his depression.

This was mind-numbing work and it always took him an hour or two to balance all the receipts for sundry expenses against the bankings, but his employer, Mrs Conliffe, examined them herself on a monthly basis and made sure that every pound, shilling and halfpenny was accounted for. On this occasion, however, he quite enjoyed the monotony of the job as it kept his mind off the various problems which were threatening him at the time.

The debt to Nicholas Delfy of fifty thousand pounds, ten grand of which had to be paid off within the month.

The loss of Leyville, its associated capital, landownings, income and rent, all of which rightly belonged to him. Stella's relationship with that fool Raymond Davis and her absurd idea about marrying him. Issue of that marriage would leave him ever further away from his rightful inheritance and the life he wanted to live. But he shouldn't care about any of that, he thought bitterly in his mind, because he'd always be welcome in her home.

He considered making his way to a noisy bar in the West End, somewhere he could slip in unnoticed to a table in the corner and drown his sorrows over an evening's drinking, but the thought of spending yet more money and waking with a hangover was too much for him. He thought about gambling, numbing the pain of these hours with the brief hope of victory at the tables or around the baize but that too seemed like it might only make matters worse. His mind drifted to the idea of a woman but his body was left behind; it had been weeks, in fact, since he had enjoyed any physical comfort but the idea was of little interest to him now. He had to do something, he realized. Something that might fix all his problems at once.

There was a tap on the door and he snapped out of it but didn't look up, assuming it was some customer checking to see whether they were still open or not and who would go away when it was clear that no one was there. He had turned off most of the lights at the front of the gallery, but some of the lamps around his desk were still on and were probably sending a ghostly signal to the street outside.

The door rattled again and he raised his head irritably, standing up to get a better look at who was out there.

'We're closed,' he shouted out, seeing a man in a hat and overcoat standing on the darkened street outside. 'Come back tomorrow.'

'Mr Montignac?' called the voice from outside. 'Owen, is that you?'

His heart skipped a beat for a moment, wondering whether Delfy had sent someone to convince him of the urgency of his repayments but the outline of the figure – regular height, regular build, smartly dressed – not to mention the politeness of the question was enough to convince him that this wasn't the case. He looked around nervously all the same, wondering whether it would make sense to slip out the back door.

'Who is it?' he shouted, trying to think of a reason why anyone would be calling on him at this time of night.

The voice called out a name but it was drowned out by a passing car so he stood up from his desk and walked cautiously through the gallery towards the door. The street light outside was broken, which made it difficult for him to make out the visitor's face.

'It's Gareth Bentley, Owen,' he said as the gallery manager came into sight; he bobbed his head back and forth enthusiastically, removing his hat and grinning pleasantly. 'We met last night, do you remember?'

Montignac nodded his head, recalling the young man who had shared his taxi home the night before. The eagerness of the boy. His desperation to escape from an enslaved existence. The way his eyes had lit up in excitement at even the possibility of being offered a job. He'd spent so much of the day worrying about the fifty thousand pounds and the meeting with Stella that Gareth had slipped his mind entirely.

'Of course I remember you,' he said, unlocking the door and opening it, a spider welcoming a fly into his web. 'Come inside, why don't you?'

Chapter 4

1

THE APPOINTMENT WAS for eleven o'clock and Montignac arrived at the dilapidated office building ten minutes early but didn't go to the door just yet. Instead he hovered on the street outside, smoking a cigarette in the bright August sunlight until, wary of being spotted by someone looking down from the window above, he moved quickly down a side alley and out of sight. He felt uncomfortable here, a noisy part of London he normally never visited, where poorly dressed children rushed past him on the street and where the smell of cooking emanating from the closely packed houses was overwhelming.

The initial contact had come through a young man who had visited the Threadbare the previous afternoon with a collection of watercolours he was interested in selling; they were rather good, Montignac had thought, and he had therefore been forced to turn them down as they would only seem out of place among the other masterpieces on display in the gallery. To his surprise, the young man didn't seem particularly disappointed by his failure to sell the pictures and Montignac asked him a few questions about the technique he had employed in one of them which made it quite clear that he hadn't painted them at all and didn't even understand some of the terms that he was using.

'There's a lot of galleries on this street, isn't there?' asked the vendor, who identified himself as Tom Sweeney.

'Well yes,' said Montignac, resisting the urge to laugh. 'That's what Cork Street is all about. It's the commercial centre of London's art world.'

'The security must be top notch around here then,' said Sweeney.

'Well not really,' he replied. 'There's never really any trouble. We don't have many bobbies coming down to check on us anyway.'

'And that gallery next door,' said Sweeney. 'I read that they'll be housing some Cézanne paintings there soon?'

'For a brief period, yes. There's a rather good restoration team who work out of the Clarion and they're going to be working on the paintings before they join a national tour. Are you an admirer?'

'Sure,' he replied, with an indifferent shrug of his shoulders. 'Isn't everyone?'

Montignac narrowed his eyes, recognizing a fishing expedition when he saw one. 'Can I ask you a question,

Mr Sweeney?' he said and the young man nodded. 'Who actually painted those pictures you're carrying?'

Sweeney opened his mouth to protest but then seemed disinterested in pursuing the deception. 'I don't know,' he said. 'I was just asked to bring them here and see whether you would be interested in them, that's all.'

'Interested in the paintings?'

'Interested in assisting a collector.'

Montignac paused for a moment to consider this before leading him through the gallery to his desk and indicating that he should sit down. 'I'm always happy to help out a serious collector in any way that I can,' he said quietly.

'My employer is an extremely serious collector,' said Sweeney.

'And who is your employer?'

'If you don't mind, I'd rather keep that private for now,' he replied.

'Of course. But why don't you tell me what it is I can do for him? Are these his paintings?' he asked, nodding at the watercolours which Sweeney had placed on the floor now, leaning against Montignac's desk. 'Is he an artist as well as a collector?'

'I couldn't tell you. I've never seen him with a paintbrush in his hands and to be honest I doubt it,' he replied with a slight smile, as if the idea of his employer engaged in something like that struck him as faintly ludicrous.

'Perhaps he'd like to come down to the gallery

himself some day and look at our pieces,' suggested Montignac.

'Actually, he's already been here,' said Sweeney. 'He spent a few hours here during the week. I believe he made a thorough assessment of all the work on display.'

'I see,' said Montignac, racking his memory to recall whether or not there had been any suspicious or noticeable people present in the gallery recently but he could remember no one out of the ordinary.

'From what he told me he was quite surprised by what he discovered here.'

'In what way?'

'The fact that everything you seem to sell is, in his words you understand, utter rubbish.'

Montignac smiled and gave an unembarrassed shrug. 'We specialize in that, Mr Sweeney. But you'll also find that this is among the most expensive and profitable galleries on Cork Street. Is your employer interested in a private viewing perhaps, so that he can purchase a few pieces himself? Their values do stand an excellent chance of escalating over future years.'

'No, I don't think so,' said Sweeney, shaking his head. 'I don't think he'd sully his collection with the work from here. No offence, of course.'

'None taken.'

'No, I believe he's more interested in the gallery next door to yours. The Clarion.'

'It's an excellent gallery,' said Montignac, nodding his head appreciatively. 'But of course only half the

Clarion's floor space is taken up with pieces that are actually for sale. The rest is made up of visiting exhibitions and, of course, the restoration room.'

'We're aware of that.'

Montignac nodded, unsure where this conversation was going. 'I'm sorry,' he said eventually, when it was clear that Sweeney wasn't intending to enlighten him any further for the time being. 'I don't see where I fit into this. The Clarion is a different gallery entirely to the Threadbare. We're not connected in any way.'

'Are you sure about that, Mr Montignac?'

'Perfectly sure,' he replied. 'Separate owners, separate businesses.'

'They seem to have a more physical connection, don't they?' asked Sweeney. 'These aren't detached buildings after all.'

Montignac nodded. 'That's true,' he said. 'In fact the galleries to our left and right were part of one large building which was knocked into three smaller units decades ago.'

'My employer noticed the staircase on the upper floor of your gallery,' said Sweeney, nodding up to the mezzanine level above. 'There's a doorway up there, I believe.'

'To our storeroom, yes.'

'Wouldn't it be connected to the galleries on either side?'

'There are thin walls between them, yes. But no doorways. There's no way through to each gallery if that's what you're getting at.'

'The plans of the buildings show that there's a small attic running across the top.'

'Well yes,' admitted Montignac. 'There's a roof panel into the—' He hesitated and inclined his head a little, looking at the young man with renewed interest.

Sweeney reached into his pocket and wrote down an address on a piece of paper and held it up for Montignac to see. 'Can you remember this?' he asked.

'Yes, of course.'

'Do you know where it is?'

'I'm sorry, no.'

'But you could find it.'

'I expect so.'

'Excellent,' said Sweeney, crumpling the piece of paper up and putting it back in his own pocket. 'My employer keeps one of his private offices there. He'd be very interested in meeting with you. Perhaps tomorrow morning at eleven o'clock.'

Montignac considered it. 'We are quite busy here at the moment,' he said.

'I think it might be to your advantage,' said Sweeney. 'More profitable than, perhaps, an evening spent at the roulette tables in the Unicorn Ballrooms.'

Montignac narrowed his eyes and stared at him. 'What do you know of that?' he asked.

Sweeney stood up and collected his watercolours. 'Like I say, Mr Montignac, it might be considerably to your advantage to meet with my employer. Can he expect you at the appointed time?'

Montignac declined to answer but Sweeney appeared to take this as an assent for he smiled, gave a quick nod, and left the gallery with his paintings under his arm. Montignac sat there for quite some time considering the matter, wishing that he could remember a man who had been looking around the gallery earlier in the week and investigating the staircases and different floors but despite his misgivings he knew that he would keep the appointment. He had nothing to lose after all.

He knocked on the door at the appointed time and it was immediately opened by Sweeney, wearing, Montignac noticed, the exact same suit of clothes he had worn the previous day.

'Mr Montignac,' he said, opening it wide and ushering him inside, and not sounding in the least surprised that he had come. 'We're delighted you could make it.'

'Strange place for an office, isn't it?' he asked, for the street they were situated was in one of the less salubrious areas of London and certainly not one where one would expect to find a serious art connoisseur.

'My employer has several different offices,' he explained. 'Sometimes he needs to use one of the more discreet ones for meetings such as this. Follow me please.'

Montignac trailed after him along a musty, filthy corridor and shivered slightly in distaste. The naked light bulb hanging from the centre of the ceiling was host to an enormous, vacant cobweb while the paint was in an advanced state of peeling from the walls; rotten floorboards were visible through a ripped carpet.

They moved in silence, going up three flights of stairs before coming to a door, which Sweeney rapped upon.

'Come in,' said a voice from inside and Sweeney opened the door, standing back to usher Montignac inside and then closed it behind him again, standing guard outside as he left the gallery manager and the buyer alone together.

'Mr Montignac,' said the man, stepping around from behind the desk cheerfully. 'I'm delighted you could come. Please, take a seat.'

Montignac shook his hand cautiously and tried to recall whether he had seen him before in the gallery but his face was unfamiliar to him.

'I'm a little in the dark as to what I'm doing here, Mr . . . ?'

'The name's Keaton,' said the man. 'And it's not actually *Mr*,' he added with a shrug. 'But we'll let it go for now. I suppose you young people think that titles are something of an anachronism in this day and age.'

Montignac shrugged. 'I think it's generally only those who don't have a title who hold them in contempt,' he suggested.

'I think that's a very perceptive analysis,' said Keaton pleasantly, sitting down behind his desk. 'I'm sorry I can't offer you anything to drink,' he added. 'We don't keep any comforts here, I'm afraid. If we were in my normal office I could give you a rather nice Glenfiddich but I wanted to meet you in private. I've heard a lot about you, Mr Montignac.'

'More than I've heard about you then,' he replied, taking the time to study the man sitting opposite him. He was in his mid-fifties with thinning dark hair and a strong, aristocratic jawline. Immaculately dressed, Montignac could see a pair of cufflinks creeping out of the ends of his jacket sleeves encrusted with what he knew immediately to be diamonds. He imagined that the man looked as pristine at the end of every day as he did at the start.

'I try to be kept informed about interesting people,' said Keaton. 'And you seem to me to be just such a fellow. I'd be right in saying that you read history of art at university, wouldn't I?' asked Keaton.

'That's correct.'

'Cambridge, wasn't it?'

'Yes.'

'I was at Cambridge myself many years ago. Reading law.'

'Indeed.'

'And now you run a gallery.'

'For four years now, yes.'

'And how do you enjoy it?'

'It's fine,' he said, shrugging his shoulders in a non-committal way. 'The lady who owns it allows me a great deal of autonomy.'

'You've recently taken on a young man, haven't you? One Gareth Bentley.'

Montignac shifted in his chair and hesitated before answering. 'Yes,' he said.

'Any particular reason why?'

'I have an eye for talent,' he replied with a smile. 'I feel that Mr Bentley might be of some use to me.'

'You know who his father is, of course.'

'Yes.'

Keaton nodded and breathed heavily through his nose. 'He may well prove to be one of your more perceptive finds,' he added after a moment. 'And you enjoy your life at the gallery?'

'There are worse jobs to do.'

'I daresay there are. You're well paid for your services?'

'Not particularly,' he admitted, unsure whether he should be answering such personal questions but assuming that there must be a point to them and that whatever game was being played out, he would be sensible to simply participate in it.

'But then you were never really in it for the money, were you?' suggested Keaton.

'Everyone works for the money,' said Montignac, confused.

'Some people do,' he replied with a shrug. 'I'm not sure that men like you and I do. And then of course there are those who are expecting to come into a large inheritance and who work in order to occupy their time while they're waiting for their loved one to pass away.'

'That's true.'

'But should that inheritance be cruelly and unexpectedly snatched from their grasp, then the idea of getting up to work long hours for someone else and for a small amount of recompense every day for the rest of their lives might begin to appear less attractive.'

Montignac stiffened in the chair. He liked to be in control of situations and felt that he almost always was. However, it was obvious that Keaton knew a lot more about him than he was comfortable with.

'Who are you exactly, Mr Keaton?' he asked. 'How do you know so much about me?'

'I am merely a connoisseur of the arts,' he said with a smile. 'And I find myself in a position where from time to time I can provide services for other like-minded connoisseurs.'

'And what service are you currently providing?'

Keaton smiled and said nothing, but looked down at a series of pages on his desk. After a moment he looked back across the table at Montignac with a look of concern on his face. 'You're quite a gambler, aren't you, Mr Montignac?' he asked. 'Not very successful at it, of course.'

'I've had some luck,' he said, a little offended.

'I'm not sure that Nicholas Delfy would agree with you on that.'

'You know him?' asked Montignac, his jaw rigid.

'Not very well. I'm familiar with his work, of course. And I believe that he wants to see you in two weeks' time. A little matter of ten thousand pounds that you owe him. For starters.'

Montignac said nothing. He set his jaw and stared at Keaton, wishing he would get to the point.

'Which is a lot of money,' conceded Keaton. 'And if the things I've heard about Mr Delfy are true, then he won't take very kindly to being disappointed. He's not a very forgiving character, by all accounts. Very unsporting. On a separate note,' he said then with a flourish, 'I believe that some of the pieces from the Cézanne collection will be passing through Cork Street in advance of their national tour?'

Montignac thought about it. 'Yes,' he said. 'That's true but they won't be on display at my gallery if that's what you're hoping for. We don't do any restoration work there.'

'No. They're going to the one next door to yours, aren't they? The Clarion, I believe.'

'I believe so.'

'There are some lovely pieces in that collection, I imagine,' said Keaton, leaning forwards and smiling. 'What do you say you find a way to steal them for me?' he asked as if this was the most natural question in the world and a perfectly acceptable thing to throw into a conversation.

2

Margaret Richmond could hardly contain her excitement. Twice during the week Stella had phoned to make sure that she would be at Leyville over the weekend as she had something of particular importance to tell her.

Of course the phone calls had been pointless for there was no other place that Margaret could have imagined that she would be; she had no home of her own after all and no family to speak of other than the Montignacs. But she hated being left alone there for days at a time, with only her memories and loneliness for company, and was pleased that Stella's London trip was finally coming to an end.

Her excitement turned to apprehension, however, when she rose on Saturday morning to find a scattering of coats and bags in the hallway, some obviously belonging to Stella but the others, she presumed, the property of Raymond Davis. She hadn't expected them until lunchtime and so hadn't planned on making the beds in Stella's room, and another in a guest room, until later that morning but assumed Stella had managed this herself when she'd got home. The thought crossed her mind as to where exactly Raymond might have slept the night before but she dismissed it quickly. It was not something she wanted to dwell on.

She was in a state of some anxiety, therefore, as she waited for them to rise and didn't want to go back upstairs in case her worst fears regarding the sleeping arrangements were confirmed. She moved around the kitchen noisily, hoping that the clanging sounds of pots and pans would wake the dormant couple, and was just preparing a pot of tea when she was surprised to see them walking towards the back door from the garden.

'Stella,' she said as they came inside. 'I thought you were still asleep.'

'Asleep? Oh no. We barely got any sleep,' she said, coming forwards and throwing her arms around her former nanny. 'How are you, Margaret? Miss me, did you?'

'Well of course I missed you,' she said, returning the hug. 'You know I hate it when you're up in London. It's far too lonely down here for me and far too dangerous up there for you. Good morning, Mr Davis,' she added, a little nervously as she turned to Stella's companion, greeting him with uncomfortable formality.

'Good morning, Margaret,' he said cheerfully. 'And haven't I told you that you must call me Raymond?'

'Raymond then,' she said with a smile, although she still felt awkward with the familiarity. 'Well I hope you're both hungry because I've got breakfast on.'

'We're absolutely famished,' said Stella, stepping across to the oven to see the frying pans of bacon, eggs and sausages that were being prepared. 'Smashing,' she added. 'I'll set the table.'

They almost never used the formal dining room or even the smaller family room to eat in any more; instead most meals were taken around the small round table in the kitchen, by the latticed bay windows with the views over the garden. It was a most pleasant place to eat and now that the full-time servants had been let go one did not have to worry about the staff interrupting all the time.

'How were the girls during the week?' asked Stella. 'No problems with them, I hope?'

'Not really,' said Margaret as they sat down to breakfast. 'Obviously they're a little unhappy about only working part-time but I told them that they were more than capable of finding full-time jobs for themselves if they wanted them and all we needed was a cleaner a few times a week and a part-time cook. It's not like the old days, is it?' she added sadly.

'No,' said Stella, recalling when there had been five members of the family living here along with the staff. In her grandfather's day there had been more than twice that number, what with all the members of the extended family tree who had taken up residence there when they'd fallen on hard times. Now it was just her, the last Montignac, actually living at Leyville.

'And how was London?' asked Margaret. 'Did you go to the theatre much?'

'Once or twice,' said Raymond. 'But mostly we dined out and caught up with some of Stella's friends.'

'But you're home for a while now, aren't you?' she asked hopefully. 'You're not going straight back to the city?'

'Raymond has to be back for work on Monday morning,' said Stella. 'But I'm not going anywhere. I intend to spend the rest of the summer lazing around here and keeping as far away from London as possible. It's too hot there and I'm sure there's a stench starting to rise up from the Thames.'

Margaret smiled; she could hardly have been happier. 'Well that's wonderful news,' she said. 'And we'll have each other for company.'

'Yes,' said Stella, who – fond as she was of Margaret, despite everything – wouldn't have minded if there were a few more young people around the village. 'But we'll be kept busy, of course. Planning, I mean.'

'Planning?' asked Margaret, looking up. 'Planning what?'

Stella and Raymond exchanged an excited look and he reached across and took her hand in his, giving it a gentle squeeze. 'I'm happy to tell you, Margaret, that Stella has agreed to marry me.'

'Well I knew that,' said Margaret, feeling a little confused. 'Didn't you decide that at Christmas?'

'Yes, but now we've set the date,' said Stella. 'We're actually going to go through with it.'

'Well don't make it sound like such a trial, darling,' said Raymond with a laugh before turning back to Margaret. 'We're thinking of the first Saturday in October. How does that sound?'

Margaret opened her mouth but found herself lost for words. She jumped up from her seat and went around to Stella, who burst out laughing as the ritual of kisses and embraces began.

'That's the most wonderful news I've heard in a long time,' said Margaret, who even went so far as to kiss Raymond before returning to her seat. 'Oh, and there was me thinking that you were the types to have one of those long-drawn-out engagements. The kind that last for years and years and the bloom has gone off the rose before you've even made it down the aisle.'

'Well we were thinking of that originally,' admitted Stella.

'But I persuaded her otherwise,' said Raymond quickly. 'We decided there was no point wasting any more time. Besides, I can't take the risk that Stella might come to her senses. So October it is, which only gives you two months to put the whole show together.'

'And that's how you and I will be spending our time from now on, Margaret,' said Stella. 'If you think you can handle it, that is.'

'Handle it? I'll be delighted!' she said. Her head was already filled with the promise of what was to come. A family living at Leyville again. Soon enough there would be children, plenty of children she hoped, and she would still be young enough to take care of them. They'd have to bring the servants back then and life would be as it once was; her own future would be secure.

'You don't think it's too soon, do you?' asked Stella after a moment, her smile fading from her face a little.

'Too soon?' said Margaret. 'No, I don't think so. You two have known each other for a couple of years now after all.'

'No. I mean too soon after Father's death,' said Stella, correcting herself. I mean it's only been a few months since . . . since he passed away. You don't think people will think it's a little insensitive to have a wedding in the same year?'

Margaret thought about it; there was no doubt there were some who would think that – had she been observing the family from a distance she would have muttered about it herself – but she couldn't afford for Stella to be discouraged from going through with this in case, as Raymond had suggested, she changed her mind.

'No,' she said. 'Not at all. By October it will have been four months since . . . since that happened.' She found herself unable to get the words out. 'It's a perfectly decent amount of time to wait.'

'Well I thought that,' said Stella. 'And after all, Father would want me to be happy, wouldn't he?'

'Of course he would,' said Margaret, reaching across and squeezing her hand in happiness. 'And if he was here he'd tell you that himself.'

'Then it's settled,' said Raymond. 'The first Saturday in October. We'll do it here at Leyville and invite the whole world.'

'Oh not the whole world, Raymond,' protested Stella, laughing. 'Let's keep it relatively small. Sixty or seventy guests at most. Family and friends.'

'Whatever you want,' said Raymond, eager to please, delighted and amazed that she had actually accepted his proposal to set the date.

'Did you tell Owen?' asked Margaret cautiously after a few more minutes had passed. 'When you were in London, I mean. Have you already let him know?'

'Not yet,' said Stella. 'We went for dinner one evening a few weeks ago and then I met him at the gallery the next day but he's been almost impossible to track down ever since. I don't know what he's up to. And Raymond and I only agreed on the date earlier in the week and I wanted to come here for the weekend to see you. I'll write to Owen on Monday.'

'You'll *write* to him?' asked Margaret.

'Yes. That's all right, isn't it?'

The two women locked eyes for a moment and it seemed to both that they were having a silent dialogue in those few seconds. Eventually, Margaret broke away and looked across at Raymond.

'You do whatever you think is best,' said Margaret. 'I'm sure Owen will be as delighted for you both as I am.'

'I doubt that very much,' said Raymond.

'Oh, Raymond, don't say that,' said Stella. 'Please. You have to make an effort with him.'

'I don't think Owen likes me very much,' explained Raymond to Margaret. 'Perhaps he thinks I'm not good enough for his sister.'

'I'm not his sister,' insisted Stella.

'No, but you know what I mean. You're as good as.'

'But I'm not,' she repeated.

'Don't worry about Owen,' said Margaret. 'He'll come around in time.'

'I hope so,' said Raymond. 'I don't have any brothers of my own. I quite like the idea of an in-law. I don't know what it is he has against me anyway, to be honest. Perhaps he finds me a bit rough and ready.'

He reached up to his face and could feel the stubble on his chin from a day and a half without a shave. Margaret bit her lip to resist laughing; Raymond Davis was one of the least rough and ready men she had ever met in her life.

'I think I'll bring the bags up, Stella,' he said. 'And have a wash and a shave. How about a walk into the village in an hour or so?'

'Perfect,' she said, accepting the kiss he planted on her cheek as he left the kitchen. Margaret watched him leave and waited until the door had closed before turning back to Stella with a smile.

'I am doing the right thing, aren't I, Margaret?' asked Stella quietly.

'Does he make you happy?'

She considered it. 'Yes,' she said. 'Yes he does. He's very kind, he makes me laugh and I know he'll never hurt me.'

'You love him then?'

Stella hesitated. 'Margaret . . .' she said with a sigh as if that was an unfair and, in the circumstances, almost cruel question.

'You can't write to Owen,' she repeated suddenly. 'That's just being spiteful.'

'Do you think he'd give me away?' Stella asked, ignoring what Margaret had just said. 'Since Father isn't here any more? Do you think he'd walk me down the aisle?'

Margaret stood up and cleared away the breakfast things, shaking her head.

'You take your mind off what he'll do and think about what you're going to do,' said Margaret. 'We have a wedding to plan, don't we? And you're the head of the Montignac family now, no one else. So let's concentrate on that.'

Stella watched her as she placed the dishes in the sink and knew that she was right. She would tell Owen herself and if he didn't like it, if he wanted to create a fuss about it or insult Raymond some more, then he was perfectly entitled not to attend the wedding at all.

Still, it wasn't a conversation she was looking forward to.

3

Gareth arrived at the back door of the Threadbare Gallery just after midnight, dressed entirely in black as he'd been instructed earlier. It had been two months since he first met Owen Montignac on the night of his twenty-fourth birthday party and the time between then and now had consisted of a cat-and-mouse game on their parts as Montignac attempted to judge the motives and courage of his new employee and Gareth set out to prove that he would do anything to keep himself away from a life sentence at the Rice Chambers.

Right from the start Montignac had made it clear to

him that there were more opportunities out there to make money than the strictly legal ones but had hesitated to imply that he himself was someone who would take advantage of them. After all, his new charge had studied the law himself and came from a family well known for upholding it; there were only so many chances one could take with a fellow like Gareth Bentley. Should he tell his father too much about Montignac's schemes, for example, there might be trouble ahead.

'The thing you have to understand about me,' Gareth told him, a few weeks into their relationship while they ate lunch together, 'is that I'm extremely lazy. I'd like to dress it up in better clothes than that but there we are. That's me. A lazy good-for-nothing.'

'You make it sound like a virtue,' said Montignac, smiling.

'Well it is in a way,' said Gareth, thinking about it. 'At least I'm honest about it. I don't pretend to be something I'm not. I'm not the sort who wants to go in and out of an office every day for the rest of his life. There are other things I want to do. Holidays, travel, cars,' he said extravagantly, waving his hands in the air.

'All things which require money,' Montignac suggested.

'Exactly. And unfortunately I don't have very much of that.'

'Every person who is honest with himself recognizes that the only worthwhile pursuit in life is the pursuit of money,' said Montignac with a shrug, looking around the restaurant as if the world agreed with him. 'All the other things that one wants out of life – happiness, friends, love, sex – they can all come out if one can afford to pay for them. In fact the most ridiculous cliché of all is that money cannot buy you happiness.'

'Do you really think so?' asked Gareth. 'Isn't that a little cynical?'

'Not at all. Show me a wealthy, unhappy man and I'll show you a man who just isn't trying hard enough.'

Gareth smiled. 'Perhaps you're right,' he said, nodding his head.

'I am right,' said Montignac with confidence. 'The only question is how far one is willing to go to achieve that happiness. So tell me,' he asked, leaning forwards, 'just how far are you prepared to go, Gareth?'

'However far I have to,' he said, betraying only a slight note of nervousness. 'Within reason, of course.'

Conversations like this one had gone on for a few weeks now until the barriers had come down and it had become clear to Montignac that Gareth, a pleasant enough boy if a little dim, would do anything to avoid the life of enslavement which was otherwise being set up for him and had no great moral compass guiding him in the pursuit of his goal. It was clear to him that he saw life as one great adventure, something to be laughed at and enjoyed; he would never do anything truly bad, of course, nothing that could actively hurt someone else but he was open to suggestion for harmless schemes.

And of course he didn't drink. Montignac noticed that from the first evening he came to visit him at the Threadbare. He had taken him out to the pub down the road but the younger man had stuck to water.

'It's bad for me,' he explained, unwilling to offer any further information on his affliction for the moment. 'It's always best that I keep a clear mind.'

Montignac pressed him on his reasons for his sobriety but Gareth just shook his head and said he didn't want to talk about them. 'Another time,' he said, laughing it off as if it really wasn't that important. 'After all, you never tell me anything about yourself, do you?'

'No,' he admitted. 'No, I never do.'

The fact that he didn't was not enough to stop Gareth from wondering. Montignac had an air about him, a confidence, something that might be termed an arrogant swagger, that made him admire him more and more each day. He tried hard to put his finger on exactly what it was but it was difficult to define. It was in the way he dressed, the way he casually despised the art in his gallery but was in awe of the works, situated elsewhere, that he considered masterpieces. It was in how he smoked a cigarette at his desk while reading the morning paper and seemed to barely notice it as it drifted to and from his lips. It was the ease with which he could sweet-talk some rich old lady into thinking that the painting she was staring at in bewilderment would make her wealthier, younger, sexier, if she just wrote him a cheque there and then and took it off his hands; as if its very presence in her home would take years off her and have young men clamouring for her attentions. It was in the way he kept himself to himself and seemed to have few friends worth speaking of and yet had somehow invited him into this august body. For years Gareth had wondered on and off what he wanted to be and was never able to define it; now all he had to do was look across the room and there, strolling around, caught up in his own schemes, stood the answer.

Montignac opened the back door and looked out on to the laneway just as Gareth arrived.

'You're late,' he hissed. 'I told you to be here at twelve.'

'Sorry,' said Gareth. 'I got held up. Anyway it's only a few minutes past.'

'If we're going to do this, we have to be punctual,' said Montignac, ushering him inside. He looked at the boy and was pleased to note that he had dressed as required. 'No one saw you leaving?'

'I went up to my room before everyone else and even wished them goodnight,' he said. 'My parents must think I'm falling ill or something,' he added with a smile. 'As far as they're concerned I'm tucked up in bed right now.'

'Good. And no one saw you come down the laneway?'

'No one. It was deserted, just like you said it would be.'

Montignac, a stickler for preparation, had spent every night for the past two weeks at the Threadbare Gallery late at night, patrolling the streets and laneways outside. From around nine o'clock they were almost entirely empty and when the nearby pubs let out just after ten-thirty there were always a few people milling around, but by midnight the place was deserted again and one could slip in and out the back door without being noticed.

They stepped inside the gallery now but kept the lights switched off. The recently repaired streetlight outside offered a little brightness but other than that they simply used a torch to make their way up to the mezzanine level and from there they continued up the steps that led to the doorway.

Montignac unlocked the door to the storeroom and immediately a rush of stale air spread out towards them. They moved back instinctively and covered their mouths.

'Good God,' said Gareth. 'It smells dreadful in here. Don't you ever clean it out?'

'We never have any cause to use it,' he explained. 'I haven't opened that door in over a year.'

Gareth handed the torch over and the two men stepped through the doorway into the darkness beyond. The bulb was dim and Montignac kept a hand stretched out before him as he walked in order to avoid crashing into anything. The ceiling seemed to sink lower and within about fifteen feet he was crouched down as he tried to make his way through. For a moment he thought the whole area was going to be sealed off but, almost at the last possible moment, the ceiling rose again and they were faced with a solid wooden wall before them.

'That's the partition,' said Montignac, turning a torch on it and frowning. 'It would be a lot easier if they'd left a door in it.'

Gareth leaned past him and knocked sharply on it.

'What do you think you're doing?' hissed Montignac quickly.

'There's no one around to hear.'

'There's also no way through a solid wall with an oak bookcase on the other side of it so let's not waste time, all right?'

He shone the torch across the ceiling and located the panel into the attic. 'Pass me that chair,' he said, turning around and indicating a chair with a broken back that was standing against the wall, alongside a heap of empty boxes, broken picture frames and age-old furniture. Gareth passed the chair across and held it carefully as Montignac stood on top, pushing the panel upwards. It shifted noisily and he ducked out of the way while a drizzle of dust particles fell down from above.

'Bloody hell,' said Gareth. 'It's filthy up here. What's it going to be like inside? And will the floorboards hold you?'

'Only one way to find out,' said Montignac, pulling himself up with great effort into the gap and pushing through until he lay in the darkened space above their heads. He rested there for a moment, waiting to see whether anything untoward would happen, but already he could feel that the boards were quite solid. 'It's all right,' he said, poking his head through the hole again and looking down. 'But I'll go across first and then you follow. There's no point risking the weight of both of us.'

Gareth nodded and Montignac crawled along the dark attic space like a caterpillar, dragging his lower body forwards first, then his upper. He reached upwards but it was no more than three or four feet high, certainly not enough for a grown man to stand erect in. There were quite a few pieces of broken wood and old paint pots in his way, discarded there perhaps fifty years before, but he kept advancing forwards until he knew that he must be over the Clarion and felt for a similar panel. Very soon, a raised square of wood was before him and he took hold of it and pulled it up, smiling as he looked down into the restoration room of the gallery next door. He adjusted his body around and carefully lowered himself down.

'I'm through,' he called back, something of a half-shout and a half-whisper. He stood there quietly as he heard Gareth's grunts as he lifted himself through the panel from the Threadbare Gallery and shuffled along the overhead corridor. A few minutes later he had jumped down too and the two men stood together and looked around.

They stood there without saying a word for a few moments, their hearts beating sharply inside their chests, and Montignac turned the torch around on the walls. In front of the wall he noticed an extraordinary bookcase, filled to capacity with hardback books, and realized that it would have been impossible to move, even if there had been a door behind it. Locating a light switch he went over and flicked it on, pleased to note that there were no windows up here to let the light out, and turned to his accomplice and smiled.

'We're in,' he said.

They looked around at the restoration room in admiration. In the Threadbare there were a couple of small storage rooms off the top floor that were in a permanent state of disarray and had become little more than glorified dumping spots. The management of the Clarion, on the other hand, obviously had a very different approach to their work. The room was spotless. One wall was lined with implements for constructing frames – brackets, nails, tiny hammers, razors, mat-cutters, frame clamps – another was filled with paints and restorative cleansers. Against the wall there was a pile of unframed canvases which had been stapled to their backgrounds but the prize, the main prize, stood on a dozen easels around them.

'The Cézannes,' said Montignac appreciatively.

The twelve paintings by Cézanne had been removed from their old frames and the canvases stood starkly on their easels. Montignac took a few moments to examine them appreciatively. He had studied them, of course, at Cambridge and had even seen some of the master's work once at the Hermitage Museum in Leningrad on a class expedition to Russia, and also at the Louvre on several occasions, but this was the most intimate viewing he had ever enjoyed. Even the sight of them made him want to return to the Threadbare and set fire to those artistic impostors he displayed there before they could pollute the aesthetic world any further.

'Magnificent, aren't they? he mused. 'Look at the restraint he shows in his portraiture, the broad use of the palette knife. Of course, they say that Cézanne—'

'Oughtn't we to get started?' said Gareth, who was feeling distinctly nervous about being here and wasn't keen on an art history lesson; he glanced at his watch with concern. 'We don't want to be stuck here all night.'

'Philistine,' said Montignac irritably. 'Aren't you even a little moved by them?'

Gareth stepped forwards and peered at the paintings, hoping that an intelligent response might occur to him that would impress his employer. But where Montignac saw colour and weight, all he could see was paint on canvas.

'Very nice, I suppose,' he muttered and Montignac shook his head.

'This is wasted on you,' he said. 'You have no idea how lucky you are to be seeing these so close-up. But I can see you're entirely disinterested. All right,' he said, giving in to commerce over art. 'Do you have the measuring tape?'

Gareth nodded and took the tape from his pocket as Montignac removed a pad and pencil from his own.

'All right,' said Gareth, measuring the first picture beside him. 'Picture of a boy looking at a skull.'

'That's *Jeune Homme à la Tête de Mort*,' said Montignac irritably.

'Fifty-one and a quarter inches vertical by . . .' He turned the tape lengthwise. 'By thirty-eight and a quarter inches horizontal.'

Montignac made a note of it as Gareth moved on to the next one.

'A bunch of naked women,' said Gareth distastefully and Montignac peered closer at it.

'I think that's *Les Grandes Baigneuses*,' said Montignac. 'Isn't it?' he asked, rhetorically.

'I don't know!'

'It can be difficult to separate the bathers' pictures.'

'Really.'

'I think it's *Les Grandes Baigneuses*, though. We'll say it is.'

'Well whatever it is it's ninety-eight inches horizontal by eighty-two inches vertical.'

This carried on until all twelve paintings were measured and double-checked and Montignac put the pad back in his pocket and nodded, satisfied. 'Arthur Hamilton keeps the place so clean,' he said, impressed with the immaculate condition of the floor beneath them. 'Perhaps I should start using our storerooms to better effect.'

'Can you worry about that another time?' asked Gareth, who was starting to grow anxious now that the initial adrenalin rush was wearing off.

'Of course,' said Montignac, helping him up into the gap above the ceiling again. 'You'll have to reach down to pull me up,' he said. 'And let's hope the ceiling holds us both.'

It did, creaking only slightly beneath their combined weights, and they replaced the panel and made their way back through the dark and dusty corridor and out to the Threadbare Gallery, where Montignac closed off the ceiling once again. Observing it from a distance and then close-up it looked as if it had never been touched at all.

'Perfect,' he said, turning to smile at his accomplice. 'That's the first part over with anyway. But we only have three days now so we have to get it right.' He looked at his watch. 'All right,' he said. 'We better go home. We'll start work tomorrow morning on the frames. I'll copy the list of the measurements for you overnight.' He hesitated before going on. 'You're sure you're prepared for this, Gareth, aren't you?' he asked. 'Because once we begin there's no going back.'

'I'm sure,' said Gareth, who thought the whole thing was a terrific hoot. 'You can count on me, Owen.'

Montignac smiled. Poor boy, he thought. Like a lamb to the slaughter.

4

Jane Bentley made her way up the stairs of the Rice Chambers, uncomfortable in a pair of new shoes which were cutting into her heels. They were a recent purchase, styled on a pair that Elizabeth, the Duchess of York, had worn to the Cheltenham Gold Cup earlier in the year; she had ordered them from Harrods in her size and they were now receiving their first outing. (Everybody hated the Duchess, of course. She was the worst kind of snob and had no way with people, but the shoes, well they were something else.) She'd made the mistake, however, of walking directly from Oxford Street to chambers when she should have taken a taxicab, and the ancient stone stairs did not help matters, every tread feeling like a knife grating against the back of her heel.

She was greeted when she walked into the reception area by Alistair, the senior clerk, who stood up respectfully when she entered.

'Good afternoon, Lady Bentley,' he said, resisting the urge to offer a bow.

'Good afternoon, Alistair. How are you today?'

'Very well, ma'am. Very well indeed.'

Alistair Shepherd was one of the chambers' longest-serving employees, having clerked for three consecutive heads since 1901. Approaching seventy years of age and less limber with his memory than previously, he had accepted the mandatory retirement which the partners had thrust upon him earlier in the month and was in his final week of service, living in dread of Friday afternoon and the enforced solitude that Saturday morning would bring.

'Looking forward to your freedom then, Alistair?' Jane asked cheerfully.

'Very much so,' he said, for he had been trained never to disagree with his betters.

'I wish I was in your shoes,' she replied, wishing in fact that she was in anyone else's shoes at the moment other than her own, which she didn't think could support her for another minute.

'Do you indeed,' muttered Alistair, who assumed that Lady Bentley's life was one long holiday, broken up only by spontaneous shopping trips and weekends in the country.

'Of course I do. I never seem to get a moment to myself. You're a very lucky man.' She glanced up at the clock on the office wall and frowned. 'Oh my. Is it a quarter past already? He's waiting for me, I expect, is he?'

'Sir Roderick never mentioned it one way or the other,' said Alistair. 'But he's alone in there if you want to go in.'

Jane nodded and passed him by, walking down the narrow corridor towards her husband's spacious office, grateful for the thick, luxurious carpet beneath her feet. (The more senior the counsel, the more luxurious was the carpet on the way to his rooms.) Turning around for a moment and seeing that no one was watching her, she reached down and slipped her shoes off in relief before continuing along, giving a polite knock on the door and stepping inside without waiting for an answer.

'Jane,' said Roderick, looking up from a file he was studying and breaking into a smile when he saw her. 'There you are at last.'

'I'm sorry for keeping you waiting,' she said, collapsing on his sofa with a look of exhaustion on her face as she massaged her injured feet. 'Don't be angry with me,' she added in the flirtatious tones of a debutante, a position she had relinquished many years before.

'Of course I'm not angry with you,' said Roderick. 'Actually I lost track of time myself. But what's happened? You look like you're in agony.'

'It's these new shoes,' she explained. 'They're a terrible fit. And I'm very angry about it. I shall get Sophie to take them back first thing in the morning. I thought I wasn't even going to be able to make it here without a pair of crutches.'

She looked down at her injured foot, where there was a deep-red bruising starting to lift from the heel, and hissed in distaste.

'Well I'm afraid there are no spare ladies' shoes at chambers,' said Roderick with a smile. 'So you're stuck with them until you get home.'

Jane smiled briefly and accepted the small sherry that her husband had poured for her from the cabinet. 'Thank you, darling,' she said, sipping it as if it was her first drop of water after a month-long trek in the desert. 'You're a gem. So tell me all.'

'Tell you all? All about what?'

'Oh don't tease me. You know perfectly well about what.'

Roderick sighed. 'Jane, you know I'm not supposed to discuss it.'

'Oh, come on,' she said, leaning forwards. 'I'm your wife. If you can't discuss it with me then who can you discuss it with?'

'Well no one apparently,' he said. 'I think that's rather the point.'

'That's ridiculous. They know perfectly well that you need someone to rely on at moments like this. They must know how discreet you are. Particularly after all that business this year with the Domson case. Look how well you carried yourself throughout that. Never spoke to the media. Never gave a hint about what you were thinking. And I never let anything slip about it either, did I?'

'You never let anything slip because I never told you anything,' he said, smiling at her, reaching across and squeezing her knee affectionately.

'I know and I still haven't quite forgiven you for that. But I understood it, Roderick. It was a murder trial. A man's life was at stake. It was terribly serious. This isn't the same at all.'

'Heavens above, woman, this is just as serious. Perhaps more so.'

'Yes, but no one's going to die because of it, are they?'

'Well, no,' admitted Roderick. 'But it's not just a salacious piece of tittle-tattle either.'

'Roderick Bentley,' said Jane, becoming stern now. 'If you don't tell me this instant what happened at that meeting I shall go next door to Quentin Lawrence and ask him to represent me in my divorce case.'

'Jane,' he said pleadingly.

'Oh go on. I promise I won't tell anyone. A problem shared . . .'

He sat back and she could see that he was relenting. 'If I talk to you about this,' he said sternly, pointing a finger at her as if he was chastising an unruly child. 'You must promise me that it will go absolutely no further.'

'It won't.'

'It's strictly between us as husband and wife.'

'Of course.'

'You can't speak of it to any of your friends.'

'I wouldn't.'

'And not to Gareth either.'

'No.'

'Especially not Gareth, in fact.'

'Roderick, you have my word,' said Jane in exasperation. 'My word as your wife. Now will you please just tell me—'

'All right, all right,' he said, going over to the cabinet and pouring himself a drink now while offering her a refill. 'Well I went to see him this—'

'Wait!' said Jane, interjecting already. 'Start at the beginning.'

Roderick stared at her in amazement. 'I am starting at the beginning,' he protested.

'Who was there first of all?'

'Are you going to let me tell this my way or not?'

Jane sat back and put a finger on her lips to indicate that she would stay silent.

'All right,' he continued. 'I went to see him this

morning as arranged. There was just Hailsham, the Lord Chancellor and Alan Altringham. Do you know him?'

'I know his wife,' said Jane. 'Awful old trout. Organized the Old Bailey Christmas Party last year. Total drip.'

'Well he was there too and Lord Keaton and also Walter Monckton.'

'Monckton was there?' she asked in surprise. 'So just Hailsham and four senior KCs then?'

'That's right. And of course Monckton is extremely close friends with the king. So in a way he was there to represent his interests.'

Jane nodded. 'Did he say whether the rumours were true or not?'

'The Lord Chancellor led the discussion of course. He said that acting under advice from Mr Baldwin he had been instructed to take opinions on the constitutionality of an event that may or may not take place at an indefinite time in the near or potentially distant future regarding a person who may or may not have a position of authority and prestige within the empire.'

'Good Lord,' said Jane in surprise. 'He put it like that?'

'That was the opening gambit, yes.'

'It's almost as difficult to understand as some of the opinions he writes.'

'That's what I thought,' said Roderick with a small laugh. 'But then Altringham leaned forwards and said, "Hang it all, Hailsham, just get on with it for the love of God." '

'Good for him,' said Jane, nodding her head appreciatively.

'Well, Hailsham didn't much appreciate that to be honest. He said there had to be a certain amount of formality to the meeting but everyone said that we would keep it to ourselves and wouldn't we all be better off if we just called a spade a spade.'

'Quite right,' said Jane.

'So then we just got down to it. Altringham asked what exactly was going on, that he'd heard the most extraordinary rumour that Stanley Baldwin had been at a dinner with the king and he was presented to Mrs Simpson and not only that but the woman's husband, Ernest Simpson, was there too.'

'No!' said Jane, shocked.

'Well that's what old Altringham heard and I must admit I'd heard the same thing.'

'And you never told me?'

'It never came up in conversation and I don't like to trade in gossip,' insisted Roderick. 'Anyway, about the dinner, Monckton piped up and said yes, apparently, that this was indeed true but that another way to look at it was that the prime minister had attended a dinner hosted by the king, which is quite right and proper. Also in attendance that evening were an American couple, Mr and Mrs Ernest Simpson. Which does rather put a different spin on things. It's all in the phrasing, you see.'

'Oh really, Roderick. It makes the whole thing sound like a game of musical chairs.'

'Naturally Hailsham piped up at this point and said that it should be pointed out that the PM didn't know who Mrs Simpson was and that therefore there had been no relaxation of attitude towards her.'

'Oh rot,' said Jane. 'Of course he knew who she was. How could he not? Everyone in society knows who she is by now. I heard that Baldwin said it's not even as if she's a decent, respectable whore. One wouldn't mind so much then.'

'Yes, well he may have known in a personal sense, but in an official capacity he didn't know her.'

'Is there a difference?'

Roderick shrugged his shoulders. 'Well, Hailsham says there is anyway.'

'That's just semantics,' she said. 'So what's she like anyway? Did he say?'

'No. Altringham pushed Monckton on it but he wasn't giving anything away.'

'I thought that she had got rid of that husband of hers two years ago when the king asked her on that cruise around Spain and Portugal?'

'He wasn't there then, that's true,' said Roderick. 'But apparently he was still in the picture. He has his own woman, you see, on the side. It's all perfectly amicable they say. They're just waiting for the nod so that they can divorce.'

Jane shook her head. 'Well that's extraordinary,' she said.

'Americans, I suppose.'

'Still. You have to admire the way they go about it. They know when to call a spade a spade while we just dance around the issue.'

'I suppose,' said Roderick. 'But it goes without saying that it'll never come to pass.'

'She won't divorce him?'

'She may do that, that's neither here nor there, but there's no possibility of a marriage. It's inconceivable. A two-time divorcée for queen? It's simply out of the question.'

'Well yes,' said Jane. 'Yes I can see that. But it's going to be awfully hard for him to give her up when it comes to it. They do say he's terribly fond of her.'

'He can be as fond of her as he likes but I can't see it going any further,' said Roderick, giving a brief thought to the question of whether he would sacrifice his own career for Jane and knowing that, in a heartbeat, he would. For Gareth or Jane. But the king was different surely. He was made of sterner stuff than a humble king's counsel.

'She needs to go back home,' said Jane determinedly.

'Yes, but then the strangest thing happened,' said Roderick. 'Keaton, who'd been silent throughout all of this—

'Now hang on,' interrupted Jane. 'Lord Keaton. I don't know him, do I?'

'I don't know if you've met him or not. He's been around for years but has never really made it into the inner circle. Terribly bitter man, I've always thought.

Belongs to a very old family of Lord Chancellors who had some sort of bitter falling out with the Hanoverians sometime in the early eighteen thirties. One of his ancestors had a dust-up with some toady of William IV's and Charles Grey got him removed from office. Anyway, the Keatons have been hoping for a chancellor in the family again ever since to avenge the family honour; I think they'd already had half a dozen until then. They seem to think they have some sort of God-given right to the office, but it's quite preposterous. He's quite friendly with the Yorks, I believe, and something of a confidant of Baldwin's too. Terribly wealthy, so why he cares about ancient history like that is beyond me. I must admit when I entered Hailsham's office I had no idea what he was doing there. He didn't seem like he had a reason to be invited but I daresay Hailsham knew what he was doing. He has an excellent legal mind, I suppose, and is a senior KC, although I would have thought Mellows or Hagan more suited to the matter at hand. Baldwin probably insisted on it.'

'Well go on anyway. What did he say?'

'He leaned forwards and of course everyone stared at him because he hadn't said a word in all the time that we'd been there and he said, "Just for argument's sake, gentlemen, should the king decide to marry this woman, what would happen then?" '

'Well it's a reasonable question, I suppose.'

'I hardly think so. Hailsham quickly told him there was no point wasting time on unrealistic scenarios. The question we were there to discuss was how much longer we could put off telling the king that he had to set the woman aside and take a wife.'

'I can't imagine he liked that much.'

'No, he didn't. And he insisted on an answer. "Just for argument's sake," he repeated. "What would happen then?" '

'And what would happen then?' asked Jane out of curiosity.

'Well none of us knew for sure,' said Roderick with a shrug. 'It felt like we were Oliver Cromwell's cabinet after the trial of Charles I, trying to decide what to do with the poor old bugger. No one wanted to be the first to suggest it. And finally, Monckton did.'

'*Monckton* did?'

'Yes, surprising isn't it? He said in a very clear voice that the point of this committee was to discuss all possible scenarios and their constitutional implications and if the king insisted on having his way then our point of view would be put to the prime minister who would in turn consult his ministers but ultimately take our advice and pass that advice on to the king. And then Hailsham said that if that ever happened they would say absolutely not, sir. And then Monckton said he wasn't sure what the king would do in a situation like that but he'd known him all his life and he wasn't a man to be trifled with.'

'He wouldn't . . . ?' began Jane, not knowing whether to say the words or not.

'He might.'

'For a woman? For an *American* woman?'

'I'm sure that's all a long way off,' said Roderick quickly. 'Hardly worth discussing now anyway. In the end Hailsham thanked us all for coming and said he'd get back to us if we needed to talk again. Monckton made a break for it, Altringham wasn't to be seen for dust, and I ended up drifting back here with Keaton in tow. And just as we left each other and shook hands he said the most extraordinary thing.'

'Yes?'

'He looked me directly in the eye and said, "He's a fine fellow, you know. A damned fine fellow." And I said, "The king? I'm sure he is. We've only spoken once, at a garden party." '

'Which we have to make sure we get tickets to next year,' interrupted Jane.

' "The king, certainly," said Keaton, "but I was talking about the Duke of York. He's a damned fine fellow." And of course I didn't know what to say to that and just stood there with my mouth open and then the impudent scoundrel gave me a wink and walked away. What do you make of that?'

Jane frowned. It all sounded very salacious and grist to a gossip monger's mill but that last part felt faintly disturbing.

'I'm not sure,' she said. 'But you'll have to keep your ear to the ground.'

'At first I didn't want any part of the thing,' said Bentley.

'But now I'm not so sure. Now I think I had better do exactly that. I mean when it comes down to it, if he wants to marry the woman, who does it hurt exactly?'

5

The process of constructing a picture frame is not a difficult one but it takes a certain amount of skill and expertise to get it right; it also takes patience. First, having checked the dimensions of the picture to be encased within, the correct amount of wood to surround it has to be measured out and divided into four pieces, each of which should equal the length of the side plus twice the width of the wood, the extra being in place for the mitred corners. The end of each piece needs to be cut to a forty-five-degree angle and then all four may be laid out with wood glue and corner clamps attached to join the corner sections of the frame. Turning the frame over, two nails should be applied along each glued corner seam with a hammer, with one nail pointed towards the inside of the frame and one nail aimed towards the outside. The midpoint of the nail rests on the seam and the open portion points towards the inside edge. At this point the clamps may be removed and the frame should be left to dry overnight. Varnishing may be completed the following day.

Owen Montignac and Gareth Bentley were novices at the art of frame-making but, working together with the aid of a good manual, they succeeded in constructing three by the end of the first day. They would have managed more were it not for the fact that their first two efforts fell apart quickly and when Gareth was hammering the nails in on a third, he placed one too close to the centre of the wood and it split. This was work that Montignac normally contracted out to a local firm when it came to paintings at the Threadbare Gallery but this was a specialist operation and could not involve any outsiders.

Gareth arrived in the early evening and joined Montignac upstairs in one of the small storerooms where they had laid out their materials; he had already told his assistant, Jason, that he was not to be disturbed and that he should lock up as usual and leave at the normal time.

'You want me to let you know when I'm off then?' asked Jason, poking his head around the door to see what was going on without him, unhappy by the presence of the new colleague in the storeroom who might be after his job; his nose was already out of joint over Gareth's apparent closeness to his employer.

'No, that's all right, Jason. Just go at six and I'll see you in the morning.'

'But what happens if—'

Montignac closed the door in the assistant's face and the boy went back downstairs to the gallery, distinctly unhappy.

'Do you really think this is going to work?' asked

Gareth as they came to the end of their third successful frame for the evening.

'Of course it will,' said Montignac, who would suffer no doubters on the subject.

'They won't check the boxes before they're shipped again?'

Montignac shook his head. 'You have no idea how painful the process of shipping paintings is,' he said. 'They have to be carefully swaddled individually in tight wrapping, which is all taped up, and then inserted into the wooden casings which are stapled shut. It takes an age to do. Trust me, once they've completed it no one will be opening them again until they reach Scotland.'

The first stop of the Cézanne paintings was the Royal Museum in Edinburgh, from where they were to make bi-weekly trips down the country from Edinburgh to Newcastle, Leeds, Liverpool, Birmingham and Cardiff before coming to a final rest for a month at the Tate Gallery in London. There were over eighty already on their way to Scotland with the last dozen, the ones being restored at the Clarion, set to join them shortly.

'And by then,' said Montignac, 'they will be gone forever.'

Gareth nodded; the plan seemed like a sensible one and he was enjoying the excitement of being involved in something illicit. Enjoying even more the promise of the thousand pounds which Montignac had promised him if everything went off without a hitch, not knowing that Montignac himself had negotiated a fee of fifteen times that amount for himself. He checked his watch; it was six-fifteen. All going well they should finish half the frames that evening and the other half by the end of the following one, which would mean they could undertake the operation at the only possible moment, on the evening of the last day.

He stood up and stretched out – his back felt sore from being crouched over for so long – and he looked at the just completed frame, which was designed to house a painting of ninety-eight inches by eighty-two, the exact dimensions of Cézanne's *Les Grandes Baigneuses*. He quite enjoyed the work and began to wonder whether he'd missed his calling as a carpenter but thought better of it immediately, knowing what his father would say if he suggested such a thing.

'I'm just running to the bathroom,' he told Montignac as he began measuring out the wood for the fourth frame. 'And then I'm going to make a cup of tea. Would you like one?'

Montignac nodded and pulled out his measuring tape as Gareth left the room. He was deeply immersed in his work and didn't hear the sound of Jason Parsons leaving the gallery a few minutes later, or the conversation he had with the young woman outside, whom he allowed to enter before he left, locking the door behind him. And he didn't hear her footsteps as she climbed to the mezzanine level and made her way up the side stairs to the small room where he was working. Given another moment he may well have recognized the scent of her familiar perfume as she stood in the doorway behind him but before that could happen he was startled by her voice and jumped, dropping the tape and wood on the floor in surprise.

'Surely the canvases should have already been painted before they're framed?' she asked, standing there and looking half in amusement and half in confusion at the three large frames standing by the door, their entirely white canvases standing out in contrast to their elaborate frames. 'Haven't you rather put the cart before the horse?'

'Stella,' he said, standing up and feeling his face begin to redden a little, as if he had been discovered while committing an illicit act. 'I didn't notice you there. How did you get in?'

'Your assistant let me in as he was leaving,' she said, looking past him as he tried to block her view. 'He knew I was your cousin and—'

'Did he indeed?' said Montignac, making a mental note to tell Jason exactly what he thought of him the next day.

'Well it's not a problem, is it?' she asked. 'You're still here after all.'

'Indeed I am,' he said, taking her by the arm and leading her out. 'Come on, let's go downstairs.'

'Why? What's wrong with talking here?'

'Staff only,' he said with what he hoped was a charming smile but only made her raise her eyebrows in surprise.

'Owen, it's only me for heaven's sake and there's no one else here.'

'Still, I'd prefer it,' he said, taking her by the arm and leading her towards the stairs. 'Come on, let's go.'

'All right, all right,' she said irritably. 'You don't have to drag me.' She turned around just as they went down the stairs and for the briefest of moments caught a glimpse of another young man going back into the storeroom carrying what looked like two cups of tea. 'Was that someone else?' she asked, but he had already disappeared inside. 'Is there someone else up there?'

'Just a trainee,' said Montignac, now that they were safely on the ground floor again. 'We're learning to make frames, you see. It's costing the gallery a bloody fortune contracting the work out to craft shops and we're never so busy that we couldn't do it ourselves if we had the skills. Hence all the . . . woodworking going on upstairs,' he explained. 'And the blank canvases. After they're secured we pull them off and start all over again.'

'Right,' said Stella, who had already lost interest in the matter of the canvases. 'Well, that's not what I came to talk to you about anyway.'

'Yes, well this isn't a good time really,' said Montignac. 'Can't we meet tomorrow perhaps?'

'No, Owen, we cannot meet tomorrow,' said Stella sharply. 'As I'll be on the morning train for Leyville tomorrow. And if you recall I phoned you yesterday and you promised to meet me for lunch today but never showed up. Which meant I had to stay here another night when I had particular business to take care of at home.'

'Oh that's right,' said Montignac, who had gone to the restaurant earlier in the day at the appointed time but turned back at the last minute, unable to face another conversation about money with his cousin when he was immersed in a new plan at the time. 'Sorry about that. We were up to our eyes here.'

'Well it seems that the only way I have of tracking you down these days is by just turning up here unannounced. Which is fine because if that's what it takes then that's what I'll do. I'm not going to let you just slip away, Owen, you know.'

Montignac licked his lips and recalled once when she had said that very line to him before; the memory seemed to have escaped her, though, as so many things had.

'Aren't you?' he asked quietly.

'No, I am not. I've told you before that I'm not going to allow the fact that Father is no longer with us to cause a separation between us. I want to see you, Owen. I want us to be friends. To be . . . family again. Like we once were.'

Montignac nodded. 'Yes,' he said, eager to move her towards the door. 'All right, but this isn't the best time for this conversation. If I don't get on with my work I'm going to be—'

'Owen, there's something I need to tell you,' she said, interrupting him.

'Do I want to hear it?'

'It's about Raymond and me,' she said, looking away from him for a moment.

Montignac felt his stomach contract a little. Even the phrase *Raymond and me*, three words which implied a connection on so many levels between them – legally, spiritually, emotionally, sexually – was enough to cause him unparalleled pain within.

'Then I'm sure I don't want to hear it,' he said bitterly.

'Well you're going to have to hear it, I'm afraid, because I have to tell you. We've decided to get married.'

Montignac laughed. 'You told me that at Christmas,' he said. 'I told you that you were a fool then and I'll tell you that you're a fool now. If you want to spend the next few years engaged to that—'

'No, you misunderstand me, Owen,' she said. 'We're not just engaged any more. We've set a date.'

Words failed him for a moment. The idea of marriage was one thing; the reality of it something else entirely. It was unacceptable.

'A date,' he said in a voice devoid of all emotion.

'Yes, a date. The first Saturday in October in fact.'

Montignac thought about this for a moment. 'Not this October, surely?' he said.

'Yes, this October.'

'But that's only . . .' He made a rapid calculation. 'Two months away.'

'Well it doesn't have to take years to prepare for, you know. Not for a simple ceremony.'

'Your father's only been dead a few months,' he said, playing a card that he didn't particularly like to play. 'Don't you think it's a little soon?'

'I discussed that with Margaret and she said—'

'She said it would be fine,' said Montignac, shaking his head. 'I can just imagine. I'm surprised she doesn't want you to elope to Gretna Green. I'm amazed she didn't find a way to get a vicar down to Leyville to marry you in the bloody kitchen before you could change your mind.'

'Owen, don't be cruel, please,' said Stella. 'Can't you be happy for me just a little?'

He stared at her without expression and made the most imperceptible shake of his head. Stella looked away and hesitated before speaking again.

'Margaret and I have both agreed that it wouldn't be a good idea for you to give me away,' she said.

His mouth dropped open in horror at the very idea.

'But Raymond obviously expects you to. As my only surviving male relative. So I wondered, if I could get him to ask you, whether you'd consider being his best man.'

'Stella, tell me you're not serious,' he said, flabbergasted that she would even suggest such a thing.

'It's the only way to explain to him why you're not walking me down the aisle.'

'I can't believe you would even think that I would want to do that,' he said, stunned now by her cheek. 'I simply can't believe it.'

'Why not?'

'You know why not,' he said, narrowing his eyes. 'I don't even want to be there.'

'But you have to be there,' she insisted. 'You're my cousin. We grew up together. We're—'

'Stella, don't you think it's a little late to play the cousin card now?' he asked with a bitter laugh. 'It seems to me that I was only your cousin when I was of some use to you. And after that . . .' He clicked his fingers in the air, like a magician performing a disappearing trick.

'And after that, what?' demanded Stella.

'Let's just say that family loyalty was hardly your strong suit, was it? You did what you did to save your own neck and didn't much care what happened to me afterwards. *Cousin*,' he added, feeling as if he wanted to spit the word on the ground and tread on it, but resisting. 'And besides, do you really think that Raymond would want me to act as his best man? What if he knew—'

'Owen, don't,' she barked, a pink dot appearing on either cheek.

He bit his lip and looked away from her. 'I don't want to do it,' he said quietly after a moment. 'I think it's heartless of you to suggest it.'

'Owen, when you think about it, it's really not that—'

A loud hammering sound came from upstairs and they both jumped and looked up there at the same time.

'I have to get back to work,' he said, snapping out of

his unhappiness and moving towards the door. 'Can you just leave please?'

'Well will you think about what I've said at least?' asked Stella. 'Will you just tell me that you'll give it some thought? Please? For me?'

He breathed in deeply and nodded. 'I'll think about it,' he said. 'But now I have to get back to work. I'll be in touch, all right?'

'Thank you, Owen. It means a lot to me.' She hesitated for a moment before turning back to stare at him. 'And for the record,' she added, her voice faltering slightly, 'you remember things entirely as you want to remember them; you do realize that, don't you? You can call me disloyal or cruel all you want but perhaps you should examine your own conscience about those days.'

Montignac snorted and looked away. 'I have and it's clear,' he said.

'Of course it is,' she said turning away. 'Because nothing is ever your fault, is it?'

'No,' said Montignac, seeing her through the door and locking it behind her.

Sometimes, he thought to himself, it's possible to look at a person and wonder how on earth you could ever have loved them in the first place.

And why it is, when they continue to hurt you, over and over again, you keep trying to make things better and you keep going back to let them take another punch at you.

It's because my love was an honest one, he thought,

answering his own question. *It was honest and true and I never would have betrayed her like she did me. No matter what she did. Cousin or not. I never would have done it. Not in a million years. I would have died first.*

6

They were unsure how to deal with him at first but it didn't take long for the Montignacs to feel that they couldn't remember life before their young nephew had come to live with them; after only two weeks at Leyville, Owen Montignac proved himself to be a favourite with his new family. The children were welcoming, Stella doting on her blue-eyed, white-haired cousin, treating him like a real-life doll who'd been thrust among them, while Andrew enjoyed the fact that he had a younger brother of sorts for the first time in his life, and one who was already grown and not a baby at that.

Of course one of the reasons he made himself so popular was because he ingratiated himself so much into their affections. He kept up a parade of jokes, tricks and good humour that had the family and the servants falling in love with him, even Margaret Richmond who didn't appreciate the kind of spontaneity that Owen brought to the house. She put that down to his French upbringing. (Or his 'wild' French upbringing as she styled it.) After only a short while it felt like a room was empty if he wasn't in it.

The first night he slept at Leyville, only a few hours after his uncle Peter had brought him there following the long drive from Dover, Montignac crawled into the enormous bed in the room he was to share with his cousin Andrew and lay awake, trying to keep his fears at bay while he decided how he would behave now that he had finally arrived.

It had been only two months since his mother was killed when the munitions factory in which she worked was blown up; five week after that his father, a soldier in the British army, was killed at the battle of the Somme. His mother's family had been caring for him ever since and had written to his uncle to inform him of his new address in case they wanted to contact him; it had not been their intention to send the boy to England but events had overtaken them.

After the letter arrived, Peter and Ann had discussed what they should do for the best.

'Well we don't have any choice in the matter,' reasoned Peter. 'He'll have to come and live here with us.'

'At Leyville?'

'Of course. Where else?' he said, rereading the letter. 'He's still a Montignac. We can't have him growing up with a different family, let alone a foreign one.'

'But he doesn't even know us, Peter,' she said. 'And he must have known the Reims family his whole life.' She reread the letter. 'They seem to be a big family too. His grandparents are looking after three grandsons and a granddaughter already. I'm sure they'll take care of him.'

'He's only five years old, Ann,' said Peter sternly. 'We can't do that to him. Montignacs should be here. At Leyville.'

Ann wasn't entirely happy with the situation but had little choice in the matter and Peter wrote to France, insisting that the boy be returned to England immediately. At first, Montignac's maternal grandmother was reluctant to let him go, but Peter threatened legal action as well as pointing out what a better position he was in to give the child a comfortable upbringing, and she finally relented. He sent enough money for the boy's passage, and collected him at Dover a few weeks later.

'All I can say is I'm glad your father's not here to witness this,' said Ann, the night before his arrival. 'He'd be rolling in his grave if he knew what was about to happen.'

'What happened between Henry and Father should never have happened,' said Peter, the beneficiary of their falling-out. 'They both lost out. For heaven's sake it's not as if the marriage between my brother and his wife didn't work out. Presumably they were happy together. The poor lad must be traumatized by losing both his parents so close together. We have a responsibility to the boy to make up for what his own father missed out on. Don't forget, Henry was my brother. We grew up together.'

'But by rights Leyville belongs to him. Don't you think he'll want it back someday?'

'It's not his by rights,' pointed out Peter. 'Father left it to me. And I shall leave it to Andrew. He'll be looked after, though. He'll be happy with that.'

The young Owen had one sepia-toned photograph of his parents and he kept it beside him on his bedside locker. It had been taken on their wedding day and they both had a ghostly pallor to them that didn't recall their faces for him at all. His mother's long blond hair and his father's wavy blond hair stood out dramatically from the dark tones surrounding them.

'You know your father was disinherited,' Andrew told him a year or two later after some fight between the two. 'He upset grandfather and was cut off without a penny.'

'No, because we always lived in France,' said Owen, with the logic of a child who bases all he believes on his own memories. 'We were never here before.'

'*You* weren't here before,' said Andrew. 'But your father grew up here. With my father. In fact yours was the elder brother but there was some sort of commotion when he chose to get married and that's when he slunk off to France.'

Montignac narrowed his eyes. He wasn't sure what the verb *slunk* meant but he didn't like the sound of it. He had worked hard at losing his own French accent over the last year or two as it had only provided the other boys in school with an excuse to tease him but on occasion it rose up again and he remembered a string of words, some of which he threw at his cousin now.

'Steady on,' said Andrew. 'Don't use that Frog speak here. Hasn't Father told you about that?'

The relationship between Andrew and Owen was always a fractious one; most of the time they got along fairly well but there was always the possibility, on an hour-by-hour basis, that they would end up rolling around on the floor, knocking the stuffing out of each other. And despite the fact that Andrew was three years older and a good deal bigger, he always came off worse in any such confrontation.

'It's ridiculous, Andrew,' said Margaret Richmond after one particularly violent session when the two boys were lined up before her, waiting for her to wash out the cuts they had inflicted on each other and examine their bruises. 'You're old enough to know better, aren't you?'

'It was him,' protested Andrew. 'It's always him. He always starts things and then comes over all angelic when we get into trouble for it.'

'You're three years older,' she said. 'You should know better. And as for you,' she added, turning to Owen and glaring at him. 'You should be grateful for all your uncle and aunt have done for you and not go around causing chaos every day. Look at your cousin's face,' she added, pointing at Andrew who had a large bruise preparing to darken beneath his eye. 'It's absolutely no way to behave.'

Owen didn't care. The only one he liked was Stella whose opinion of him seemed to change on a daily basis. At first she enjoyed the fact that there was another child in the house. He was her junior by less than a year and they could play together perfectly happily. As she grew older she decided to resent his presence and would evict him from her room whenever he came to talk to her and in fact spent the best part of a year or two ignoring the boy.

And then, when she was about twelve, they grew close again and remained increasingly intimate for several years. Then Andrew was killed and the family broke down into its separate components, afraid to mix together in case of an explosion, Ann taking to her bed for weeks on end, Peter retiring to his study to consider the wreckage of his family, and the heart-broken Stella to her room. Only Owen managed to keep his composure during those difficult months despite the fact that he had been the one who had been present during his cousin's final moments.

'What happened exactly?' Peter asked him in tears within hours of the tragedy. 'How did it come about?'

'It's hard to say,' he said. 'He loaded his gun and waited until he saw a rabbit. I wasn't even watching him and then when he pulled the trigger he flew back against the grass. It was horrible. The gun mustn't have been cleaned properly or perhaps it just misfired.' He broke down in tears too and refused to discuss it any further and the doctor advised that he should not be asked to describe it any longer for fear of traumatizing him further.

Stella was taken dramatically from school a few

months later, just before her seventeenth birthday, and sent to a finishing school in Geneva. It had been Margaret Richmond's idea and she had used all her wiles to persuade Peter Montignac that the move was a sensible one. Neither parent was sure at first but with a little clever persuasion on her part the move was secured.

Owen didn't see her for almost two years after that. He wrote to her, of course, but she ignored his letters. When he saved up his money to phone her in Geneva she wouldn't take his calls and refused to return them. When she finally returned to Leyville he was at Cambridge and their paths did not cross as much as they had in the past. When they did see each other she was distant with him, afraid to be left alone in the same room together, and he felt devastated by the way she treated him.

That had been how things had stood between them then for several years now. Two cousins, once very close, who now barely spoke to each other for reasons neither one fully understood, both feeling betrayed by the other but perhaps only one feeling the great loss. When Owen thought of her he thought of someone he had once been ready to lay down his life for, the only one of his English relatives who had ever meant anything to him, but who had betrayed him badly. Who, apparently over the space of one night, had decided to have nothing more to do with him and to treat him with contempt. When he thought of the maliciousness and vindictiveness of her actions, it took his very breath away. It was as if she wanted to hurt him and go on hurting him forever.

But Stella knew differently. She knew the truth about why she found it difficult to be alone with him now, but could never tell him. It would only hurt him more than she had any right to do. And she wasn't sure what the consequences of revealing the truth to him would be.

7

Having been opened four nights earlier, the upstairs room in the Threadbare Gallery did not smell quite so damp nor feel so dusty on the night that Owen Montignac and Gareth Bentley used it as their thoroughfare on their return to the Clarion Gallery. It was the night before the Cézanne pictures were due to be shipped to Edinburgh and the two men had managed to construct twelve sturdy frames during that time which, should their measurements prove correct, would match the various sizes of the masterpieces.

'Let's hope that they've packaged the paintings today after all,' said Montignac as they made their way up the stairs. 'And that they're storing them in the same room. If they've moved them at all, we're done for.'

The panel above the room gave way easily and although the narrow opening above it leading to the gallery was still difficult to negotiate, at least they knew where they were going this time and after a few minutes Montignac came through first into the restoration room of the Clarion with a minimum of fuss.

All day long Gareth had been in a state of heightened expectation, waiting for the evening to arrive. Until now the plan had seemed like a great adventure, the kind of mischief he might have got up to back in his boarding school days at Harrow, but as the night approached the thought began to cross his mind that what he was actually about to do was to commit a crime.

He cast his mind back to his law books and tried to remember what kind of sentence was passed on thieves such as the one he was about to become. Unfortunately he had not always been a regular attendee at his lectures – something which no doubt contributed to his lower second-class degree, a standard by which he would never have been considered for a pupillage at chambers had his father not been head thereof – so he could not render a guess at the likely punishment.

There was no doubt that it would be a custodial sentence in the unlikely event that they were discovered, but Gareth found it hard to believe that they were really doing anything too terrible. After all, it wasn't as if they were breaking into someone's home and robbing their possessions, or holding up a bank and clearing out the investors' savings accounts. These were paintings which for the most part belonged to financial institutions rather than collectors and which were no doubt insured for large sums of money. If they were stolen the heads of the various banks that had an interest in the Cézanne estate would simply collect on the insurance and not give the matter of the lost art a second thought. And the ultimate recipient of the goods was undoubtedly someone who would treasure them as the painter had intended. Thus did Gareth Bentley justify his actions that night.

They left the set of twelve frames they had constructed back in the Threadbare, wanting to make sure that they would be able to execute their plan first before dragging them across, which would be no easy task in itself. Some were quite heavy and bulky and it would take several trips back and forth to transport them.

Montignac switched on the light and looked around the room to where the easels had stood three nights earlier and his heart sank. There was nothing there. He looked around at the neat stores of implements on the walls, the rows of restorative paints and cleansers facing him, but the Cézannes were missing.

'Over here,' said Gareth, who had walked to the back of the room where a large tarpaulin was draped over what appeared to be an enormous box. He lifted it off and standing in a holder underneath were twelve wooden boxes.

'That's a relief,' said Montignac, who even in the few seconds of despair had been considering whether he had enough money to leave England indefinitely and without delay. 'All right, let's lift one out.'

Gareth reached down and picked up the smallest of

the twelve and released it from its moorings, carrying it to the centre of the floor and laying it down. Montignac took the staple remover from his pocket and lifted out the heavy steel clips that kept the casing in place. The wood made a sharp cracking sound as the top came away and revealed the packaging beneath. They picked it up and took the wrapping off to reveal a painting.

'Perfect,' said Montignac, breaking into a rare smile as he looked across at his accomplice. 'All right, we better do these one at a time so the boxes are placed back in the same order. That's a small one. Go back and get the canvas and the box.'

Gareth nodded and jumped up, and struggled back into the ceiling gap and across to the Threadbare.

Montignac inspected the picture closer, running his fingers lightly over the surface where Paul Cézanne's brush had hovered a half century before and that old urge inside him to be an artist himself reappeared. *If only I'd had the talent,* he thought, imagining the life of an internationally successful painter that he could have lived. The glamorous friends, the love affairs with European heiresses, the hospitality offered by kings and presidents and prime ministers around the world. Instead he was reduced to this. Stealing the great works in order to pay off a portion of his gambling debts. How had it come to this, he wondered, before remembering that the answer lay in two words: Peter Montignac.

The previous evening he had calculated that the paintings themselves could be worth up to about one hundred and fifty thousand pounds when taken together. He had no idea who the final buyer was – only the intermediary, Lord Keaton, had spoken to him so far, and they had agreed on a payment of fifteen thousand pounds for his services. One thousand of this he had promised to Gareth – who was under the impression that Keaton had only offered five in total – ten was earmarked for Nicholas Delfy, which would leave him four thousand pounds in the black as he considered how to raise the final thirty-six thousand he owed him.

'Here we are,' said Gareth, reappearing and struggling under the weight of the fresh canvas and new box of the same size that he'd brought back with him. 'I think this is the right one.'

Montignac took the Cézanne and laid it on top of the blank, framed canvas and smiled in relief. They were a perfect match. 'Good job,' he muttered, taking the packaging from the floor and wrapping it around the blank. 'Fetch me that tape from the wall over there,' he said, looking up. Gareth brought it over and they wrapped it round several times.

'You can't even see through that,' said Gareth appreciatively. 'Even if they were to open the boxes.'

'They won't open them,' said Montignac, shaking his head. 'You can rely on that.'

The operation to transfer all twelve paintings took almost four hours. It became more of a complicated business than had originally been thought of as several of the canvases were of similar but not exactly the same proportions and when ten had been wrapped and sealed in fresh boxes, the two that were left were clearly the wrong size.

'Let's just put them in other boxes,' suggested Gareth, who had grown weary of the whole thing. 'No one will know the difference.'

'We'll know,' said Montignac, shaking his head. 'It's best to get it right. We'll have to take some out again.'

They reopened a few until the elaborate jigsaw puzzle they had laid out for themselves finally started to make sense and the twelve blank canvases had been swaddled in wrapping and placed inside new boxes and returned to their moorings in the holder beneath the tarpaulin.

'What time is it?' asked Montignac, who was only starting to feel tired now that the operation was nearly over.

'Almost ten past five,' said Gareth.

'All right. Enough time to clean this place up and get back. Watch out for splinters,' he added as they started to collect all the broken boxes which they had taken off, and carry them back to the storeroom in the Threadbare. 'Now the paintings,' said Montignac.

One by one, they collected the Cézannes and carried them carefully through the ceiling into the next-door gallery, leaning each one side by side against the wall. The light was starting to break outside as the sun came up but time was still on their side.

Gareth went back to the Clarion and swept the floor to rid it of any small pieces of wood that remained and then between them they inspected the room, happy that they were leaving it exactly as they had found it. They climbed back into the attic space and made their way back to the Threadbare.

'Now,' said Montignac. 'You see those desks in there?' He pointed towards four old desks that stood in the second storeroom, two standing on the floor, two resting upside down on top of each other.

'Yes,' said Gareth.

'I want to put all of them in this room,' he said. 'To fill it up.'

Gareth sighed in exhaustion. 'Why?' he asked petulantly. 'That will take ages.'

'In the unlikely event that anyone ever considers the fact that the attic space is easily accessible, I want it to look as if it has been blocked up for years,' he said patiently. 'Now come on. If we put our backs into it, it won't take long.'

Knowing that he had no choice in the matter, Gareth grudgingly followed Montignac and they pulled the desks down, loading up the corridor and filling in the final gaps with some spare chairs and various bags of rubbish and bits of wood that they found about the place. By the time they locked the door again the storeroom housing the attic panel appeared virtually inaccessible.

'A job well done,' said Montignac with a smile as the Cézanne's were freshly wrapped and left in the downstairs storeroom overnight, which he locked and then pocketed the key. 'Now, young man,' he added with a smile, 'I suggest you go home and get some sleep. I'll take care of all this tomorrow and then you will be one thousand pounds better off.'

Gareth rubbed his hands together in glee. 'Can't wait,' he said in delight. 'When do we get the money?'

'A couple of days, I imagine,' said Montignac with a shrug. 'I'll speak to the middle man tomorrow' – he had not revealed Keaton's name to his accomplice – 'and let him know that the job is done. In the meantime, don't contact me, all right? I'll be in touch with you.'

Gareth nodded and walked towards the door, eager to get home and to bed, where he could think about how to spend his money.

'I'll see you soon,' he said as he left.

'Yes, but don't contact me,' repeated Montignac. 'Wait until you hear from me. I don't want anyone knowing that you were here.'

Gareth nodded, shook his hand, and drifted off into the night while Montignac locked the door and returned to the gallery. He let out a deep yawn and longed for bed himself. He couldn't help but smile at how well this part of the plan had all gone. He only hoped that the next would be as successful.

8

Jane Bentley was still growing accustomed to seeing her son up and dressed this early. At first she hadn't dared to believe that he would continue to take his new responsibilities seriously, but it appeared that he had, for every morning for some weeks now he had risen at the same time as the rest of the working world.

'Good morning,' she said. 'I'm pleased to see that you're sticking with it.'

'With what?'

'This new-found sense of responsibility. Being up and about with the lark.'

'I told you, I've turned over a new leaf,' said Gareth, smiling at her as he placed a couple of slices of bread under the grill. 'You don't have to keep expecting the worst from me, you know.'

'I don't, I just—'

'Of course you do, Mother,' said Gareth with a good-natured shrug. 'But perhaps I've given you cause.'

'Well, whether you have or haven't, there's no question that this new job of yours is doing you the world of good. Your Mr Montignac is a good influence on you. You should invite him to dinner some evening. I'd like to meet him.'

'Really, Mother,' said Gareth, a little embarrassed. 'We're not engaged to be married, you know. I don't have to invite him over to meet the parents.'

'No, of course not,' she replied. 'That's not what I meant.' She sighed; her son could be so prickly sometimes. He always had to be handled with kid gloves. 'I just meant that you seem a lot happier in yourself since you started working with him.'

'I am,' said Gareth. 'Everything seems . . . different suddenly. I'm starting to think the future might be brighter than expected.'

'I'm pleased to hear that,' said Roderick Bentley, strolling into the kitchen with the Saturday newspapers under his arm. 'What are we talking about?'

'Gareth was just telling me about his new job,' said Jane.

'About time he had one too.'

'Oh really, Roderick—'

'It's all right, Mother,' said Gareth, sitting down with his toast and pouring some tea from the pot. 'He's quite right. Well I think from now on I'm going to be a lot less bother to you.'

'Glad to hear it,' said Roderick, scanning the headlines on the front page of *The Times*.

'In fact, I'm thinking of getting a place of my own.'

'What's that?' asked Jane, spinning around. 'A place of your own?'

'Yes, I thought about taking a flat somewhere. Not too far away, of course. Perhaps around Bedford Place.'

'What on earth do you want to move there for? asked Roderick. 'When you have a perfectly good home here?'

'Well I'm twenty-four years old now,' said Gareth. 'I think it's about time I had a little independence, don't you?'

'Oh, don't be so ridiculous, Gareth,' said Jane, who couldn't bear the idea of being without him. 'You have all the independence you want here. We don't give you any bother, do we?'

'Well no,' he admitted. 'Short of getting a pitchfork to get me out of bed every morning—'

'You come and go as you please and no one says anything to stop you. And now that you've got a job you have even more independence.'

'It's not just about that, Mother,' he said. 'A fellow of my age should have his own flat, I think.'

'Oh nonsense,' said Jane. 'Which of your friends do?'

'Alexander Keys, for one,' said Gareth, thinking about it. 'Owen Montignac for another.'

'But you just said you're turning over a new leaf. It's pointless you getting a place of your own when we have so much space here.'

'Perhaps he has a romance on the go,' suggested Roderick with a gentle smile. 'Do you, Gareth?' he asked mischievously. 'Have you fallen in love and don't want to tell us about it yet?'

'That's not it, is it?' asked Jane, glaring at him, unsure how she should feel about such a development. 'Have you met someone special?'

'It's just something I'm thinking about,' said Gareth, his face flushing bright red and stepping away to the grill so as to be able to turn his back on them. 'I haven't decided on anything for sure.'

'Flats are a lot more expensive these days than they used to be,' said Roderick, considering the matter. 'There's a young chap just come to work for us in the clerks' office and he's paying two pounds a week for a bedsit in Clapham. Two pounds a week! Can you imagine what you would have got for that in our day?'

'Your day maybe, darling,' said Jane with a smile. 'Your day was ten years before my day.'

'Anyway I don't want to live in Clapham,' said Gareth.

'Bedford Place is only around the corner,' said Roderick. 'Seems a bit pointless to move out of here and into there. And I imagine it would be a damn sight more expensive than Clapham when it comes to that.'

'Well it was just a thought,' said Gareth quietly. 'Owen Montignac lives there and he seems very comfortable.'

'Ah, I might have known,' said Roderick. 'Been putting ideas into your head then, has he?'

'Now, Roderick, don't say anything negative,' said Jane quickly. 'I was just telling Gareth what a good influence I felt Mr Montignac had been on him.'

'What is it exactly you do for him anyway?' asked Roderick, putting the papers down and staring at his son. 'You know you've never actually told us.'

'Well it's all sorts really,' said Gareth in a hesitant voice. 'He has an awful lot of interests and I help him with . . . the books and so on. Plus I help out around the gallery. It's terribly interesting, you know. I'm learning an awful lot. About art and whatnot.'

'I've been to that gallery myself,' said Jane. 'Some very exciting pieces there. We should go together someday, Roderick. Pick out something for that space on the third-floor landing. All the artwork is very contemporary there, isn't it, Gareth?'

'That's one way to put it,' he said.

'One gets so tired of landscapes and seascapes and portraits of dead aristocrats,' said Jane.

Roderick grunted and looked back at the papers. He was checking to make sure there was no further gossip about the king in there and for the time being there didn't seem to be anything; he lived in dread of a leak and his getting the blame for it, particularly since he had confided rather more than he intended in his loose-tongued wife. The prime minister had put the papers under a blanket embargo on discussing the matter of Edwards and Mrs Simpson but the American newspapers and their continental counterparts talked of nothing else and it had become the common currency of discussion among the people on the streets. It was only a matter of time, he felt, before one of the newspapers broke the prohibition and challenged the government to act.

'Nothing in there?' asked Jane, following his line of thought.

'Not a word,' said Roderick. 'They're all covering this paintings business, though.'

Gareth looked up from his toast, his blush of a few moments before saving him from a second embarrassment. 'What was that?' he asked.

'Haven't you heard?' said Roderick, pointing at an article that filled a third of the page on the front of *The*

Times, beneath the fold. 'It's awfully funny in a way, although one shouldn't laugh at such things of course. It seems that there's an exhibition touring the country of paintings by some dead French artist and a part of the collection was in London for some restoration work and reframing. Once they were finished the paintings were transported up to Edinburgh to join the rest of the collection but when they got there the canvases were entirely blank.'

'Blank?' asked Jane in surprise.

'That's right.'

'How could they be blank?' she asked. 'Do you mean the restorers wiped them clean?'

'Well no,' he said, stifling a laugh. 'No, I don't think that's what anybody thinks. They were packed away in cases and were apparently fine when they were going up there but then they reached their destination and the real paintings were gone. They must have been switched en route, I expect. They went on a train, of course, and you know the type that travels on them. The whole thing's a terrible mystery. All the employees of the railway line are being questioned and the stations searched. It's going to cost the insurers a pretty packet. And of course the gallery that were doing the work are in terrible trouble too. There's talk of a lawsuit against the owner for not providing adequate security. This chap here,' he muttered, running his finger along the article for the name. 'Arthur Hamilton. Poor fellow's getting all the blame.'

'Well I don't see how it's his fault once they've left the gallery,' said Jane.

Roderick continued to read further through the article, the mischief of which had rather intrigued him. 'Hello,' he said. 'It's on Cork Street. That's where your Mr Montignac has his gallery, isn't it?'

'Yes that's right,' said Gareth casually. 'What gallery was it?'

'A place called the Clarion. Do you know it?'

Gareth narrowed his eyes and hesitated for a moment. 'Yes, I think so,' he said finally. 'I think it's a few doors down from Montignac's. Same side of the street.'

'Well there'll be hell to pay, that's for sure,' said Roderick. 'These insurance companies don't like paying out a penny. Of course they're worse scoundrels than the thieves, if you ask me. And the police are baffled, it says here.'

'The police are always baffled, aren't they?' asked Jane, pouring some more tea. (This, she had a sudden realization, was exactly as she had always wanted her life to be; interesting conversation over the breakfast table about the news of the day. The odd *bon mot* to show they were lively people. A sensation of pure happiness descended on her.) 'Whenever anything mysterious happens, they end up baffled. If you ask me the London constabulary are in a permanent state of bewilderment. God forbid we should ever be in need of their help.'

'Yes,' said Roderick, turning the pages to find the

crossword which could occupy him for the next half-hour or so.

'But there's nothing in there about . . . the other business?' asked Jane after a moment.

'Nothing. They're toeing the line for once, it seems.'

'Well I daresay it's only a matter of time.'

'Is this the king you're talking about?' asked Gareth, looking up.

'You know about that?' asked Roderick, looking across at his wife irritably who made a sign to indicate that it had nothing to do with her and she hadn't let anything slip.

'Everyone knows about it,' said Gareth, laughing at his father's naivety. 'It's all anyone talks about any more. All this Queen Wallis business.'

'That's never going to happen,' said Jane irritably.

'Of course not,' said Roderick.

'But it's utterly pointless the papers not being allowed to discuss it,' said Gareth. 'When all the foreign ones can. It only takes a few days or a week at most for the latest rumours to hit people.'

'Have you heard from Hailsham again?' asked Jane quietly, sitting down beside her husband. He shook his head.

'Not in the last week or so. But Lord Keaton came round the other day and said we should expect another meeting any time soon. It seems that she really is going to go through with divorcing the fellow.'

'I'm not surprised,' said Gareth. 'He's the most famous

cuckold in England right now. He should have had some pride and divorced her long ago. I know I would have.'

'Let's not get into it,' said Roderick. 'I have a horrible feeling that it will be a matter to prey on my mind for long enough over the next few months without discussing it now. Is there any more tea in the pot?'

Gareth slipped out of the kitchen a few minutes later and made his way up to his bedroom. He'd risen early for the last few days expecting to hear from Owen Montignac arranging when he should call around to collect his thousand pounds but there had been no word as yet. Still, it had only been a few days and Montignac had specifically told him not to contact him but to wait until he heard from him.

But it had been three days already and he was starting to grow nervous. He decided that if he hadn't heard from him by Monday evening, he would pay a visit to the Threadbare at closing time and remind him of his existence and the money that was owed to him.

9

It had been almost a month since Owen Montignac had been to the Unicorn Ballrooms and he arrived there on Sunday evening in mixed spirits.

He had arranged to meet Lord Keaton at lunchtime at the office where they had spoken twice already and they drove together to a lock-up near King's Cross where the dozen Cézannes had been hidden since the switch had been made a few nights earlier. Together they took the boxes off a selected few and Keaton examined them.

'Very good, Mr Montignac,' he said. 'Do you know that when your name was mentioned to me in association with this job I wasn't really very sure.'

'Really?' asked Montignac. 'May I ask why not?'

'Well I don't mean any offence,' said Keaton with a shrug. 'But I knew your uncle quite well and he was something of a straight-shooter. He never would have involved himself in an operation like this.'

'My uncle was not quite the saint that people like to portray him as,' said Montignac.

'Sons never like to hear people speak well of their fathers. I bet if I had criticized him you would have defended him soundly, though.'

'He wasn't my father,' Montignac pointed out.

'Well be that as it may, I wasn't sure that I was doing the right thing approaching you. I see now that I was wrong. You've done a very efficient job.'

Montignac nodded. 'Well I'm glad that I managed to impress you,' he said. 'Can I ask you who recommended me in the first place?'

'Of course you can ask,' said Keaton, smiling. 'But it would be entirely inappropriate for me to tell you. Let's just say that it was someone who was familiar with your character and who believed you would be happy to provide me with this service.'

'All right,' said Montignac, who understood the rules regarding transactions like this. 'And what about where they're going to then? Whose walls are these going to end up on?'

'I'm afraid it would be improper for me to tell you that either,' he replied with a laugh. 'I'm sorry, Mr Montignac, but there we are. It was nothing more than a discreet business arrangement. Perhaps we should leave it at that and not ask each other any more questions.'

'That's fine,' said Montignac. 'Although please do stress to your buyer that he won't be able to put any of these pictures on general display. If anyone should see them—'

'Let me assure you that they are for his private collection only, and once these have left here today any association they may have to you or your gallery will be completely forgotten. No one would be able to prove a connection anyway.'

'Good,' said Montignac. 'Which leaves us with only one matter left to sort out.'

'Indeed it does,' said Keaton, reaching inside his jacket to remove the envelope. 'Fifteen thousand pounds to do with what you will.'

Montignac took the envelope and looked inside it.

'You can count it if you want,' said Keaton but Montignac shook his head.

'I'll trust you,' he said, extending a hand and they shook on it. 'If there's any other business deals you can put my way you know where to contact me.'

'Indeed I do, Mr Montignac, and now that you have proved your value and discretion, I may very well be in touch again. In fact, you can count on it. I think there's another matter, a far more important and financially beneficial matter, that you could help me out with.'

'Oh really?' he asked. 'Can I ask what it is?'

'Your debt to Mr Delfy still stands at an extraordinary figure, does it not?'

Montignac hesitated; he hated admitting to his failures like this. 'Yes,' he said finally, through gritted teeth.

'Well there may be a way that I could help you clear the entire amount.'

'Go on.'

'Not here,' said Keaton, shaking his head. 'I'll contact you shortly about it. It's a much riskier venture than this one, of course, but then the remuneration will be a lot higher. And it has far greater importance too.'

'Sounds mysterious,' said Montignac.

'Let's just say that it will take some ingenuity to pull it off.'

Montignac nodded. 'I'll wait to hear from you then,' he said.

They shook hands again and Montignac left the lock-up; there weren't many people who made him feel uncomfortable but Keaton was certainly one. Despite his corpulent build and aristocratic bearing, he had a chilly manner and fixed smile that made Montignac think that under the right circumstances he could be quite brutal.

Throughout the rest of the afternoon, while relaxing at his flat on Bedford Place, it had been a battle of wills between Montignac's good and bad nature to hold on to the money he had just earned. He laid it out on his bed when he got home and counted it. As it turned out Keaton had been wrong, there was not fifteen thousand pounds there, but fifteen thousand one hundred. He smiled as he double-checked. It was a trivial amount in relation to the total but twenty-four hours earlier a hundred pounds would have meant a lot to him.

He separated the money into three piles. Ten thousand for Nicholas Delfy, one thousand for Gareth Bentley and four thousand one hundred for himself, and put the first bundle back into the envelope and sealed it.

The idea of taking the entire amount to a card table at another club and doubling, tripling or quadrupling it by teatime was very attractive but he managed to resist it. He had only left himself with two days to go before the payment was due and if he lost it now there would be nowhere to hide. On the other hand, the thought of taking all the money and disappearing to Europe was also a possibility but he couldn't trust that he wouldn't be found there too. In the end, proud of his determination, he stayed at home until nearly eight o'clock and then, to prevent any further temptations, left for the Unicorn.

'Mr Montignac,' said Henderson as he approached him on the street outside, the same man who had escorted him from the pub some weeks earlier when Delfy had made contact to demand repayment. 'We didn't expect to see you tonight.'

'Really?' said Montignac. 'I have some outstanding business with Mr Delfy.'

'Yes, but he thought you would wait until the last possible minute to arrive which, by my calculations, would be two days from now.'

'Well I have plans two days from now,' said Montignac with a casual air. 'So I thought I'd come now. He is in, isn't he?'

Henderson smiled and led the way down the corridor and told Montignac to stay put while he went into the office. He stood there and looked across at the club which was surprisingly busy for early on a Sunday night. He saw the barmen loading up the cash registers with the money that was being spent on bottles of wine and champagne; he could see the croupiers in the distance raking in thousands of pounds' worth of chips and wondered how one managed to set oneself up in a business like this. The income from it must be extraordinary and could make a tall and powerful man out of a runt like Nicholas Delfy.

The doorman stepped out of the office and moved back on to the corridor, nodding Montignac in the direction of the door. 'Go on in,' he said.

Montignac walked slowly towards the door, stepped

inside and closed it behind him. He felt a sigh of relief descend on him that he had got this far with the money intact, despite all the temptations, and that this meeting would be a lot more pleasant and a lot less threatening than their last had been.

'Mr Montignac,' said Nicholas Delfy, leaning back in his chair and smiling broadly. 'Or shall I start with Owen and see how we get on?'

'Owen's fine,' he said. 'Hello, Nicholas. Nice to see you again.'

'Is it?' asked Delfy in surprise. 'That's not something I hear very often.'

'Well I don't really mean it,' said Montignac with a shrug. 'I'm just being polite for form's sake.'

Delfy stared at him, unsure how to take that, but gave a gentle laugh; there was something about Montignac that he couldn't help but like.

'Sit down, Owen,' he said. 'Take the weight off. Can I get you a drink?'

Montignac was about to shake his head, the urge as strong as ever to stay for as short a time as possible, but then reconsidered. 'All right,' he said. 'I'll have a glass of whisky if you're having one.'

'No, I like to keep a clear head,' said Delfy, walking across to the small bar in the corner and pouring one for his guest. 'But you have one by all means. Ice?' he asked.

'Please,' said Montignac, accepting the glass a few moments later and tasting it appreciatively. 'Very nice,' he said.

'Aged twenty-five years,' said Delfy, sitting down again. 'Just like you.'

'Sadly I have a birthday coming up shortly,' said Montignac. 'I'll be twenty-six.'

'Feeling confident you'll make it that far then?' asked Delfy.

'More confident that I was a month ago.'

'Well that's good. No one likes unnecessary violence,' said Delfy. 'More than I,' he added with a laugh. 'But I am hearing wonderful things about you, Owen,' he said with a flamboyant gesture. My spies keep me well informed of course and they tell me that you've been working terribly hard at raising the money you owe me and there's a possibility, a slim possibility of course, that you may have ten thousand pounds in your pocket for me right now.'

'Indeed,' said Montignac, enjoying the cat and mouse. 'And what else do your spies tell you then?'

'They say you've trapped an innocent little fly in your web and you're just waiting for an opportunity to swallow him up.'

'Well I don't know where they got that from,' Montignac replied. 'But it's true that I have the money I owe you.'

'The whole fifty thousand?' asked Delfy in surprise.

'No, no,' said Montignac quickly, laughing nervously. 'Just the first payment. That's what we agreed upon, isn't it?'

'It is indeed,' said Delfy. 'So there's no need to look so

nervous, Owen. And you've managed it with two days to spare. That's very impressive. Very impressive indeed. It fills me with confidence about your trustworthiness and our future relationship.'

Montignac nodded and they stared at each other for a minute before Delfy made a come-hither gesture with his left hand. Montignac frowned, unsure what he meant by it, and leaned forwards in his seat.

'Not you, Owen,' sighed Delfy. 'The money.'

'Oh yes,' he said, reaching into his inner pocket and extracting the envelope and handing it across. 'It's all there,' he said, relieved that it had been handed over now and he couldn't possibly risk it any further. 'All ten thousand pounds. Count it if you like.'

Delfy laughed. 'I'm sure you wouldn't be that stupid,' he said.

'No.'

'Well, like I said I'm very impressed,' he said. 'Now you must promise to stay out of casinos from now on until the debt is fully paid off. Clearly, Owen Montignac and gambling do not go hand in hand.'

'No,' said Montignac, not appreciating the sensation that he was being chastised like a child. 'No I don't think we do.'

Delfy reached into a drawer and extracted a ledger and thumbed through it for the page he needed. 'Ten thousand pounds,' he said as he wrote the figure down. 'Paid in full. Excellent. Now we should probably talk about the balance.'

'The balance,' said Montignac. 'Yes, I'm working on that. But if you could give me a little more time I'd appreciate it.'

'Well we agreed on Christmas, didn't we?' asked Delfy, looking up. 'And since you've been so successful with the first instalment I think we should stick to our original arrangement.'

'Christmas will be fine,' said Montignac, who had been slightly worried that Delfy would turn around and change the conditions; it had been one of his motivating factors in bringing the ten thousand two days early.

'Do you want to know the outstanding balance, Owen?'

'Just over forty grand, I would imagine,' said Montignac.

'Forty thousand one hundred and fifty,' said Delfy. 'And if you can organise ten in a month I'm sure you can sort out the rest, which will mean you'll still be around next year to celebrate your twenty-seventh birthday.'

'Don't worry,' said Montignac, draining his glass. 'I'll sort it. It won't come to that.'

'Then I thank you for your time and will wish you goodnight, Owen,' said Delfy, reaching across and shaking his hand as if this had been a perfectly friendly business meeting and not a potentially fatal one. Montignac nodded, stood up and left.

He considered his options as he left the club. He had four thousand one hundred pounds left, plus almost six hundred in personal savings, and of course there was

Gareth's thousand which he wouldn't need where he was going. That made almost six thousand. Nowhere near enough. He hoped that Keaton had not been joking when he'd suggested that he might have another scheme for him to be involved in.

As things turned out, he only had to wait until the following lunchtime to hear from him again.

10

Gareth Bentley arrived at the Threadbare at seven o'clock precisely, just as Montignac had told him to.

'Perfectly punctual,' said Montignac with a smile as he let him in.

'I was delighted when you phoned,' said Gareth. 'I was starting to worry.'

'Worry? About what?'

'Well it's just that you told me not to contact you. You said you'd be in touch. But then I hadn't heard from you and it had been almost a week since—'

'Shh, Gareth,' said Montignac. 'Let's not talk about it here. Let me just go and grab my jacket and I'll take you out for dinner and then I may have something to give you at the end of it.'

Gareth gave a sigh of relief. His biggest worry was that he would arrive at the Threadbare Gallery to find the place closed up and Montignac disappeared to places unknown with his money. But not only was he still there but he seemed to be in an uncommonly good mood and in possession of the payment. Immediately his mind was set at ease and the dreams he had been imagining over the past few days danced before his eyes again; he felt uncommonly happy.

'You got it then?' he asked.

'Got it?'

'The money, of course.'

'Yes, I got it,' said Montignac with a laugh. 'You didn't doubt me, did you?'

'No, no, of course not,' said Gareth quickly. 'I just can't believe it was so easy, that's all. I was worried that—' Something caught his eye and he looked down at Montignac's shirt sleeve. 'Good God, Owen,' he said. 'Have you hurt yourself?'

Montignac stared at him in surprise. 'No,' he said. 'What do you mean?'

'But you're bleeding,' he said. 'Look at your arm.'

Montignac looked down and saw a thin line of blood, perhaps two inches long, running along the white sleeve and cursed himself for not collecting his jacket before answering the door. 'That's nothing,' he said. 'A slight accident with Jason and a frame cutter earlier.'

'Oh dear. Was he all right?'

'He'll live,' he replied quickly. 'Had to bandage him up and send him on his way. I'll have to throw this damn thing out, though, and it didn't come cheap either.'

Gareth nodded, accepting the explanation, and

waited while Montignac ran back upstairs to collect his jacket. He walked into the storeroom and looked around to make sure that he hadn't forgotten anything.

Lying on the ground, his arms tied behind his back, his legs bound together, his mouth covered with masking tape, lay the unconscious body of Raymond Davis, the young man who had had the temerity to propose marriage to Stella. Montignac leaned down and placed a hand against his chest; his breathing was perfectly normal.

'Right,' he said, running back downstairs having locked the storeroom door behind him. 'Let's go.'

They left the gallery and walked towards a pub near Piccadilly Circus where Montignac ordered two steak and kidney pies at the bar and brought a couple of pints of beer to the table.

'I better just have some water,' said Gareth, eyeing the glass nervously.

'Nonsense! We're celebrating, aren't we?'

'Yes, I know but—'

'Oh one won't kill you. Come on. Your very good health,' he added, raising his glass and holding it there. Gareth picked his up, torn between reluctance and desire, and they clinked glasses.

'And yours,' said Gareth, taking his first happy sip.

'Before you get even more anxious about it,' said Montignac, handing across a thick envelope. 'Here's your share. It's all there but don't open it in here, all right? You never know what kind of people are lurking around.'

'Thanks,' said Gareth gratefully, sticking the money in his inside pocket. 'You've seen the newspapers have carried articles about it every day?'

'Yes,' said Montignac. 'It's rather funny, isn't it?'

'I'll say. My mother says the London constabulary are in a state of constant bewilderment.'

'She's not far wrong.'

'Apparently the Clarion are going to be sued for the cost of the paintings.'

'Oh that's ridiculous,' said Montignac, dismissing the idea. 'The insurance will cover it.'

'Well they're not very happy.'

'No, I wouldn't imagine they would be. No one likes to be robbed. Here, let's have another drink.'

'Steady on, Owen,' said Gareth. 'I haven't finished this one yet.'

'Well drink quickly then, this is a celebration.'

Two more drinks arrived and Gareth finished his first in a couple of quick mouthfuls before bringing the second to his lips as well. He felt giddy with excitement and thrilled with the amount of money in his pocket; his nervousness about alcohol had disappeared as quickly as that first pint.

'So what's next?' asked Gareth.

'Next?'

'Yes. There must be other ways to make quick money like this. Haven't you got contacts?'

Montignac laughed. 'My dear Gareth,' he said. 'You must disabuse yourself of the notion that I am some sort of underworld operative. Opportunities like the Cézanne job don't come along very often, you know.'

'Oh,' said Gareth, disappointed, for he had imagined earning a thousand pounds a week and had already put it to good use in his mind.

'Well that's not to say there won't be others. You're a valuable part of my plans, you know, Gareth. In fact I wouldn't be able to imagine the next few months without you being part of them.'

'Is that so?' he asked, brightening up. 'So I should just wait to hear from you then?'

'Oh no,' said Montignac, shaking his head. 'That would look far too suspicious. I'll give you a regular job in the gallery to begin with and we'll see what comes along. I was looking for a way to get rid of Jason anyway. He's a liability. Not half as much use to me as you.'

'I wouldn't want to put him out of a job,' said Gareth.

'That's not for you to worry about.'

'No, but . . .' He frowned slightly, wondering how to phrase this best. 'I can't tell you what all this means to me, Owen,' he said.

'All what?'

'All this. What you've done for me.'

'I'm not sure I've done very much,' said Montignac. 'Other than get you involved in a criminal conspiracy, that is.'

'Well no one got hurt, did they?' said Gareth,

justifying his actions. 'And, well you've given me some focus in my life. Something I was missing before.'

Montignac nodded. He took a sip from his own drink, uncomfortable with the confidential tone that Gareth had adopted.

'I know we haven't known each other very long,' he continued, his voice betraying a little nervousness. 'But I have to say I'm glad I met you.'

'As am I. Now should we order some more drinks?'

'I could tell the night I first laid eyes on you,' he said, refusing to be put off. 'The night of my birthday. I knew when I looked at you that you were someone who could help me achieve something. Someone who could break me out of the . . . out of the soul-destroying lethargy that my life had become. Do you realize that, Owen? Do you realize how much you've done for me? How you've changed things for me?'

Montignac looked away and shook his head; he didn't want to hear this. 'You're responsible for your own actions,' he muttered, unhappy to be the focus of so much undeserved adoration.

'I know I am. But you've shown me the way. I really . . .' He laughed and his hands curled into fists on the table top. 'I really want to tell you, Owen, how much I admire you. How much I respect you. You . . . you're a person I—'

'Barman!' Montignac called out before another embarrassing word could be uttered, raising his hand and pointing at the glasses. 'Two more of these please.'

'My God, Owen, you're going at a pace tonight, aren't you?' Gareth asked nervously as more beer and whiskies arrived; he seemed to have snapped out of his dreadful speech and was preparing to embarrass himself no further. 'I'll be drunk within an hour at this rate.'

'And when was the last time you had a thousand pounds burning a hole in your pocket?' Montignac asked. 'Let's make it a night to remember, what do you say?'

Gareth hesitated, knowing what a bad idea it was for him to drink, especially to excess like this but shrugged it off, putting his fears to the back of his mind. He would be sober from tomorrow, he decided. Sober, rich and employed, with a great future ahead of him. A great future and a great friend. He lifted his glass and held it in the air.

'To the future,' he said.

'The future,' said Montignac. 'May it bring everything we deserve and more.'

Two mornings later, Montignac rose early in the hotel room he had taken the night before and felt a mixture of relief and anticipation. Relief that the murderous hangover of the previous day had finally abated overnight. Anticipation that the morning's newspaper would bring the news he was hoping for. The clarification of where things stood. He shaved quickly but carefully and took a quick bath, dressed exactly as he always would for work, and left the hotel, walking without haste to a corner shop a few streets away. There he purchased a copy of *The Times* and used all the willpower he could summon not to look at the front page until he was back in his room with the door firmly locked behind him, sure of his privacy.

He laid the newspaper out on the desk and the headline jumped out at him immediately; he gasped in a mixture of excitement and panic at the sudden truth of it. The fact that he had actually gone through with the plan and things were starting to work out already.

Judge's Son In Murder Probe

said the headline in large font across the top of the page. Montignac settled into the chair and read the opening paragraphs quickly:

> The son of a prominent High Court judge was arrested yesterday in connection with the murder of horticulturalist Raymond Davis. Gareth Bentley (24), a recently graduated student barrister, was taken into custody after the body of Davies (28), his head apparently beaten in with a candlestick, was found at a flat where the accused was staying. Bentley is the son of Sir Roderick Bentley KC, best known for presiding over the trial this year of Henry Domson, third cousin to His Majesty King Edward VIII; the judge was both criticized and praised in equal measure for sentencing Domson to death after his conviction for the murder of a policeman. With his own son standing accused of a similar

crime and facing the same punishment, Bentley was unavailable for comment yesterday evening. The victim, Mr Davis, a fellow of the Royal Horticultural Society, was rushed to Charing Cross Hospital within minutes of his discovery but was declared dead on arrival. His family were being contacted last night.

Montignac set the paper down and closed his eyes for a moment, breathing heavily. He held his hand out flat in the air and was pleased to see that it sat there perfectly still, not a nervous flicker in sight.

Chapter 5

1

THE ONLY THING that made it even slightly bearable was that they had finally moved him to his own cell. During those first three days when he had barely been able to remember his own name let alone piece together what had happened on the night in question, Gareth had been kept in a cell with two other prisoners, both of whom were considerably older than him, and he had crouched quietly in the lower bunk, terrified and filled with horror at what he had been accused of. The rough stone walls felt perpetually damp to his touch, despite the fact that no water appeared to be seeping through.

His two cell-mates had kept themselves to themselves for the most part but viewed him with suspicion as he spoke with a more upper-class accent than they did and yet was being held on a more serious charge. But their very presence had offended him; the dry, stale stink of them, the language they used, the casual threats of violence they threw at each other, the sound of their snores and breathing while he lay there, unable to sleep.

Taken with thirty other prisoners for an hour's exercise in the courtyard the previous afternoon, word had quickly spread that he was the son of Mr Justice Bentley, a man who had been responsible for the incarceration of more than a few of them, and he had been set upon when the warders' backs were turned. Boots had been kicked into his ribs, fists flung into his face. The afternoon was spent in the luxury of the hospital wing and from there he had been brought back downstairs in the evening time where his reward for suffering a beating had been to be given a cell of his own; nothing would have persuaded him to have taken that beating back.

The room wasn't very big, no more than twelve feet by fifteen, and held a cot, a chair, a small table and an open toilet, but when the door was locked the sense of relief he felt at being left alone outweighed the feeling of panic at being locked up in there in the first place. The cell smelled of disinfectant and the sheets of cheap soap powder; he stank of dried-in perspiration and fear.

It had been almost a week since he'd woken up in a strange bed in a strange flat, that familiar thumping behind his eyes threatening to lay waste to his brain at any moment, and cursed himself for getting drunk yet again. So many times he had promised himself that he would not succumb to it and for long periods he managed to resist quite successfully but then there was always a slip. Something happened that made him feel that it could only be celebrated by alcohol, and the first always led to another and a third and then oblivion. He could remember almost nothing about the night before and tried to recall how he had got there. The last thing he could remember for sure was turning up at the Threadbare Gallery to see Owen Montignac and the fact that they had gone for dinner where he had started drinking copious amounts. But everything after that was a blank.

He shifted in the bed and glanced beneath dark covers. He was almost fully dressed but he'd managed to kick his shoes off and loosen his belt before falling asleep. His tongue was stuck to the roof of his mouth; he felt desperately in need of a glass of ice-cold water.

'Hello?' he grunted, turning his head slowly to look around the bedroom as he tried to make sense of things. It was a very tidy room, with no clothes lying around as there were in his own bedroom at home. The wardrobe door was closed and a dressing table in the corner seemed to be very neatly maintained. To the left of the window there was a print he recognized of a painting by Claude Monet. A girl in a white dress with a parasol standing in front of a tree as the sun beat down on her. Other than that, there was nothing in the room of any familiarity to him at all and he couldn't understand where he was or how he had arrived there. 'Hello?' he called out again but there was no response.

And then the noises started.

He lay in the bed and didn't think much of it at first as what sounded like two cars pulled up noisily on the street outside. Then there was the sound of people rushing up the path towards the front door and a loud banging.

'Police,' shouted one of the voices from outside. 'Open up!'

He frowned and closed his eyes, hoping he could either fall asleep again or the noises would go away. He didn't know what neighbourhood he'd ended up in last night but wished he was at home in Tavistock Square.

Footsteps from downstairs in the hallway ran towards the door and opened it and the sound of frantic conversation from the floor beneath drifted up the stairs but he couldn't quite make out what was being said; however by the tone of the voices it occurred to him that the door of whatever flat he was in must have been left slightly open. Feeling a sudden movement of unexpected panic he sat up in the bed, putting a hand to his forehead as the hangover kicked into life, and groaned, turning a little sideways as he thought he might suddenly throw up. But something inside him told him it was important to get outside and close that door as quickly as possible so he twisted in the bed and got out, climbing unsteadily to his feet as his aching body and thumping head competed with each other to see which could cause him the most pain. Standing up with the light streaming through the slightly parted curtains he looked down at himself for a moment and his mouth fell open in surprise.

His clothes were covered in blood.

'Good God,' he said, teetering slightly, worried that he would fall over. He pulled at his shirt in fright, ripping it open to discover where he had been injured but his skin beneath was perfectly smooth and showed no signs of distress. There was a mirror in the corner and he examined his face in it but, with the exception of dried, streaked daubs of blood on it too, he did not appear to have cut himself. Quickly he realized that the blood was not his own, was merely on his clothes, but the whole thing made no sense and filled him with a sense of dread, a feeling that only increased as the footsteps began to charge up the stairs outside. Without knowing why, he knew it was important to get into the next room and close that door before the police made it any further.

He turned and lunged for the doorway, stepping outside to see the rest of the unfamiliar flat, and nothing there made any sense. It looked like a place that was normally kept well ordered but had recently been unsettled by someone. Bookcases were knocked over, a vase of flowers from a writing bureau had crashed to the floor, leaving the porcelain in shards and the flowers crushed. But all of this was nothing compared to what lay on the floor between him and the half-open door: the body of a man, his skull crushed, the congealed blood on his forehead turning black and stiff as he lay there, one eye open, staring up at Gareth in horror.

Gareth gripped the doorframe to the bedroom, unable at first to process what he was seeing. The whole thing was like some ghastly, surreal nightmare. An unfamiliar flat, blood everywhere including all over himself, a dead body of a complete stranger at his feet. He narrowed his eyes, unable to look away from the ghastly sight. Blinking suddenly, snapping back into life, he understood the scene that was before him and looked across at the half-open door, his body lunging forwards to kick it shut just as the policemen appeared in the hallway outside. Everyone froze for a moment, staring at each other, before the first policeman kicked the door fully open, sending him tumbling backwards towards the wall behind him, his hands outstretched before him in self-defence, the sight of the corpse on the ground and the bloodied individual shouting at them causing everyone to hesitate now, to stand still and take in the gruesome nature of the scene, before two of the policemen rushed forwards to grab him. With a rare sense of self-preservation he pushed forwards, thinking that if he could only get to the door, and through it and down the stairs and out on to the street – whatever street this might be – then he could run and run before they could identify him, run all the way home, back to Tavistock Square, and crawl into his own comfortable bed in his warm house and wake up in an hour's time, shivering at the memory of the nightmare that had seemed so vivid and real at the time but would already by then be dissolving from his mind.

The policeman caught him as he jumped forwards and he yelled out in fright as they pushed him to the floor. For a moment they lost their footing in the struggle and he landed directly on top of the corpse with his face pressed down only inches away from the horrible gaping hole in the dead man's head and he found his voice then and started screaming, a piercing scream that ran through the house, as the policemen lifted him again and pushed him against a wall and then there was a sensation like the world coming to an end and he sank to his knees as everything went black.

When he came to a little later it didn't take any time for him to remember what had happened. The hangover was still there but was being complemented now by a pounding on the back of his head where one of the policemen's truncheons had connected with him, and he knew that this was no nightmare. That whatever had happened was no dream.

He found himself in the back of a police van now, the type with one barred window on either side, and he stood up and gripped the poles as it pulled away from the kerb. He noticed two things as the van drove away. The first was the man's body, covered now in a sheet, being carried from the house on a stretcher to a waiting ambulance while spectators gathered on the pavement to watch, glancing from the dead body with pity to the young man in the van with disgust and back again. The second was the sign on the corner of the building which told him exactly where he was: Bedford Place.

A key turned now in the lock of his cell and he shunted back on the bed, pushing his back to the wall. The knowledge that no one could come through and injure him here was as nothing compared to the horror of being here in the first place. He had barely been able to speak or comprehend what had happened since he had arrived there.

'Hello, Bentley,' said the warder, stepping inside with a tray carrying quite a decent breakfast. Ham and eggs. Toast. A pot of tea. Not at all the kind of mush he would have expected to be served from the traditional fictional accounts of prisons he had read. 'How are you feeling today?'

'When am I going to see my parents?' asked Gareth. The warder gave a small laugh but he didn't mean it unkindly.

'Do you know,' he said. 'It's the funniest thing. I have a son about your age and he gives me a hell of a time, he really does. He never listens to a word I say, and anything I tell him to do he'll go and do the opposite, just to spite me I think. And all you young people are the same, it seems to me. You all want to think you're big men on your own but every one of you that gets into trouble and lands in here with me, you always end up asking the same question: *When am I going to see my parents?* It's nice to know we're good for something anyway.'

Gareth kept his face steady and didn't move from the bed. He didn't want to be looked at or touched or spoken to. He just wanted an answer. The warder sighed.

'I don't know,' he said finally. 'I'm sure it's all being arranged through your solicitor.'

'It's been three days since I've seen them. When are they coming back? I haven't seen anyone since then.'

'Well that's not true, is it?' said the warder. 'You've seen the inspector, haven't you? Wasn't he the one who arraigned you?'

'Arraigned me?'

'Told you the charges you were facing.'

'Yes,' said Gareth. 'He said I murdered someone. Someone I don't even know. Why would I do that?' he asked pleadingly, as if the warder would see the sincerity of his words, realize the terrible mistake that had been made and release him without any further trouble. 'Why would I kill someone I don't even know?'

'No point asking me, sunshine,' said the warder with a friendly shrug as he went back to the door. 'I'm not much more than a glorified waiter around here. Enjoy your breakfast.'

He pulled the door shut and it sealed heavily, like a bank vault, but Gareth found he still couldn't move. He was starving, he hadn't eaten in almost twenty-four hours, and the food both smelled and looked good but it was on the other side of the cell and the idea of stepping off the bed, unravelling himself from his coarse blanket and giving himself up to the room, was impossible for him, as if the floor beneath his feet was shark-infested waters.

What happened to me? he asked himself, feeling the tears start to build up behind his eyes again and not for the first time over the past six days. *How did I end up in here?*

2

While Gareth Bentley was staring across his prison cell at his breakfast growing cold, Annie Daly was standing in the kitchen at Leyville preparing an extravagant breakfast with an air of worry and disappointment. Dismissed from her full-time position almost three months earlier after Peter Montignac had died, she had been struggling to make ends meet on the part-time hours that she had been offered ever since. The news that Stella was about to marry Raymond Davis and live at Leyville had been very welcome to her as she thought they might go back to needing a full-time cook then, especially when children came, but now that that was no longer a possibility she began to think about whether she would have to leave the house entirely. She was too old, she decided, to start all over again. Too old and too tired.

'Good morning, Annie,' said Margaret Richmond, entering the kitchen and sniffing the air judgementally as she noticed an unwelcome smell. 'You weren't smoking a cigarette in here, were you?' she asked.

'No, Miss Richmond,' said Annie, who had put her cigarette out only a few minutes earlier. 'That was one of the delivery boys from the village as came up with the groceries. I told him to put it out, of course.'

Margaret nodded, not believing a word of it, but unwilling to engage in an argument at this time of day.

'There's fresh tea in the pot there if you want some,' said Annie, nodding towards the table and Margaret poured herself a cup and sat down by the bay window, looking out at the garden.

'Such a beautiful morning,' she said, lost in thought. The outside world seemed so calm to her in comparison to the things that were going on elsewhere.

'Will Miss Stella be coming downstairs for her breakfast this morning then?' asked Annie.

'No, I don't think so, Annie. I'll bring it up to her when it's ready.'

Annie nodded. 'You know she can't stay locked away up there for ever,' she said finally, after considering whether she should say anything or not. 'It's not healthy for a person. When my George died, I wanted to do the exact same thing but I told myself to snap out of it and get on with life. It's the only thing you can do.'

'I hardly think the loss of a favourite labrador can compare to losing a fiancé,' said Margaret with a sigh. 'Particularly when barely three months have gone by since she lost her father. The whole thing's been a terrible shock to her.'

'Well I'm just saying,' said Annie, a little offended. 'Mourning's important, of course it is. But she's still young. She'll meet someone better. And I'm sure Mr Davis was a very nice chap, at least he was always polite to me when we met, but I don't hold with a man that takes that much interest in flowers. It can't be healthy, can it?'

Margaret was barely listening but she shrugged her shoulders and looked away in the hope that Annie would stop talking for a moment. She too had often been surprised by Stella's choice of Raymond Davis; not because of his passion for horticulture but because he was never a particularly exciting or spontaneous fellow and that, Margaret had always believed, would have been what Stella looked for in a husband. She had broached the subject once in an indirect way but Stella had rebuked her, saying that Margaret didn't know Raymond like she did, that his decency and kindness were what attracted her to him, and besides hadn't she had enough excitement in love for one lifetime, enough disappointment, a statement that had silenced Margaret on the subject entirely.

She had been the unlucky person who had had to deliver the news of his death to Stella three days earlier. A policeman had phoned from London and told her what had happened and she had to sit down to take it in. The violence of it. The horror. Stella was buying some groceries in the village at the time and could see by Margaret's expression when she returned that something had happened.

'What is it?' she asked, coming towards her, seeing Margaret standing there pale and wringing her hands as she always did when she had bad news to deliver. 'Goodness, you're as pale as a ghost, Margaret. What's happened?'

'You'd better sit down,' said Margaret, leading her to the table.

'Just tell me,' said Stella, taking her hands, not wanting to be left in the dark for any longer than was necessary. 'Something's happened to him, hasn't it?'

Margaret nodded slowly. She had spent the best part of the previous hour trying to find the right words to use at this moment. It was bad enough breaking the news to someone that a loved one had passed away, trying to phrase it so slowly and peacefully that by the time the unhappy truth was revealed the listener might feel that it was a peaceful end. But a situation like this, a murder . . . there was no good way to phrase it. There were no suitable words at all. The best thing was to stay quiet and let her piece it together for herself.

'He's dead, isn't he?' asked Stella after a moment, her face blank.

'Margaret nodded again. 'I'm so sorry, Stella,' she said. 'There was a phone call. While you were out. The police. It's terrible news.'

Stella looked away and seemed to be struggling with her breath for a moment. As a child she had had a tendency towards asthma but it was an affliction she had grown out of; Margaret hadn't heard her breathing like this since she was very young, and worried for her.

'Try to stay calm, Stella,' she said, rubbing her back. 'Breathe slowly.'

Stella's body seemed to crumble where she sat and she buried her face in her hands. 'But how?' she asked finally, trembling, holding back the tears for now. 'How did it happen?'

'They're not sure yet,' said Margaret. 'They weren't able to tell me very much. I'm afraid you're going to have to be very strong when I tell you.'

Stella looked across again; in her mind she knew she could not afford to fall apart until she had heard all the details. Then and only then could she face her loss. 'Go on,' she said.

'I'm afraid . . .' began Margaret, at a loss as to how to explain such a terrible thing. 'I have to tell you that he was murdered,' she said.

'Murdered?' asked Stella, gasping, feeling her stomach turn in revulsion. 'How? Why? Who did it?'

'They're very unclear about things right now. It's a bit of a mystery. We'll probably have to go to London to find out more. They were able to contact Owen, thankfully, and—'

'What?' asked Stella, who had turned away from

Margaret as she faced the full horror of what she was saying. 'What did you just say?'

'The police,' explained Margaret. 'They contacted Owen and he identified the body and—'

'He . . . ?' Stella stared at her, her mind swimming, as if the whole thing was an enormous puzzle that she couldn't understand. 'Owen identified . . . ?' She stopped and considered it. 'It's not Owen then who—'

'Apparently Raymond came around to visit Owen,' continued Margaret. 'But he wasn't in. He'd gone out for the evening with some friends and a colleague of his from the gallery was staying overnight in his flat. The fellow was drunk, it seems, and Raymond showed up and—'

'Raymond,' said Stella with a sigh, closing her eyes and keeping them sealed for the best part of a minute as she tried to shift her emotions from where they had been a moment before to where they had to rest now. 'Raymond's dead,' she said quietly.

'I'm so sorry, Stella,' said Margaret.

The story had come together in the days in between. Owen Montignac had hired a young man named Gareth Bentley to work with him in the gallery. He'd been doing a good job so they went out one evening for dinner and, according to Montignac, Gareth got so inebriated and so quickly that he gave him the keys to his flat on Bedford Place and sent him there in a taxicab to sleep it off. In the meantime Montignac met up with some other friends and was in their company for the entire rest of the night, leaving their home at eight o'clock the following morning and heading straight for the gallery, which he opened up and where he stayed until the police called on him later in the day.

Montignac went with them to examine the body and identified it as Raymond Davis, a young horticulturalist engaged to marry his cousin. He must have come round to see Montignac in the night, the police deduced, and when the drunken Bentley found him there a fight ensued, leading to the vicious death. Bentley, of course, was claiming his innocence but also maintaining that he could remember nothing of the night before due to the amount of alcohol he had taken. In the circumstances it wasn't a very satisfying alibi, particularly since not only did it not seem to be an accident, but the fellow's brains had been smashed in by a candlestick in a particularly brutal way.

Stella had taken to her bed then but, Margaret noted, she had cried very little. Instead a great sadness seemed to descend on her and she just lay there. She had managed to keep herself composed during the funeral but had come straight back to Leyville afterwards, not even attending the wake, a formality which she said she hated.

'There we are,' said Annie, serving up the breakfast on to a plate. 'I put in a couple of extra eggs for her too. See if she can't build her strength up. Wait there till I fetch the tea.'

'Thank you, Annie,' said Margaret standing up. 'I think I'll encourage her to get up after breakfast.'

'Quite right too. All this lazing around is no good for anyone.'

'No.'

'I don't suppose you know,' began Annie after a polite hesitation. 'Whether Miss Stella will be staying full-time at Leyville from now on?'

Margaret frowned. 'I expect so,' she said. 'Why? Where else would she go?'

'Well no, I didn't mean that,' said Annie. 'Just with her not getting married after all. She's not going to up sticks and head off to London to Mr Owen's, is she?'

'I think that's the last place she'd want to be right now, don't you? After everything that's happened.'

'I just need to know for my own situation,' explained Annie. 'If there's not going to be the work—'

'Oh please, Annie,' said Margaret in frustration, reaching down for the tray as Annie placed tea on it. 'Can we not have this conversation just now? All I can think about is Stella for the moment, I can't be expected to worry about everyone else's rotas. You'll get paid if that's what you're worried about.'

'That's not what I'm worried about,' said Annie angrily. 'And there's no need to be so rude.'

'I wasn't being rude,' said Margaret in an exhausted tone. She sighed. 'Look, if you're really that concerned I can have a word with Stella when the moment's right and find out exactly what her plans are.'

'If that wouldn't be putting you to too much trouble,' said Annie archly.

'Fine then,' Margaret said, leaving the room. 'I'll speak to her about it as soon as possible.'

She left with the tray and made for the staircase. The atmosphere was so gloomy that it threatened to overpower her but she understood only too well the worry that Annie was feeling. They had had so much death in this house, she considered, and even now, when there was the chance of a marriage and children, of a happy event, it had been stolen away. As she left, she clutched the tray so tightly in her hands that she could feel a painful sensation in her bones.

3

Montignac took the keys and wallet from his pockets and laid them in the tray, moved against the wall and stretched his arms out wide while the warder patted him down for any contraband materials that he might be smuggling in. Passing inspection, he followed the other visitors down the long, cold corridor and shivered slightly with the uncomfortable sensation that comes from being in a prison. Of all the places in the world where he would not have wanted to go by his own choice, this was at the top of the list.

He glanced at the other visitors and couldn't help but feel superior and out of place among them. They were, for the most part, a lower class of person, dressed in cheap clothes, the women with stringy hair, the men who hadn't even bothered to shave or put on a tie; those who had looked like they wore the same suit every day of their lives, from morning till night. The corridor itself smelled of disinfectant and the stone floor, walls and ceilings could scarcely have made the place seem less welcoming.

At the end of the corridor they turned left and were escorted into a large room where small tables and plastic chairs stood at regular distances from each other and his fellow visitors started to scatter hesitantly in different directions as they spotted their loved ones. Montignac looked around the room slowly and finally found his prey sitting in a corner, at the most distant table, and walked towards him.

'Hello, Gareth,' he said, sitting down.

'Owen,' he replied, his voice betraying enormous amounts of relief. 'I'm so grateful that you came. I didn't know whether you would or not.'

'Of course I would come if you wanted me to,' he said with some concern. 'How are you anyway? Gareth laughed and shrugged his shoulders as if to suggest that the answer was obviously. 'I must admit I was surprised that you wanted to see me,' continued Montignac after a moment. 'But I was intrigued.'

He looked across the table and tried not to give away the fact that his appearance was harrowing. Although he had hardly been overweight before, he had lost a good ten pounds since being incarcerated and his skin was a pale, waxy colour. His hair had been cut quite short and he hadn't shaved for a couple of days; the stubble was irregular, thick around the chin but straggly and inconsistent about the cheeks and throat. The youthful good looks that he had sported were starting to fade at an incredible rate, the effect, Montignac believed, of an altogether too comfortable life having been suddenly destroyed. To his surprise, Gareth was smoking a cigarette, something he couldn't remember him ever doing before.

'This whole thing . . .' began Gareth nervously, looking around to make sure that he wasn't being overheard. 'This whole thing is a tremendous mistake.'

'Is it indeed?'

'Of course it is,' he said, faltering, 'I don't know how it happened. It . . . it must have been a terrible accident.'

Montignac sighed and sat back in his chair. He noticed that there was the faintest hint of trembling in Gareth's fingers as he put the cigarette between his lips and drew on it inexpertly, like a schoolboy having his first drag. He sucked in the nicotine too deeply and held it in his mouth too long but somehow managed to control his coughing.

'Why don't you tell me what you remember?' asked Montignac. 'From the beginning.'

'Well that's just it,' said Gareth. 'I don't remember anything much from that night so I don't know what to say. Everyone keeps asking me but what can I tell them? I remember going to the Threadbare to meet you, and I remember you suggesting that we go and have some dinner and we went to the pub at the end of the road—'

'You drank an awful lot there, Gareth,' he said, interrupting him. 'I couldn't get you to stop. I've never seen someone get through so much alcohol in so short a time.'

'I've done that before,' said Gareth sadly. 'I should have learned my lesson. Alcohol and me . . . well we don't mix. I black out, I get violent—'

'Apparently.'

'But I've never done anything like this before. Nothing even approaching this. You have to believe me, Owen.'

'I tried to stop you,' protested Montignac. 'I said you should either slow down or stick to water but you got quite aggressive then.'

'I did?'

'Well, yes,' he replied apologetically. 'You said you weren't a child, you told me that I wasn't your father and if you couldn't celebrate earning a thousand pounds, well what was the fun of life anyway?'

Gareth shook his head and then placed it in his hands, bereft now. 'I'm so sorry,' he said. 'I should have listened to you. But once I start, it seems that there's no stopping me.'

Montignac sighed and looked around. He noticed the way that all the guards who were either standing by the walls or parading between the tables looked directly ahead of themselves all the time, as if they didn't want anyone to think that they were evesdropping on conversations, but something about the way they held themselves implied to him that they could hear every word that was being said and were ready to interject if any trouble broke out.

'You have to understand,' said Montignac, leaning forwards a little and lowering his voice. 'This is very difficult for me. Being here, I mean. After all, Raymond . . . well he was engaged to my cousin. And Stella's like a sister to me.'

'I know that, Owen, and I'm so sorry. Did you know him well?'

'I knew him a little. He was a sterling chap.'

Gareth bowed his head, biting his lip in regret. 'I don't even remember him coming round. For that matter I don't even remember arriving at your flat.'

'I gave the taxi driver my address,' said Montignac. 'He's since spoken to the police to confirm that,' he added quickly.

'But why didn't you come with me? Why did you leave me on my own?'

'For heaven's sake, man, it was barely half past nine and you were on another planet of drunkenness. I hadn't been drinking very much at all and I wanted to celebrate too. That was the plan, for both of us. I didn't want to call it a night yet. I never suspected that . . . well, anything like this might happen. Do you think I'd have left you alone if I had? In fact I was trying to do you a favour. I knew that if you went home to Tavistock

Square in that condition, there'd be hell to pay. I figured I'd never see you again, that you'd be locked up in your father's chambers until your retirement party forty years from now. So I sent you off to Bedford Place and met up with some friends myself. I was with them all night. In fact it got so late that I stayed with one of them and then went straight from there into work the next morning. It was only that afternoon that the police came to see me.'

'The whole thing has been an absolute nightmare,' said Gareth. 'I woke up . . . I didn't know where I was . . .'

'Well it's not exactly been a barrel of laughs for me either,' hissed Montignac, looking around to check the position of the guards. 'For pity's sake, Gareth, how could you just throw your life away like that? You know people are saying you're going to swing for this?'

Gareth let out a low groan, a sound of such pain and agony that it might have come from an animal that needed to be put down.

'Are you sure you didn't know Raymond Davis?' he asked after a moment.

'Of course I'm sure,' said Gareth. 'How could I have known him? I'm not a horticulturist and that's what he was, right? I've never been to the RHS or Kew Gardens or any of those places. They don't interest me. And why would I want to kill him anyway? I have no motive.'

'Well I don't know, but that's what the police are trying to find out. And the newspapers.'

'The newspapers are on to the story?' he asked,

looking up with tears in his eyes; he had had no access to the papers in jail, despite the fact that he had asked for them on a daily basis.

'Of course they are,' said Montignac with a gentle laugh, as if the whole thing was entirely obvious. 'Remember who your father is, after all. Remember how he sentenced that fellow to die earlier in the year when everyone said that his connections would get him off, but your father said no, the law's the law. Well that's coming back to haunt him now. Now they're all using his words and throwing them right back in his face. They're saying that just because it'll be his son in the dock he can't turn around and say—'

'But I didn't do it!' protested Gareth.

'Oh for heaven's sake. You were found alone with Raymond's dead body, covered in his blood, alone in the flat, and your fingerprints were all over the candlestick. The evidence is damning.'

'Well if I did do it,' said Gareth, looking lost and shaking his head from side to side even as he verbally accepted the possibility of guilt. 'Then I certainly didn't mean to.'

'Well that's not much use to Raymond Davis,' said Montignac. 'Now is it?'

'No, of course not, but—'

'Nor is it of any comfort to my cousin, who's been devastated by this. You know she lost her father earlier in the year?'

Gareth looked around in despair and as he did so, he

caught the eye of one of his fellow inmates who gave him a salacious, gap-toothed grin.

'I hope she knows how very sorry I am.'

'I very much doubt that she cares.'

'Owen, you've got to help me,' he said, leaning forwards and trying to grab the other man's hand. Montignac recoiled instantly. He could see the filthy nails and wondered when he'd last dared to wash. The last thing he wanted was to be touched by him; he began to wonder why he'd even come here but then remembered. It was to find out exactly how little Gareth remembered from the night of Raymond Davis's death and the interview had proved a very satisfactory one so far. 'You've got to help me get out of here,' he repeated quickly.

'Me?' asked Montignac. 'What on earth can I do? Stage some sort of prison break? Smuggle a file inside a cake?'

'Well you can tell them what you know,' he said. 'That I'm . . . that I'm a good person. That I would never—'

'Gareth, listen to me,' said Montignac, adopting a more sympathetic voice now; it was clear that the younger man was in absolute torture and it gave him no pleasure to witness this. 'I can see that you're in pain here but I have no doubt that you're filled with remorse. But let's be honest; I don't really know you.'

'But we're friends, aren't we?'

'I . . .' Montignac looked away in despair; he could feel Gareth's eyes burning into him, could sense his longing to believe that theirs was a friendship that superseded all other loyalties or responsibilities. 'We haven't known each other very long,' he said finally, regretting having come here at all now. 'Even if I did have any influence, which I don't, how on earth could I possibly be a character witness for you when—'

'But we worked so well together. All that business with the Cézanne paintings,' he added, lowering his voice at the risk of being overheard. 'I was loyal to you during that, wasn't I? I did a good job?'

Montignac laughed and shook his head. 'Gareth, we broke the law when we did that. You do understand that, don't you? You can't turn around and tell them that you were a part of that little misadventure; it would only make things worse for you. And I can hardly say, "Oh yes, Your Honour, he's a good fellow; when we stole all those paintings he kept his mouth shut and never let on to anyone. He had a real future in crime, please don't send him away now. What a promising career you'd be ruining." '

'Of course not, that's not what I meant,' said Gareth angrily. 'But we could work together again maybe if I could just get out of here. I was useful to you, wasn't I? Please, Owen, somehow I feel you're the only one who can help me. My God, you don't want to see me rotting away in here, do you? Or . . . or being hanged for this?'

'You leave me in a very difficult position,' said Montignac after a long silence. 'You have to understand that I love my cousin very much. We grew up together. We're like . . . well, she considers me to be like a brother to her. My first loyalty has to be to her. We're cousins, after all; how can I turn my back on my own cousin? What kind of man would that make me? If she even knew I'd accepted your invitation here today—'

'Owen, I'm begging you,' pleaded Gareth, starting to cry now. 'Please do something. I know you can help me. I don't know who else to turn to.'

'Surely your own father can do more for you now than I can,' he suggested. 'After all, if anyone has influence—'

'He's trying. He's hired a top barrister to defend me. But everything they do will be by the book. I need more than that.'

Montignac shook his head. The tears were flowing across the table now and he wanted nothing more than to make a run for it. 'Gareth, please stop. You'll make yourself ill.'

'Who cares if I'm ill?' he snapped, lunging forwards and trying to grab Montignac's hand again. 'Please, Owen, how many times can I say it? You have to help me. You have to find a way.'

Montignac breathed heavily through his nose and considered it. This was not what he had been expecting at all; he had never seen such devastation or such fear before. And he found that, despite everything, he rather liked Gareth. He failed to understand why he looked up to him so much, that misplaced devotion of his, but it was a rare and not entirely unwelcome form of self-approbation.

'I just don't know what I can do,' he said finally. 'If I could think of something . . .' he added, his words trailing off into quietness.

'You know what the strangest thing is?' asked Gareth finally.

'What?'

'The thousand pounds you gave me. Earlier that evening, my payment for the job we'd done—'

'Yes?'

'Well it wasn't on me when the police arrested me. And they never found it when they searched the flat.'

'That's strange,' said Montignac, remembering how, after stepping towards a terrified Raymond in the living room and bashing his brains in with the candlestick, his eyes had caught sight of the envelope on the ground and he'd taken it with him as he left. 'But for your sake, it's probably for the best. It would have been difficult for you to explain to the police what you were doing with so much money and at the scene of a crime too. They might have thought you'd stolen it from Raymond. It could only have hurt you, I think.'

'I suppose so,' he said. 'But that's gone now too. I must have left it in the taxicab. Or dropped it on the street. Can you imagine? After all that work, and it's just disappeared into thin air. It was all for nothing. Can you imagine if I'd never met you, Owen? How much different my life would have been?' Finally the prospect of being a pupil for Sir Quentin Lawrence KC did not seem so appalling.

Montignac stood up and pushed his chair back under the table.

'I'll do what I can for you, Gareth,' he said. 'Truly I will. I'm not sure what it is I can do but give me a chance. I know that you didn't mean to do it and I'll try to help you.'

'You will?' he asked, looking up hopefully. He reached forwards with both hands to take one of Montignac's in his, but Montignac pulled away, unwilling to be infected by his guilt.

'I promise,' he said. 'In the meantime, try to keep your spirits up.'

'Thank you, Owen,' said Gareth, his voice betraying breathless relief. 'I just know that if anyone can help me out of this it's you. You're the most ingenious person I've ever come across.' He gave a gentle laugh as if the entire thing was ridiculous. 'You're my best friend.' He said quietly.

Montignac felt his stomach sink a little and turned on his heels to leave. Once out in the corridor again he walked as fast as he could down the corridor, anxious to get out of the prison. The closer he got to the exit the more he found himself breaking into a stride, the more he found himself choking in its claustrophobic atmosphere. He hated it there. He could only imagine how it felt for Gareth being caged up between four walls for twenty-four hours a day. If it was him he would welcome the blessed relief of the hangman's noose.

Released back out on to the street he breathed in the

fresh air deeply and stood quietly for a few minutes, recovering his equanimity, before walking away. Gareth was exactly where he needed him to be and, more importantly, so was Raymond. But one thing that he himself had said in there came back into his mind now. *Surely your own father can do more for you now than I can.* It was always a possibility. But his new partner, Lord Keaton, had that matter in hand already, he knew. Still, it would be a good idea for them to talk, he decided, and to make sure that nothing could go wrong.

4

Sir Quentin Lawrence was a gruff but likeable barrister in his early sixties who had devoted his life to the law, had never married or fathered children during that time in case they came between him and his work, and had taken silk when he was only thirty-three years old. What had been a prodigious early career, however, had – for some inexplicable reason – failed to score many triumphs during its second half and he had maintained a stewardship of decent criminal trials, all the time waiting for one to come along which might connect his name to glory.

He had never quite forgiven Roderick Bentley for beating him to the position of head of chambers fifteen years earlier. The crucial partners' vote, which had seen him run against a rival and Roderick elected as a compromise candidate, had left a bitter taste in his mouth for a long time and he had considered it a long-overdue olive branch some months earlier when he had been asked to take Roderick's son Gareth in as a pupil, a position he was never destined to fill. As he sat in the living room at Tavistock Square it was hard for him not to dwell on how different things might have been had Gareth followed his father's advice and come with him to Newcastle for the fraud trial earlier in the year.

'Thank you,' said Quentin as Jane poured him a cup of tea and took a seat on the sofa opposite with her husband Roderick by her side.

'It's us who want to thank you,' said Jane anxiously. 'When Roderick said that you had agreed to represent Gareth, well it came as a tremendous relief to us both.'

'Did it?' asked Quentin, fishing for a compliment. 'How flattering.'

'Well Roderick has always said what a brilliant advocate you are. And of course you've been linked to so many high-profile cases.'

'Which is one of the unfortunate things we have to deal with here,' he said, resting the cup on the table as he removed a pad of paper from his briefcase to take a note. 'The newspapers are making quite a story out of this, aren't they?'

'Those bastards,' said Roderick bitterly, who rarely used language like this but was finding it increasingly difficult to maintain his temper in the face of the latest media onslaught. 'You know I thought we were through with all that nonsense after the Domson case ended. Reporters camping out on the doorstep, shouting at one as one leaves for work. The neighbours are up in arms of course. Again.'

'Really?' asked Quentin, who rather envied Roderick the celebrity his cases had brought him. 'I didn't notice any journalists or photographers outside as I arrived.'

'They seem to have given us a day off today,' said Jane in a relieved tone. 'There'll be a few around later, I dare-say. Or if I was to leave the house for any reason they'd just appear out of the bushes and start firing questions at me. They seem to know my habits better than I do myself.'

'Well you mustn't tell them anything,' said Quentin sternly. 'They won't report what you say anyway so it's best to stay silent.'

'I've told her that already,' said Roderick.

'And it goes for you too,' said Quentin, pointing a finger at his colleague. 'However much you feel like getting angry with them and telling them where to place their pads and pencils you must keep entirely silent.'

Roderick nodded. He knew full well what the appropriate way was to behave but found it difficult to maintain his composure with them screaming remarks at him about his son every time he set foot outside.

'Now,' said Quentin, poising his pen over his paper like a reporter himself. 'How about we begin by you telling me a little bit about Gareth.'

'The only thing you need to know,' said Jane, attempting

to sound as determined and unflappable as possible, 'is that he didn't do it.'

'Well yes,' said Quentin with a slight laugh. 'But I don't think we can convince the trial judge with that. I might need a little bit more.

'Who is it going to be anyway?' asked Roderick. 'Not Carter, I hope. We've never got along.'

'I believe it will be Patrick Sharpwell,' said Quentin, consulting his file. 'Do you know him?'

'A little,' said Roderick, who had spoken before him as a barrister on a few occasions and had never liked him; he had always struck him as being biased from the start. Neither a defence judge nor a prosecutor's darling, Roderick believed him to be one who simply picked a side at the start and stuck with it, regardless of the evidence. 'I don't know him very well but he's never been top of my list.'

'Oh he's perfectly reasonable,' said Quentin, dismissing this remark. 'I've argued before him myself on many occasions. He'll give us a fair crack of the whip, you can count on that. Of course one of the main problems facing us is the statement that your son gave to the police on the day of his arrest.'

'Yes, I've seen that,' said Roderick. 'It's not very helpful, is it?'

'Why?' asked Jane quickly, who had thus far been kept away from some of the more explicit evidence. 'What did he say?'

Quentin sighed and looked across at her. 'He was

either terribly foolish or terribly honest,' he explained. 'Throughout the whole thing, while they were quizzing him about what had taken place after he arrived at the Bedford Place flat he never once denied having killed Mr Davis.'

'Well of course he didn't kill him,' said Jane, as if the entire thing was beyond absurd. 'What possible reason would he have for harming the man anyway? He didn't even know him.'

'Yes, he's said that himself subsequently. But on that first morning and afternoon, while he was being questioned, it never seemed to occur to him to deny it. Instead he seems to have staked his initial defence on the fact that he couldn't remember what had happened the night before. Now that's not a very solid start for us because it implies that he was at least open to the possibility that he might have been involved in the . . .' He searched for the right word, not wanting to play it out too graphically in front of the boy's mother. 'In the incident,' he settled on eventually.

'I think he must have thought that no one would have suspected he had any involvement,' suggested Roderick. 'And therefore it didn't occur to him to focus on that aspect of it. That would make sense, wouldn't it? I mean who would even think that a young man such as Gareth—'

'Well you could argue that, I imagine,' said Quentin doubtfully. 'But under the same circumstances I daresay I would be protesting my innocence from the start.'

'It was the drink,' protested Jane. 'Gareth has always had difficulties with alcohol. It runs in the family. Roderick's father and grandfather were just as bad. How it skipped a generation with Roderick, I don't know.'

'Jane, I don't think we need to bring that up,' interrupted Roderick quickly, who hated to acknowledge this flaw in his lineage.

'And then the other problem we're facing,' said Quentin, 'is Gareth's general lack of stability in the world.'

'What do you mean?' asked Jane, anxious to defend her cub. 'Gareth is a wonderful boy. You don't even—'

'He hasn't held down a job since graduating. It seems he had been doing very little before taking a position at this . . . what was it called?' He consulted his notes. 'The Threadbare Gallery.'

'Yes, but that will count for something, won't it? That he had found suitable employment?'

'It's hard to say. He was only there for a very short while after all and seems to have had no specific responsibilities. The fact that he'd thrown in the career he'd studied for doesn't help. The idea that he would reject the law at all looks suspicious. Why on earth didn't he come and join us in chambers when you arranged it, Roderick?' he asked, as if he failed to understand why anyone would not choose such a path for themselves.

'I don't know,' Roderick replied. 'I think he was exhausted with the law by the time he finished his studies. Originally he just wanted to take a break and we said that was all right, there was no harm in him having a little time to himself, but then the weeks drifted into months, I was snowed under with the Domson case, there was just no easy way to take the matter in hand. But we were delighted when he went to work for Mr Montignac because—'

'Yes, Montignac,' said Quentin, consulting his notes again. 'That's something of a mixed blessing. If we could get him to give a character witness that would be a good thing. He's a very respectable fellow – I met with him myself a couple of days ago – and of course his name is one that will impress the judge and the jury. But on the other hand this Davis fellow was engaged to marry his cousin.'

'Yes I'd heard that,' said Roderick sadly. 'And I imagine he'll put the interests of his cousin first.'

'Well one would think that any decent human being with a sense of loyalty or a conscience would,' said Quentin. 'But when I spoke to him he did express the fact that he thought Gareth a very good sort. He found it hard to imagine that he would have done such a thing. But it's all very difficult for him. Not only is there the family connection but he had sent Gareth back to his flat that night, which is where the crime took place. All in all, I'm not sure that Montignac is going to be someone we can call on.'

'But if he would only say a word in his favour,' begged Jane, close to tears now. Quentin stared across at her; he had been able to tell immediately when he walked into the room just how difficult the last few weeks had been on her. She was quite clearly a beautiful woman but she was losing some of her sheen having to go through such a public trauma. There were dark bags forming under her eyes and he suspected she hadn't slept very well over the previous week.

'Well we'll have to wait and see,' said Quentin. 'But there is one other matter. Something I hesitate to bring up with you both but I daresay the prosecution will get hold of it too so . . .'

'Go on,' said Roderick, knowing exactly what was coming.

'It's this business back at Harrow,' he said, sounding almost apologetic for the intrusion.

'Oh not that again,' shouted Jane in frustration. 'That was all so long ago, I don't see what possible connection that can have—'

'It has a connection in that it can show a pattern of behaviour,' explained Quentin patiently. 'Particularly since it correlates directly with the events of the night of the murder. And if the prosecution get hold of it – which they undoubtedly will – they're sure to make hay. On the plus side, he wasn't expelled for his actions.'

'That was only through a lot of careful negotiation on my part,' admitted Roderick. 'It was extremely difficult in fact. One of the hardest cases I've ever fought. But to be fair to Gareth, the whole thing was an aberration. He never behaved like that either before or since.'

'Until now,' said Quentin.

'But he didn't do it now,' protested Jane.

Quentin nodded; he was accustomed to parents refusing to recognize that their young prodigies were capable of any wrongdoing but it was his job to find out the truth and employ it artfully before a jury. 'Can you tell me what happened there?' he asked finally, directing his question towards the boy's father.

'Well it's all such a long time ago,' said Roderick apologetically. 'It's difficult to remember exactly.'

'Try. You know that they will only ask about it at some point.'

Roderick sighed. 'The boys had been drinking,' he said. 'Not very much, I don't think, but perhaps Gareth had more than the others, I don't know. Either way it went directly to his head. He can't handle it, you see. My father had the same problem. Then there was some sort of altercation and a fight broke out.'

'From what I've been told he broke a boy's arm and dislocated his shoulder.'

'No,' said Roderick firmly. 'That was the crux of the matter. In the course of the ensuing fracas,' he said in a legalistic voice, 'one of the boy's arms became broken and his shoulder became displaced from its socket. But Gareth himself did not break it. Or rather, no one could prove he did.'

'He denied it, of course?'

'He couldn't remember. He'd had so much to drink that he blacked the whole incident out of his mind. It was late at night and when he woke to face the consequences the next day he couldn't remember anything about it. Of course the head wanted to send him down but I wasn't having that and fought his case staunchly. And then I made a hefty contribution to the school benevolent fund and the matter was finally dropped. He received a suspension but I promise you, Quentin, he never put a foot wrong again between then and now.'

'Then and now. The two bookends of when he has put a foot wrong, though,' said Quentin sadly. 'It's a terrible shame he didn't come to chambers, isn't it?' he asked brightly. 'He might have been my pupil now, rather than my client.'

'You will save him, won't you?' asked Jane anxiously, and for a moment he feared she was going to reach across and take his hand.

'I'll certainly do my best,' said Quentin. 'But it's a very difficult case.'

'Just so long as you know, I couldn't live without him,' she said fiercely. 'I wouldn't want to live without him.'

Roderick stared across at his wife and narrowed his eyes. It was almost as if he wasn't in the room, he felt. All her questions were now directed towards Quentin; all her faith was placed in him.

5

Montignac didn't often come to White's and he felt slightly self-conscious sitting there today. As much as he enjoyed the atmosphere of wealth and privilege that pervaded those luxurious rooms he felt like an outsider with his lowly salary, diminishing savings and enormous debts. White's, he felt, was a place one needed to earn the right to sit in, although he wondered how many others were there for having a reputation for wealth rather than actually being rich themselves; the place was like a dosshouse for the aristocratic homeless. Rather than roaming the streets, buying infinite cups of tea, or spending endless hours asleep in libraries pretending to read newspapers, they were granted access to a place where they could spend their afternoons perfectly comfortable with cigars, brandies and card games. Quite a few had been friends of Peter Montignac and when he had arrived a few minutes earlier some had glanced in his direction but looked away quickly rather than have to speak to him. Too many months had passed for it to be appropriate to offer any further condolences and it may have seemed somewhat ludicrous to them that suddenly there was another tragic death attached to the Montignac name, albeit at something of a distance.

'Owen,' said a voice from behind and he looked up as a man stood before him. 'It's Charles Richards. I hope you remember me.'

Montignac opened his mouth and tried to place him. He was an older gentleman, quite brutal looking, and so could have been no one other than a friend of his late uncle's. But there was more to it than that, a memory of their most recent encounter that he was trying to recall. It came to him then. He had been at the funeral earlier in the year and had cornered Montignac in the hallway as he was leaving, mumbling some claptrap about the eulogy he'd made, saying it was 'damn fine' or some such rubbish, that he didn't normally hold with the expression of emotion but that he'd been moved by what he'd said about his uncle and benefactor. It had been all Montignac could do to keep his temper.

'Of course I remember you,' he said, standing up to shake the older man's hand. 'We talked at my uncle's funeral.'

'That's right. Haven't seen you in here before, though. Are you a member?'

'Yes, but I'm afraid I'm kept so busy with work that I don't often get a chance to come here.'

'Oh I know what that's like. Retired now, of course. On your own, are you?'

'Actually I'm meeting a friend,' he replied, checking his watch. 'But he seems to be late.'

'Well I'll just join you for a minute then,' said Richards, sitting down as if he'd been invited. 'How are you holding up?' he asked after a moment, a look of genuine concern in his eyes.

'Perfectly well, thank you,' said Montignac.

'I read about this new business in the paper. Shocking stuff, wasn't it?'

'Very shocking.'

'How's Stella coping with it all?'

'Well she's bearing up, which is all we can hope for.'

'And so soon after losing her father too. The poor girl must be grief-stricken.'

A thought came into his head; it was always worthwhile planting seeds when such an opportunity could be found. 'She is,' he said. 'She's finding the whole thing very difficult but the doctor has prescribed something for her and—'

'Oh you don't want to get her into all that rot,' roared Richards. 'Exercise, that's what she needs. Brisk walks every morning and evening. That'll clear the cobwebs out and make her face up to the world again. Cold baths too. They work wonders for the soul.'

Montignac smiled and tried to stifle a laugh. 'Well I'll pass that on,' he said. 'Thanks for your concern.'

'Oh not at all, old boy. Not at all. Your uncle was a very dear friend of mine, you know.'

'Yes.'

Montignac glanced to the side and saw Alexander Keys arriving, scanning the room carefully.

'Ah,' he said. 'There's my friend now.'

'What's that?' asked Richards, spinning around as Alexander arrived. 'Ah yes. Right you are. Well I'll leave you two young chaps alone then. Do pass on my best wishes to Stella, though, won't you?'

'Of course I will,' said Montignac. 'And thank you.'

Alexander greeted Richards quickly as he left them and then sat down in the seat opposite Montignac and let out a deep sigh. 'Sorry I'm late,' he said. 'Got a bit of a telling-off in work and it went on longer than was strictly necessary.'

'Oh yes? What have you done now?'

'Nothing important. I only wrote a highly negative review of a novel by a debutante author and it turns out she's the niece of the editor.'

'Ah. That can't be good.'

'Well the novel was rubbish. So bad I only made it as far as chapter two and I make it a point of honour always to read as far as chapter three. Regardless of how awful it is.'

'You need to learn a little discipline,' said Montignac. 'If a job needs doing, just devote yourself to it. That's what I do. Anyway, thanks for meeting me. I know it was short notice.'

'Oh, no problem at all. Glad of the break if I'm honest.'

'I'm sure you can imagine what it's about.'

'Let me guess,' said Alexander. 'Gareth Bentley.'

'The very one.'

Alexander shook his head and looked extremely contrite. 'I don't know what to say to you about that, Owen. I feel terribly guilty about the whole thing.'

'You do?' asked Montignac, surprised. 'Why?'

'Because I was the one who introduced him to you.

That night at the Unicorn. It was his birthday, wasn't it? If I hadn't introduced you both, then he wouldn't have followed you outside, he wouldn't have struck up a relationship with you, you wouldn't have given him a job and then young Mr Davis would still be alive, tending to the rhododendrons at Kew Gardens.'

'I don't believe he worked at Kew Gardens,' said Montignac, correcting him. 'It was the Royal Horticultural Society. And I think that roses were more his passion. But yes, I take your point. Although really, Alexander, you have no need to feel guilty about it. No one could have guessed what was going to happen.'

'He's always been an odd one, though,' Alexander said with the benefit of hindsight, shaking his head sadly. 'I can spot them a mile off, you know.'

'How did you come to know him anyway?'

Alexander breathed heavily through his nose and tried to cast his mind back. 'He was at university with my younger brother, he said. 'And he often used to be around the house when they were between terms. Then Daniel went off to Burma, of course, and about two years ago I ran into Gareth on Chiswick High Street and we got talking about old times and I suppose a sort of friendship just built up between us. We'd meet every so often for dinner. We were similar souls, I thought. Neither of us doing very much with our lives. Trying to live the life of a dandy without really having the means or resources to cover it. We talked about Daniel a lot. I suppose we both missed him.'

'And did he ever show any signs of this kind of thing before?'

Alexander shook his head. 'Not this bad,' he said. 'I mean I knew that he had something of a drink problem. It stretches right back to his schooldays apparently. I think there was some sort of incident back then that was all covered up—'

'Yes, he mentioned something about that to me.'

'I don't remember the ins and outs of it to be honest but I believe one of the boys in his class was quite badly hurt. But Gareth's father made sure it never got out. But other than that . . . well he had changed a little in recent years. In the old days, whenever we went out, he would knock back three or four drinks for every one that I got through. And he insisted on my buying rounds despite that. And then he started not to drink at all, claiming that he'd turned over a new leaf.'

'Yes, I knew about the drink problem,' said Montignac. 'It became clear to me early on.'

'The night we met you at the Unicorn, the night of his birthday, that was the first time I'd seen him drinking in quite some time and I must admit I thought he'd got a handle on it because he only had a few and then stopped. And he left quite early. He met you outside, didn't he?'

'Yes. He followed me out.'

'How's Stella handling the whole thing anyway?' asked Alexander, his voice adopting that level of concern which is appropriate with such questions.

'Not very well,' said Montignac, who had barely seen her since Raymond's death.

'The poor creature. Were they very close?'

Montignac stared at him in amazement. 'Well they were engaged to be married,' he said. 'So yes, I would assume so.'

'Quite, quite. Well I just hope we're not going to be dragged into the whole thing,' he added cautiously.

'How do you mean?'

'The trial, of course,' said Alexander, leaning forwards. 'I mean obviously they're going to want to call you as a witness. You were there on the night in question, weren't you?'

'I was there at the start of the evening. I left him quite early.'

'And it happened at your flat?'

'Yes, I made the mistake of giving him a key.'

'So you will no doubt be called as a witness. Do you suppose they'll ask you how you met Gareth in the first place?'

Montignac shrugged. 'I don't know,' he said. 'I suppose they might. I can't see how important it would be.'

'Well try to keep my name out of it anyway if you can, will you? The last thing I need is any more trouble from my editor and I don't think he'd appreciate finding his least favourite reviewer linked to the Unicorn Ballrooms, which you won't be surprised to hear do not have a tremendous reputation, let alone to a murder. I'm hoping to start writing profiles soon of dead writers whom I never meet and essays about books that I've never read and I don't want to jeopardize that.'

'I'll do my best,' said Montignac. 'I saw him, you know.'

'Who?'

'Gareth.'

'You saw him?' asked Alexander, sitting forwards in surprise. 'You mean recently?'

'Yes. Quite recently. Yesterday afternoon, in fact.'

'Good Lord. Where?'

'Where do you think?' asked Montignac with a smile. 'Walking down Carnaby Street in a top hat and tails? In prison, of course.'

'Why on earth did you go there?'

'I don't know,' he replied. 'He asked for me to visit and something . . . a sort of morbid curiosity took me over.'

'Well I'm not sure I would have been quite so forgiving in your shoes,' said Alexander. 'I think I would have left him to rot. Does Stella know?'

'Oh God, no.'

'Well I'd keep it that way if I was you. How is the old fellow anyway? How's he looking?'

'Absolutely dreadful. A shadow of his former self.'

'Well I daresay he doesn't look half as bad as Raymond Davis,' said Alexander.

'No. I imagine not.'

'And was he repentant?'

'Very. He doesn't remember any of it, of course, but he seems to think that he might have been capable of such an act even if he never meant to do it.'

'They do say that it's always the quiet ones.'

'He was hardly quiet, Alexander. He was a raving alcoholic. He'll be no loss to anyone.'

'Loss?' he said in reply, raising an eyebrow at the word. 'You think he'll swing for it then?'

'I think it's a possibility,' said Montignac. 'They'll certainly push for it.'

Alexander shuddered; the whole thing was proving far too real for him. 'Well anything you can do to keep me out of it, Owen, would be much appreciated,' he said. 'I don't even want to think about it.'

'What a good friend you are, Alexander. Deserting our young Gareth in his hour of need.'

'He's not *my* young Gareth,' said Alexander, glancing around at the company to make sure that no one could overhear them. 'And you shouldn't think of him as *your* young Gareth either, if you've any sense. Anyway, enough of this. I don't want to talk about him any more. The whole thing is too horrible and he's old news now. Let's just leave him to his own repentance and punishment. Shall we have some tea?'

Montignac nodded; he was feeling hungry. It struck him how cruel people could be to their former friends. How once they had outlived their usefulness they were dropped, almost as if they had never existed in the first place. When Gareth was gone, Montignac knew that his entire history among them would be rewritten by these so-called friends, all the good things he'd ever done for them forgotten, all his kindnesses ignored. Scandals would be invented, non-existent conversations recounted until he had become more of a cartoon figure, a Dickensian villain, than a person with blood and feelings, a man who had once meant something to them and who had cared for each one in return. It seemed odd to him that the only member of Gareth's circle who probably cared at all whether he lived or died was he himself and he, after all, was the one who had put him in that position in the first place.

Still, there was nothing he could do to fix that now. This was what Lord Keaton had needed him to do and that was what he had done. It would earn him forty thousand pounds. And if someone had to die, Montignac reasoned, better him than me.

6

Stella wasn't in her room when Margaret brought her breakfast up but it was such a beautiful day outside that she had an idea where she might find her and carried the tray up the stairs to the roof garden, where she discovered her walking around the parapet, using the hose that was kept up there to water the dozens of pot plants which were dotted around the area.

'I thought I'd find you up here,' said Margaret,

resting the tray on the table. 'I brought you some breakfast.'

'I'm not very hungry,' said Stella, eyeing the plate of bacon and eggs warily.

'You don't have to look at it like that, it's not poisoned,' said Margaret with a smile. 'And you should untangle that hose,' she added, looking at the coils of tubing gathered like a nest of snakes around her feet. 'You'll trip over it one of these days.'

Stella gave her a brief smile, her first in days.

'I'm sorry, Margaret. I don't think I can manage food.'

'You have to eat. I'm not having you wasting away.'

For a moment they had reverted to their old roles, with Margaret as nanny and Stella as truculent child and after a moment Stella relented, switched the hose off and came to the table. She picked up her fork, mostly in order to evade further discussion on the subject.

'I was just thinking,' she said, 'of how much Raymond could have done with the grounds here had we married. He spoke to me of it once, you know. Of how he would re-landscape them and all the different trees that he'd like to plant. He wanted to build some greenhouses too so that we could grow our own tomatoes, and talked about a herb garden under our bedroom window. It would have been beautiful, I think.'

'There's nothing wrong with it the way it is,' said Margaret, a little irritated by Raymond's presumption. 'Your grandmother designed the gardens and to my way of thinking she did a lovely job.'

'Yes, but it would have made a nice change. It's all very staid as it is. Anyway, it would have been an interesting project to have worked on, don't you think?'

'Well, perhaps you could still do it yourself?' suggested Margaret. 'It would take your mind off things.'

Stella shook her head. 'I couldn't face it now,' she said. 'I wouldn't even know where to begin. Raymond had all the plans in his head. And besides, I don't know how much longer I'm going to stay here anyway.'

Margaret stared at her in surprise. 'What do you mean by that?' she asked.

'I've been thinking about it,' said Stella, shrugging her shoulders. 'What's the point in maintaining such a big house just for me? I'm thinking of closing it down and moving away.'

Margaret's mouth dropped open, horrified by the prospect.

'You can't be serious,' she said.

'I am.'

'And what would you do? Move to London?'

'Oh no,' said Stella quickly. 'No, I couldn't face London. Too many people. I thought perhaps I could travel. There's so few places that I've seen, other than England and Switzerland. Obviously I'm not allowed to sell Leyville but I could donate it to a trust perhaps. It could be turned into a museum.'

'Stella, you're not thinking straight,' said Margaret, who had visions of being turned out of her home on the whim of a grieving girl. 'You can't do something like that. You'd regret it for ever.'

'I've always loved it here,' Stella said dreamily. 'But there's been a lot of unhappiness in this house and I'd be glad to say goodbye to that. When you think back to what Grandfather did, cutting off Owen's father like that, well that must have been a horrible time to have lived through. And then when Father took the place over and Owen had to come to live here and he was frightened at first, do you remember?'

'I remember,' said Margaret quietly, recalling the look of terror on the child's face that had taken months to drift away.

'And then Andrew died,' she continued. 'And Mother. Then Father. And now Raymond.'

'Raymond didn't die at Leyville, though. He's not connected with it in any way.'

'If he hadn't met me, he wouldn't have met Owen. And if he hadn't met Owen, he wouldn't have been going to his flat that night and he'd still be alive. It's as much my fault that he's dead as anyone's'.

'That's nonsense,' said Margaret in a stern voice. 'You had nothing to do with it. The only person to blame for Raymond's death is that young man who killed him.'

'Gareth Bentley,' said Stella quietly.

'Yes and you don't have to worry about him because he's safely locked up in prison and will no doubt be found guilty and that'll be the end of him.'

Stella grimaced; she hated the idea of executions.

There was something so medieval about them, she thought.

'I don't want that,' she said.

'Well you may not have a say in it. The law's the law.'

'If he did kill Raymond,' said Stella. 'I would prefer for him to live a long, long life and spend all of it in jail. Hanging would be too swift a release for him.'

'*If* he killed him?' asked Margaret, surprised by the qualification. 'What do you mean "if"?'

'Well he hasn't been found guilty yet, has he?'

'It's only a matter of time,' replied Margaret, who was following the case avidly in the daily newspapers, although she was keeping them far away from Stella's sight. To read the details would, she knew, only upset her.

Stella sighed and said nothing for a while, picking at her breakfast without making any great inroads into it.

'Have you spoken to Owen lately?' she asked after a while.

'I've left messages for him. I haven't heard back from him.'

'Will you do something for me?' asked Stella. 'Will you call him again and ask him to come down for the weekend? There's something I want to talk to him about.'

'If you like. But you're not going to talk to him about this ridiculous idea of leaving Leyville, are you?'

'No, it's not that. It's something else.'

Margaret narrowed her eyes suspiciously. 'What is it, Stella?'

She shrugged her shoulders and wouldn't look Margaret in the eye; the moment took her back in time ten years to when Stella was a teenager, to that dreadful time just before she was sent away to Geneva. When she had sat down with them both and they had confided in her. Just before Margaret had taken the matter in hand.

'It's nothing special,' said Stella. 'Just something I want to discuss with him.'

'I'll call him if that's what you want,' said Margaret. 'Just be careful with him, that's all I ask.'

Stella stared across the table. 'Be careful with him?' she asked. 'Be careful with what? He's my cousin, isn't he? He's not going to harm me.'

'Yes,' said Margaret forcefully. 'That's my point exactly. He's your cousin. Perhaps you should leave him to live his life in London and you should get on with yours down here.'

'Anyone would think you don't like to see the two of us together.'

'I don't.'

'Margaret—'

'Well, do you seriously expect me to say anything else?'

Stella shook her head. 'Really, Margaret. Anyone would think that it was you who—'

'Stop that,' said Margaret, slapping her hand down on the table. 'Stop it this instant. You know that I don't like to talk about those days.'

'Feeling guilty, are you?' she asked, aiming to hurt.

'Of course I don't feel guilty. What do I have to feel guilty about?'

Stella raised an eyebrow and stood up from her chair and walked over towards the side of the roof, resting her arms on the low stone in front of her.

'I wonder if things had been different, whether Owen and I would have been friends at all,' she said. 'If we would have even known each other.'

'How do you mean?'

'Well if Grandfather had accepted Uncle Henry's marriage. If they had stayed on here. If Owen had been born at Leyville rather than in France. Of course, none of us would have grown up here then. Father might have moved to London. We would have had a house there. Everything would have been the opposite of what it is now. I would have been the one coming down to visit him. This would have been his home and Andrew and I would have been the poor relations.'

'If that had happened, then Owen might not have been the boy he is.'

'You've never liked him, have you, Margaret?'

'That's not true,' she replied, offended and pausing a moment to consider it. 'When he first came here, I welcomed him as much as anyone. If anything I gave him extra attention so that he wouldn't feel like he didn't belong.'

'Which is how he's always felt,' said Stella.

'There's no one was as kind to that boy as I was. He owes this family a lot, if you ask me. He owed your father a lot. Look at all your father did for him! Took him in when he didn't have a home. Gave him a decent education. Set him up for life. And how did Owen repay him?'

'That wasn't just Owen,' said Stella quickly, turning around in frustration. 'Good God, Margaret, you've never been willing to accept that have you? You always view him as some sort of predatory beast who—'

'You were only sixteen, Stella.'

'And he was fifteen! He was younger than me! If anyone was the predator—'

'I'm not listening to this,' said Margaret, rising to her feet. 'I told you ten years ago that I would never discuss this matter again and I don't intend to change that now.'

'All right, all right. There's no need to get angry about it. I'm just saying that if you looked at things from his perspective—'

'I've been doing that for years, Stella, and it gets me nowhere,' she said, growing upset now. 'You have no idea of how much I've worried about that boy. Both of you, all three of you, Andrew too, were like my own children. I was like a second mother to you—'

'Of course you were.'

'Albeit a second mother who was on the staff and could be dismissed on a whim. I spent years worrying about Owen. Ten years ago I did what I did not just out of concern for you, you know, but out of concern for him too. I did it for you both.'

'Your best intentions may have ruined us both.'

'And what Owen became then,' Margaret continued, ignoring what Stella had said, 'is no fault of mine. If he's unhappy because your father disinherited him, well that's nothing to do with me. If he's bitter that things went so wrong between the two of you, that's not my fault. I refuse to take responsibility for his failings.'

'Why did Father cut Owen off, Margaret?' asked Stella quietly and Margaret stopped talking for a moment and stared at her, open-mouthed.

'What was that?'

'I asked why Father cut him off. He was always so passionate about tradition. And the tradition indicated that the Montignacs inherited on the male line.'

'Perhaps he had a change of heart,' said Margaret, stumbling over her words. 'Perhaps he wanted to leave his estate to his only surviving child.'

'Did he know, Margaret?' asked Stella, wondering if she would be able to tell from her face whether she was telling the truth or not. 'Did you tell him?'

A silence descended between them. The two women stared at each other, Stella wondering whether she had stumbled across a secret entirely by chance, Margaret asking herself whether she had wasted her life on this ungrateful lot.

She didn't answer and Stella turned around for a moment, shaking her head in frustration; when she turned back Margaret had already gone back inside, leaving the door swinging open and – unusually for her

– the breakfast things on the table for Stella to bring back to the kitchen herself.

7

From across the street on Cork Mews, Montignac could see the way his young assistant was looking at the woman and couldn't help but smile and shake his head. Jason Parsons had a habit of falling in love with the various older ladies who spent time in the gallery, although he became flustered and unable to look them in the eye if they started asking him questions or quizzed him about a painting. For all his longing stares he had never yet managed to impress one sufficiently and, to the best of Montignac's knowledge, his social life was not particularly expansive. Still, on this occasion he seemed to be getting along quite well with the women who was, he could see even from a distance, an extremely attractive middle-aged lady, the type that often frequented the art galleries along Cork Street but who was usually more of a browser than a purchaser.

Montignac kicked the butt of his cigarette out on the street just as Arthur Hamilton stepped out of the Clarion Gallery next door. He cursed his timing and tried to double-back into the doorway of Pollen house but the older man saw him and raised a hand in greeting, and he had little choice but to continue across the road.

'Hello there, Owen,' said Hamilton. 'Haven't seen you around the gallery recently.'

'I've been rather busy, Arthur,' he explained. 'Some family issues to take care of.'

'Oh yes,' he replied, frowning and lowering his voice, despite the fact that there was no one listening in to their conversation. 'I read about your . . . unpleasantness in the newspaper. Very bad business.'

'Indeed.'

'Coping all right, are you?'

'Tolerably well,' said Montignac. 'Any luck with those missing Cézannes?'

Hamilton shook his head. 'Not a sausage,' he said. 'The whole thing's a terrible mystery. And, would you believe, I'm having a hideous argument with the insurance people over it. They say I didn't provide enough security.'

'Really? I would have thought that was a very secure room.' The words were out before he realized what he was saying and he tried to keep his face still so as not to betray his regret.

'What was that?' asked Hamilton.

'I'm assuming you kept the paintings in your restoration room upstairs,' said Montignac quickly.

'Well yes, but—'

'I mean that's exactly where I would have kept them if I'd been in your shoes.'

'Yes, it is the safest place. It's very secure. I'm the only one with a key. But how did you know about it?'

Montignac smiled at the man as if he had become senile overnight. 'Well you showed it to me, Arthur, don't you remember? About a year ago. I was browsing among your stock one day and you told me that you were working on some restorations for the Tate and would I be interested in taking a look.'

'I did?' asked Hamilton, looking away as if to try to recall the encounter.

'Yes, don't you remember?'

He thought about it and shook his head. 'The old brain isn't what it used to be,' he said finally with a shrug. 'You should value your youth, Owen.'

'I do,' said Montignac with a smile. 'I'm trying to enjoy it as much as possible as it happens.'

His eyes darted in the direction of the Threadbare where the lady had moved away from the counter and was now standing in front of one particularly repulsive self-portrait by a Shoreditch artist, her head inclined as she silently judged it. Behind the counter he could see Jason Parsons staring at her with barely disguised longing.

'I had a look around your place the other day,' continued Hamilton, oblivious to the fact that Montignac wasn't fully paying attention. 'Some very interesting pieces you have there.'

'Nice of you to say so, Arthur,' said Montignac with a laugh. 'Anything you'd be interested in? I could do you a nice deal on one since you're a neighbour.'

'Eh, no,' said Hamilton quickly. 'No thank you.

Probably not quite right for me. They're more for the young people, I imagine. Would they be your regular customers?'

'Not at all. The young people don't have any money, do they? No, we're more for the undiscerning middle-aged couple with aspirations towards maintaining their fashionability and impressing their Parisian friends when they come on a visit.'

'Which would explain why we're never in competition then,' said Hamilton with a laugh. 'Well I'd better get along. Good to see you again anyway.'

'You too, Arthur,' said Montignac, shaking his hand. 'And sorry to hear about the insurance problems.'

'Oh we'll sort them out. Never you worry.'

He disappeared down the street and Montignac watched him for a moment. The man was nearly seventy and still working five days a week, eight hours a day in his gallery. He didn't know whether it was because he loved his work so much or because he couldn't afford to retire but he had a quick realization that in forty years' time he did not want to be anywhere near Cork Street, unless he was redecorating his home.

'There you are, Mr Montignac,' said Jason as he stepped through the door. 'Thought you'd run away on us altogether.'

'I don't have to answer to you, do I?' he asked sharply and the boy reddened and shook his head.

'No, sir. No, I didn't mean that. I was just—'

'I'll be at my desk doing the books if you're looking

for me,' he said, walking past him without a glance.'

'Hold on, sir,' called Jason. 'There's a lady here to see you.'

'A lady?'

'She's been here for quite some time. Says she needs to talk to you about something.'

'Which one?' he asked, looking around at the half-dozen or so ladies walking slowly from picture to picture and gesturing at the sculptures in between.

'That one,' said Jason, pointing across.

Montignac studied her; it was the same lady he'd seen talking to Jason from across the street. She was still engrossed in the Shoreditch painting and hadn't noticed him come in. He frowned, trying to understand why she looked vaguely familiar.

'I'll be at my desk,' he said. 'You can send her over to me there.'

He went across and sat down and felt an urge to do a quick tidy of the top of the desk, moving the catalogues and folders out of his way and on to the chair to discourage her from sitting and taking up too much of his time as Jason approached the woman and pointed in Montignac's direction. She stared down at him as if trying to get a sense of him from a distance before looking suddenly relieved and walking through the gallery towards him.

'Mr Montignac?' she asked and he nodded in reply.

'That's right. We've met before . . . ?' he began, sure that they had but she shook her head.

'No I don't think so. I'm Jane Bentley. Gareth's mother.'

He felt a slight chill inside and couldn't find a response for a moment. I thought you looked familiar,' he said finally. 'He has the look of you.'

'Do you think so?' she said, brightening up considerably. 'People usually say he takes after Roderick's side of the family. Roderick's my husband of course.'

'Of course,' said Montignac, taking her in. Close up he could see why Jason had been captivated. She was a startlingly beautiful woman, the type who probably looked even better now in her fifth decade than she had in her third or fourth. 'I'm so sorry,' he said, reaching for the catalogues from the chair and aware that he had been staring. 'Please sit down.'

'I apologize for calling in unannounced,' she said, sitting down. 'But you never seem to be here when I phone.'

'I have been rather busy lately,' he admitted. 'And as my assistant will no doubt tell you, I'm dreadful at returning calls.'

'You must know what I'm here about,' she said.

'Gareth, I assume.'

'He tells me you've been to see him.'

Montignac sighed and pulled a face; he wasn't sure how much of this he wanted to talk about. 'He asked me to visit him,' he said, correcting her slightly. 'And I obliged. I didn't stay very long, I'm afraid.'

'I never stay long myself,' said Jane, looking tired and drawn. 'I hate the place.'

'Well I think . . . that's the idea,' he said quietly.

'How did you find him?' she asked, swallowing hard and recovering her poise.

'Scared,' said Montignac, considering his answer carefully. 'Bewildered by what had happened. Guilty.'

'He's not guilty, Mr Montignac,' she interrupted quickly. 'Whatever my son is capable of, he's not a killer.'

'No, I meant that he *felt* guilty,' said Montignac correcting himself. 'Whether he is or not . . .' He wanted to suggest that that was for a jury to decide but he felt no urge to cause this woman any further pain and so pulled back.

'I need to ask you about that night,' said Jane. 'I need to know for myself what happened.'

'I have told the police this,' he protested. 'Haven't they talked to you about it? Or Gareth's barrister?'

'I need to hear it from you, Mr Montignac,' she said firmly. 'Those few hours you spent with him were the last hours of his freedom. By the end of that night, whatever took place has destroyed him. It's destroyed our entire family. I just need you to tell me yourself. Please.'

Montignac sighed; he had little desire to relive the events of that evening.

'Have you any children, Mr Montignac?' she asked after a moment when it became clear that he was hesitating.

That question – that most hated of questions – snapped him back and he felt his lip curl involuntarily.

A burning sensation tore through his stomach and as each second passed he willed himself to speak.

'No,' he said finally, through clenched teeth.

'Well if you did have children, you would understand how important this is to me. How I can't just let it go.'

Montignac sighed. There was something about her that made it clear to him that she wouldn't be going anywhere until he talked her through it, so he shrugged his shoulders and relented.

'Like I told the police and Gareth's barrister,' he began, 'I really wasn't with him for all that long. There's a pub on Piccadilly that I sometimes go to, the Bullirag. Do you know Air Street?'

'No,' she said, shaking her head. 'I'm not overly familiar with the public houses of this area,' she added in a dry voice.

'No, of course not. Well they do a decent dinner there in the early evening and I took him along. We ordered some drinks but Gareth . . . well he kept ordering more and more. Every time I looked away he was at the bar, buying another one. Within an hour or so, he was very drunk.'

'And you weren't?'

'I wasn't matching him drink for drink,' he explained. 'He wanted me to, of course, but if I drank like that I'd collapse on the floor and I told him so. But it didn't seem to matter to him. After a while it became clear that we couldn't stay any longer, he was starting to become quite loud and the landlord was giving us daggers' looks, so I called him a taxicab and sent him back to my flat to sleep it off. And then I met some friends and spent the night with them and the next thing I knew, the police arrived here the following afternoon telling me what had happened.'

Jane closed her eyes quickly, not wanting to hear that part of the story recounted again. She had heard it described one too many times already.

Montignac watched her and wondered how she was managing to keep control of her emotions as well as she was. He was impressed by her fortitude but resented her presence there. The last thing he had expected was for a grieving mother to come calling on him. But he was relieved that his story was holding up as well as it was. He had become quite adept at telling it.

8

The truth about that night was, of course, slightly different.

Montignac had waited until Jason Parsons was on his lunchbreak and he was alone in the Threadbare before phoning the Royal Horticultural Society and asking to be connected to Raymond Davis. It had taken some time and he'd grown increasingly frustrated with the delay, worrying that he would be interrupted by a customer at any moment; this was a phone call that he did not want to be overheard. After a few moments an operator came back on and told him that Raymond had taken the day off to be with his fiancée. Frowning as he hung up, he dialled Leyville, hoping that luck would be on his side and Stella would not answer the phone.

'Raymond Davis.'

'Raymond,' he said, relieved and trying to sound as friendly as possible. 'It's Owen Montignac.'

There was a slight hesitation at the other end, the result, no doubt, of Raymond's apprehension at hearing who his caller was. 'Owen,' he said finally. 'This is a surprise.'

'Yes, I imagine it is. Raymond, I thought I should call you up to apologize.'

'Apologize?'

'Yes, and to congratulate you. I'm afraid I haven't been terribly friendly to you in recent times. That whole business at Claridge's a while back . . . well, it was inexcusable.'

'Really,' said Raymond, trying to keep the note of amazement out of his voice. 'There's nothing to apologize for, Owen. I understand it's been a difficult few months for the family.'

'The family. Yes. But I shouldn't have taken it out on you. In truth, I was a little worried about your intentions towards Stella. I was afraid you were going to keep stringing her along on this engagement of yours forever but now I understand you've set a date.'

'That's right, we have,' said Raymond enthusiastically. 'Yes, she mentioned that she'd told you.'

'And I couldn't be happier for you, I really couldn't.

You know it's only because Stella means so much to me that I've been . . . a little hard on you. You do understand that, don't you?'

'Oh certainly,' he replied. 'It's very good of you to call and say so.'

'But it's not enough, Raymond. Not enough at all.'

'It's not?'

'No. Look, I think we should have a chat. Man to man. What do you say? Now that Uncle Peter isn't with us I feel we should run through a few of the formalities, don't you? Your intentions, how you plan on supporting Stella, things like that. Oh I know she's wealthier than Croesus but I'm something of a stickler for tradition and it would set my mind at rest to know that Uncle Peter was looking down and feeling I was doing the right thing by everyone. What do you say, Raymond? Are you game? We could settle it with a nice bottle of wine. Toast the happy couple.'

There was a long pause on the other end of the line that momentarily worried him; he wondered whether Raymond had hung up or collapsed in surprise at what he had said. But finally there was his reedy little voice again, sounding positively choked up with emotion. 'Owen, I can't tell you what that means to me,' he said. 'The last thing I ever wanted was to feel that I was coming between you and Stella.'

'Oh that wouldn't be possible,' said Montignac with a laugh.

'I'm just terribly touched that you've called. We

should definitely meet up and follow the traditions, as you say. Perhaps later in the week?'

'Why wait?' asked Montignac quickly. 'How about later this afternoon?'

'Well I'm down here at Leyville,' said Raymond, considering it. 'And I'd made plans at the RHS tonight. Perhaps we could meet tomorrow or the next day and—'

'No, this is too important to put off. What do you say you come around to the gallery this evening. Around six? We can have a good talk then.'

'Yes, well, all right,' said Raymond, who didn't sound convinced by the need for such urgency. 'I was supposed to be going to a lecture tonight, a visiting botanist, Gustav Linden. Have you heard of him?'

'No.'

'Well I don't suppose you would have, but he's something of a genius in the field. Still, I don't suppose I'd be missed. All right then, yes. I'll see you at six.'

'Just one other thing, Raymond,' said Montignac quickly before he could ring off. 'Let's keep this between ourselves for now, yes? Not a word to the missus, if you understand me. We'll get everything settled, then head back down to Leyville at the weekend, brothers-in-arms, give her the shock of her life. She'll be thrilled. What do you say?'

'Absolutely,' said Raymond, sounding increasingly delighted by the turn of events. 'I won't say a word. And I'll see you at six.'

'Sharp,' said Montignac, placing the phone back on the receiver. He breathed a sigh of relief that he hadn't been interrupted and looked to his left, through the large windows leading on to the street, but the light had faded a little and he could see his own reflection there and, without giving the matter much thought, he turned away quickly.

Knowing how important it was not to let Montignac down, Raymond showed up promptly at the Threadbare at five minutes to six. Jason had been sent home an hour earlier and he had closed the gallery then, preparing the room upstairs for its upcoming visitor, the same room where Gareth and he had prepared the twelve frames for the Cézanne paintings they had stolen some weeks earlier. He took off his jacket and rolled up his sleeves and was clearing a space on the floor when the knock came on the door.

He waved at Raymond when he saw him and turned back to his desk for the keys, fumbling through them as he walked towards the door, not looking up or catching his visitor's eye.

'Come on in,' he said, opening it and locking it again behind him, throwing a quick glance up and down the street which was, happily, deserted. 'Glad you could make it.'

'Well I wouldn't have missed it for the world, old man,' said Raymond, glancing around at the gallery, which he had never visited before. 'So this is the famous Threadbare Gallery that I hear so much about.

Montignac laughed. 'Yes,' he said. 'This is it. In all its glory. Take a look around if you like. See what you think.'

Raymond nodded and started to stroll past the walls, glancing up at the paintings and studying them for a few moments each. 'I have to say I don't know much about art,' he said.

'Then you should feel right at home,' said Montignac, picking up Raymond's coat and carrying it with him. 'Neither do any of the artists.'

'Mother's quite keen of course. Gives her an interest, I suppose. She sponsors a student every year at RADA, did you know that?'

Montignac blinked. 'I didn't,' he said. 'But RADA's an acting school.'

'No, it's for artists,' said Raymond.

'It's for actors,' he insisted with a smile. The Royal Academy of Dramatic Arts.'

Raymond turned around and frowned at him. 'Is that so?' he said. 'And all these years I thought she was sponsoring some starving artist in a garret and all the time it's been some ponce in tights shouting Shakespeare and Oscar Wilde.'

Montignac nodded and smiled to himself, suddenly feeling even more justified in his plans; the man really was unworthy of Stella.

'This one's dreadful,' continued Raymond, pointing at a rather small oil painting which had been purchased that morning by the Duchess of Argyll for three hundred pounds and was being collected the following day. 'The colours clash terribly.'

'They do,' admitted Montignac. 'Yes, it's a very weak piece.'

'And this,' he said, pointing at its neighbour. 'Is that supposed to be a person?'

'An orang-utan, I'm told.'

'Well it would put you off going to the zoo, wouldn't it?' asked Raymond with a shudder. 'This one's not bad, though.'

'No,' admitted Montignac. 'You have more of an eye than I thought you would.'

'Not really. I know what I like, I suppose.'

'Indeed you do, Raymond. Stella, for one thing. And flowers.'

Raymond turned around, suspecting a slight. 'There's a lot more to what I do than that,' he said. 'Nature is every bit as valuable as the art that you enjoy. Nature *is* art. Well, artists paint nature, don't they? All those fellows with their landscapes and still lifes.'

'Yes,' said Montignac. 'Yes, they do. I suppose we're not as different as we think.'

'No,' said Raymond. 'I've always felt that. Which was one of the reasons I was so delighted to get your call. I mean if we can put any differences we have to bed – or rather, if I can settle your mind on any worries you have regarding my suitability for Stella – then that would be an evening well spent, don't you agree?'

'Raymond,' said Montignac, leaning forwards and clasping his arm for a moment. 'I couldn't have put it better myself. Settling this business once and for all is the only thing that matters to me right now. But before we do I wonder if I could impose on you for just a few moments.'

'Of course,' said Raymond. 'What do you need?'

'Nothing more elaborate than brute strength,' he replied with a laugh. 'There's a large bookcase in a storeroom upstairs that I particularly want to drag out on to the floor before I leave tonight. My assistant's gone home. I wonder if I could impose . . . ?'

'No problem at all,' said Raymond cheerfully, delighted to be of help. 'What are brother-in-laws for anyway? Or is it brothers-in-law?'

'Cousins-in-law,' said Montignac quickly. 'She's not my sister.'

Raymond nodded; it didn't seem the moment to laugh now. 'No. No, of course not.' He rolled his sleeves up and Montignac was a little surprised to see the strength in his adversary's forearms and the surging muscle from the bicep as the arm was revealed. *There must be a lot more heavy work goes on at the RHS than I knew,* he thought to himself, realizing he probably had one chance only to get this right.

'It's upstairs,' said Montignac, leading the way. 'Follow me.' They climbed the stairs together and Montignac flicked a switch, leaving the downstairs part of the gallery in near darkness. 'By the way, you didn't tell Stella we were meeting, did you?'

'Didn't say a word,' said Raymond.

'Good man.'

'She'll be delighted, though,' he continued. 'I'm sure she wants us to be friends.'

'A man can never have enough friends,' said Montignac, opening the door to the storeroom and switching on the light. He pointed across at the bookcase on the opposite wall. 'What do you think?' he asked.

'Doesn't look too bad,' said Raymond, stepping inside, his back to Montignac.

'It's heavier than it looks,' said Montignac. 'Lean down and try to move it and you'll see what I mean.'

Raymond nodded and stepped across the small storeroom and crouched down, placing his hands beneath the bookcase, and attempted to lift it. It was heavy but manageable, particularly with two of them.

'Shouldn't be a problem,' he said, turning around to speak to his intended cousin-in-law. 'If we each take a side and—'

That was a sentence he didn't get to finish for at that moment he was hit across the back of the neck by a large steel rod and he fell slowly to his knees, a low groan emitting from his mouth. He knelt there for a few moments, a hand reaching around to find what had caused the pain before lurching heavily to the ground and into unconsciousness.

Montignac breathed a sigh of relief. He had counted on one sound blow doing the job. It was important that he didn't kill him, just knocked him out, and he checked his pulse, which was a little quick but active. Quickly, he got some masking tape and taped his hands behind his back and his legs together and covered his mouth with another strip. All going well he figured he had hours before he recovered consciousness.

A little blood had come from the side of Raymond's mouth and stained Montignac's shirt but he didn't notice it as another knock was heard on the door downstairs and there was Gareth Bentley on the street outside, hands up to the glass, face pressed to it as he peered in, waiting to meet his fate.

Montignac had deliberately chosen a seat in the Bullirag pub which was slightly out of the sightlines of the bar, and had been the one to make sure that the drinks kept coming.

'No more, no more,' Gareth said, each time a fresh beer or whisky came his way. 'I told you I can't drink like this.'

'Oh come on, man, we're celebrating,' Montignac said cheerfully. 'You've got a thousand pounds in your pocket. You can't allow your employer to drink alone. That's just bad staff relations.'

He could see the look of concern in Gareth's eyes as his last remnants of resistance began to wear down and his taste for the stuff took over. Watching him was a study in itself. The worry, the disintegrating self-knowledge, the lack of control, slowly replaced by a desire for more, by faster drinking, by more animated and even vitriolic conversation. The sudden and embarrassing confessions of admiration. Montignac had no idea how many drinks he had had that night but there was no question that if he didn't get him home soon, he would collapse on the floor of the pub and that would not be a good thing; he had to be seen to be leaving standing up.

'Come on, Gareth,' he said, dragging him outside after settling the bill. 'Let's get some fresh air into you.'

There was a wind blowing as they opened the door and stepped out on to the street and Gareth lost his footing for a moment, his hands pressed to the sides of his head as the alcohol and air mixed through his system.

'I don't feel very well,' he mumbled as Montignac struggled to keep him erect. He whistled for a passing taxicab and opened the back door, pouring his friend inside.

'Best you don't go back to Tavistock Square. I don't think they'd be impressed, do you?'

Gareth looked up at him with bleary eyes, barely aware of what he was saying.

'You can go back to mine,' said Montignac. 'Sleep it off there, all right?'

'Thanks, Owen,' said Gareth, collapsing into the back seat of the cab. 'You're a pal.'

'Bedford Place,' he said to the driver, giving him the number of the flat and passing him his keys. 'Give these to him when you get there, will you? And be careful, they're my only set,' he added, slipping a few shillings across which the driver accepted gratefully before speeding off.

From there, Montignac walked back to the Threadbare Gallery and unlocked the door, revelling in the peace and quiet of the darkened space. He hadn't drunk anywhere near as much as Gareth but enough that he was starting to feel a buzz from it and drank several glasses of water in quick succession in order to maintain his equilibrium. He glanced at his watch. It was only nine-thirty and Keaton wouldn't be there until it was dark, well after midnight.

A little nervously, he made his way up to the storeroom and opened the door tentatively, convinced for a moment that Raymond would have vanished, but he was still there, lying in the same position he had left him in, sleeping soundly and appearing none the worse for wear. Montignac closed the door quietly and went back downstairs.

To pass the time he sat down at his desk and began to work his way through the gallery accounts, a process which took him the best part of an hour and a half and took his mind off what was to come.

By eleven o'clock he was thoroughly bored and began reading a novel that Alexander Keys had lent him, something he had said was surprisingly good despite the fact that it was written by a textile worker from Milton Keynes, but his mind wasn't able to focus on the words and no matter how often he read the same paragraph over and over again he couldn't seem to remember what had just taken place. His eyes kept glancing in the direction of the storeroom and he got a chill, worrying that Raymond would wake too soon. In the end he spent the remaining time pacing the floor, trying to decide which of the pieces he would ensure got left behind in the event of a fire.

The phone rang just after midnight and he picked it up quickly, his heart starting to beat faster as the night's events began to play out.

'Montignac,' he said, answering it quickly.

'I'm not far away,' said Lord Keaton. 'Just outside the Museum of Mankind. I'll pull in down the laneway.'

'Is there anyone out there?'

'Not a soul. We're in luck.'

Montignac nodded. 'Good,' he said. 'I'll be right out.'

He ran to the back door and unlocked it just as Keaton arrived and he stepped inside, rubbing his hands together briskly. 'Chilly night, isn't it?' he said.

'Is it?' said Montignac. 'I've been in here for hours. I hadn't noticed.'

'Well it is. So how did things go with our young friend?'

'Very well, I think,' said Montignac. 'He was pickled by the time we left the pub and he's gone back to mine as arranged. I made sure the taxi driver would remember that I was staying behind.'

'Good, good. Well I've organized your alibi for the

next few hours so you've nothing to worry about on that score. It came quite cheap too. Decided where you're going to sleep yet?' he asked.

'I thought I'd just come straight back here,' he said. 'There's nowhere else I can go. A hotel would be too risky in case someone remembered seeing me there.'

'True. Well it won't be a very comfortable night for you but there we are. That's the price we pay to get the things we want,' he added pleasantly. 'Shall we get on with it?'

Montignac nodded and led the way up the stairs towards the mezzanine level, where the small store-room was. 'He's in here,' he said, unlocking the door and pulling it open.

The man stared inside at the body of Raymond Davis which lay on a plastic sheet on the floor, and grimaced. 'Poor chap,' he said. 'He looks quite peaceful, doesn't he? How much longer do we have, do you think?'

'Not long,' said Montignac. 'I think we need to get him back to Bedford Place as soon as possible.'

'Right you are,' said Keaton. 'Well let's get on with it then. I don't want to be late home, I have an early start in the morning. Should we untie him first?'

'Yes, I think so. Just to be safe.'

They removed the masking tape from his arms and legs and with one quick pull, from his mouth. The action of doing this seemed to jolt Raymond for a moment and he emitted a loud groan, although his eyes remained firmly shut. Montignac and Keaton stared at him for a moment before judging it was safe to continue.

They picked him up under each arm and walked him carefully down the stairs and out into the laneway, where they propped him up in the back seat of the car as if he was simply a passenger, and drove on towards Bedford Place.

'Poor bugger,' said Keaton at one point, catching sight of him in the rear-view mirror. 'What did he ever do to you anyway?'

'Does it matter?' asked Montignac. 'You said we needed a victim. He got the job.'

'Well it doesn't matter to me. I'm just interested, that's all.'

Montignac breathed heavily through his nose and considered it. 'He was an unwelcome intruder,' he said finally. 'Someone I should have taken care of a long time ago but never thought would become such a regular fixture in my life.'

'Well he's not going to be now,' said the man.

'No.'

'As long as we both get what we need, that's all that matters,' said Keaton. 'It's been very convenient that we can help each other out like this. First with the Cézannes, you made a nice little bundle out of that, didn't you?'

'It came along when I needed it, certainly,' admitted Montignac.

'And now we get to help each other again. What's this Gareth fellow like anyway?'

Montignac shrugged. 'He's all right, I suppose,' he conceded. 'One of life's losers. No goals, no ambitions. But fairly harmless. Looks at me like I'm some sort of god. Every time I turn around he's standing there, desperate for my approval. I think he just lacked direction in life. Positive role models, as they say. Still, he won't have to worry about it now, I suppose.'

'No. I blame the parents of course,' said Keaton. 'And they'll be paying for it. It's unfortunate for the lad but it was the only way I could be sure of influencing his father. If only he wasn't such a stickler for formalities I wouldn't have had to take things this far. If he was just corruptible, just a little bit, then none of this would have been necessary. Most of them are, you know. I'm one of the more honest judges in the system.'

'That says a lot.'

'Don't be sarcastic,' said Keaton quietly. 'There are greater principles involved here.'

'Do you really hate this American woman that much?' asked Montignac. 'I'm just interested that's all,' he added, echoing Keaton's earlier phrase.

'Wallis Simpson doesn't matter to me one way or another,' said Keaton with a shrug. 'In fact I've never even met her. Personally I couldn't care less if the king wanted to marry a donkey. It doesn't make a blind bit of difference to me. But the man has a way about him that has to be stopped. All this business with the miners in the North-East. The little visits he makes. This nonsense of "something has to be done". He thinks the monarchy is there to be shared with the people. He understands nothing about our ways. It's as simple as that. But Baldwin . . . now he understands. He can see the damage the man is doing.'

'But the people love him,' said Montignac.

'The people!' snorted Keaton, shaking his head as he drove along. 'Who cares what the *people* think? The people, as you put it, are an ill-educated, senseless mob. They look for leadership, they need it, and they see this prancing fellow going up and down the country, patting them on the heads, looking terribly sympathetic, drinking mugs of tea in their tiny cottages and they think he's one of them. Or that they're one of us. And by extension that makes *me* one of them, and I'm not. You know what the last king said about him, don't you? His father? He said that six months after he was dead his son would have destroyed the monarchy. And believe me, if he's not stopped that bloody man will tear down all the palaces in the land and share out the wealth among every poor man and woman in the country, every starving tramp on the streets.'

'And would that be such a bad thing?' asked Montignac with a smile.

'You know damn well it would,' he replied. 'So don't pretend otherwise. No, the man has to be stopped and this ridiculous infatuation of his with Wallis Bloody Simpson has given us the perfect artillery. Still, the PM needs the judiciary to back him up. I help him and he's ready to help me in return.'

Montignac frowned. 'Help you with what?' he asked. 'What's he going to do for you?'

'Have you ever had anything stolen from you?' asked Keaton after a lengthy pause, feeling that perhaps he owed his co-conspirator an explanation.

'I've had things taken away from me that I expected to be mine.'

'Then you'll know how I feel,' he said. 'Until you've had your birthright taken away from you by people who have no right to it, you won't understand how bitter it can make you.'

'But I have had that happen to me,' pointed out Montignac. 'When my grandfather cut off my father and mother he left us with nothing. The irony of it is that the entire inheritance was not his to decide upon. He'd just come into it like everyone else, it wasn't as if he'd actually earned it. The right and proper thing was to leave it to my father and then to me. It wasn't his place to make such a decision. They stole it.'

'Then perhaps you do understand,' said Keaton thoughtfully. 'But I'll get mine back when I put York on the throne.'

'It sounds like we're back in the Middle Ages.'

'The same principles are involved,' insisted Keaton. 'The monarch doesn't just represent the country, Owen. He's not just there to open church fêtes and meet with the prime minister for tea and coffee every week and wave from the balcony of Buckingham Palace every so often. Think of your history, boy. The monarch has a greater responsibility than that. Think of all the wars that have been fought for the Crown, the lives that have been lost. And your young Mr Davis is just another casualty of that war. No, by Christmas I will have one man off the throne and another man on. And the country will be a safer place for it, you mark my words. The present king will destroy us all if he's left in charge. He'll make communists of everyone. He'll bring the whole system crashing down about our heads and the poor man's too stupid to see that when it falls, it's his head that gets crushed in the vice first. Of course my rewards will begin when he's gone, but that's neither here nor there. I'm serving a greater cause than just my own.'

'Crowning a king isn't reward enough?'

'Goodness me, no,' said Lord Keaton. 'That will be York's glory, the poor bugger. And Baldwin's triumph. Mine will be in all the things he can do for me then. I will have the position that was always owing to me.'

'And will he thank you for it?'

'Oh, he'll hate me for it,' replied Keaton with a laugh. 'He no more wants to be king of England than the man in the moon. But he won't have any choice and he won't know that it was down to me. And once he's installed . . .' He shook his head and laughed. 'Well I haven't cultivated him for all these years for nothing, put it that way. I will have a great deal of influence at court. The influence my father should have had. And his. But I will have saved the country, can't you see that? This is patriotism at its finest. What we are doing is in everyone's best interests. We are protecting our way of life from ignorant princes who know nothing of the real world.'

Are we only here to avenge the crimes against our fathers? wondered Montignac.

'And Roderick Bentley?' he asked. 'You're sure you'll be able to get what you want out of him now?' asked Montignac.

'Oh yes, certainly I am. We'll have him over a barrel. See his own son hanged when he has the power with a simple word to stop it? You obviously don't have children, Mr Montignac, or you wouldn't even ask.'

Montignac turned to look out of the window.

'No,' he said. 'Perhaps if I did I'd understand.'

Raymond Davis jolted into life suddenly, his eyes opening wide, incredibly alert, before slumping back in the seat, half asleep. His head turned to his right and he tried to focus on the man sitting beside him. 'Owen . . .' he groaned.

'It's all right, Raymond,' said Montignac, patting his arm. 'You had a little accident, that's all. We're taking you to a doctor. Just try and relax. Go back to sleep if you like.'

Raymond groaned again, deeply, and his hand moved to the back of his head, but a moment later he seemed to be immersed in sleep again although his eyes remained slightly open.

They arrived at Bedford Place a few minutes later. It was entirely deserted and the two men pulled Raymond from the car as quietly as possible. He was more alert now and his feet moved as they brought him up the stairs but he said little, just emitted deep sounds from somewhere within his chest. They went up the stairs and into Montignac's flat, which he opened with the spare key he kept over the door. Montignac went in first to check on Gareth and, sure enough, the young man was asleep in the bedroom, still in his clothes, wrapped up in the sheets. Montignac smiled and closed the door on him for a moment.

'Sleeping like a baby,' he said to Keaton as they closed the door of the flat behind them and settled Raymond on a sofa.

'All right,' he said. 'Let's throw a few things around. Make it look like there was a struggle.'

He unsettled a bookcase and broke a vase, then upended the coffee table, resting them on the carpet quietly so as not to disturb the rest of the building, and cleared a space on the floor.

'Now for the hard part,' said Montignac, taking the candlestick from the fireplace.

'Rather you than me,' said Keaton, turning away as Montignac moved towards his prey and shook him roughly.

'Raymond,' he said. 'Raymond, can you hear me? Wake up!'

He opened his eyes blearily and tried to focus. 'Stella . . . ?' he muttered.

'You have to stand up, Raymond,' said Montignac, enunciating each word clearly. 'Stand up. The doctor is here to see you.'

'Can't you just do it there?' asked Keaton but Montignac shook his head.

'He needs to fall the right way. You don't attack intruders who are sleeping on your sofa. He needs to be standing up. It needs to look like there was a struggle.'

He took Raymond's hands and pulled him to his feet, no easy task as he wanted nothing more than to remain prostrate on the sofa.

'Oh here, let me help,' said Keaton, taking one side and between them they pulled him upwards and dragged him to the floor.

'Raymond, turn around and look at the door,' said Montignac, and now the words seemed to have more meaning to him because his eyes opened wider and he licked his lips as he wondered where he was.

'Owen?' he asked clearly. 'What . . . ? Where am . . . ?

'Raymond, over there,' said Montignac, pointing towards the door. 'Turn away from me. Look over there.'

'What's over there?' he mumbled, turning as Montignac had asked him.

'Stella's over there,' said Montignac quietly and as he said that Raymond turned around again, his mouth open, his eyes questioning, and at that moment Montignac brought the candlestick crashing down on his head. He fell to the floor immediately, heavily, his hands going to his temples for a moment before falling at his side. Standing over him, Montignac lifted the candlestick again and brought it down on his forehead with as much force as he could muster. There was a sickening sound of broken bone and Keaton turned away in disgust. Montignac looked down, aware that his hands were trembling now and his stomach churning but the blood did not seem to be pouring quite as much as he would have wished so he hit him again, at which point he was certainly dead. Reaching down with a towel he wiped up much of the blood and carried this into the bedroom, smearing Gareth's clothes and hands with it. The young man lying in his bed barely stirred.

'Are we done?' asked Keaton when he reappeared, and Montignac nodded.

'I think so,' he said, looking around. 'You'll drive me back to the gallery?'

'Yes, of course,' he said. They stepped outside and made sure to leave the door ajar so that the first person to leave the building for work in the morning would see the body and alert the authorities.

They drove back in relative silence. Montignac felt a sensation of sadness at all that had happened but his resolution was firm. He had had no choice, he reasoned. It was kill or be killed. And he was saving Stella from a life with that fool.

'And the forty thousand pounds?' asked Montignac as they pulled up in the back lane.

'Will be yours when the plan has worked,' he replied. 'You've got what you want, Mr Montignac, now it's time for me to get what I want. And it will be money extremely well spent too.'

'I need it by Christmas,' said Montignac. 'Or my life will be on the line.'

'By Christmas, I guarantee it.'

'You'll be ready by then?'

'Oh yes. Certainly if Roderick Bentley plays along. Your Mr Bentley will be saved from the noose and I will have saved the country.'

'Then everyone wins.'

'Except young Mr Davis, yes.'

Montignac nodded and went back into the gallery as the Rolls Royce drove away into the night.

9

'The whole thing is just such a terrible tragedy,' said Jane Bentley. 'Were you expecting Mr Davis to call around to see you that night?'

'Not at all,' said Montignac. 'He'd never said anything about it to me at any rate.'

'But you were friends, the two of you? It wouldn't have been unusual for him to call around that late at night? He'd done it before?'

'I wouldn't go so far as to say that we were friends,' he said, not wishing to imply something that she could easily discover to be false. 'As you know, he was engaged to be married to my cousin. I wasn't entirely in favour of the match if I'm honest.'

'Can I ask why not?'

'No special reason,' he replied. 'I suppose I just didn't know him very well and I wasn't happy that he proposed so soon after my uncle died. He left rather a lot of money to Stella, you see.'

'Yes, I heard that.'

'I was only looking out for her best interests. I'm sure you can understand that. But I think that in time Raymond and I would have got along fine.'

Jane nodded and her body seemed to slump in the chair for a moment. 'And your cousin?' she asked finally. 'How is she holding up?'

'It's been very hard on her.'

'I wish I could tell her how sorry I am.'

Montignac shook his head quickly. 'I don't think that's a very good idea,' he said. 'She's down at Leyville at the moment, our family home. I think she just wants to be left alone to come to terms with things.'

'Of course,' said Jane. 'I wouldn't know what to say to her even if we did talk.'

'It's best if you leave her alone for now.'

'That's what my husband said. I wanted to write to her, to tell her that we were sorry for her loss, but he wouldn't allow it. He said it might prejudice the case.'

'I suppose it might.'

'Roderick's a judge,' she said. 'But I expect you know that.'

'Yes.'

'Gareth trained for the law too. As a barrister. He should have stuck with it.'

'That's something I never quite understood,' said Montignac. 'Why did he study for so many years and then not take it up as a profession?'

'Children are strange, Mr Montignac,' she said, offering him a bittersweet smile. 'At a certain age they want you to be proud of them and so they follow in your footsteps. And then a few years later they want nothing to do with you and reject it all. Even if it causes injury to them.'

Montignac nodded. He reached across and started tapping a pencil against his desk nervously, wondering how much longer she would be staying.

'I'm keeping you from your work,' she said, slowly snapping back to the moment and noticing his discomfort.

'Not at all,' he said and then immediately contradicted himself by saying. 'I do have rather a lot to do today, though.'

'One last question,' she said. 'Will you be testifying at the trial?'

'I believe I'll be called as a witness, yes.'

'A prosecution witness?'

He hesitated before giving her a gentle nod. 'It doesn't really matter who calls me,' he said then. 'I don't really have an awful lot to say about it. I simply wasn't with him long enough.'

'No, but you could testify to the fact that he was so inebriated, yes? Perhaps they will take that into account when it comes to sentencing.'

Montignac noticed that she had already decided the verdict would be guilty. If even the poor boy's mother didn't believe him, what chance did he have? He felt almost sorry for him.

'I'll testify as to what I saw,' he said. 'And what the judge does with that information . . . well you must know only too well from your own husband.'

'Yes,' she said. 'But if they ask you about his character, Mr Montignac? You'll be able to say good things about him, won't you?'

'I'm afraid that will be rather difficult for me. For one thing, we didn't really know each other long enough for me to form an opinion about him. And for another, I can hardly stand there and have my cousin hear me say nice things about the man accused of murdering her fiancé.'

'But you did know Gareth,' she insisted. 'You liked him. You employed him.'

'Of course, but—'

Jane leaned forwards, her eyes searching his face for some connection with her. 'You're a successful young man, Mr Montignac. And your name is a well-respected one. If the court heard you say that you didn't believe Gareth was capable of such a crime—'

'Mrs Bentley—'

'If you told them that you had heard that Raymond Davis had enemies, for example, then maybe—'

'But he didn't have any enemies,' insisted Montignac.

'How do you know that?' she pleaded and then, aware that she was starting to shout, she lowered her voice and spoke in a more confidential tone. 'You have to help him, Mr Montignac,' she said, reaching forwards and taking his hand in both of hers. Her skin was terribly soft to the touch but he could feel the tension in her grip, her unrelenting horror at what was happening to her life. 'You *have* to help him. If you do, if you could do something to stop all this . . . you understand there's nothing I wouldn't do to help my son, don't you? There's nothing you could ask of me—'

Montignac pulled his hand away and stood up, turning his back on her and looking out the window. He bit his lip, wishing he could just disappear into another life, another world, anywhere that didn't involve any of this. He'd never seen someone so desperate for help and yet there was nothing he could do.

'So you won't testify on his behalf?' asked Jane Bentley finally, her voice adopting a more robotic tone of resignation now.

'I will say what I witnessed and I'll answer any questions that are put to me,' he insisted. 'But other than that I can't help you.'

Jane nodded and stood up. He turned around and watched as she walked away and then, to his annoyance, she stopped for a moment and turned back to look at him.

'I was looking at your paintings earlier,' she said. 'The paintings in the gallery, I mean. While I was waiting for you.'

'Yes?' said Montignac. 'Did one of them interest you?'

'None of them did,' she said, shaking her head. 'I don't mean to be rude but I don't think I've ever seen worse in my life. Is it supposed to be some sort of joke?'

She stared at him for a moment but then, aware that he couldn't find an answer, she turned and walked away slowly.

He sat there musing over her visit for some time. Remorse was not an emotion that Montignac was familiar with, and he examined his conscience to find out whether it would visit him now. He decided not. He'd been dealt a difficult hand twenty years before when his parents had been killed. He, like his father, had had his entire fortune and inheritance stolen away from him by his cousin's family. But he had taken control of his life and worked to win it back. He was responsible for Raymond's death, that was true, but Stella was no innocent either. She had killed someone close to him, even if she'd never acknowledged it as such. Gareth Bentley was responsible for his own actions; as Lord Keaton had pointed out about Raymond, he was little more than a casualty of war.

He felt nervous doing so but picked up the phone

and dialled the Westminster number, waiting for a long time before it was finally answered.

'Hello?' said a voice on the other end in a rushed tone, as if he was just about to run out the door.

'It's Montignac.'

A slight hesitation. 'Hello, Montignac,' said Lord Keaton, not entirely pleased to hear from him. 'We don't have any further business to conduct yet, do we?'

'I've just had a visit from Jane Bentley.'

'Roderick's wife.'

'Yes. Naturally she's very concerned about what's going to happen to her son.'

'Well I would imagine she would be,' said Keaton with a gentle laugh. 'Get all weepy on your shoulder, did she?'

'No,' he said, offended for her. 'She's a very determined woman actually. I quite liked her.'

'Well don't like her too much. We can't afford for anything to go wrong at this stage. It's good that she came to see you, though. She's obviously willing to go down any route to get her boy off. Did she offer to bribe you to change your story?'

'No,' he said, unwilling to spell out exactly what had been on offer. 'Would you have expected her to?'

'I wouldn't have thought it impossible. They're a fairly wealthy family.'

Montignac considered it but dismissed the idea as unreasonable. 'I couldn't do it anyway,' he said. 'The only way the case holds up is if I stick to the story. Otherwise I'd look guilty as hell.'

'That's true. Well don't worry about her. I'll start working on her husband from this side and she'll start from the other side and between us we'll get to him.'

'But where are we on this anyway?' he asked, glancing at the calendar on his desk. 'It's almost November. I told you at the start that I only had until Christmas before I'd need the money.'

'Relax, my boy, it's all in hand.'

'It seems to me a lot to hope that you can resolve matters by then. In eight weeks? What are the chances of an advance payment anyway? Say fifty per cent?'

'Twenty thousand pounds?' asked Keaton sharply. 'Are you joking?'

'You know as well as I do what Delfy is capable of.'

'I know what you're capable of too.'

'Not against him. He has too many people on his side. I wouldn't survive it.'

Keaton sighed. 'My dear boy, you have to start trusting me. It's not going to come to that, I guarantee it. The trial begins in a couple of weeks and I can't see it lasting too long. Two weeks perhaps at the most, which brings us to the end of November. If I can't persuade Roderick in that time then—'

'Is he starting to crack?'

'Actually, you caught me just as I'm on my way to a rather important meeting. I need to take stock of exactly how staunchly he stands behind the king. I'll know better then. I intend to start working on him immediately, though.'

Montignac nodded. 'So you won't give me an advance,' he said finally.

'I'm afraid I can't. You'll receive your money when the king renounces the throne. But it wouldn't matter anyway. I know Nicholas Delfy of old and if he says he wants the rest of his money by Christmas, well then, that's exactly when he wants it by. And he's not going to accept anything less than the full amount. He's been fairly generous with you so far anyway. He must like you. But you shouldn't test his patience any further.'

'All right,' said Montignac irritably. 'Well keep in touch with me, will you? I need to know what's going on.'

'I'll let you know, don't worry,' he said, hanging up the phone.

Montignac replaced the receiver in the cradle and sat there nervously staring at it for a moment, racking his brain for a way to raise the money should the plan not come to fruition. There was always one other option but he wasn't sure he wanted to take that. Not yet anyway. The phone rang again a moment later and he picked it up anxiously.

'What?' he said. 'Did you forget something?'

'Owen?' said a voice on the other end of the phone. 'Is that you?'

'Margaret,' he replied with a sigh, running his hand before his tired eyes. 'Hello.'

'I can't believe I've got you at last. You're not very good at returning phone calls, are you?'

'I'm sorry about that. I've been very busy.'

'Well there's been a lot happening here too. What are you doing this weekend?'

'Why?'

She sighed and spoke to him as if he was a child once again. 'Do you have any plans for this weekend, Owen?'

'Nothing special,' he said.

'Right. Well Stella has asked me to ask you to come down on Saturday. She wants to see you.'

'This Saturday?' he asked, regretting not having said that he was busy.

'Yes, of course, this Saturday.'

'How is she doing anyway?' he asked, ignoring the question.

'She has her ups and downs. But she's talking about doing some crazy things. Things that she'll regret.'

'How do you mean?'

'She'll tell you herself, Owen. Will you just come down and see her? Perhaps you can make her see the foolishness of her plan.'

He nodded and glanced at his diary which was empty for the weekend, as he preferred it.

'All right,' he said. 'I'll be on the lunchtime train.'

'Good. We'll see you then.'

She rang off without a goodbye and Montignac put the phone down irritably. He found himself wishing that it was New Year's Day, that all this business was either behind him or he'd faced the consequences of his actions. Either way, it was getting close to the time when he wanted the whole business to draw to a close.

10

The atmosphere in the room was electric when Lord Keaton entered it.

'I won't walk away from my duties just because of a family tragedy,' Roderick Bentley was saying in a forceful voice. 'That's just not the man that I am. I couldn't do it.'

'Keaton, come in,' said the Lord Chancellor, Lord Hailsham, as he stepped inside.

'I'm sorry I'm late,' said Keaton, sitting down and glancing around anxiously at the other men's faces. 'I was just leaving my office when I got a call and I couldn't get the bugger off the phone.'

'Well you're here now and that's what matters,' said Hailsham. 'We haven't got started anyway. I was just telling Roderick here that in light of his . . .' He searched for the appropriate and most inoffensive words. 'Present difficulties, that if he wanted to recuse himself from this advisory committee that it would be entirely understandable.'

Keaton frowned and looked around at their faces. Sitting directly to the right of the Lord Chancellor, like Peter on Christ's right hand, sat Walter Monckton, the king's most important adviser and his representative in the room. To his left sat Lord Altringham and beside him Sir Roderick Bentley.

'And I told him,' said Roderick, turning to look at Keaton, 'that there were no circumstances, no circumstances at all, in which I would even consider such a thing. That this is an extremely important group, considering the future of our country, and I won't compromise it in any way by stepping away from it.'

'Quite right too,' said Keaton nervously. 'And if I may say so, Hailsham, it's not fair to ask him to. You're suggesting that Roderick won't be able to give this matter its due consideration and I think we all know him better than that. It's something of an insult in fact.'

'That's not what I meant at all,' said Hailsham, sounding a trifle offended. 'I was only trying to be helpful, actually. I didn't think he'd want to have to worry about this as well as everything else.'

'Well he's made his decision,' said Keaton gruffly, who couldn't afford to lose him now. 'So let's get on with things.'

'Thank you,' said Roderick, looking at him gratefully, a little surprised by his show of support. In all the discussions they'd had so far it had become clear that Keaton and Roderick were the two most extreme representatives of both sides of the case. It comforted him, therefore, that the other man set so much store by his own integrity.

'Well I do have something important to tell you,' said Hailsham in a gruff tone, as if he was being blamed for something when he was only trying to be kind. 'Now that you're all here, I went to Downing Street yesterday evening to meet with the prime minister. Slipped in by the cabinet office so that I wouldn't be seen by the press—'

'They're on to the story now anyway,' said Lord Altringham. 'You've seen the editorials, I presume?'

'I've seen them,' said Roderick. 'Lot of rot, if you ask me. Who do these fellows think they are anyway?'

'I imagine they think they have as much right to discuss the future of their king as a group of judges sitting around in a stuffy room in Westminster,' said Walter Monckton with a shrug. Hailsham threw him an irritated glare.

'Well they should keep their noses out of it,' said Hailsham firmly. 'It's too much, it really is. Anyway, I went to see Baldwin and he knew we were meeting this morning and wanted me to make a few things clear to you all.'

'Oh, let's not waste time on that,' snapped Monckton irritably. 'We all know that he's opposed to the king. Well no one's stopping him from resigning if he feels so strongly about it.'

'That's what he wanted me to let you know,' said Hailsham with a sigh. 'The PM has no intention of stepping down over this matter and if he did, you'd find that the country would end up in a state of anarchy overnight.'

The other men frowned and leaned forwards as the Lord Chancellor lowered his voice and spoke in a more conspiratorial tone.

'He held a meeting the night before last,' he confided in them. 'Baldwin invited Attlee to Downing Street in his role as leader of the opposition. And Sinclair too, to represent the Liberals. And also Winston Churchill.'

'Churchill?' roared Keaton in exasperation. 'What in blazes was he doing there? Who does he represent?'

'Mr Churchill's a fine man,' said Monckton quickly.

'Mr Churchill is the *king*'s man,' pointed out Keaton. 'Everyone knows that. He's a sycophantic has-been who loves clinging on to the shirt tails of power in the deluded hope that he may get some himself one day.'

'It hardly matters what you think of him personally,' said Hailsham irritably. 'The point is that they were all there. And both Attlee and Sinclair agreed that should the government have to resign over the matter, then neither of them would form an alternative government in its place. The whole system, you see, would come crashing down.'

'Ha!' said Keaton. 'Don't be so naïve. Churchill would be over to the palace before the deed was done looking to install himself as PM with his friend Beaverbrook pulling the strings.'

'No,' said Hailsham. 'Churchill stated clearly that he would not do that.'

'I wouldn't trust that man as far as I could throw him,' muttered Keaton. 'And you've all seen him. That would be a short throw. Now listen. Before we get on to who's resigning and who's forming governments and who isn't, can't you let us know whether any of these things that we're reading about are true or not? The papers may write a lot of rot, as Roderick suggests, but it can't all be rot, can it? Walter, where exactly does the king stand right now?'

Monckton let out a long sigh and nodded, accepting their right to know. 'As Lord Hailsham would no doubt tell you,' he began, 'the king and Mrs Simpson remain very much an item.'

'Disgrace,' mumbled Altringham.

'Their relationship, if anything, is stronger than ever,' he continued, ignoring him. 'Particularly now that she's divorced her first husband.'

'*Second* husband,' said Keaton. 'Ernest Simpson was her second husband. She does get through them, doesn't she? Quite the merry widow.'

'Trading up all the time,' said Altringham.

'Second husband, you're quite correct,' said Monckton, ignoring the jibes. 'The king and Mr Baldwin have discussed the matter and His Majesty came up with a proposal concerning a possible resolution to the country's concerns. And that, gentlemen, is what we are here to discuss today.'

The judges sat forwards eagerly. They, like most of the citizens of the island, had become fascinated with the developments in the matter of Edward and Mrs Simpson but it was so difficult at times to get any fresh news. Here, direct from the king's own plenipotentiary, was the latest development.

'The king proposes that he and Mrs Simpson

marry but that their marriage be a morganatic one—'

'A what?' said Altringham, his face frowning at the unfamiliar word.

'A morganatic marriage,' repeated Monckton. 'Whereby the issue of the marriage would not be in line for the throne.'

'Good God,' said Keaton. 'She's not pregnant, is she?'

'No she's not,' said Monckton quickly and angrily. 'And let us remember that we are discussing the king here and that a certain level of decorum needs to be maintained. As I was saying, the issue, should there be any,' he added loudly, 'would not be in line for the throne. After the king's death, the throne would pass to the Duke of York or, should he predecease him, to the Princess Elizabeth.'

'He can't be serious,' said Altringham.

'He's perfectly serious,' said Monckton, sitting back. 'And it seems a perfectly fair proposal if you ask me.'

'It would satisfy both sides of the debate,' said Roderick, nodding his head. 'And Mrs Simpson. What title would she expect?'

'She would be willing to reject the title of queen; instead she could use the consort equivalent of one of the king's other titles. The Duchess of Cornwall is the preferred option.'

'And the king would be happy for that to be the case?' asked Roderick.

'I think it would be stretching things to say that he would be happy,' said Monckton with a laugh, knowing the character of his master only too well. 'Between ourselves he would prefer to make her queen and for their children to be the heirs but—'

'That would be unacceptable!' shouted Keaton. 'Unacceptable!'

'Hear, hear,' said Altringham.

'I said that would be what he would *prefer*,' said Monckton, clarifying that. 'Not what he is willing to accept. He knows that the government would never agree to that, even if the British people appear to be on his side, and so he is willing to accept their demands should they be willing to agree to the marriage.'

'Well I think that under those circumstances,' said Roderick, 'a deal could be brokered.'

'Hold on a moment,' said Keaton, sitting forwards. 'What exactly is the function of this group? To advise the prime minister, am I right?'

'Of course,' said Lord Hailsham.

'And he would pass that advice on to his ministers and together they would effectively tell the king what he can and cannot do?'

'Well it's a rather blunt way of putting it,' said Hailsham. 'But I suppose that's the long and the short of it.'

'Well then I don't think we can just decide on a whim, in one meeting, whether or not such a thing is acceptable. We're talking about the throne of England here, not a decision on whether or not he should visit the Italian Riviera for his summer holidays.'

'Of course,' said Monckton. 'But in principle, the idea would seem an acceptable one?'

'To me, yes,' said Roderick.

'And to me, no,' said Altringham.

'And to me, definitely no,' insisted Keaton. 'Don't you see that a proposal like this could lead us back to the Middle Ages?'

Monckton sat back in his seat and raised an eyebrow quizzically. 'The Middle Ages? he asked. 'How do you mean?'

'I mean that it's all well and good to say that the king accepts such an idea and that his offspring can go off and live dilettante lives somewhere when they grow up with no concern for their duties but who's to say that that's what will happen?'

'Well . . . we are, I suppose,' said Hailsham. 'That's the whole point.'

'We'll be dead and gone in forty years' time,' protested Keaton, his voice rising in anger. 'Let's say the king dies, and the throne passes to York or his daughter—'

'Yes.'

'And then the king's son, should he have one, decides that he himself never made any such agreement and refuses to renounce the throne.'

'Well he'd be legally obligated to,' said Monckton irritably. 'We would draw up a document to ensure that it was the case.'

'My God, man, haven't you read your history? You think that a legal document would suffice? Any son of

Edward VIII would have built up his own court and his own following. He's not going to be foolish enough to sell away his birthright for an American woman. He's going to demand it. When someone's birthright is stolen from them, they will go to extraordinary lengths to win it back. We'd be going back to the days of Lancaster and York. The War of the Roses.'

'Keaton, I hardly think that would happen in this day and age,' said Hailsham. 'Don't you think you're over-reacting a little bit?'

'I most certainly do not. Wars are fought over thrones, Hailsham. They're fought all the time. We're talking about the empire here. Do you seriously think that the king's son, the natural heir to the throne, would not set about winning it back? Wouldn't *you*?'

The men went silent for a moment as they considered it.

'We could have a situation where the king's son is leading one army, the Princess Elizabeth is leading another—'

'Oh come on, Keaton!'

'What?' he protested. 'Why is it so difficult to comprehend? The law would say that the throne is hers but the natural law would say it's his! And the moral law . . . well that would be open to conjecture. And whatever happens, whoever ends up winning, the other side would always make a case that their man, or woman as the case would be, is the rightful monarch. You would be creating a schism that might take centuries to resolve itself.'

'He's right,' said Altrincham, nodding his head forcefully. 'He's absolutely right. The morganatic marriage doesn't work.'

Hailsham inclined his head slightly and shrugged. Keaton was not one of the people he most admired – after all he had made no secret of wanting his job and his talk of schisms was no doubt prompted by his belief that his own family had long ago been robbed of high office – but he was a senior judge and the prime minister had insisted on his being appointed to this committee. And, he had to admit, he might have a point.

'If such a thing were possible,' said Roderick, the voice of reason, 'I think it would be foolish of us to discount it. And Keaton makes a powerful argument.'

Monckton's mouth fell open. He had hoped that the idea was a reasonable one and they would give their consent. He tried to imagine the scene that would ensure if he went back to his master with this response and he dreaded it; the man's temper was appalling and infantile at times.

'But there is another possibility,' suggested Roderick after a suitable pause, while they were each considering the green fields of Albion lying splattered with their English dead. 'We could simply allow the king to do as he pleases.'

The other four men stared at him, Keaton and Altringham in horror, Hailsham and Monckton in interest.

'Go on,' said Hailsham. 'What do you mean?'

'Well,' said Roderick, 'throughout this whole business the question has always been whether the people would accept the marriage, whether the government would accept the marriage, whether Stanley Baldwin would accept the marriage—'

'I wouldn't worry much about him,' grunted Monckton, no supporter of the prime minister.

'But maybe we should just step back from it and say the king is the king, he has been anointed by God, and whom he chooses to take as his wife, and when, are matters for him and his conscience. And, come that day, he can explain them to his maker if needs be.'

The room went very silent for a moment as they took this in.

'After all,' continued Roderick. 'What are the people going to do?' Take to arms over a wedding? Pull down the palaces? Personally, I don't believe they really care all that much. Have you seen the letters they've been writing in support? They've been goaded into it by the secrecy that's surrounded this relationship from the start but if it was over and done with they'd get used to it very quickly. If the whole matter was finished and put to bed, so to speak, then they'd be back to worrying about the price of fish tomorrow or the conditions in the pits. Is it really too ridiculous to suggest that the whole thing might just blow over?'

Keaton could hardly contain himself. His own argument had been powerful, if bellicose, but surely these were the rantings of a madman. He looked around, waiting to see who would kick Roderick from the room first.

'There may be something in that,' said Hailsham after a moment.

'The mob do get bored very quickly,' said Monckton.

'He is the king, I suppose,' said Altringham, the least convinced. 'But still, the idea of an American woman—'

'I think we need to call this meeting to an end for today,' said Keaton immediately, sensing the tide beginning to turn against him. 'It's inconceivable that we make a decision of such importance without due consideration. We need to step away and consider things. You've all heard my argument and I believe it stands strong—'

'Yes, it's a powerful case,' said Hailsham. 'And we've heard Roderick's, which is unusual but also persuasive.'

'Then I suggest we allow cooler minds to make a decision and consider both sides of this debate over the next week. And then return here to make a decision.'

'A decision I can then take to the prime minister?' asked Hailsham, looking around at them. 'Because he wants an answer as soon as possible.'

'A decision I can take to the king?' asked Monckton. 'Because he's losing patience.

'We all vote next week,' said Keaton. 'And the majority rules.'

'Very fair,' said Altringham.

'I think so,' said Roderick, convinced he had won the debate anyway.

'All right,' said Monckton and Lord Hailsham together.

'One week from today,' said Hailsham quietly. 'And I cannot stress how important it is that you do not reveal anything of this discussion to anyone.

'Of course not,' they said, filing out.

Keaton watched as Roderick slipped down the stairs, glancing at his watch anxiously. He probably had a meeting with his son's barrister to get to, he considered. But it all depended on him. It wouldn't be difficult to bring Altringham back from the other side. Monckton obviously wouldn't change and Hailsham was an unknown quantity. So Roderick was the one.

It was time for end game.

Chapter 6

1

BREAKFAST WAS SERVED at seven o'clock but he was allowed to shower before it was brought to him and to change into the new suit that his mother had brought to the prison the previous day. Although he had barely left his cell since his incarceration, he felt physically exhausted and stood with his head under the spray for a long time, appreciating the rare privacy offered there as he tried to wash the sleep from his eyes. Afterwards, dressed and alone in his cell, he found that he couldn't sit still and paced the floor over and over, wishing they had allowed him a watch so he would know how much longer he had before it was time to leave.

On most nights over the previous two months he had managed to sleep quite comfortably, desperate to return to that state when his eyes opened in the morning to face another tedious day, but the night before the trial began he was too nervous to fall asleep. His old life –

that aimless, peaceful, uneventful existence – seemed like a dream now, something that he had taken so much for granted but had been stolen away from him without his even knowing why.

The sound of a key was heard in the lock and his stomach churned with tension as one of the warders walked in, followed by Sir Quentin Lawrence and James Lewis, the instructing solicitor.

'Not too long now, gentlemen,' said the guard, collecting the breakfast tray and leaving them alone together in the cell. 'I'll give you a call when it's time to go.'

'What's the matter?' asked Sir Quentin, sitting down on the only chair in the cell while Gareth sat on the bed and Lewis stood. 'You look like you've seen a ghost.'

'No, it's just you,' explained Gareth. 'In your wig and gown. I haven't seen you dressed for court before. Did you get it from Ede and Ravenscroft?'

'Why on earth do you want to know that?'

'It doesn't matter,' said Gareth, smiling to himself. He had given up wishing he could go back to the day of his own fitting and attend it after all. 'The whole thing seems a lot more real suddenly. Like it's actually going to happen.'

Sir Quentin snorted. 'Well of course it's going to happen, my boy,' he said, pulling his timepiece from his waistcoat pocket and flipping it open. 'In about twenty or thirty minutes in fact. I just wanted to check on you. See that you were feeling all right.'

Gareth shrugged. 'I suppose so,' he said. 'I don't have

much choice, do I? It can't be much worse than what I've been through already.'

The barrister and solicitor exchanged an anxious glance before looking at him again.

'I should warn you,' said Sir Quentin. 'There's probably going to be rather a lot of people in court today. In the spectator's gallery, I mean. But you shouldn't let it worry you. Just ignore them and keep your eyes focused directly ahead.'

'Really?' asked Gareth. 'Why would there be so many people?'

'Well there's been rather a lot of reporting on this matter. Your father being who he is and all that. You must remember he wasn't very helpful to the reporters earlier in the year when the whole Domson case was running. I think they're rather getting their own back on him now by rubbing his nose in it.'

Gareth felt his whole body slump and he wanted to bury his face in his hands. 'He doesn't deserve that,' he said quietly. 'Neither of them deserve what I've done to them.'

'You haven't done anything, remember?' said Sir Quentin sharply. 'Or are you having a last-minute change of heart and changing your plea to guilty?'

'No, no,' he said quickly. 'I still want to plead not guilty.'

'Quite right too.'

'The fact that I can't remember doing it surely counts for something, doesn't it?'

'Well, we'll have to wait and see what the judge and

jury think of that,' said Sir Quentin, who had worked long and hard on his defence of Gareth Bentley but still knew that it would be an uphill battle; he wasn't feeling particularly hopeful.

'They still have to prove it, though, don't they?' asked Gareth.

'Beyond a reasonable doubt, yes,' he replied.

'And it's going to be difficult to prove, right?'

Sir Quentin didn't like to answer that; considering that he had been found alone in the flat with the dead body, smeared in the blood of the deceased and with his fingerprints all over the murder weapon. It all came together, he knew, to form damning evidence.

'You do know the procedure for when we get into court, don't you?' asked James Lewis, the young but promising solicitor that Roderick had hired to instruct Sir Quentin.

'Yes,' said Gareth.

'Stand up when the judge comes in,' said Lewis, ignoring what Gareth had just said. 'And when he asks how you plead, answer him in a loud, confident voice. Other than that, don't say a word. If a witness says something that you disagree with or you know to be false, you are not to say anything at all. Not under any circumstances. There's nothing worse than a defendant who makes a scene in court. Just write a note and hand it to me and I'll see to it that Sir Quentin gets it.'

'I did study law at Cambridge,' pointed out Gareth irritably. 'I know the procedures.'

'You may have studied it but you never practised it,' said Lewis. 'And you're the defendant here, not the barrister, so you need to be careful you don't confuse your role. That's all I'm saying. The worst thing that could happen is that the jury sees you in a negative light.'

'All right, Lewis, that's enough,' said Sir Quentin irritably, seeing how little of this Gareth was actually taking in. 'He knows what he's doing.'

'It's a funny thing, isn't it? said Gareth quietly. 'If I had simply used my senses I would be your pupil now, going into cases like this with you and afterwards . . . afterwards going for celebratory drinks, I suppose,' he added.

'It was too many drinks that got you into this mess in the first place, young man. I wouldn't spend too much time thinking about things like that if I was you.'

'Do you know who's up first?' asked Gareth.

'The pathologist,' said Sir Quentin. 'That'll probably take most of the morning anyway. We're looking at two weeks in total, I would think, until jury deliberations.'

'And then the sentencing,' said Gareth.

'Don't be so pessimistic. We haven't even started yet. 'You need to cheer up, only don't look too happy out there. Feel free to look outraged and appalled by the whole business. As if you can't believe the injustice of your being there.'

'It's kind of you to say. Somehow I don't have a good feeling about this, though.'

In fact no one in the room, if they were honest with themselves, did.

* * *

Some miles away, Roderick and Jane were getting into their car and escaping the phalanx of reporters who had been waiting on their doorstep for them since early morning. When they managed to close the doors and drive off, Jane was close to tears.

'Catherine Jones phoned this morning,' she said bitterly, referring to the next-door neighbour who had seen red over the encampment of reporters earlier in the year. 'First thing too. Can you believe it? I was hardly out of bed. And said that she hoped that everything would go all right for us today but would it be possible to ask the young men on the street to move along to the Old Bailey instead? It lowers the tone, according to her. If I hadn't been in my dressing gown I would have gone next door and throttled her.'

'That would be all we need,' said Roderick. 'Two trials.'

'Don't be flippant, Roderick.'

'Well just ignore her then,' he replied. 'We have more important matters to worry about than the neighbours' concerns for the value of their houses.'

They drove on in silence for a few minutes until Jane broke it with a quiet comment.

'I'm frightened,' she said. 'I never knew I could feel quite so frightened.'

He opened his mouth to reassure her but found that the words wouldn't come; he had been in the law long enough to know how a case looked and the last thing he wanted was to offer false hope.

'We'll be there together,' he told her instead. 'Both of us. And we'll be there for Gareth, whatever happens. You simply have to block everyone else out of your head.'

'It's not everyone else I'm worried about, Roderick. It's Gareth. It's our son. It's the thought of what could happen to him if . . . if he's found guilty.'

She could barely bring herself even to suggest it but the possibility was there, it was more than a possibility, she had been married to a barrister for long enough to know that.

'It's what they'll do to him then. At the sentencing.'

'I told you that you can't worry about that now,' said Roderick his vision blurry with tears as the idea came into his head too. 'Remember, there's no mandatory sentence here. Even if he was found guilty – and there's no guarantee of that – but even if he was, well he could be sentenced to a few years perhaps—'

Jane laughed. 'That's not what you would have done,' she pointed out. 'It's not what you did. You sent that Domson boy to his death. And two others,' she added, recalling the other murder cases that had lead to the death sentence during her husband's tenure on the bench.

'That was different,' he said. 'That boy was no good, he didn't have a job, he sponged off his wealthy parents, he'd committed a horrible murder . . .' His words trailed off; they were both struck by the fact that this was not so very different at all, that the cases were very much alike, and neither wanted to acknowledge it. They drove up towards the courthouse and both their hearts sank when the crowds outside came into view.

'It's like déjà vu,' said Jane. 'It's like a punishment for what happened before.'

'Stop it,' said Roderick bitterly. 'I won't have you talking like that, do you hear me? Now just keep your head down, hold my hand, and don't speak to anyone until we're inside the court, do you understand?'

She nodded, recalling the last occasion he had used those words to her and how that day had ended.

As they stepped from the car, Mr Justice Patrick Sharpwell KC finished robing in his chambers and checked his appearance in the full-length mirror, pleased by what he saw. Not as grossly overweight as some of his colleagues on the bench, he always believed he cut a rather fine figure in his red ermine. An experienced barrister and judge, he had woken early that morning too, quite looking forward to the case that lay ahead. Despite the fact that it was frowned upon, he had read some of the newspaper reports of the murder of Raymond Davis and had already formed an opinion on the case. Not that it mattered much; if the boy was found guilty the question of what would happen to him was not entirely in his hands. In that event, he would receive his instructions.

There was a brief knock on his door and the bailiff informed him that the court was in place.

'Right you are,' he said, following him out, down the corridor and up the steps to his seat, while the packed courtroom rose noisily to their feet and the case of Rex vs Gareth Bentley was called to be heard.

2

When they were children, Peter Montignac's office was out of bounds to Andrew, Stella and Owen, and even after his death his only daughter avoided the room out of a mixed sense of awe and respect. From as far back as she could remember her father had run his estates and various businesses from that office, flunkies coming to and fro on the morning and evening trains or, for those who could afford it, in their motorcars. He maintained an office in London of course, where his managers were employed, but rarely visited it, preferring to spend his days and nights around the grounds of Leyville and in the company of his wife, children and nephew.

So Stella's decision to enter the room to plan her trip came as a surprise to Margaret Richmond who had also rarely set foot inside.

She had combed the house looking for Stella and couldn't find her anywhere, not even on the roof garden that she loved so much, and was returning downstairs when she saw the door to the office slightly ajar and went to investigate. She pushed it open, saw the figure sitting behind the desk and screamed.

'Good God, Margaret,' said Stella, screaming in response and looking up in fright with a hand to her breast as if she feared a heart attack. 'What on earth are you yelling about?'

'You gave me a shock, that's all,' said Margaret. 'You had the look of your father, when he was a young man, sitting behind his desk. What are you doing in here anyway?'

'I came in to organize some things,' she said. 'Do you know, this is the room in the house that I've spent the least amount of time in? Except when I was getting a telling-off as a child. Other than that, I've almost never been in here.'

'Me neither,' said Margaret, maintaining her position at the door and rubbing her hands quickly up and down her arms. 'It gives me the chills being in here,' she added.

'It does?'

'Well I've spent forty years in this house and always knew that this was your father's private place. I don't feel like I have any business being in here.'

Stella nodded; she had felt the same way coming inside but the room couldn't stay sealed off for ever. 'There are so many things here,' she said. 'Documents, files, account papers. The London office is always asking for them. I think the thing to do is to get them to come up and organize to move everything down there, don't you?'

'You're not going to manage his affairs yourself then?' asked Margaret in surprise.

'I told you, Margaret. I'm not going to stay here.'

Margaret sighed; she had hoped that this idea had been dropped but realized now that Stella had been perfectly serious. So serious in fact that she had taken a trip to London the previous day to visit the London office that her father had set up, and had spoken to his – her – manager there and informed him of her plans. He was to take over all the day-to-day running of the business from then on, with an increased salary of course, but he would have access to all the papers that Peter Montignac had previously stored at Leyville.

'You're serious about this then?' she asked.

'Perfectly serious. This might come out like a joke, Margaret, but do you have any idea how wealthy I am?'

'I'm sure I don't,' said Margaret with a sniff.

'Well neither do I,' said Stella. 'There's so much money, there's so much land, that I simply can't keep track of it all.'

'What about Owen? Why don't you ask him to look after some of it?'

'I tried,' said Stella, shaking her head. 'I suggested it briefly to him shortly after Father's death but he turned me down flat. Said that if he hadn't been trusted enough to inherit it, then he wasn't going to act as an employee. So I could try to do it myself, which would be a bore, or I could pay professionals to do it for me, and then I could start to enjoy some of my money. Why not, after all?'

Margaret opened her mouth to protest but found that her conscience bothered her. In truth, she thought, why shouldn't she enjoy it? If she had had access to a fortune of that size when she was a young woman, wouldn't she have wanted to travel the world and have adventures of her own and meet interesting men rather than acting as an underpaid nanny to three children who weren't even her own? Three children who had never shown the slightest amount of gratitude to her for all she had done. Of course she would. But her selfish half, the half that feared being left alone, got the better of her.

'You're walking away from your responsibilities,' she said. 'Your father would never have approved.'

'Then he should have left the lot to Owen,' said Stella – who wasn't to be dissuaded – in a distracted tone. 'Rather than to me.'

'Perhaps he should have,' muttered Margaret.

'What was that?'

'I just think you'll regret it, that's all. The world's not a safe place at the moment. Why, look at the newspapers every day. All that trouble going on in Spain, the ructions in Germany—'

'Oh come on, Margaret. I don't know what newspapers you've been reading but all I can see when I pick up *The Times* or *The Daily Telegraph* are editorials either denouncing the Simpson woman or calling on Stanley Baldwin to keep his nose out of another man's affairs.'

'And don't get me started on that harlot,' said Margaret angrily.

'I don't intend to. But what I do need you to do is speak to Annie for me.'

'Annie?'

'Yes. We're going to have to let her go.'

Margaret's mouth dropped open. 'But you've already cut her hours to part-time. How am I supposed to explain this to her?'

'There's no point having a cook on the staff if there's no one to cook for, is there, Margaret? Come on now. Be reasonable about this.'

'And what about me?' asked Margaret. 'Am I to be dismissed too?'

Stella sighed and came around from behind the desk. She could see the tears forming in her old nanny's eyes and felt bad for her. Of the three children she had always had the trickiest relationship with her. Not when she was a child, perhaps. But when she was a teenager, things had changed. It was true that the decisions Margaret made for her might have been meant for the best – in retrospect she didn't know what she would have done in her shoes had she been faced with a similar situation – but nevertheless it had damaged her and she had never been able to forgive.

'Well you're not to be turned out of course,' she said. 'This is your home, Margaret. It's yours for as long as you live. And you'll keep your salary. You'll be perfectly comfortable.'

'Living all alone in a house this size? Good Lord, when I think back to when you were all children—'

'Which was twenty years ago,' said Stella with a sigh,

returning to her chair. 'Father's dead, Mother's dead, Andrew's dead, Owen never visits—'

'He's coming, though, I called him.'

'You called him?' asked Stella in surprise, looking up.

'Yes, you asked me to.'

'He took the call?' she asked.

'Well he answered the phone and there I was. He didn't have much choice in the matter.'

Stella smiled. She knew only too well how difficult it was to get hold of her cousin.

'And what did he say?' she asked. 'Is he coming down?'

'Well he made an awful lot of excuses. You know what he's like. But yes, he said he'd see us in a few days' time.'

'Good,' said Stella. 'Because it's only fair that I let him know my plans.'

'And what are your plans exactly?' asked Margaret. 'Where do you intend on going?'

Stella shrugged her shoulders. To the right of the desk there was an enormous globe, an old-fashioned one with a wooden base and she twirled it slowly, watching as the multicoloured countries spun past her, the blue of the oceans catching her eye as it rotated.

'I thought America,' she said, as it slowed down. 'Perhaps New York. That's where everybody goes nowadays, isn't it?'

'New York?' asked Margaret, shivering again. 'Isn't that terribly dangerous?'

'No more dangerous than London,' said Stella in a

cold voice. 'Haven't you heard? Innocent young men get murdered there all the time.'

Margaret frowned; she didn't like to hear Stella speaking like this. She hated the idea of her being turned cold and bitter by what had happened.

'Don't,' she said quietly.

'Don't what?'

'You mustn't torture yourself so. By thinking about Raymond like that.'

'I've lost more important things than Raymond, Margaret,' she said. 'And I've survived. Or don't you remember?'

Margaret felt herself grow angry and turned away just as Stella started to spin the globe again.

'Of course,' she said after a moment, 'I could go east rather than west. Perhaps visit old friends in Switzerland.'

'I hardly think that's a good idea, do you?'

Stella shrugged. 'I don't know,' she said. 'What harm could it do after all this time?'

Margaret opened her mouth to speak but didn't want to get drawn on the topic. 'Well I don't want to get into all that,' she said finally. 'You know what I think. But if you're determined to make mistakes—'

'I'm determined to do what I think is best.'

'Well then it's none of my business at the end of the day.' She sighed in a grumpy way and looked around the room, shivering slightly. 'It's so cold in here,' she said. 'Why don't you sit in the drawing room?'

Stella shook her head. She had been just about to leave in fact but changed her mind when it was suggested.

'I think I'll stay a while,' she said. 'But you go if you want to.'

Margaret turned and looked at a case of legal books that stood to her left and ran her finger along one of the shelves, examining it afterwards and shaking her head. It was only on the rarest of occasions that Peter Montignac had even let anyone in here to clean. He claimed that he knew where everything was and he didn't want a single item to be disturbed. 'And it's so dusty too,' she said. 'I'll have to get someone in to clean it. It's been ignored all this time. That bin is overflowing,' she added, reaching forwards to pick up a wastepaper basket at the side of the desk that was full to the brim and taking it with her. 'I'll see you later,' she said as she left.

'And you'll speak to Annie?'

'If you're sure you want me to.'

'I'm sure.'

'Then I'll speak to her. But will you do one thing for me? Will you just think about what you're doing? Or at least speak to Owen about it. You're still grieving, you know, for both your father and your fiancé and if you only realized that—'

'Thank you, Margaret. I'd like to be left alone now.'

Margaret opened her mouth to speak again, thought better of it and turned and left.

Stella sat at the desk for a few minutes, doodling on a pad of paper with a pen. Her mind drifted to her dead fiancé and she wrote his name down in the centre of the page:

Raymond

She stared at it for a few moments before writing a phrase on top of it:

Living without
Raymond

She tapped her fingers against the desk and thought that this was what she would have to get used to from now on. Living without Raymond. No one had ever realized just how special he really was, not even – she decided – herself. She picked up the pen once more and wrote three words beneath it:

Living without
Raymond
is too painful

She stared at it, frowning at the self-pity of the words, and ripped the piece of paper from the top of the pad, crumpling it up to throw in the bin but Margaret had taken it away. Shaking her head irritably, she stuffed it in the top drawer of the desk instead and stood up, shivering in the chilly atmosphere of the room, and went out and locked the door behind her.

3

Richard Smith had taken over as clerk in the Rice Chambers after the forced retirement of Alistair Shepherd and the position had turned out to be a lot more controversial than he had ever imagined it would be at the outset. In his previous chambers, where he had been a junior clerk, the phone only rang when there was an instructing solicitor on the other end trying to book a meeting with a barrister to represent one of their clients; that, after all, was the business of chambers. Here, however, every second call was from a newspaper editor or a reporter looking for a comment from their venerable head on the murder case involving his son. Richard had quickly learned not to put these calls through to Roderick and told each one in as polite a tone as he could muster that they were not to call back, but it had reached the point where he was beginning to answer the phone in a tetchy manner himself. It was his considered opinion that Roderick should do the decent thing and resign before bringing chambers into further disrepute.

The first call of that day, however, had been from

another senior member of the judiciary, Lord Samuel Keaton, wanting to know whether Mr Justice Bentley would be available to see him later that day.

'His schedule's a little awkward at the moment,' said Richard, flicking through the diary where whole mornings and afternoons had been scored out. 'I'm sure I don't need to tell you that—'

'The trial of course,' said Keaton quickly. 'I know he's there most of the day but does he pop back to chambers at all?'

'Sometimes on the lunch recess,' said Richard cautiously, who would not have given this information out to anyone but a judge of Keaton's seniority. 'You might perhaps find him here then if you wanted to drop by.'

'Well don't book any appointments for him today,' ordered Keaton. 'I need to speak to him on a matter of urgency.'

'Right you are, sir,' he said, making a note of it as he rang off and hoped that his employer would not be angry with him.

As it turned out Lord Keaton arrived at chambers before Roderick and was waiting for him when he came up the stairs, hunched forwards, head bowed, looking like a man with the weight of the world on his shoulders. He walked right past his colleague without even noticing his presence and gave only a cursory nod to the clerk's desk out of habit; the desk could have been inhabited by a two-hundred-pound gorilla and he would scarcely have noticed.

'You have a visitor, sir,' said Richard, nodding past Roderick towards Lord Keaton.

He turned around and seemed surprised to see him there. 'Keaton,' he said, not entirely happy. 'This is unexpected. Did you want to speak with me?'

'If you can spare me a few moments, I would appreciate it,' said Keaton with a smile.

Roderick nodded, his eyelids heavy from lack of sleep, and indicated that he should follow him and they walked up the stairs together towards his office.

'I'm sorry to intrude on you,' said Keaton. 'I know this is a difficult time. I can't imagine what you're going through. How are things developing anyway?'

'Not very well,' said Roderick as they stepped inside and hung their coats on the stand. 'Please, take a seat, Keaton.' He paused and let out a deep sigh as he sat down behind his desk. 'The prosecution are still presenting their case but it doesn't look good. Harkman's doing a wonderful job. He's making Gareth out to be some sort of combination of Jack the Ripper and Attila the Hun. They're bringing up the alcohol, events from the boy's past—'

'He's a prosecutor,' said Keaton, not without sympathy. 'You know it's nothing personal. He's just doing his job. You've done the same thing in the past.'

'Well it's very difficult to listen to,' explained Roderick. 'To hear your own son labelled in those terms. A boy you brought up, educated, had so many hopes for . . . You have children, don't you, Keaton?'

'Five.'

'Well there you are. You can only imagine what it's like to hear someone you love so defamed.'

Keaton nodded; in a small corner of his heart he felt bad for Roderick, a decent man who had had the misfortune simply to be picked for the wrong advisory committee. Gareth Bentley's imprisonment, he realized, could be directly related back to the choices that Lord Hailsham made and to Owen Montignac's gambling debts.

'And Jane?' asked Keaton. 'How is she coping?'

'She's not,' he said with a shrug. 'She goes through the day like a zombie. She hasn't cried very much but it's like she's visibly ageing before my eyes. She's in a state of blind panic and I want to help her, I want to be there for her, but I simply don't know what to do. It's all I can do to keep my own head above water. If this ends badly—'

'It's something you have to prepare yourself for,' said Keaton. 'If the evidence mounts up.'

'Do you think I don't know that?' he snapped. 'I'm sitting there, listening as they present their case and wondering how I would feel if I was presiding over it and by this stage I would be thinking to myself that it's open and shut. I'd be starting to think about the sentence.'

'Ah,' said Keaton. 'Well there's the crux of the thing.'

'Don't, please,' said Roderick, raising a hand. 'I can't even bear to think about it. Even the idea of—' He found himself unable to complete his sentence. Tears were welling up in his eyes and he blinked them back in shame and embarrassment as he looked across at Lord Keaton with an attempt at a smile on his face. 'You know, all I can think about is the families of those three boys I sentenced to death during my career. Their parents. I used to look at them in the courtroom and their faces were filled with devastation and horror but it never affected me. And the ridiculous thing is that I always congratulated myself on the fact that I could be so unmoved. That it made me a better judge, when all it really did was make me ignore the effect these sentences can have on the actual families. That it's their sentence as well. I'm so sorry,' he said, aware that he was growing more and more distressed with each sentence. 'I must seem like a dreadful ass behaving like this.'

'You're behaving like any father would.'

'Yes, well . . .' he said, clapping his hands together to indicate that portion of the conversation was over as he coughed and tried to move on. 'Anyway, what can I do for you? I'm sure you didn't come all the way over here just to hear my troubles.'

'Actually, to an extent I did,' said Keaton. 'But I also wanted to discuss the other matter.'

'The king?'

'The king.'

'That's not for another few days yet, though, is it? Our next meeting?' Roderick flicked through his diary, looking for the appointed date.

'No, that's right,' acknowledged Keaton. 'But I thought it might be worthwhile for us to have a little chat in advance. You know we both seem to be the standard-bearers for the armies of the left and right.'

'I suppose we are,' said Roderick. 'One of us behind the king, one of us behind York.'

'Just so. And Monckton is obviously on the king's side, the two are inseparable. While Altringham is much closer to mine. Hailsham will only make the casting vote if it's a tie, which will inevitably be for the status quo if we can't reach an agreement. Which really means that you have the casting vote. The most important vote of all, you might say.'

'I don't quite see that,' said Roderick with a frown. 'To be honest, as I've considered it recently I feel that I am as adamant in my support for the king as you are opposed. I'm not sure that I can be convinced otherwise.'

'Really?'

'Yes. You made a strong argument last week, conjuring up images of the two armies meeting on the battlefield as in days of old, but somehow I just can't believe that would happen. The world isn't the same as it was in the fourteenth or fifteenth centuries. Parliament and the law would decide who was the legal heir and that would be the end of the matter. Civil war wouldn't be tolerated. And besides, look around the country. Can you really see the people answering a call to arms to fight against each other like that?

People don't have that level of selflessness any more.'

Keaton smiled. 'Actually, I can,' he said. 'But as you pointed out, it wouldn't be in our lifetime anyway. The question remains who best serves the British people now. A layabout wastrel who thinks only of his own pleasures and puts the entire future of the empire in jeopardy—'

'Steady on, Keaton!'

'Or a quiet, decent family man, with two heirs already provided, who will always put duty before . . . personal pleasures.'

'The king is the king,' said Roderick in frustration, beginning to grow irritated at having to discuss this while his son was on trial for his life. 'We don't have the right to unseat him. And as you say, if my vote is the crucial one, then you're asking me to be entirely responsible for removing him from the throne. I might just as well say that your vote is the crucial one if I could persuade you to my side.'

'Oh, but that's impossible,' said Keaton with a laugh.

'And it's impossible for me to change my mind too,' said Roderick with finality. 'I will stand behind him. I don't pretend that I much like the idea of the marriage because I don't. I've never met the woman but I can't say I care for her. But nevertheless I have an overriding feeling that it's simply none of my business. Who am I to say who a man can and can't fall in love with? So I'm going to vote in favour of it. I'm sorry, Keaton, but my mind is made up.'

Keaton nodded; he had hoped that he might be able to persuade him to change his vote but it was clear now that Roderick was as staunch in his opinions as Keaton was in his. There was nothing left to do now but to lay his cards on the table.

'Very well,' he said. 'Of course I have to admit I am a little surprised by your support of him. After all, it's not so many months ago that you were sentencing his cousin to the gallows.'

'Henry Domson was the king's third cousin,' said Roderick defiantly. 'He was hardly what you would call a close relation.'

'I know, I know. But nevertheless I was rather impressed by your decision at the time.'

'You were?'

'Of course,' said Keaton with an honest shrug. 'I followed the case quite closely actually and thought you handled it extremely well. I could see that the fellow was guilty as hell and showed no remorse. And I knew that if any other fellow was standing in the dock there would be no question that he would swing for it. But I really didn't think you'd sentence him to death.'

'Like you say, if it was any other fellow—'

'Yes, but with the mass of public opinion to contend with. All the people who thought it was somehow going against God's will to execute a member of the royal family, albeit such a distant one.'

'Hardly a member of the royal family,' said Roderick with a laugh.

'And then all the people who said he should be treated the same way as the common folk. As themselves. You had the weight of the aristocracy on one side and the voice of the mob on the other and you chose the mob.'

'I chose my own sense of judicial righteousness.'

'It was a brave thing to do.'

'I didn't see it like that,' said Roderick.

'And now here you are,' said Lord Keaton. 'The father of a son in the exact same position as Henry Domson. Fighting to prove his innocence. Knowing that if he is found guilty, he will be executed for the crime.'

Roderick gasped; to hear it put in such stark language shocked him.

'*When* he is found guilty,' Keaton said, correcting himself. 'Because you know that he will be. He hasn't got a prayer.'

'I'd rather you didn't . . .' Roderick found himself stumbling over his words. 'Please don't . . .'

'There's an ironic inevitability about it, though, isn't there?' asked Keaton, settling back and starting to enjoy himself now. 'That you should lose a son to the same fate. Mr and Mrs Domson must be loving every moment of it.'

'Keaton, I don't wish to discuss this any further,' said Roderick, appalled by how cold-hearted the man was being; he was aware that they were fighting different sides in a debate but to speak so callously to him was unacceptable.

'Well you're going to have to face up to it sooner or later, Roderick. Unless someone comes along who can change things for you, they're going to have a noose around your boy's neck in a matter of weeks.'

Roderick frowned. 'Unless someone comes along . . . ?' he began.

'What would you say,' asked Keaton so quietly that both men had to lean forwards, closer to each other, 'if I was to tell you that I could see to it that a conviction in this case would definitely lead to a less severe sentence?'

Roderick didn't know what to say; he was unsure what his colleague was trying to tell him.

'What if I was to tell you that I have the means to ensure that your boy gets a much lighter sentence, say a number of years in prison with time off for good behaviour. Mitigating circumstances and all that. What if I could give your son back to you and spare him his life?'

'You could do that?' asked Roderick, sitting back slowly, his face covered in confusion at what was being suggested.

'I can do that,' acknowledged Keaton. 'I have the power and authority to influence the sentencing in this case. And all I would need is for you to do one simple thing for me.'

Roderick's mouth opened slowly. It hit him immediately and he could scarcely believe that this was being asked of him.

'You want me to change my vote,' he said in an awed voice. 'You want me to vote against the king.'

Keaton sat back and smiled, raising an eyebrow to acknowledge that yes, that was exactly what he wanted him to do.

4

The train was surprisingly busy and Montignac was irritated that he could not locate a compartment of his own; instead he found one that was less crowded than the others and opened the door to it, revealing a young couple sitting very closely together and laughing at a shared joke.

'This seat is empty?' he asked, poking his head through the doorway, and they looked up at him with a look of disappointment on their faces to be intruded upon, but nodded. He had almost missed the train and as it had pulled out, they probably thought they were going to have the place to themselves.

Montignac settled down opposite them, watching as Liverpool Street Station disappeared in the distance, and took the newspaper from his bag. Two headlines caught his eye. The first was above the fold and said in stark black letters:

Judge's Son Has Violent Past

He read on:

It emerged in court today that Gareth Bentley, son of the eminent High Court Judge Mr Justice Roderick Bentley KC, has a history of violent behaviour brought on by overconsumption of alcohol. Bentley, who is standing trial at the Old Bailey for the murder of Raymond Davis of the Royal Horticultural Society in August of this year, sat expressionless in the dock yesterday while Mr Justice Harkman questioned Aidan Higgins, a former schoolboy friend of Bentley's who had been seriously injured in an assault some years ago. Higgins testified that he was part of a group of Harrow boys who, at the age of fifteen, had indulged in an evening of drinking and that a fight had ensued later that evening which resulted in Bentley fracturing his arm in a number of places and dislocating his shoulder. Prosecution counsel questioned why Bentley had not been sent down for the offence but Higgins was unable to provide an answer. Another school friend, Paul O'Neil, also stated that Bentley had claimed to remember nothing of the attack the following day and that he had blamed the violent outburst on his excessive alcohol intake during the evening in question. Mr Justice Harkman pointed out to the court that on the night of Mr Davis's murder, Bentley had been observed drinking approximately twelve pints of beer and half a dozen shots of spirits at the Bullirag public house on Air Street.

The article went on with some further details of the afternoon's business but Montignac tired of it; it was clear that no one was in any doubt regarding Gareth's guilt. It occurred to him for the first time that his defending barrister should have persuaded him to plead that way, as the sentence might well be lighter.

Below the fold, there was another short article, bearing the headline:

Further Talks in Simpson Matter

More gossip, thought Montignac as he scanned the article.

> London society is abuzz with rumours that an announcement is expected before Christmas regarding the possibility of a marriage between His Majesty, King Edward VIII, and Mrs Wallis Simpson, an American divorcée. Although there is some public support for the union between the two it is believed that the Prime Minister, Mr Stanley Baldwin, is firmly opposed and that he has empowered a committee of leading legal minds to discuss the proposals and rule on their legitimacy.

'Excuse me,' said a voice from across the compartment and he looked up and saw the young woman, who couldn't have been more than about twenty years of age, speaking to him. 'There's nothing in there about the king, is there?' she asked.

'Actually I was just reading about it,' said Montignac.

'Oh tell us what it says,' she said eagerly. 'It's so hard to get any information on it and I'm fascinated. They never talk about it on the wireless at all.'

Montignac nodded and read the article aloud. The young couple listened intently, shaking their heads.

'Well it's not right, is it?' she said when he reached the end. 'Imagine him going after a harlot like that. It don't bear thinking about.'

'We just got married yesterday,' explained the young man, reaching for his wife's hand and holding it up to display her wedding ring as if to confirm their legitimacy. Montignac wasn't sure if he had ever seen such a tiny diamond before, if diamond it was. 'So why Jenny's so opposed to him doing as he pleases is beyond me. Why not, if he can have a bit of happiness, that's what I say.'

'Oh no, I don't hold with that,' said Jenny. 'Surely there's plenty of European princesses out there who would do anything to land the king. I think he's just doing it to be clever, don't you?'

'I'm sure I don't know,' said Montignac, who had an hour's journey ahead of him and wasn't sure he wanted to get involved in a long discussion about the rights and wrongs of regal matrimony. He closed the newspaper and handed it across. 'Here,' he said, hoping to distract their attention. 'Please. Be my guest.'

They took the paper gratefully and started to read it between them as Montignac looked out of the window at the countryside rolling by. It was extraordinary, he thought, how time could change a person's emotions. Ten years ago when he was fifteen he had loved the train rides back and forth to Leyville during term breaks or the long vacation. He could never sleep on the nights leading up to it, the idea of getting home, getting back to the freedom of Leyville, returning to Stella.

Their relationship had changed after a fight he had with Andrew when he was fourteen and his cousin was seventeen. It had been over something trivial and whether the older boy was in a particularly bad mood or had just built up a resentment against his young cousin, Montignac did not know, but he had had the better of him in the fight and he went home with blood pouring from his nose and from a gash above his eye.

'Good God,' said Stella when she saw him slink unhappily through the front door. 'What on earth happened to you?'

Montignac shrugged; he didn't want to admit that Andrew had been able to overpower him. She could see that he was embarrassed and so didn't push him further.

'There's no one else at home,' she said. 'We better get you cleaned up before Mother and Father get back. Come upstairs with me.'

He followed her up to the bathroom where she washed out his cuts and dabbed a little iodine above his eye, where some grit had stuck in the wound, before covering it with a plaster. 'There,' she said. 'You don't look so bad now.'

The whole process had taken no more than ten

minutes but in those ten minutes, their lives were to change. They had never sat so close together, nor touched in this intimate way before. Stella had found that the more she reached across and wiped at her cousin's skin the more she wanted to touch it. The more she looked at that shock of white hair on his head, the fringe of which held flecks of red from the blood, the more fascinated she became by it.

When she was finished they sat there for a few moments, staring at each other and then, as if it was the most natural thing in the world, they leaned forwards and kissed.

'We're going on our honeymoon,' said Jenny and Montignac snapped out of his daydream and glanced across at her.

'What was that?' he said.

'We're going on our honeymoon,' repeated her husband, Jack. 'Off down to Cornwall. I have family down there, you see, so like as not they'll have a spread laid on for us when we get there.'

Montignac smiled and tried to resist a laugh; they obviously wanted to share their good news with someone and he was the only available person.

'We're both in service at a house in London,' said Jack. 'That's where we met. We got twenty pounds as a wedding present from the master and mistress. Can you believe it? Twenty pounds,' he repeated as if the fact of his good fortune was still a matter of amazement to him and he should have considered marriage years before.

'Congratulations,' said Montignac. 'But you're very young, aren't you?'

'I'm nineteen,' said Jack.

'And I'm twenty-one,' said Jenny. 'I'm his older woman.'

Montignac smiled. The older woman. They had spent eighteen months making jokes about that, he and Stella. She was less than a year his senior but it didn't matter, it amused them to think of it in those terms; it made their relationship even more exciting.

On one occasion he forged a slip from his uncle and aunt and left the school for the weekend, meeting Stella from her school and they spent an illicit Saturday together on the beaches at Brighton, hiding in coves together, making love furtively. They were enraptured with each other, with the surprise of a physical relationship, the lust they felt. Montignac woke one morning with the certain knowledge that Stella was the only thing in the world that gave his life any meaning. He loved her, passionately, a love that made him feel weak inside and electrified him when she walked into a room. He just wanted to look at her all the time, to feel her presence, to receive that thrill that came when she turned in his direction and smiled or reached out for him and kissed him.

She said she was smitten by him, a word that vibrated within his soul, and they repeated it to each other for more than a year. It was the single word they used to describe their relationship. Smitten. Always smitten.

'Of course,' said Jenny. 'People thought we were crazy getting married so soon—'

'We've only known each other a few months,' explained Jack.

'But we just thought, when you've met the right person, you know it, don't you? You know that no one else can ever match up to him. So there's no point looking. Are you married, Mr . . .'

'Montignac,' he said. 'Yes,' he added after a moment. 'Yes I am.'

'Oh that's good. How long for?'

'A few years now,' he lied.

'And what's her name?'

'Stella.'

'That's a posh name,' said Jenny. 'Where is she then? Isn't she travelling with you?'

'Actually, I'm just on my way home to her,' he said, wondering whether it really was his home any more. He turned his head to discourage further conversation and wished he'd picked a different compartment. The two young people seated opposite were smitten with each other too, he could see that, and it tore at his insides to have lost the only woman he had ever loved or ever would.

Of course, he knew that their relationship had never really stood a chance. But that it had come to an end in such a dramatic fashion made the memory of it even more painful. First there had been that awful morning, that most terrible morning of his life – he had to close his eyes to block the memory as it poured in upon him – when Andrew . . . Andrew . . .

He shook his head to dismiss it; he had done many unpleasant things in life but thinking of that was not allowed. It was, he had decided long ago, injurious to his health.

And then a month or two later Stella had told him the awful truth and they didn't know what to do. They had nowhere to turn, no one to turn to, and so she had taken a chance and called Margaret Richmond to her room and confessed everything to her, becoming almost hysterical with tears and upset as she did so, and Margaret had sat there, growing paler and paler as the story progressed, as they told her the things they had done, of what they should never have done, and the consequences that had suddenly landed on them.

She was shocked, of course. Almost speechless. Paced around the room, reeling from disgust and panic. She went to the bathroom and threw water on her face. But finally she had agreed to help them, the children she had never had. It was Margaret who had laid the seeds of doubt in Peter and Ann Montignac's minds about the school Stella was in and it was she who had first suggested the finishing school in Switzerland. She only had to mention the names of the aristocrats who sent their daughters there for them to be convinced and then soon enough, before she could begin to show, Stella had left Leyville, not to return for almost two years.

She hadn't said goodbye to Montignac before going

and had never spoken to him about the matter since. Once again it was left to Margaret to tell him what had happened. That she was safely in Switzerland and would remain there for now, and that the problem was behind them, there would be no baby now, and he must forget about it and never discuss it again with anyone. Not ever.

A sharp taste entered his mouth and he licked his lips, putting a finger to them which he drew back coated in blood. He had bitten right through his lip as he thought of the events of the past.

'Oh my, you're bleeding, Mr Montignac,' said Jenny, reaching in her bag and extracting a handkerchief. 'Here, hold this to it.'

She pressed forwards and went to hold it there herself – as Stella had done all those years ago – but he pulled back and took it off her with a grateful nod.

'Thank you,' he said. 'I can do it myself.'

The train was slowing down; they were two stops away from Leyville, a good hour's walk or more. It was cold outside but something told him that if he sat there for a minute longer he would put his fist through the window in anger and he quickly grabbed his bag and, without so much as a goodbye, charged through the compartment doors and out on to the platform outside, where he gasped in the fresh air and hated his life and his history and everything he had become and everything they had turned him into. The young couple stared at him through the window in surprise as the train pulled away.

The Montignacs, *those* Montignacs, had stolen everything from him. His house, his money, his land, his family, his inheritance, his peace of mind, his child.

And here he was, answering a summons from the worst Montignac of all, as if he was little more than a servant. Why did she treat him like this? He wondered. Why couldn't she see how much he loved her? How they were born to be together?

5

While Roderick Bentley was learning just what he needed to do in order to save the life of his only child, his wife Jane was also taking a break from the Old Bailey to speak to Sir Quentin Lawrence during the lunch recess. She had waited for him after the morning session but he had disappeared from sight as the judge had risen and the crowds of spectators blocked her view of where he went.

'I'm going over to chambers,' Roderick told her as he stood up to leave and collected his bag. 'Do you want to come with me?'

'No,' she said, shaking her head. 'I'll have a sandwich here and see you later.'

He nodded and went on his way, grateful that he would not be forced to make hopeful conversation, and she waited for him to leave the courtroom before following him out and looking up and down the corridor for her son's barrister. He was nowhere to be seen but then, by chance, she spotted James Lewis, the instructing solicitor, descending a staircase and she ran in his direction, her high heels making loud noises in the otherwise deserted corridor. Before she could reach him, however, he had stepped through the door of the gentleman's lavatory and she stood outside, waiting in desperation for him to emerge. After a few moments that felt like a lifetime, and looking to her left and right to ensure that no one was around, she followed him in.

It was a strange experience, walking inside. It occurred to her that she had never been inside a Gents room before in her life; it was colder than the Ladies and less well laid out. Standing with his back to her at one of the urinals, whistling a tune under his breath, stood the young solicitor.

'Mr Lewis,' she said and he jumped, startled, turning his head in amazement to see her standing there.

'Lady Bentley,' he said. 'What the—?'

'I'm sorry to burst in on you, Mr Lewis, but—'

'Lady Bentley, this is the Gents! You can't come in here!'

'There's just something that I—'

'It's for men only,' he insisted. 'You'll have to wait outside until—'

'Oh I don't care about that, you stupid boy,' she roared. 'I need you to tell me something.'

Lewis glared at her and turned back to gather himself together and button his trousers up before stepping over to the hand basin, his youthful face scarlet with embarrassment. 'This is most improper,' he muttered under his breath. 'A chap goes to the bathroom, he should be allowed—'

'Do you know where Sir Quentin has gone?' she asked, uninterested in his rules of etiquette.

'To lunch, I imagine,' he replied.

'Yes but where?' she insisted; she had a slightly manic look in her eyes that unsettled James and he gave her the name and address of a pub down the road where he knew Sir Quentin often went for a steak and kidney pie during a trial.

'I can't guarantee he'll be there,' he shouted after her as she ran through the door again, just as an aged barrister stepped inside and stared at her departing figure in surprise before turning back to Lewis contemptuously. 'Don't ask,' he said, shrugging his shoulders and making for the door himself.

Fortunately for James, Sir Quentin was indeed in the pub he had suggested, sitting alone at a discreet corner table with a pie in front of him and a half glass of beer, *The Times* crossword laid out on the table beside him.

'There you are,' said Jane, sitting down opposite him. 'I was waiting for you after court.'

'Jane,' he said, not entirely happy to see her there; he relished the peace and quiet of these brief breaks in proceedings and wondered how she had tracked him down. 'Dear lady,' he added in a patronizing tone.

'Don't "dear lady" me,' she said crossly. 'What is going

on in there, Quentin? This morning just seemed . . . I've never heard such . . . what kind of people . . . ?' Her mind was so filled with misery and confusion that she could find no expression for her many complaints. Her hundreds of questions fought to be heard, like a crowd of angry villagers screaming in unison at a town-hall meeting.

'Please, Jane,' he said quickly. 'Settle down. Let me get you a drink. What would you like?'

She sighed and tried to compose herself. 'I don't need to settle down,' she cried in frustration. 'I just need to—'

'Sit down,' he insisted. 'I'll get you a gin and tonic. That will calm your nerves.'

'All right,' she said, taking the chair opposite him and brushing her hair from her eyes; she caught sight of her reflection in a mirror for a moment and her skin looked pale and dry. Three months earlier she would never have allowed herself to leave the house looking like that. She looked away quickly.

Sir Quentin called over the waitress to place the order and she returned a few moments later with a glass that Jane started to sip from anxiously.

'This morning,' she said in a more even tone now. 'It didn't go well, did it?'

'Those two boys, Higgins and O'Neill, they didn't help matters, that's for sure. It's very unfortunate that the prosecution got hold of them.'

'Oh they probably contacted them themselves,' she

said bitterly. 'I remember them well enough from when Gareth was in school. Terrible influences. They were the ones who were always goading him into doing these things. Drinking and causing trouble. Although they seem to have been able to hold their alcohol better than him. They probably read about the case in the newspapers and thought they'd make names for themselves.'

'Young Mr Higgins did end up with quite severe injuries,' said Sir Quentin carefully. 'The prosecution were able to make a lot of hay from that.'

'But you made no objections,' complained Jane. 'That's what I don't understand. Why didn't you get to your feet more often?'

'Because, dear lady,' he said, 'I objected at the outset. I told the judge that the evidence of misdemeanour ten years earlier had no relevance to this case whatsoever and he over-ruled me. He felt that it spoke to the character of the defendant.'

'Gareth,' insisted Jane. 'His name is Gareth.'

'Yes, to the character of Gareth. He wanted the evidence to be laid out for the jury to hear. And having ruled on that I could hardly object to any of the young men recounting what had happened, could I? Harkman hardly had to lead them at all. But I couldn't allow the jury to think we were afraid of it.'

'It damaged us, though, didn't it?'

'Very badly, I fear.'

Jane sighed; she had hoped that he would say no, that

it was not too important either way, but his tone said differently.

'Well what are we going to do to counter it?' she asked. 'What will our defence be?'

'Our defence remains what it has been all along,' said Sir Quentin. 'One, that there are no witnesses to the attack and no one, for that matter, even to say that the victim died in Mr Montignac's flat.'

'Well of course he died there,' said Jane irritably. 'That's ridiculous.'

'Yes, but no one saw it. It's a valid point. Two, that the defen—' He quickly corrected himself. 'That Gareth would not have been able to summon enough strength in his condition to fight and kill another person, let alone a sober, strong young man like Raymond Davis.'

'That's good,' said Jane, nodding her head.

'And three,' said Quentin, 'and perhaps most importantly, that he had absolutely no motive whatsoever. He didn't even know who Davis was.'

'Isn't that enough?' she asked. 'Isn't that a valid defence?'

Sir Quentin breathed heavily through his nose. He wasn't sure how truthful she wanted him to be but if she was going to push him then he would not hold back. 'Well that's rather the problem, isn't it?' he said. 'There are those who will see our third defence, the lack of motive, as potentially quite damning. It implies that Gareth was so drunk and out of his senses that in a blind fit he simply murdered an innocent man who had come to call on a friend. His future brother-in-law.'

'He's not her brother.'

'Cousin-in-law then. If there's such a thing.'

'I wondered,' began Jane, looking around to ensure that no one could overhear her, but the bar was relatively quiet at this time of the day, 'whether there was any chance we might be able to do a little more than what we are doing?'

Sir Quentin frowned, 'I assure you, dear lady, I'm doing all I can. As you know I've been practising at the Bar for over twenty-seven—'

'I don't just mean in terms of our defence,' said Jane, holding his gaze. 'I mean in terms of ensuring a favourable verdict.'

He stared at her and shook his head. 'I'm sorry, Jane,' he said, baffled. 'I don't follow you.'

'Sir Quentin, you must have looked at them,' she said.

'Looked at whom?'

'The jury, or course.'

He nodded. 'Well yes,' he said, 'I've looked at them. But I don't—'

'Where do they get these people from anyway?' she asked with a bitter laugh. 'They're a rotten-looking bunch, don't you think?'

Slightly offended for the integrity of the judicial system to which he had devoted himself throughout his life, Sir Quentin drew himself up in the chair and shook his head. 'They seem like a perfectly sensible jury,' he said. 'Twelve good men and true. That is the foundation on which we base our system of justice after all.'

'There's a man in the front row who's worn the same suit every day of the trial,' she said. 'The same shirt even. He must wash it out overnight and leave it on a hanger to dry. There's a woman seated behind him who wears a hat that was in fashion for about three weeks in nineteen twenty-eight. There's an older gentleman at the end of the front row who cycles to court every morning on an old boneshaker and brings his own sandwiches for the recess. Do you see what I'm getting at now, Sir Quentin?'

'No,' he said in a clear voice. 'I haven't the first clue if I'm honest.'

'These are people who are not of solid means,' she explained. 'They are lower-middle-class, upper-working class folk who are no doubt struggling from week to week to support themselves and their families. Trying to give their children a decent upbringing but finding that economic circumstance or just plain bad luck is getting in their way all the time.'

'Perhaps,' he granted her. 'But that's the way we do things. We don't recruit our juries from the food halls at Harrods.'

'Surely there's a way that some of these people could be helped,' she said gently, ignoring his attempt at humour. 'Surely they would appreciate it if a charitable donation was made to them to help them out with their lives, with their children's lives?'

Sir Quentin narrowed his eyes and laid down his

knife and fork, his appetite for the steak and kidney pie destroyed at last. This was exactly why he didn't like to be disturbed at lunch. 'Jane, I'm going to stop you before you say anything else,' he said.

'Just listen to me,' she said, interrupting him quickly.

'No, I don't believe I will—'

'It wouldn't have to be the whole jury, just two or three of them. Four or five at most. Enough to swing things our way. If we could just let them know, offer them—'

'Jane, stop it!'

'In a way it would be like making amends for what Gareth has done, trying to improve the lives of some needy people—'

'Jane, I must insist,' he shouted, his voice rising so high that the few other people in the bar turned and glanced coolly in the direction of the arguing couple in the corner, suspecting a love affair gone awry. Jane stopped talking and bit her lip, looking away from both them and him.

'We're not wealthy by any means,' she said now, reaching forwards and pinning his hand to the table with her own. 'But we're extremely comfortable. We have the money. I have it myself if need be.'

'Does Roderick know that you're having this conversation with me?' he asked suspiciously.

'No, of course not. He'd lose his mind.'

'I daresay he would,' said Sir Quentin. 'And for what it's worth you could go to jail for what you've just suggested and while you're at it you could ensure your son's conviction and execution.'

She turned to stare at him again, her face suddenly pale as if he had slapped her.

'That's right, Jane,' he repeated. 'Execution. And if you ever make a suggestion like that again and anyone overhears you, that's exactly what could happen. And I have to tell you, I am offended, mortally offended that you think I would go along with such a scheme.'

She leaned forwards, her lips seeming to recede slightly as she bared her lips, the lioness defending her cub. 'Don't play the high and mighty with me, Quentin,' she said. 'You don't have any children, do you?'

'No, but—'

'Then don't you think for a moment that I wouldn't do everything in my power to defend mine. If they want to hang him, they'll have to hang me too.'

He sat back and took the napkin off his trousers and laid it on the table, standing up.

'I'm going back to court now, Jane,' he said, barely able to look at her; she seemed like she was losing her reason entirely. 'Because I have known and respected your husband for so many years I will do you the courtesy of pretending that this conversation never happened. However, if you ever broach this topic with me again I shall resign from the case and will have no alternative but to report my reasons to the judge. Do you understand me?'

She stared at the table, no tears now, just a sense of

total and utter impotence, unable to control what was going on around her. The frustration of seeing her life disappearing, her son's life on the point of extinction. He, on the other hand, refused to budge until she confirmed it.

'Do you understand me?' he repeated and then a third time.

'Yes!' she said quickly and angrily. 'Yes, yes, yes. Yes, I understand you. What do you care anyway? You get paid no matter what happens, don't you?'

She turned and looked at him and he shook his head and left the bar, leaving her alone in the seat. The fact that she was unable to do anything to save her son felt like a ticking time bomb inside her and it was all she could do not to overturn the table and scream as loudly as possible; it was what she wanted to do. Scream and scream and scream until they came to take her away and lock her up and fill her full of enough medication that she would forget about all of this and be transported back to a time when the only thing that mattered to her, the only things of any importance, were securing invitations to garden parties at Buckingham Palace and finding the right hat to wear to Ladies' Day at Ascot.

6

He found her sitting in the roof garden, reading a travel guide to America; it was a beautiful day and she was wearing a sleeveless dress, dark sunglasses and had a glass of white wine on the table beside her. She looked for all the world like a woman without a care or concern. She was luminous, Montignac thought. The most beautiful woman he had ever known. On a whim he re-enacted that favourite game of his from when they were children; he stood silently for a moment, then stamped his right foot forwards loudly and she jumped in her chair, dropping her book as she let out a small cry of alarm.

'Hello,' he muttered, his voice barely carrying.

She looked towards him, laughing a little as she did so. 'I didn't hear you arrive,' she said, reaching down to recover the book. 'Actually, I think I'd drifted off into some sort of trance.'

'I took the lunchtime train,' he said, sitting down opposite her and wishing he had a pair of dark glasses too, not just to ward off the sun but because he felt she suddenly had an advantage over him by being able to see his eyes when he could not see hers. She glanced at her watch.

'It must have come in late, did it?' she asked. 'When you weren't here by two-thirty I thought you weren't coming at all.'

'I got delayed,' he explained, not wishing to recount how or why he had got off the train two stops early and walked the remaining six miles to the house.

'Well you're here now and that's what matters. Would you like some wine?' she asked, lifting the bottle and holding over the glass she had set out for him. He nodded and she poured one for him, which he tasted carefully, allowing it to linger on his palate for a few moments. 'It's from Father's cellar,' she said as he looked impressed. 'I decided to start trying some of it rather than just letting it go to waste. I have no idea how many bottles there are down there but there's an awful lot of them. They go back to our great-grandfather's day, some of them.'

'There's almost four and a half thousand,' he said quickly and she looked at him in surprise.

'Really?' she asked.

'Really. Less whatever you've managed to get through, of course.'

'I haven't gone through that many. Don't worry. How was your journey anyway?'

Montignac sighed; he was in no mood for small talk. 'I'm sure you didn't ask me here to talk about the train trip,' he said.

'Well, no.'

'How have you been anyway?' he asked, not wishing to sound aggressive from the start. 'I wondered whether I would see you in London during the week.'

'For the trial, you mean?' she shook her head. 'I thought about it,' she admitted. 'But in the end I couldn't see the point. It seems like a foregone conclusion that he's going to be found guilty, doesn't it?'

'I'm afraid it does,' he said.

'What do you mean by that?' she asked, taken aback.

'Well, it's a tragedy, for all concerned, isn't it?' Raymond's family, Gareth's family. Gareth himself. You.'

'And Raymond,' said Stella harshly. 'Let's not forget him. He was the victim here, remember?'

'Of course,' he replied quickly. 'I meant alongside Raymond.'

'Well forgive me if I don't have a lot of sympathy for your young friend—'

'He's not *my* friend, Stella. He simply worked for me, that's all. And he didn't even do very much of that.'

'I know, I know,' she said sadly, shaking her head. 'Sorry, Owen. I didn't mean to imply anything by that. You could hardly have known that things would work out the way they did. He came from such a good family too.'

'I'm giving up the flat in Bedford Place,' he said. 'I didn't tell you that, did I?'

'No,' she said, a little surprised for he had been there for about four years and it was convenient and comfortable. 'When did you decide this?'

'A week or so ago. I told my landlord I'd be moving out in about a month. I couldn't stay there any longer. I didn't feel that it was appropriate to stay any longer after what happened.'

Stella found herself touched by his decision and had an urge, which she resisted, to reach across and squeeze his hand. 'I think that's very kind of you,' she said. 'Do you know where you'll go yet?'

'Not really. I have to start looking. I dread it.'

An idea came into her head. 'What about Father's apartment?' she asked. 'The one in Kensington? It's all bought and paid for and there's no one in it at the moment.'

'Father's apartment, as you put it,' he said 'is your apartment now, remember? He left it to you.' He resisted the urge to add the suffix: *along with everything else*.

'Yes, but I'm not using it. Oh, Owen, you should take it. It's so beautiful there and you'll have three times as much space.'

He shook his head. 'He left it to you,' he repeated. 'He obviously didn't want me to have it.'

'But it's not his to decide about any more,' she said.

He looked away and stared out over the grounds of Leyville. 'Do you remember when we were children and we used to come up here to hide from Margaret or your parents?' he asked with a smile. 'And then we'd get into worse trouble because they were always afraid we'd fall off and kill ourselves. And your mother wanted to put up a railing so that couldn't happen but Uncle Peter refused, he said it would destroy the view.'

'I remember,' said Stella.

'I think the only reason why they didn't want us up here was so that it could be their own refuge. All the little lunches they had up here with their friends. The wine receptions. They didn't want us interfering with them.'

'Well we're here now,' said Stella.

'Yes, we are.'

'And no one can stop us any more.'

'No.'

He seemed to be drifting off into his own thoughts and she snapped him back to her. 'Owen, I'm glad you came down. I wanted to talk to you about something.'

He looked across at her and took another sip of wine. 'Go on,' he said.

'Well it's about Leyville. 'What's to become of it.'

He sat back in surprise. 'What's to become of it?' he asked. 'I don't follow you. Why, what are you thinking of doing to it?'

'I'm not thinking of doing anything to it as such,' she explained, a little nervously. 'But I've decided I don't want to live here any more.'

The news could hardly have surprised him more. 'Why not?' he asked.

'After Father died, and particularly after Raymond died, I just started to think that the place was no good for me. I had this vision of myself hiding away for the rest of my life, only rising above the parapet for food and water, and dying surrounded by a hundred cats, not being discovered for weeks on end. Don't you think this place has caused only trouble for people?'

'Not at all,' he said with certainty. 'I love Leyville, you know that. My father loved it too. Our grandfather—'

'Yes, yes, I know they did. But I don't. Isn't that strange? After all these years to suddenly feel like you don't belong in your own home? No, I've decided I don't want to stay here any longer. I'm thinking of going travelling in fact.'

'Hence the book,' he said, nodding towards the travel guide on the table.

'Exactly.'

He frowned; he found it extremely difficult at times to be around Stella but the idea of her being elsewhere, in another country or continent, a place where he could not keep track of her and the lowlifes who tried to get close to her, was anathema to him.

'You can't be serious,' he said.

'I'm perfectly serious.'

'And what would you do with the house? Just close it up?'

'Well that's what I wanted to talk to you about,' she said, a little irritably he thought. 'I had an idea about donating it. To the National Trust. Letting them make a sort of museum out of it. A place that the public could come to visit. What would you think of that?'

His mouth dropped open in surprise. The public, those millions of nobodies with mud on the soles of their shoes and cigarettes dropping ash on the floors, marching through his ancestral home, searching for a coffee shop or a convenient bathroom; his father's birthplace, the birthright that was stolen from him . . . the idea was too much.

'I think it's obscene,' he said. 'And I don't for a moment believe you mean to go through with it.'

'Obscene?' she asked, a little taken aback by his choice of words. 'I don't see what—'

'Your father did not leave you Leyville in order to see you throw it over to the government or the Crown,' he said, pointing a finger at her. 'Good God, if he thought you were going to do that he never would have cut me out of the will.'

Now it was her turn to look surprised. 'I can't believe you just said that,' she said.

'Well, believe. And anyway, I don't think you have the right to do any such thing. The will made it clear that you couldn't sell any of the land or estate, that you had to live off the income and only your heirs—'

'Actually, I've already spoken to Denis Tandy about that,' she said defensively. 'It's true that I'm not allowed to sell Leyville, but I can give it away. I can create a trust whereby the house becomes the property of the nation with a board to oversee its activities over which I would preside. And I had very much hoped that you would want to be a board member too.'

'Not if my very life depended on it,' said Montignac.

She stared at him, truly surprised by his attitude. I don't understand you, Owen,' she said. 'I didn't think you'd react like this at all. I thought you might be sad at my going away but—'

'Don't flatter yourself, Stella. You may go to the Arctic Circle, the Kalahari Desert or the North Pole for all I'm concerned but if you think I am going to allow you to sell my birthright out from under me to a bunch of overpaid politicians and a man who's ready to throw in his country for some tart from Maryland then you've got another think coming. Grandfather may have done that to my father, and your father may have done it to me, but I won't allow it to happen again. The theft stops here, all right?'

'My father took you in,' she insisted, standing up and raising her voice. 'When you had nowhere to go, he gave you a home. He educated you.'

'And he had the money to do so because he had stolen it from my father. After Grandfather died, why didn't your father seek to bring mine back into the family again then? Why did he wait until after he had died to bring me here?' Now his voice rose in anger. 'Because he didn't want to give up what he had, that's why. For all his faults, he valued this place at least. And if he knew that you were considering such a thing, he'd be rolling in his grave right now.'

She stared at him and breathed deeply, counting to ten in her head. She could feel something inside of her ready to let rip at him but wanted to control it.

'Well I'm sorry you feel that way,' she said. 'But I've made my decision.'

'You can't.'

'I can and I have. I'm sorry, Owen, but there we are.'

'This is being done purely out of grief,' he said, protesting. 'You're still missing Uncle Peter, you're grieving over Raymond—'

'Leave Raymond out of this.'

'You brought him into it, Stella. You're the one who said that Leyville only had bad memories and he was one of them. Well he's a bad memory for me all right.'

'Don't you talk about him like that.'

'Oh please,' said Montignac. 'We're all better off without him. Let him prune the rose gardens in Heaven and leave the grounds of Leyville alone.'

She narrowed her eyes and walked past him towards the door that led back inside. 'I won't talk to you while you're in this mood,' she said. 'I asked you here today out of courtesy, I told you my plans out of courtesy, I wanted you to be part of them because your last name is Montignac too. But if you think I am going to allow you to sit there and criticize my father and my fiancé just because you feel that things went wrong between us—'

He leapt up from the seat, lunged towards her and slapped her face. A white mark appeared across her cheek, almost as white as the hair on his head. Stella stood there, frozen to the spot, and he stared at her, biting his lip for a moment before returning to his seat and finishing his glass of wine in one mouthful. When he turned to look in her direction again, she was gone.

7

Jane Bentley found her husband, Roderick, sitting alone in the living room with only a table lamp switched on, not reading, not listening to the wireless, just sitting and drinking whisky.

'Roderick?' she asked, stepping forwards nervously. He was sitting in his chair without moving and for a moment the thought went through her head that he was dead, that the stress of recent events had finally got to him and he had suffered a stroke or a heart attack. She could barely breathe through nervousness. 'Roderick?' she repeated. 'Roderick, are you all right?'

After a moment his head gave the slightest nod and she realized how tensely she had been holding herself in too and breathed a sigh of relief, exhaling loudly. She switched on a second lamp and the room became bathed in the pale cerise light of the shade.

'What are you doing sitting here all alone?' she asked. 'You gave me a fright when I came in.'

'Sorry,' he said. He looked up at her and was pleased that the light was so poor in the room; it meant that he could imagine the beautiful, youthful woman he had been married to and loved for almost thirty years and not the frightened, pale and drawn lady she had turned into in recent months. 'I couldn't stay there any longer.'

'When you didn't come back after the recess I thought perhaps you'd arrived late and had just taken a seat at the back,' she said.

'No,' he replied. 'I couldn't take it any more. I couldn't hear them talk about him like that for another moment.' He leaned forwards and although she was still a few feet away from him she suddenly realized that he was crying quietly and she went to him, kneeling on the floor beside him and taking his hand in hers.

'Oh, Roderick, don't,' she pleaded. 'Don't. Not now. I can't get through this if you're not strong.'

He nodded and breathed heavily and managed to contain his tears for now. 'Well?' he asked after a moment. 'What did I miss? Did it get any worse?'

'Not really,' she said. 'There wasn't too much of note in the afternoon. They called Maud Williams to the stand, of course.'

'Who?' he asked.

'Maud Williams. The lady who called the police that morning. She lives in the flat two floors up from Owen Montignac and was coming down the stairs to leave for work when she saw the door half open and peeped inside.'

'Prying neighbours,' said Roderick, only too familiar with the curse of them.

'She seemed like a sweet old thing actually,' said Jane. 'Still quite traumatized by . . . by what she found.'

'Did she make things worse?'

'Not especially,' said Jane. 'She was only reporting on what she saw and that had already been established. Quentin tried to discredit her a little by suggesting that she was entering a residence that she had no business entering but he gave up after a few minutes. It was clear that the jury had warmed to her and he was doing more harm than good.'

She stayed on her position on the floor and rested her head against her husband's lap and he allowed his hand to stray to her hair, smoothing it down with tenderness and affection. Her own day had been so traumatic, so difficult, that a moment of peace and respite like this was worth a thousand sunshine holidays. First there had been the destructive elements in Gareth's school friends' evidence and then her disastrous lunchtime conversation with Sir Quentin Lawrence. It was only fair, she thought, that the afternoon should provide a little relief.

'What made you change your mind anyway?' she asked. 'Did something happen at chambers over lunch?'

He shook his head, loath to tell her the facts. 'I just couldn't face it,' he said. 'I'd had rather a disturbing meeting.'

'How do you mean?'

'It doesn't matter. By the time I got back to the Old Bailey it was preying on my mind too much and I knew I couldn't enter the courtroom. So I just came straight home and I've been sitting here ever since.'

Jane had spent the afternoon debating in her mind whether or not she should tell her husband about the conversation she had had with Sir Quentin earlier in the day and the suggestions she had made to him but had decided against it. She knew him only too well to know that he would be appalled by her willingness to bribe jury members. She had cornered the barrister at the end of the day as he left the courtroom and begged him not to say anything.

'Quentin,' she said.

'Jane, not here,' he said quickly, looking at her with as much offence in his face as he could muster.

'Quentin, I came to apologize. What I said was—'

He grabbed her by the arm and dragged her into a quiet alcove before she could utter another word.

'Will you please shush, woman?' he said, for the first time in their long acquaintance behaving in a less than gentlemanly fashion towards her. 'There are people here trained to overhear every whispered conversation.'

'I just want to say I'm sorry,' she said. 'And I won't mention it again.'

'Good. You know my position.'

'And ask you not to tell Roderick.'

He nodded. 'Fine,' he said. 'Let's just pretend it never happened. Now go home and try to get some sleep. You look dreadful.'

Despite everything, she had felt offended when he said that and found herself dwelling on the remark all the way home in the car. She dismissed it now as pointless vanity.

'You'll be coming on Monday, though?' she asked.

'Of course.'

'Good. Quentin is putting Owen Montignac on the stand and then it will be Gareth's turn to defend himself and he needs to see that we're both there for him. We can't let him down.'

Roderick nodded. He was barely listening to her. He was fifty-two years old and faced with the most difficult decision of his life and didn't know where to turn with it.

'Jane,' he said quietly after a moment. 'Jane, you do know that things aren't looking good.'

This was no moment for hysterics; she simply nodded her head and held his hand tighter. 'I know that,' she said. 'I can sense it in there every day. I just don't know what I can do to help him. I'm his mother and for the first time in my life I cannot think of a single thing I can do to make things right. Do you know what I spend my time thinking?'

'What?'

She gave a gentle laugh. 'That I spent so many months complaining about how the boy wouldn't get up in the morning, wouldn't get out of bed, wouldn't find a job. And now it all seems so pointless. What I wouldn't give to have him lying in his bed until noon every day.'

Roderick laughed too. It was strange, he felt, how the things that annoyed one most in one's children became the most endearing memories when the chips were down. They sat there in silence for a few minutes and Jane felt very warm and hoped the moment would never end, that they could just sit there alone for ever and never get hurt again.

'What was your meeting about?' she asked eventually.

'Which one?'

'You said you had a disturbing meeting at lunchtime. What was it about?'

He held his breath and considered his options. Earlier, he had resolved to say nothing about it. But now, faced with the question, he knew that he couldn't keep it in. For the life of him he didn't know what was the right thing to do and, although he knew how she would react, he found that he had to speak.

'Lord Keaton came to see me,' he said.

'Keaton?' she asked, without sounding at all surprised. 'He picks his moments, doesn't he? He must know what we're going through here.'

'Yes, he does. But he came anyway.'

'About the king?'

'Of course.'

She shook her head; these were yet more things that had once seemed so important to her and now she could scarcely have cared less about them. 'Perhaps you should just resign from the committee,' she said.

'Resign from it?' he asked, surprised.

'Yes. With all we have to deal with, you can hardly be expected to concern yourself with whether or not he marries some woman who no one even really knows. My God, it all seems so trivial when you think about it, doesn't it?'

'But it's not trivial,' said Roderick with determination. 'It's not trivial at all. It's a matter of vital public concern. It's the throne, the empire. It's history. How can I just step away from that?'

She shrugged her shoulders; she didn't really care too much either way. 'I suppose not,' she said. 'Well if you're sure you can handle it.'

He took a deep breath and decided to lay his cards on the table. 'Lord Keaton,' he began, 'told me that the results of our committee will be taken to the prime minister and he will act on that advice to tell the king either to renounce the lady or renounce the throne. At the moment the opinions are dead-locked with Hailsham's tie-breaking vote most likely to go towards allowing him to marry. Keaton informed me that if I changed my vote and sided against the king, effectively forcing him to make that choice, then he will see to it that, should Gareth be convicted of murder, he would receive a light prison sentence rather than be subject to the death penalty.'

He felt Jane's head move a little by his leg as she stifled a brief laugh at the intricacies of the monarch's love life; although it was only seconds, it felt to him that it took an eternity for the meaning of his brief speech to seep into her brain and for her to realize the enormity of what he had just told her. When that eternity was over she sat up slowly and turned to look at him, blinking her eyes in the dim light.

'What did you just say?' she asked very quietly.

'You heard me,' he shrugged. 'I just have to change my vote.'

'Keaton said . . . he told you . . .' She looked away, her brow furrowed, trying to understand how this might have all come about. 'Why would he say such a thing?' she asked.

'Because he believes that under those circumstances the king will renounce the throne and the Duke of York will ascend. And if he does, then he will be appointed Lord Chancellor. He's in Baldwin's pocket, or perhaps it's the other way around. I don't know, and they both want the king out. He's interfering with their narrow view of what England ought to be. They see the whole system crashing down about their heads and will stop at nothing to get rid of him. It's all about power, Jane, and unfortunately because of the trouble that Gareth has got himself into, he's in a position to bribe me.'

Jane stared at him. She could scarcely believe it. 'And he can do that?' she asked. 'He can influence the judge?'

'He says he can. And I don't suppose I have any choice but to believe him.'

She leaned forwards and her voice dropped quite low; when she spoke it was the purr of the lioness. 'Then do it,' she said.

It was his turn to stare now. 'I can't, he said.

'You can't? What do you mean you can't?'

'Jane, I have served at the Bar for my entire adult life and I have never once compromised my integrity or my ethics. Not once. I have made difficult decisions, such as the ones that have led to men's executions, and I have learned to live with them. I have followed my heart and the law. I cannot give in to bribery now.'

'Our son's life is at stake!' she shouted, standing up. 'And you're just going to sit there and—'

'I can't do it.'

'But why not? Oh for heaven's sake, Roderick, who cares who the king is anyway? Who cares whom he marries? Who cares who follows him? Let them decide themselves who the heir should be. It means nothing to us.'

'I can't compromise my integrity. *That* means something, surely.'

'It means nothing,' she roared. 'He's only been the bloody king for a wet weekend anyway. He's nothing to us. Just change your vote.'

'I can't,' he said, beginning to regret having told her in the first place. 'I won't. No matter what.'

She stared at him. He was not looking at her and his jaw was set in that way that she knew indicated that he meant business; suddenly her own decision to try to bribe the jury did not seem so terrible after all. She tried to steady herself and compose her thoughts. Finally she spoke, quietly but effectively.

'If you don't do what he asks you, Roderick, then on the day that Gareth hangs, I will pack my bags and leave this house and I will never return to it, nor will I ever lay eyes on you again. You will lose your son and your wife on the same day. You will be alone.'

He looked at her now. 'Jane, you can't be serious. You'd have me go against everything I've ever—'

'I've told you what will happen,' she said, standing up

and moving slowly towards the door. 'The decision now is yours.'

She left the room without another word but he remained seated, knowing that despite all his heavy-handed principles and belief in his own integrity, he had hoped for an ultimatum like this, something that would make him feel less guilty if his resolve crumbled and he gave in to Keaton's demand.

8

The car pulled up alongside him as he walked around Russell Square on his way to his flat in Bedford Place. At first he barely noticed it slowing down behind him, assuming that someone was trying to locate a house number along the street but then it moved forwards abruptly and stopped about twelve feet ahead of him and he feared the worst. As he approached it the front door opened and Henderson, Nicholas Delfy's enormous henchman, stepped out and smiled at him.

'Good evening, Mr Montignac,' he said politely.

'Hello,' he replied with a sigh. 'Is this a coincidence or were you looking for me?'

'I came looking for you earlier this evening but you were nowhere to be found. For a moment I was a little worried that you'd run away on us.'

'Of course not,' he said, adding a gentle laugh for the

sake of bravado. 'I was just away from London for a few hours. And now I'm heading home.'

'I don't think so,' said Henderson, opening the back door where another of Delfy's goons was sitting. 'Why don't you come for a ride with us instead?'

Montignac began to feel nervous and shook his head. 'I have until Christmas,' he said forcefully. 'Nicholas told me that I didn't have to pay the money back until Christmas.

'Mr Delfy just wants a word with you, that's all. Just a gentle reminder.' He paused and the smile faded from his face. 'Get in the car, Mr Montignac,' he said and it was clear that he wasn't going to take no for an answer.

He had no choice now and stepped inside. They drove to the Unicorn Ballrooms in silence and Montignac could feel a knot of apprehension in his stomach as they got closer. It occurred to him that he should take pride in the fact that he had managed to stick to his plan throughout the year and had not allowed any of his vices to drag him down. There had been no gambling whatsoever since the disastrous evening which had led him to build up his initial debts, and on the evenings when he had an irresistible urge to go to a different casino he had exerted all his willpower to ensure that he did not. When all this is over, he thought, just imagine what I can achieve.

He was led down a corridor past the doormen and Henderson told him to wait for a moment while he stepped inside. After a few minutes he was ushered inside where he found Delfy sitting behind his desk.

'Owen,' he said with a wide smile. 'I haven't seen you in so long. Thanks for coming in.'

'That's all right, Nicholas,' he said, sitting down opposite him, trying to affect the air of bonhomie that might be seen in an old friend rather than a debtor. 'I wasn't expecting the summons, however.'

'Well I thought tonight might be of interest to you in a way. There's someone I want you to meet.'

'Who?'

'I'll introduce you in a few minutes. First I thought it would be a good chance for us to catch up with each other and make sure we know where we both stand. Do you know what date it is today, Owen?'

He glanced at the calendar on the wall although he was well aware of the date; the countdown to Christmas was engrained on his mind. 'December the eighth,' he said.

'December the eighth, that's right. The season of Advent is already upon us and I haven't done any of my shopping yet. Have you?'

Montignac smiled to himself. 'No,' he said.

'Well we both need to get on to that,' said Delfy happily. 'Because by my calculations there are only seventeen days left for you to raise the forty thousand pounds that you owe me. By the way,' he added, almost as an afterthought, 'how is that going?'

'You don't have to worry, Nicholas. You'll have your money.'

'Oh I'm not worried,' he said with a shrug. 'Why should I be? I don't have anything to worry about. No one's going to put a bullet through my head if I haven't raised the money by then.'

Montignac nodded; he doubted very much that it would be as clean and painless as a bullet through the head.

'No, I have every confidence in you, Owen,' continued Nicholas. 'From what I hear you've been engaged in a most ingenious plan.'

'Really,' said Montignac, raising an eyebrow.

'Indeed. I believe that there's an unfortunate young man standing trial for his life at the moment in order that another man can achieve his life's ambitions and you can clear your debts. Quite an extraordinary sea change he'll produce too if the plan works. You wouldn't have anything to do with that, Owen, would you?'

'I don't know what you're talking about,' said Montignac, stunned that their scheme was not entirely confidential. After a moment he had to add: 'How did you know about that?' he asked.

'Oh I hear a lot of things. I pay a lot of people to keep me informed. Actually, I think it's quite ingenious. I feel sorry for the Bentley boy, of course, but there we are. All's fair in love and war and all that. And I happen to have known Lord Keaton for quite a long time. He's quite mad, of course, but determined.'

'Yes,' said Montignac. 'Well I'll get paid when the plan

reaches completion. And then you'll get paid. And that will be an end to it.'

'Marvellous,' said Delfy, coming around from behind the desk and ushering Montignac to his feet. 'Then come with me. Now I think I'll make that little introduction. I only called you here because I knew he was coming and I thought, for future reference in your life, you might be interested to know who it is that you've been working against.'

He led him out of the office door and through the corridor and into the bar area of the club where the booths were, as ever, mostly full. Delfy stopped at the bar and ordered a couple of bottles of champagne to be sent over to table four, which was where they were headed. They stopped a few feet away, Delfy with his arm protectively around Montignac's shoulder, and nodded in the group's direction.

'Well?' he said. 'What do you think?'

Montignac stared at the table in amazement before turning back to look at Delfy. For a moment he could scarcely believe whom he was looking at and wasn't sure he could go through with it.

'Come on,' said Delfy, pushing him forwards. 'There's nothing to be nervous about.'

There were three people seated at the booth and they all looked up as Delfy and Montignac walked towards them. They seemed to be engaged in a serious and almost argumentative conversation and didn't look happy about being interrupted but they knew their host and had to say hello.

'Your Majesty,' said Delfy, giving a polite bow of the head as he stood before him. 'So sorry to interrupt. I just wanted to introduce a young friend of mine who's a great admirer.'

'Of course, Delfy, of course,' said the king, who stood up and offered his hand, which Montignac took nervously. 'Sit down for a moment if you like.'

He stressed the word 'moment' and they knew they would not be welcome for long; he was obviously experienced at greeting and dismissing his minions. Delfy sat on the other side of the table beside the other man, while Montignac took his place beside the king. In the centre of the group, decked out in a fine gown and lavish jewellery sat the former wife of both Mr Earl Spencer of Kansas and Mr Ernest Simpson of New York City. Wallis.

'This is Owen Montignac,' said Delfy. 'Peter Montignac's boy.'

'Montignac, of course,' said the king. 'Yes, I knew your father a little—'

'My uncle, actually,' said Montignac, wondering why no one could ever get it right.

'No,' said the king quickly, unaccustomed to being corrected or interrupted. 'I knew your father.'

Montignac frowned. 'You mean—'

'Henry was your father, wasn't he? Peter's brother?'

'Yes,' said Montignac, intrigued. 'Yes he was. How did you know him?'

'Oh, it was a long time ago. When I was a boy. Your grandfather and my father, the late king, were friends and Henry and I used to see each other from time to time. He was a fine fellow, I admired him very much. I was terribly sorry when he died.'

'Thank you, sir,' said Montignac, a little overcome by such a personal memory. 'It's very kind of you to say so.'

'Well it's the truth, that's all. These are two dear friends of mine by the way. Walter Monckton,' he said, indicating the man. 'And Mrs Wallis Simpson.'

Delfy and Montignac shook their hands and exchanged hellos.

'And what do you do, Mr Montignac?' asked Mrs Simpson. 'Are you one of the idle rich like Walter and David?'

'Idle, indeed,' said the king with a laugh. 'As if I ever get a moment to myself!'

'I have aspirations towards indolence,' said Montignac, 'but unfortunately not the reserves to back them up at the moment. No, I run an art gallery in Cork Street.'

'Really?' she asked, leaning forwards, interested now. 'Which one?'

'The Threadbare Gallery,' he said. 'Do you know it?'

'I'm afraid I do,' she said. 'I'm a great fan of the galleries on Cork Street but I must say yours has a very distinctive taste.'

'We cater for those with more money than taste,' he replied, unsure whether he was supposed to end the sentence with the word 'ma'am' or not. He felt an urge to, out of respect. He liked her immediately.

'Wallis is a great supporter of the arts,' said the king. 'You should hear the way she talks about some of the pieces in the royal collection. It's like attending a lecture, only without having some moth-eaten old buffoon at the lectern.'

The guests laughed and Montignac watched as Mrs Simpson laid a hand gently on the king's arm, an affectionate gesture, entirely truthful and unpossessive, and the manner in which he used his other hand to tap hers affectionately while she did it. He observed them in their intimacy and envied them.

'I haven't been here in a long time, Delfy,' said the king. 'I hope you're not going to rob me blind at the roulette table.'

'I'm sure you'll have luck on your side, sir,' said Delfy obsequiously.

'I've never understood the urge for gambling,' said Mrs Simpson. 'Do you, Mr Montignac? Isn't it true that the house always wins?'

'She says this,' interrupted the king before Montignac could reply, 'despite the fact that last summer she lost nearly twenty thousand at the tables in Monte Carlo and had the night of her life.'

'It's true,' she admitted with an embarrassed smile. 'I did get rather caught up in the moment. It was terribly exciting but I was awfully ashamed of myself afterwards.'

'You should have seen her face, Montignac,' said the

king, dissolving into laughter. 'The more she lost, the pinker she got. I thought we were going to have to carry her away kicking and screaming.'

'Oh, David, stop it,' she said, laughing too. 'You're embarrassing me.'

Montignac watched them, absolutely fascinated by the easy affection between them. This was what the newspapers never reported on, he realized. They were like a couple of teenagers in love; they reminded him of Stella and himself when they were fifteen. But the world was telling them that they could not be together, and for what?

'Sir,' said Walter Monckton, from across the table, speaking for the first time as he tapped his watch. 'We do need to finish discussing . . .' He trailed off his words without completing the sentence.

'Of course, of course,' said the king. 'Sorry, gentlemen, but there are matters of the greatest importance under consideration at this table. I'm sure you're in no doubt as to what they are,' he added.

'Indeed,' said Delfy, standing up and nodding at Montignac to do the same. 'I'll see you before you leave anyway.'

'Mr Montignac,' said the king, shaking his hand again. 'It was a pleasure to meet you.'

'And you, sir,' said Montignac. 'And good luck,' he added spontaneously.

The king frowned. 'Do you think I'll need it?' he asked after a moment, looking across at Mrs Simpson.

'On the roulette tables, I meant,' he said quickly, blushing slightly at the familiarity.

The king nodded. 'Do you know,' he said, before the two men could walk away. 'You have the look of your father. His hair wasn't quite so startling as yours but it was white all the same. And your face. You could be mistaken for him.'

'Thank you, sir,' said Montignac. 'I take that as a great compliment. I was only a child when he died so—'

'If I recall correctly, your grandfather opposed his marriage.'

'That's right, sir.'

The king shook his head and looked down at the table sadly. 'It seems to me,' he said quietly. 'That the world is full of interfering, busybody bastards. Do you think that would be a fair assessment, Mr Montignac?' he asked, looking up.

Montignac hesitated. 'My father did as he pleased in the end,' he said finally. 'And I think he never regretted it for a moment.'

'Sir,' said Monckton, unhappy with the subtext of the conversation.

'Good evening, Mr Montignac, Mr Delfy,' said King Edward VIII with a smile, nodding to dismiss them.

'Good evening, sir, Mrs Simpson,' said Montignac, looking across at her, and she wore a radiant smile and for a moment he was sure that she had given him a wink of thanks.

Delfy and Montignac walked back towards the club door.

'You did very well there,' said Delfy. 'I think he liked you.'

'I'm almost trembling,' said Montignac, who could feel a line of perspiration making his shirt cling to his back. 'I had no idea—'

'I thought you might enjoy it,' he said. 'Since you're so heavily involved in what happens to them.'

'He'll never give her up,' said Montignac, who had observed them closely in the few minutes allotted to him. 'That's clear.'

'I would think not. So it's all down to Mr Justice Bentley now, isn't it?' He shook Montignac's hand. 'I'll see you at Christmas, Owen, if not before.'

Montignac nodded and walked out of the club. For the life of him he wasn't sure if he was doing the king a good turn or not.

9

It had been Montignac's intention to go straight home when he left the Unicorn Ballrooms but the events of the weekend were preying on his mind – the argument with Stella, the fact that he had raised his hand to her, the apprehension of the Delfy summons, the meeting with the king – and as he passed by White's he stepped inside and signed his name in the book before repairing to the bar for a stiff drink. If today had been bad, he thought, he could only imagine what the next day would bring. He checked his watch; it was just after eleven o'clock. In the mirror behind the bar he could see Alexander Keys reading in a corner and debated going over to join him but decided to finish his drink alone first. After a few minutes he ordered two more and made his way over to the table.

'Hello, Owen,' said Alexander. 'You just caught me, I was about to leave.'

'I can't stay long myself,' said Montignac. 'I just stopped in for a quick one and saw you over here. You'll have this with me before you go?' he asked, handing over the whisky.

'Well it would be rude not to,' said Alexander, settling back into the chair again. 'Settling your nerves for tomorrow, are you?'

'Something like that,' he said.

'You're definitely being called?'

'Definitely,' he said with a nod. 'The prosecution told me to be in court first thing.'

'You're not worried about it, are you?'

Montignac shrugged and felt a sudden great rush of pain make its way across his shoulder blades, forcing him to let out a brief cry and put his hand to his neck.

'Are you all right?' asked Alexander in concern.

'It's just stress,' said Montignac. 'The last few months, well they haven't been easy to say the least.'

Alexander gave a brief laugh. 'Well just imagine how

poor old Gareth is feeling right about now.' he said.

'Yes,' he said, although he was trying not to.

'Do you know what you're going to say yet?'

Montignac shrugged. 'Well I don't know what they're going to ask me, do I? But I suppose I just have to tell the truth,' he said. 'Just tell them what happened on the night in question. Are you going to be there?'

'Oh yes,' said Alexander. 'I wouldn't miss it for the world. Not just for you, of course, but for what comes after you.'

'How do you mean?'

'Don't you know? Gareth will be testifying in his own defence. I believe Sir Quentin Lawrence is going to put him on the stand.'

Montignac nodded. 'Do you think he'll be happy when it's all over?' he asked.

'Happy? Well if he gets off I think he would, but otherwise, I doubt it.'

'His life was so meaningless when he met me,' said Montignac, his brow furrowed as he considered it. 'He had nothing going for him. He was a wastrel. What purpose did he ever serve in the world anyway?'

'Just because you lack direction doesn't give you the right to go around killing perfectly innocent people, though, does it? Poor old Raymond Davis, after all, never did a bit of harm to anyone, as far as I can see.'

'Raymond Davis was a fool,' said Montignac bitterly. 'He tried to take hold of things that didn't belong to him.'

Alexander sat back in his chair in surprise. 'Such as what?' he asked.

'I don't believe that he and Stella could ever have been happy,' said Montignac, ignoring the question. 'They were different types of person altogether.'

'Look here,' said Alexander, leaning forwards in concern. 'I know this is a difficult time but you can't start saying things like that on the stand tomorrow. People might get the wrong end of the stick altogether. Just stick to the facts.'

'I will, I will.'

'And don't get sidetracked by your emotions.'

'No.' He thought about it and an idea came into his head and he looked across at his old friend. 'Alexander,' he said. 'What do you make of this whole business of the king and the American woman?'

He let out a snort and shook his head. 'Good Lord, Montignac, if there was one man in London who I didn't think would be interested in the tittle-tattle and gossip about Edward and Mrs Simpson, I thought it would be you. It's hardly your line, is it?'

'No, I'm just interested in what you think, that's all.'

Alexander shrugged. 'Well it doesn't really make any difference to me,' he said. 'I'm not quite sure what he sees in her if I'm honest, considering he could have his pick of half the ladies in the world. She always looks a little haggard to me.'

'They seem to love each other, though.'

'Well how are we to know that?' asked Alexander. 'Because some people want to portray them as the lead players in some great love story? No, I imagine she's a gold-digger. She's an American, after all. They're a strange breed. Anyway,' he added, leaning forwards so as not to be overheard, 'I've never understood what we need with him anyway.'

'With who?'

'The king. Although I have to say I always find it hard to think of him as the king, don't you? He's been the Prince of Wales all my life so it's difficult to suddenly think of him with a different title.'

'Yes, but what do you mean by what do we need with him?'

'Well what's the point of him anyway?' asked Alexander. 'We pay for him, we pay for all of them, and we can't get within fifty feet of them. They're our employees, you might say. Without us, they wouldn't even exist. Talk about your wastrels; Gareth has nothing on that crowd. It's an odd business. Don't you think the Russians might have had the right idea? Or the French in the eighteenth century? Unseating their masters and ruling their own destinies?'

'Only a member of the landed gentry such as yourself, Alexander, could suggest such a thing. You'd be the first to start screaming if the tumbrel came to collect you for the trip to the guillotine.'

'Actually, I've always felt this way,' he replied, offended. 'Get rid of them all, I say. Let them marry monkeys or chickens if they want to, it doesn't make a blind bit of difference to me.'

Montignac nodded. This was no time for a debate on the relevance of the monarchy. He finished his drink and wiped his eyes in exhaustion.

'Well,' he said, standing up. 'Time to head home. Are you going my way?'

'No,' said Alexander, 'but I'll walk you out. Let me just get my coat.'

They stepped out of White's together into the chilly night air.

'I could pick you up in the morning if you like,' suggested Alexander. 'On my way to the Old Bailey. Say around ten?'

'I have to be there at nine-thirty, I'm told,' said Montignac.

'Too early for me then. Keep an eye out for me all the same. I'll be somewhere near the back. I want to avoid running into either Bentley *père* or *mère*.'

'Very wise,' said Montignac. 'I'm hoping not to have to face them myself.'

'You're not . . .' Alexander hesitated, wanting to choose his words carefully. 'You're not feeling guilty about all this, are you?'

'Guilty? No. Why should I be?'

It's just that whenever you talk about Gareth you seem, I don't know, a little troubled.'

Montignac shook his head. 'No it's not that,' he said. 'I'm just worried about something going wrong, that's all.'

'Going wrong? I don't follow you.'

'No, that's the wrong choice of words,' he said, instantly regretting them. 'I mean, I'm worried about landing him in trouble with what I say.'

'Owen,' said Alexander, shaking his head and smiling as if the whole thing was just a piece of trivial drama to be played out for all their delights. 'You worry too much about other people. That's one of your flaws. Gareth may not have meant to have done what he did, the whole thing might be a terrible tragedy, but it's hardly your fault.'

'You're sure about that?'

'Of course I am. And remember, I hate to say it but there's always the chance that if Gareth had woken earlier and realized what he'd done he might have got out of there as quickly as possible and you could have ended up getting the blame. Put yourself in his shoes, waking up with a dead body on his hands. If that woman from upstairs hadn't called the police who knows who would be standing in the dock now?'

Montignac nodded. 'I expect so,' he said. 'Anyway I'll see you in court in the morning.'

'Until then,' he said. They shook hands and parted, walking off in different directions.

December the eighth, thought Montignac as he headed for home. Tomorrow is December the ninth. A verdict in a day or two's time, all going well. Then Stanley Baldwin gets his answer, the king makes his choice, I get my money and Nicholas Delfy gets paid.

But where do I go from there? he wondered.

10

The innocent slept well or not at all; the guilty tossed and turned or fell directly to sleep.

Back in his comfortable apartment, Alexander Keys changed for bed and set his clock for an early start in the morning. He wasn't accustomed to rising before eleven or twelve but the following day promised more drama than he ever got from any of the tedious novels he was forced to review. He set it for eight o'clock, a time he hadn't seen in several years, and resolved to have a hearty breakfast and arrive at the Old Bailey in time to get a good seat, albeit one where he would not be noticed by the Bentleys. As he closed his eyes he wondered about his own part in the whole affair, recalling how earlier that year, at Gareth's birthday party, he had introduced him to his oldest friend, Owen Montignac, a man he had never fully understood. That was the moment, he realized, when Gareth had been doomed. Perhaps, he thought to himself as he drifted off, it's time for me to write my own book. The story of the Gareth Bentley trial. A title sprang to mind – *The Bentley Decline* – and he considered rising again and making a note of it but he was too comfortable now and was sure he would remember in the morning.

In a well-appointed house in Highgate, overlooking the woods, Mr Justice Patrick Sharpwell drained a mug of cocoa and double-checked that he had all his files correctly ordered in his briefcase for the following morning. He was sure that he would be able to send the case to the jury by the end of the next day and hoped that the young defendant would have given them enough cause to debate his innocence before finally condemning him. After all it would make it all the more reasonable then when he commuted the death sentence to a custodial one, as agreed in the arrangement he had made with Lord Keaton, should he be given the word. Otherwise, of course, he would be perfectly happy to send the boy to the gallows. He would wait patiently before passing sentence.

As ever, Nicholas Delfy was the last to leave the Unicorn Ballrooms and made his way in his chauffeur-driven Rolls Royce to his spacious apartment overlooking the Thames. It had been a special night; there was never anything better for business than when the king came for the evening. As Prince of Wales, his visits had guaranteed packed doors for months afterwards with people hoping to meet him and be introduced. Now that he was king it was even better. For as long as he remained king, of course, which by his reckoning would be a matter of weeks at most.

* * *

Mr Justice Harkman, chief prosecutor in the case of Rex vs Bentley, ran his eye over his list of questions on two separate sheets of paper. One for Owen Montignac, who would no doubt try to stand up for his friend and former employee, and one for Gareth Bentley, the accused. The case had not been difficult so far; the evidence was clearly against him. He felt terribly sorry for Roderick Bentley, an old friend for whom he had a great deal of respect, but then the law was the law and one could not allow personal feelings to influence one's deliberations over it. What happened to Gareth Bentley after – as seemed inevitable – his conviction would be down to the judge and he could hardly be held responsible for that.

In his own house, no more than a mile away, Sir Quentin Lawrence finished composing his own list of questions and hoped that the boy would answer them honestly and not go to pieces on the stand, as he had been showing increasing signs of doing lately. His greatest fear was that the boy's mother, Jane, would create a scene in court, something which would only play into the prosecution's hands, and he hoped that she had forgotten her foolish ideas about bribing the jury and had not tried the same trick with the prosecution counsel; he didn't relish the idea of another Bentley trial in the new year.

* * *

Lying in her bed in Leyville, Margaret Richmond's eyes were wide open and she knew that she would be deprived of sleep with the weight of all the worries on her mind. In a few weeks' time there would be no Montignacs left there and she would be alone. The house would be given over to the National Trust and how long then would it be before she was told to leave? Although the words were never spoken, she knew that this was nothing more than an act of vengeance on Stella's part for what had happened ten years earlier when she had done nothing more than try to act in the girl's own interests. And what if she did go to Switzerland and try to find her son, the boy that Montignac thought had never been allowed to enter the world, the boy she had told him was lost for ever, what miseries would the future hold then?

In the Lord Chancellor's luxurious suite in Westminster, Lord Hailsham resolved to call a meeting of the advisory committee for early in the week, when a final decision would have to be made. The country could no longer take the pressure of scandal and gossip and the prime minister was pressing him urgently for an answer. He hoped that the Bentley case would be resolved in time but regardless of that, it was time to bring the matter to a close.

Lord Keaton slept very well and dreamed of that very suite in Westminster, and of the future that lay before him, the birthright of his ancestors which had been stolen from him, a birthright that was only days away from being his. And a stable country, untroubled by a foolish monarch.

In Buckingham Palace, King Edwards VIII slept alone but lay awake now, his mind torn by the twin tortures of duty and love. He didn't know why he wasn't simply allowed to do as he pleased – no one had ever denied him anything before – and he thought of his late father's prophetic words that after he was gone, his heir would destroy himself within a twelvemonth. But he knew what he wanted and he knew whom he could not live without. And if that meant giving up the throne, his own birthright, then so be it. But he would wait no longer to be married. They had plagued him for so many years to take a wife and now that he had chosen one, they claimed that she was unacceptable. The whole thing was a ridiculous irony.

Stella Montignac dreamed of America and the luxurious liners that would take her there. She thought of the fact that she was not yet thirty, and wealthy, intelligent and beautiful. She missed Raymond Davis desperately, she knew she always would, but she was damned if she was going to waste her life mourning him. There were other lives to live, other men to meet. Perhaps she could fall in love again. She hadn't loved Raymond, of course, but she had liked him well enough. Her hand reached to her face; the sting of the slap had faded now. It had been a rare intimacy between her cousin and herself.

Roderick and Jane Bentley lay in bed but separate from each other, neither one speaking, breathing quietly so as not to encourage conversation, lost in the trauma of their lives. He hadn't told Jane yet but he was almost sure that he would have no choice. He could not change his vote. His entire life had been built around his integrity and belief in the judicial system and he simply could not walk away from that now; his son must take responsibility for his actions and he himself would live with the consequences. He would inform Keaton at the next meeting. On her side of the bed, Jane lay with her eyes open, her mind blank, completely lost.

Alone in his cell, Gareth Bentley felt relatively calm. He could only testify as to what he remembered. He could only apologize for what he had done. He could only live – or die – with whatever verdict and sentence was reached. There was nothing for him in life any more than this.

And Owen Montignac, the rightful heir of Leyville, climbed into bed and wondered what the next few days would hold. He had made up his mind that there was something he could perhaps do still, something that might relieve what remained of his conscience. He would never feel guilty for Raymond; no, not for that.

But Gareth was a different matter. Or would it be simpler to let him take the fall and close the business once and for all? Once Keaton was satisfied, once the king was prepared to go, then what did it matter any more? As long as the money came his way and his debts were clear. He should never have hit Stella, he knew that now. But she had said something to him on the rooftop that had stayed his mind: *no one can stop us any more.*

Was there still a chance for them? he wondered as he tried, and failed, to sleep.

Chapter 7

1

HE SAT ON a small bench at quite some distance from the courtroom doors but watched as the people streamed in – interested busybodies, newspapermen, legal representatives, a desperately unhappy-looking couple who had the look of Raymond Davis about them, Alexander Keys, the once beautiful Lady Jane Bentley, who now appeared exhausted and terrified, with the man he took to be her husband, Roderick – until the bailiff closed the doors to the court and he was left almost alone in the echoing silence of the stone corridor. There was a staircase at the end and a young lady in high-heeled shoes ascended them noisily, her heels making clacking sounds on the stone floor that reverberated around him. He felt an urge to run as far away as possible from the ordeal ahead but steeled himself, knowing that the most crucial moments of the matter lay ahead.

He heard a loud cry from inside the courtroom and then the doors swung open and the bailiff stepped outside it and repeated in a deep voice:

'Call Owen Montignac.'

He stood up and walked towards the doors, took a deep breath, and stepped inside.

The room was packed, there were even a few solicitors and bewigged barristers watching proceedings on their feet from the back, but he made his way purposefully through the crowd, looking directly ahead at all times, and walked towards the steps of the witness box, climbed up and looked out to the courtroom, holding on to the bar in front of him as he did so.

A young man approached him with a Bible and he took the oath, and then Mr Justice Harkman rose for the prosecution.

'Good morning,' he said in an amicable voice. 'Can you tell us your name and address please?'

'Owen Henry Montignac,' he said, speaking in a clear voice that carried nicely through the marble acoustics of the room, and he gave his Bedford Place address.

'And can you tell us your occupation, Mr Montignac?'

'I run an art gallery on Cork Street, the Threadbare Gallery.'

'I see,' said Harkman. 'The Threadbare . . . and that specializes in the sale of contemporary paintings, is that correct?'

'It's mostly paintings, yes,' said Montignac. 'But we handle a lot of sculpture too. We only sell art that has been produced in the twentieth century, however, that's what makes us different.'

The judge leaned over towards Montignac. 'I wasn't aware that there had been any art produced in the twentieth century,' he said, coming over all curmudgeonly and avuncular, a favourite pastime of judges, and one which made the courtroom erupt in sycophantic laughter.

'Well, you might be surprised, Your Honour,' said Montignac with a smile in order to be amiable. 'There are some very fine young artists at work today, I believe.'

Just none of them on display at the Threadbare, he thought to himself.

'And can you tell us how long you've been employed there?' asked Harkman.

'Just over four years.'

'You're the manager?'

'That's correct.'

'And the gallery is owned by a Mrs . . .' He strolled casually over to his seat and consulted a file. 'A Mrs Rachel Conliffe, is that right?'

'Yes, Mrs Conliffe is the owner but she has very little involvement in the day-to-day running of the gallery.'

'She leaves that up to you?'

'That's right.'

'She must have a great deal of trust in you, Mr Montignac.'

'I believe she does, yes. We have a very cordial relationship.'

'Excellent,' said Harkman, pleased that the formalities were over with. 'Now can you tell us whether you are familiar with the defendant?'

For the first time since stepping into the courtroom, Montignac's eyes drifted in the direction of the dock, a surprisingly small cage-like area where, seated alone with a policeman standing on either side of him, was Gareth Bentley. Montignac stared at him and was momentarily taken aback. Although he had hardly been overweight before, he appeared to be severely undernourished now. His face had grown gaunt and his eyes appeared to have sunk further into his skull. The expensive suit he wore seemed entirely ill-fitting, as if it was designed for a much larger man. He gave Montignac the impression of a drunkard in a cheap tavern, unshaven and semi-conscious, who nonetheless wears a tweed suit and tie every day of his life.

'Yes,' said Montignac. 'Yes, I know Mr Bentley.'

'Can you tell us how you first met him?'

Montignac nodded. 'It was earlier this year,' he said. 'Sometime in July, I believe. I was visiting an acquaintance at a club that he owns and while there I met a friend of mine who was part of a small birthday gathering in Gareth's . . . in Mr Bentley's honour. We were introduced.'

'I see,' said Harkman. 'And you talked a lot that evening?'

'Not really,' said Montignac. 'There were a few of us there and we chatted about a few things. Gareth mentioned some of the things that were frustrating him in his life but I couldn't stay too long as I had an early start in the morning and so I left before the others.'

'I'm sorry,' said Harkman, picking up the strand that Montignac had deliberately left hanging for him. 'You say that Mr Bentley expressed some frustrations?'

'Well,' said Montignac with a gentle laugh, as if this was the most natural thing he could imagine. 'Nothing that any young man of twenty-four doesn't feel, I suppose. I didn't think too much of it.'

'Can you be more explicit? What exactly did he mention?'

Montignac breathed in heavily as he considered it, acting for all the worlds as if he hadn't thought about this for a long time. 'Let me see,' he mentioned. 'I remember him saying that he was under a certain amount of pressure at home to find suitable employment. I believe he had graduated some time earlier with a law degree but had chosen not to pursue this—'

'Objection, Your Honour,' said Sir Quentin Lawrence, rising to his feet. 'We've already established Mr Bentley's educational history and his prospects in July of this year.'

'Yes,' said the judge, turning to Montignac. 'If you can just stick to what the defendant actually told you as opposed to what you understood to be the case.'

'Of course,' said Montignac with a nod. 'Apologies.'

'You say you left the club before anyone else that evening,' continued Harkman.

'Yes, that's right.'

'And did you travel home alone?'

'No,' said Montignac. 'No, I was waiting on the street for a taxicab when Gareth came out and continued to talk to me.'

'He left his own party?'

'Apparently.'

'I see. And what did you talk about?'

'Well it was something of a continuation of the conversation we were having inside,' said Montignac. 'About how he wanted to do something to make his own money and not be beholden to his family.'

'And how did you react to that?'

'I found him very refreshing,' said Montignac. 'I've always made my own way in the world and suspected that I had found a kindred soul. I could see his enthusiasm and I gave him my card when we arrived at my flat.'

'Why did you do that?'

'I thought it might be interesting to talk to him again.'

'And did you expect him to contact you?'

'I didn't think about it one way or the other,' said Montignac. 'I thought it was just one of those pleasant chats one has with the friend of a mutual acquaintance and that we might run into each other from time to time, but other than that . . .' He drifted off and shrugged his shoulders to imply that he hadn't given the matter any further thought.

'Very good, Mr Montignac,' said Harkman, who was

pacing back and forth and remaining steady and methodical in his questioning. 'Now the next time you saw Mr Bentley was when he came to visit you at your gallery, is that right?'

'That's correct, yes. He came one evening, just after we'd closed.'

'He arrived when the streets were dark and the shop was deserted?' asked Harkman.

'Objection, Your Honour!' cried Sir Quentin. 'Prosecution counsel seems to be equating my client with a villain directly from the pages of Mr Dickens.'

'Quite so, Sir Lawrence,' said the judge. 'Please, Mr Harkman, there's no need to be quite so melodramatic.'

'I'm extremely grateful to Your Honour for his advice,' said Harkman obsequiously, bowing his head. 'Mr Montignac, can you tell us why the defendant came to visit you that night?'

Montignac scrunched up his face as if trying to recall. 'Yes,' he said. 'He mentioned that I had said there was the possibility of employment with the gallery and whether I had been serious about it.'

'And had you?'

'Well, sort of,' said Montignac. 'It's the kind of thing one says without expecting to be taken up on it. It's rather like inviting someone to your house for Christmas; you don't actually expect that they'll say yes but you feel rather good about yourself for extending the invitation in the first place.'

Some of the jury members laughed at that and even

the judge and Sir Quentin allowed themselves a smile.

'Indeed,' said Harkman, who was pleased with how his witness was carrying himself. He could see that the jury liked him very much. His stance, his youthful handsomeness, that startling crop of white hair, only endeared him to them while little jokes like this made them trust him.

'But you did in fact offer him a position?' continued Harkman.

'I did, yes.'

'And what was that position?'

'Well it was a sort of jack-of-all-trades job,' said Montignac. 'He didn't know much about art but I have an assistant who . . . well it's difficult to say to be honest.'

'I'll have to press you, Mr Montignac.'

'Well my assistant isn't always as reliable as I would wish him to be. Timekeeping, professionalism, that sort of thing. I rather thought that in time I might replace him with the defendant, teach him the ropes and so on. I had a notion at the back of my mind about speaking to Mrs Conliffe regarding the possibility of opening a second gallery for more traditional fare and thought that Gareth could help me in that.'

'You offered him a lot of opportunities, didn't you, Mr Montignac.'

'I suppose I did, yes.'

'Now if I may turn to the night of August the eighteenth. You and the defendant went to the Bullirag pub in Piccadilly Circus for dinner after work, is that correct?'

'Yes,' said Montignac.

'And the defendant drank an awful lot that night.'

Montignac did his best to look uncomfortable in the witness box and threw an apologetic glance towards the dock.

'Mr Montignac,' repeated Harkman. 'If you can just let us know what happened on the evening in question.'

'I was rather hungry,' said Montignac who needed no more prompting, 'but Gareth seemed more interested in drinking. He was getting through quite a lot but to be honest I didn't think much of it. I'm not a heavy drinker myself but I have friends who enjoy such things and it doesn't seem to have much effect on them so I assumed Mr Bentley would be fine too.'

'Quite so, but the effect it had on him . . . ?'

'Was extreme. He started to slur his words, to shout quite loudly, he became quite aggressive in fact.'

'Aggressive?'

'Well the barman asked me to quieten him down and when I asked him to, Gareth seemed to get quite angry.'

Without meaning to, his eyes glanced in the direction of the dock where Gareth sat with an expression of confusion mingled with regret at his lack of memories of the night.

'And how did this anger manifest itself?'

'In words, at first. And then he said that if I wanted

him to quieten down why didn't I come over there and make him.'

'I see. He threatened you, in other words?'

'I think that might be overstating the case a little,' said Montignac with a smile.'

'But you felt intimidated by him?'

He considered this. 'I felt that it was best for our future relationship if I put a stop to the evening's festivities. However, knowing the difficulties he was facing at home I thought it would be best if I let him sleep it off at my flat. It's the kind of thing one does for one's friends, you know.'

'Of course.'

'So I called a taxicab and put him into it, despite his protests, and then I contacted some friends and went to see them for the evening. My intention was to return home later and sleep on the sofa but, to my eternal regret, I stayed over at my friends' house.'

'And, Your Honour, we have provided you with affidavits to confirm Mr Montignac's residence that night,' said Harkman, referring to the documents that Lord Keaton had purchased.

'Very good,' said the judge.

'And the next thing you knew about the defendant?' asked Harkman.

'Was when the police came to see me at the gallery the following afternoon and told me what had happened.'

'I see. Thank you, Mr Montignac. No more questions for now, Your Honour.'

Montignac nodded at him and took a sip of water, bracing himself for what was to come, Sir Quentin's cross-examination.

2

Sir Quentin Lawrence rose to his feet and looked across at Montignac with a vague expression of surprise on his face, as if his evidence so far had been so irrelevant that he had barely noticed him standing in the witness box until now.

'You say that you've always made your own way in the world, Mr Montignac?'

'That's right,' he replied.

'Is that an entirely accurate statement?'

Montignac smiled. 'I believe it is,' he said.

'I only ask because your surname is quite familiar to me. You are a member of the Montignac landowning family, are you not? Quite a wealthy family, if memory serves.'

'My grandfather was William Montignac,' he replied. 'Who inherited the estate from his ancestors, that's correct. After his death it passed to my late uncle, Peter Montignac. And when he died earlier this year it passed in turn to his daughter, Stella.'

'But not to you?'

'No.'

'But you were supported by Peter Montignac during his lifetime, is that right?'

Montignac bristled at the word. 'He paid for my education,' he said. 'As most parents do for their children. But I went to work as soon as I left Cambridge. And I was not remembered in his will.'

'Most parents, yes,' said Sir Quentin. 'But he wasn't your parent, was he?'

'No, he was my uncle.'

Harkman stood up slowly to protest. 'My Lord, does this have any relevance? The witness's family history is hardly pertinent to this case.'

'Yes, I'm not sure where you're going with this, Sir Quentin,' said Judge Sharpwell.

Sir Quentin frowned and changed tack.

'Mr Montignac, you say that you hired Mr Bentley for a position in your gallery after meeting him on a night out with friends.'

'That's correct, yes.'

'Do you always hire employees when knowing so little about them?'

Montignac hesitated. 'He was introduced to me by a friend of many years' standing. I assumed that if he vouched for him, then I could trust him.'

'And how many applicants for the job had you already turned down at the time?'

'Applicants?' asked Montignac in confusion.

'Yes,' said Sir Quentin. 'For the position you offered my client. How many applicants had you already interviewed and rejected?'

'Well, none,' he replied cautiously. 'It wasn't an advertised position as such.'

'I see. So a young man you don't know approaches you outside a nightclub where you've just met, informs you that he is looking for work and you simply take him on without a second thought. Does your employer approve of such hiring practices?'

'My employer is perfectly happy for me to make the decisions regarding staffing. That's why she made me manager.'

'I'm sorry, Mr Montignac,' said Sir Quentin. 'I'm still confused. I can't quite see why you would take someone on for an important position when you don't even know him.'

'Well because he was a very personable young man,' said Montignac, trying to cover his frustration. 'He struck me as intelligent, friendly and with an eagerness to learn. The kind who might do very well in our business.'

'Yes indeed,' said Sir Quentin. 'Intelligent, friendly and eager. I see. Now if I may, let me move on to the night of the incident.'

'The murder,' said Harkman, rising to his feet. 'Your Honour, let us at least call things by what they are.'

'Sustained,' grunted Judge Sharpwell.

'The night of the murder then,' said Sir Quentin, correcting himself. 'How many drinks did you say Mr Bentley had that night?'

'I couldn't say for sure,' said Montignac. 'But I would

guess somewhere around eight or nine pints of beer and perhaps half a dozen spirits.'

'And you weren't drinking at all?'

'I had a few, but nowhere near that amount.'

'How many exactly?'

'Perhaps three.'

'And when you arrived in the pub, do you recall who bought the first round of drinks?'

'I imagine I did,' said Montignac. 'That would certainly be my custom if I was taking an employee out.'

'And did my client reciprocate by buying the second round?'

'Yes, I think so.'

'And from then on?'

'It's hard to recall . . .' said Montignac.

'Is it? I believe the barman from the Bullirag pub can recall. Perhaps I should bring him to the stand and ask him?'

Montignac narrowed his eyes. 'I think I bought the majority of the drinks,' he admitted.

'Did you indeed?' Any reason why that was the case? Or are you just uncommonly generous?'

'Because I was Mr Bentley's employer. I thought it unseemly for him to be spending his wages on me.'

'And even after he started to get more and more inebriated, and even after he became loud and attracted the attentions of the landlord, you continued to buy him drinks, did you not?'

'I may have bought one or two but that was because

he was protesting so much that I thought it simpler to humour him. I never imagined that—'

'You got him drunk, Mr Montignac, didn't you?'

Harkman rose to his feet again. 'Your Honour,' he cried, appalled by the line of questioning. 'Perhaps defence counsel could specify what charges exactly are being made against the witness. He has already testified to the events in the pub that night.'

'Yes, Sir Quentin, what are you implying exactly?'

'I'm simply trying to establish whether my client was the type of man to enter a pub and purchase drink after drink after drink until he is in a paralytic state. And I find that he is not.'

'Your Honour, I believe it is for the jury to find whether he is or isn't, protested Harkman. 'It's hardly the job of my learned friend to do so.'

'Indeed,' said the judge, glancing at his watch as his stomach began to wonder about lunch. 'Do you have any more questions for this witness, Sir Quentin?'

'Just one or two more, Your Honour,' he said. 'If I may?'

'Carry on,' he sighed, as if the whole thing was a monstrous inconvenience.

'Mr Montignac,' he began again with a flourish. 'Can you describe for us the condition that Mr Bentley was in when you left the pub?'

'Well he could barely stand up,' said Montignac. 'He was extremely inebriated. His legs were going from under him, he was spouting a lot of gibberish. In truth,

I had difficulty finding a taxicab that would take him.'

'I see. And had Mr Bentley been to your flat before that night?'

'No.'

'But you gave him the address?'

'I gave it to the taxi driver and asked him to ensure that he got in safely.'

'Your Honour,' said Harkman, rising to his feet in frustration. 'Mr Reeves has already testified to that.'

'I'm almost finished, Your Honour, if I may?'

The judge nodded.

'Mr Montignac, to move away from my client for a moment, can you tell me about the relationship you had with the deceased, Raymond Davis.'

'I had no particular relationship, as you put it, with the victim,' said Montignac, stressing the last word.

'None at all? You didn't know him?'

'He was a friend of my cousin's,' he replied. 'I only knew him through her. We weren't close ourselves.'

'Your cousin?' he asked. 'That would be Stella Montignac, is that right?'

'That's right.'

'Who inherited the Montignac estate . . . ?'

'Yes.'

'And you grew up in the same house as Miss Montignac?'

'From the time I was five, yes. After my parents' death.'

'I see. And Mr Davis was just a friend of Miss Montignac's, was he?'

'Yes,' he said, unwilling to acknowledge any deeper relationship between the two.

'Weren't they engaged to be married, Mr Montignac?'

'I believe they had discussed it, yes. I'm not sure that any firm date or plans had been set in place.'

Sir Quentin inclined his head a little, intrigued by the witness's disinclination to admit anything further between the two. He pursued this for a moment.

'Did you like Mr Davis?'

'Did I like him?' he asked, surprised.

'Yes. Were you happy that he was going to marry your cousin?'

Montignac hesitated. He was quite pleased with the fact that so far he had managed to avoid perjuring himself entirely. He racked his brains to recall any conversations with others that he may have had about Raymond that could implicate him.

'My feeling about the matter was somewhat . . .' He searched for the right word. 'Fluid.'

Sir Quentin laughed. 'I beg your pardon, Mr Montignac,' he said. 'Did you say *fluid*?'

'Well at first I didn't take to him,' he replied in explanation. 'He was a perfectly pleasant fellow, of course. He was always polite and tried to ingratiate himself with the family. But I didn't think he was entirely Stella's type. I wasn't sure he could make her happy. But then after a while I became a little more ambivalent towards him and by the time of his *murder*' – he raised his voice a little with the word, lest anyone should forget the circumstances of Raymond's death – 'I suppose I thought he was a decent enough sort. I'm quite protective of my cousin, Sir Quentin,' he said with a smile, hoping to win back the jury a little, feeling that he might have lost them slightly during the cross-examination.

'The three of you dined together not so long before his untimely passing, didn't you?' asked Sir Quentin.

'I'm sorry?' he asked, starting to panic a little.

'The three of you – your cousin, Miss Montignac, her fiancé, Mr Davis, and you. You dined together a few weeks earlier.'

Montignac shrugged. 'We may have,' he said. 'I can't remember a specific meal—'

'Can't you? I have it here that you dined at Claridge's on July the sixth, the same night in fact that you met Mr Bentley, but you left the restaurant early that evening, before the puddings were served.'

'I may have done.'

'Any particular reason why?'

'None that I can recall.'

'I see. And when he died, Mr Davis was coming to visit you in your flat. Do you know what he wanted to see you about?'

'I haven't the faintest idea,' said Montignac. 'You would have to ask him. Of course he was murdered, so—'

'Yes, one last question, Mr Montignac,' said Sir Quentin, interrupting him gruffly. 'Just so I'm clear about what you're telling us. You have stated that the defendant was intelligent, friendly and eager. Is that correct?'

'Yes.'

'And that you bought most of the drinks on the night of the murder?'

'Yes.'

'And that he was so paralytic that he couldn't even get into a taxi without assistance or climb the steps to your flat without the help of a driver?'

'Yes,' said Montignac reluctantly.

'And that you sent him to that flat alone where your cousin's fiancé mysteriously arrived later and, despite his condition, the defendant is alleged to have murdered him?'

'Your Honour, the witness has testified to no such thing,' shouted Harkman, rising to his feet.

'Indeed not, Your Honour,' said Sir Quentin triumphantly. 'I do apologize, I was simply trying to get the matter straight in my head. I have no further questions.'

'Thank you, Sir Quentin,' said the judge, eager for the beef, potatoes and two veg that would be waiting for him in his chambers. 'Nothing further, Mr Harkman?' he asked hopefully.

'Just one quick question, Your Honour,' he replied, rising to his feet. 'Mr Montignac, you gave this young man here an opportunity for a career, did you not?'

'Yes.'

'And you would have continued to support him as he learned the business?'

'Indeed, yes.'

'And after you offered him the comfort of your flat, a murder took place there.'

'That's right.'

'And your cousin lost a fiancé.'

'Yes.'

'And you a friend.'

'Yes,' he said quietly.

'Mr Montignac, do you regret the night that you met the defendant?'

Montignac narrowed his eyes and looked towards the dock where Gareth sat looking miserable and lost. Enough damage had been done, he decided; the last thing he needed was for Gareth to think that he was his enemy.

'No I don't, Mr Harkman,' he said. 'I believed then and believe now that Mr Bentley had many fine traits. I regret the fact that I didn't take him home myself that night. I regret that I didn't return to my flat earlier. I regret that I wasn't there to stop him when he attacked Raymond. But I don't regret meeting him. I believe the events of that night constituted a moment of madness for Gareth and are not part of his true character. The whole thing, if you want my honest opinion, is a terrible tragedy for all concerned.'

He looked towards Gareth again who nodded his head and gave a small smile of appreciation towards his former employer.

'Yes, thank you, Mr Montignac,' said Harkman in frustration who had anticipated a more damning reply and regretted asking it now.

'Thank you all,' said the judge, rising before any further questions could be asked. 'Let's say two o'clock.'

3

Montignac did a double take when he saw Margaret Richmond waiting on the street outside the Old Bailey. He was coming down the steps, looking for a phone box to call the gallery before going for some lunch when he saw her familiar figure standing there, speaking to someone through the open window of a car before it drove off. She seemed smaller to him as she stood on the busy London street, away from her natural habitat of Leyville, and more vulnerable.

'Margaret?' he said, approaching her and she spun around in surprise.

'Owen,' she said.

'What on earth are you doing here?' he asked, surprised that she was there at all.

She was dressed formally and carrying her most expensive bag, even wearing a hat; he guessed that she must have been inside the courtroom during his testimony but he had spent most of his time in the stand deliberately avoiding catching the eyes of any of the spectators so as not to distract himself from his main mission.

'We just came out,' she explained. 'Stella's just left this minute.'

'Stella?' he asked. 'Stella was in court?'

Margaret shook her head and looked quite sad as she explained. 'I tried to persuade her not to go,' she said. 'I knew it would only bring up bad memories for her. Of course I've tried to keep a lot of the more lurid details away from her, hiding newspapers and so on, but you know what she's like. When she's determined about something there's no changing her mind. She came expecting to hear Gareth Bentley testify and then, instead of him going into the witness box, there was you.'

'Gareth is testifying after lunch,' he explained. 'Will she be coming back for that?'

'I don't think so. She's gone back to Leyville. I said I'd follow on the later train. She found it all terribly upsetting. Listening to you up there acting as if Raymond was just a friend of hers and nothing more.'

Montignac frowned. 'I didn't want to desecrate his memory,' he said.

'Really.'

'Come on,' he said, taking her by the arm. 'Let's get some tea. We can talk in private there.'

They settled into a small tea shop at the corner of the street and Margaret explained the events of the night before.

'Sir Denis Tandy came to Leyville yesterday afternoon,' she said. 'Stella wanted to talk to him.'

'Not about this idea of hers, surely?'

'She told you about it?'

Montignac nodded. 'She said she wants to give the house over to the National Trust,' he said. 'The National Trust!' he repeated with a laugh. 'She's made some poor decisions in her life, but this one . . .'

'She claims she's going to travel,' said Margaret, equally appalled. 'She wants nothing to do with the place any more. Not since Raymond's death. They had such plans, you see, the two of them. You know he was going to take some time off from the RHS and devote it to re-landscaping the grounds?'

Montignac tried to contain his natural inclination to point out that as far as he was concerned Raymond Davis had no business even entering the grounds of Leyville, let along redesigning them, but he let it slide.

'It's as if she sees nothing worth staying for any more,' continued Margaret. 'I don't know what will become of me. Or her,' she said, correcting herself quickly.

Montignac nodded; it was clear to him where her real concerns lay. 'You're worried that you're going to be left homeless?' he asked.

'She might never come back,' said Margaret, sidestepping the question. 'She's a beautiful, rich young woman. You don't think she'll meet a handsome, eligible young man in America? I imagine there are many there, just waiting for someone like her.'

'I would think it's extremely likely,' said Montignac bitterly.

'After all, if an English king can find an American woman, then an American man can surely capture an English princess.'

'Indeed.'

'You have to find a way to stop her.'

'Me?' he asked, surprised. 'But what can I do about it? We're not even talking at the moment,' he added, wondering whether his former nanny knew about the incident at the weekend when he had slapped Stella's face.

'There was a time,' said Margaret cautiously, 'when you would have wanted to stop her.'

He stared at her, unsure what she was getting at. 'How do you mean?' he asked.

'Stella doesn't think there's anything to stay here for,' she said. 'She's brokenhearted, can't you see that?'

'She liked him,' he conceded. 'But she didn't love him. I don't believe that for a moment.'

'No, she didn't love him,' said Margaret, leaning forwards. 'I've seen her in love. I've seen how she behaves when she's in love. And what she felt for Raymond wasn't that.'

'I thought you were in favour of him?' he asked.

'Oh I was. He was a very pleasant fellow. And they would have settled down at Leyville, had a family there. That was what I wanted. But she didn't love him. That's why she feels so guilty now. I don't think she's ever loved anyone the way she loved you.'

He breathed in heavily; he felt as if he'd just been

slapped himself. 'That was all a long time ago,' he said.

'Ten years ago this summer,' she said. 'But she hasn't forgotten it. And I don't think you have either.'

'Of course I haven't forgotten it. How could I forget something so . . .? But I don't . . .' His mind was confused; to hear Margaret talking like this, bringing up the great unmentionable subject between them, baffled him. 'Why are you bringing this up now anyway? You were the one who . . . put a stop to everything.'

'I put a stop to it because it was wrong then,' she said. 'You were just children. And cousins too. I was trying to protect you both. If Stella's father had found out, he would have killed you. I don't exaggerate, Owen, he would have taken a gun and shot you dead.'

'He would have tried, certainly,' said Montignac.

'Do you remember the day you both came to me?' she asked. 'When you told me what had happened and asked for my help?'

He felt a lump form in his throat. The memories of that afternoon were amongst the worst in his life. Stella and he had spent almost a week discussing the problem they faced, not knowing what to do to make things right, terrified at what would be the outcome of what they had done. Andrew had only been dead a couple of months. Peter Montignac was barely himself. Had they gone to him and told him that she was to have a baby . . . it would have been catastrophic.

'You promised never to mention that time again,' said Montignac, looking away.

'Unless I had to. And I have to now. Because she's making the worst mistake of her life and you're allowing her to do it.'

'You're sure that you're not just worried about losing your home? Being alone? Being left out in the cold like you left us?'

'I didn't leave you anywhere,' she said angrily. 'I did what I did for the best. If I hadn't persuaded your uncle to send Stella away, Andrew wouldn't have been the only Montignac killed that summer.'

'But he wasn't, was he?'

'What's that?'

'I said he wasn't the only Montignac killed that summer. Thanks to you and Stella.'

Margaret sighed. She had considered telling him the truth, that the child was alive and well, but was unsure how he would react to it. Owen had a volatility that she could not control. If he was to find out that both she and Stella had lied to him ten summers ago, then there was no knowing what he might do out of vengeance.

'Owen,' she said. 'It was so long ago. You can't hold me responsible for—'

'Margaret, I don't know what you expect from me,' he hissed. 'I can try to talk to Stella if you like but I don't think it will do any good, do you? If she wants to go, I don't see what I can do to stop her. If she wants to get rid of the house, I don't see how I can prevent her. My hands are tied. Uncle Peter saw to that.'

'But it's your house, Owen,' she protested, her hands curled into fists on the table. 'It's rightfully yours, isn't it? Not hers? It was stolen from you, just like it was stolen from your father thirty years ago.'

'Of course that's true, but I don't see what I can do about it now.'

'You can tell her how you feel about her.'

Montignac sat back in the chair, wide-eyed. 'Tell her how I—?'

'You told me once that you loved Stella. When she went away, you wept for weeks on end. You lay on your bed as if the whole world had come to an end. Don't you remember?'

He curled his lip in distaste at the memory. 'I remember being a bloody fool,' he said. 'I remember thinking that she loved me and being bitterly disappointed. I remember her betrayal.'

'But she does love you, Owen. Can't you see that?'

He shook his head. 'No,' he insisted. 'That's all over now. It was too long ago. We've hurt each other too much in the time in between.'

'It doesn't have to be,' she said, reaching forwards and taking his hand. 'If you want Stella to stay, then just tell her so. Your uncle's dead, your aunt's dead, Andrew's dead. There's nothing to stop you now. Nothing at all.'

He looked at her, amazed that the very person who had ripped them apart was trying to piece them back together again so long after the event. 'I can't believe you're saying all this,' he said. 'Are you really that afraid of being alone?'

'Yes,' she said bitterly. 'Yes I am. You children never even took notice of me, and I did everything for you. Where were your aunt and uncle when you were growing up? Can you tell me that? How often did you see them? Almost never. It was me who was there for you, wiping your tears, helping you with your homework, bandaging your knees. It was me, Owen, not them. You think you were the only one left embittered by your uncle's will? You three were like my own children. And you never, not one of you, even looked at me like I was anything other than a paid employee.'

'But that's what you were,' said Montignac.

'And the only time you ever came to me was when you were in need. When you and Stella were in trouble. Now I want something back. I didn't get so much as a pension left to me after all my years of service. Was that fair? We're in the same boat now, you and I, like it or not. We were both treated badly. So is it too much to hope that you will help me now like I once helped you? I don't want to be left on my own and I don't want to have to leave my home. You have to make her see sense. You protect me, Owen, and I'll protect you.'

'Protect me?' he asked in surprise. 'And what's that supposed to mean?'

'Do I have to spell it out?'

Montignac frowned; he wasn't quite sure what she was getting at. 'I think perhaps you do,' he said.

Margaret sat back in her chair and poured some more tea. 'Oh, it's stewed,' she said in disappointment, looking at the dark stream emerging from the pot.

'Protect me from what?' insisted Montignac.

'You're not going to believe this, Margaret,' said the former nanny quietly, leaning forwards so that no one else could hear. *'But that was Owen on the phone. He wants to make things right with us. Says he wants to apologize and make a fresh start. I'm to go up to his gallery to meet him this evening and we're going to talk it all out. Not a word to Stella now, all right? Not until I'm sure that he means it. I'll take the late afternoon train and leave a note for her; there was a lecture I was planning on attending anyway so I'll say I've gone to that.'*

Montignac almost stopped breathing for a moment. He sat back and looked around anxiously; he could feel his face grow pale with shock.

'He told you,' he said finally. 'You were there when I phoned him.'

'I was there.'

'He said he hadn't told anyone.'

'He lied,' said Margaret. 'Although as far as all of you have ever been concerned, I'm not anyone. I'm nobody at all.'

'What do you want?' asked Montignac, whose mind had already begun to skip through the possibilities; if she knew, then she had known since the morning after Raymond's murder and she had said nothing. There was no reason she was going to go to the police now. But she obviously wanted something in return.

'I don't want anything very much,' she said. 'I've been confused about what to do in fact. It took me a few days to realize the truth but I didn't say anything to the police because I didn't want the family name dragged through the mud. Nothing was going to bring Raymond back and I didn't want to hurt Stella any more. But now that she's going away . . . it's made me realize how worthless I am to her. How she simply doesn't care. So I don't have any choice. I have to turn to you. You have to stop her giving the house away.'

'You're worse than I am,' said Montignac quietly.

'Hardly,' said Margaret.

'And if I do this, if I can persuade her, then you won't say anything.'

'I won't watch that boy hang, if that's what you mean. I won't go that far.'

Montignac frowned. It was all too difficult suddenly; there were too many people to consider. 'I have to save him too?'

'There has to be a way,' said Margaret. 'He's an innocent.'

'All right,' said Montignac, realizing he had no choice in the matter. 'I'll do what I can. I'll speak to Stella. I'll try to persuade her.'

'Do you still love her?'

'Of course I love her!' he shouted, without even considering the words. Others in the tea shop turned to look at him and he stared down at his cup in embarrassment. 'Of course I love her,' he repeated in a quieter voice. 'You've got no idea of what my life has been without her. Of the things I've . . . of what I've shown myself capable of. There's never been anyone but Stella.'

'Then tell her,' said Margaret quickly. 'Tell her and she'll stay. I know she will.'

Montignac sat back and stared at her. 'There are times when I've questioned my actions,' he said quietly. 'When I've wondered what kind of man I am. But I know one thing for sure. I'm nothing like you.'

'What do you mean?'

'You sit there and say that you loved all three of us, that you took care of us . . .' He shook his head bitterly. 'You did nothing but look out for yourself. The things you said to Stella and me all those years ago when we came to you, the names you called us . . . And now you have the nerve to say that I should return to her and try to win her back, just so you can fulfil your dream of remaining lady of the manor? I don't blame Uncle Peter for forgetting you. I'd forget you myself.'

Margaret's lips pursed and she glared at him. 'You don't have any choice, Owen,' she said. 'You either help me or you lose everything. There's finally a chance for you now, for you both. It's up to you if you want to take it.'

For a moment he felt a pang of remorse for the things he had done in his life, for what was happening right now. The chain of events he had set in progress. And as he looked across the table at this old lady who was terrified of what the future held, he wondered whether there wasn't at least one person who was more to blame for the mess that was his life than he was.

He glanced at his watch; it was nearly ten to two.

'I have to go,' he said, standing up. 'The court will be back in session shortly. Are you coming too?'

She shook her head. 'I've seen all I wanted to see,' she said. 'And said all I needed to say. You'll think about what I've said?' she asked.

He shrugged. I could hardly fail to,' he said, walking away without looking back at her, walking out on to the street where he had an uncommon urge to scream at the top of his lungs, to bring the traffic to a standstill with his cries.

4

The courtroom seemed a lot bigger to Gareth Bentley when he was actually standing in the witness box. Throughout the trial so far he had managed to keep his eyes focused on two distinct places: either directly at the witness who was testifying on the stand or down below, at the ground beneath his feet. He was aware of the hundreds of people who attended court each day to hear the evidence and to judge him silently; he could feel their eyes burning into him as they stared in his direction, trying to decide for themselves whether or not he had the appearance of a brutal killer, but he never once looked back at them. Only now, standing on the raised dais with the courtroom coming to an expectant silence did he feel able to look out at them all and wonder what on earth he had ever done to deserve such unwelcome attention.

Like Montignac a few hours earlier, and like the stream of witnesses who had already appeared, he placed his right hand on the Bible and swore that the evidence he would give would be the truth. His stomach was in knots as Sir Quentin Lawrence, counsel for the defence, rose to question him.

'Mr Bentley,' he began without any further ceremony. 'Can you tell us where you were on the night of August the eighteenth, nineteen thirty-six?'

Gareth nodded and cleared his throat. 'I was in the Bullirag pub by Piccadilly Circus with my employer, Mr Owen Montignac.'

'I see. And can you tell us what you remember of the events of that night?'

'No, I'm afraid not.'

'I beg your pardon?' asked Sir Quentin in surprise, as if this had not already been discussed and rehearsed several times already in Gareth's cell.

'I said that I can't remember, sir.'

'And can you tell us why that is?'

'I drank too much alcohol that night, to my regret, and unfortunately when I drink too much I find that the next morning I can remember very little of what happened the night before.'

'So you have no memory of the evening at all?'

'Very little, sir.'

'And what is your first subsequent memory?'

'I woke up in a strange bed, in a strange flat,' he said. 'I had no idea where I was. I had a terrible hangover. I lay there for some time and then I could hear footsteps outside on the street and cars pulling up. I got out of bed and when I did I discovered that there was blood on my shirt.'

'Someone had attacked you in the night?'

'Objection, Your Honour,' shouted Harkman. 'Counsel is leading the witness.'

'Sustained. Please don't make conjectures for your client, Sir Quentin,' grumbled the judge.

'My apologies, Your Honour. Mr Bentley, can you tell us in your own words what happened next?'

He nodded. 'I heard someone come into the flat. I still had no idea where I was and so I stepped out of the bedroom and that's when I saw him.'

'Him?'

'The man I later discovered to be Raymond Davis. His body was on the floor. It was . . . horrible. And before I knew it there were policemen coming in and they jumped on me and it's all a bit of a blur from then on.'

Sir Quentin nodded and his voice rose louder as he approached the box. 'Can you tell us, Mr Bentley, whether you had ever laid eyes on Raymond Davis before that morning?'

'Never, sir.'

'You had neither met with him nor spoken to him?'

'No, sir.'

'And you had no grudges against him?'

'Of course not.'

'Can you tell me, Mr Bentley, whether you killed Raymond Davis?'

'No, sir,' said Gareth emphatically. 'I don't believe I did.'

It was all that Sir Quentin could do not to strike the witness himself. He had coached him on this moment a dozen times. The answer to the question as *No, sir*. Full stop. Nothing else. He was allowed to lean forwards to sound more emphatic if he liked but two words were all that were needed. No amendments. No editorials. Sir Quentin stared at his client, his mouth open in astonishment that he should destroy this necessarily melodramatic moment so completely. It beggared belief.

'No further questions, Your Honour,' he said quietly and the court buzzed in surprise at his brevity, his climax robbed from him, as it so often was, by an unhelpful client.

Mr Justice Harkman rose to his feet a little sooner than he had expected but he had been handed a very convenient thread and he picked it up immediately.

'You don't *believe* you killed Mr Davis?' he asked politely.

'No, I . . . I didn't kill him,' he replied, aware of the mistake he had made. 'That's what I was supposed to say.'

'What you were—'

'What I *meant* to say,' said Gareth, his voice rising as he grappled with confusion. 'I meant to say . . . did I kill Raymond Davis? No. No, I did not.'

'But you don't know that for a fact, Mr Bentley, do you? You couldn't swear to it?'

He opened his mouth and glanced at his own barrister who raised an irritated eyebrow back at him; immediately he recalled the advice he had been given in advance and cursed his own forgetfulness.

'I . . .' he began, hoping to backtrack. 'I could swear to the fact that I consider myself incapable of hurting someone in that way. I never even knew—'

'Thank you, Mr Bentley. If you could just confine yourself to answering my questions we'll all get out of here a lot sooner. Now, are you familiar with Aiden Higgins?'

Gareth nodded his head sadly.

'Can you tell us how you got to know him?'

'We were at school together,' he said. 'When we were children.'

'And can you talk us through the incident that occurred back then that led to your suspension from Harrow and can you recount the story strictly from your own memories of it?'

He opened his mouth to answer and then the second half of Harkman's question struck him. He had enough experience of the law to see exactly where the barrister was heading on this and shook his head again.

'I'm sorry,' he said. 'I can't do that.'

'And why is that?'

'I can't remember the incident.'

'Really, Mr Bentley, we've already had testimony from two of your school friends, Aiden Higgins and Paul O'Neill, both of whom have described in lurid detail how you violently assaulted Mr Higgins and left him with a fractured arm and dislocated shoulder. Are you telling us that you have no memory of the incident at all?'

'I was drunk,' said Gareth quietly, his head bowed.

'Could you speak up please? I can't quite hear you.'

'I said I was drunk,' he repeated, louder, and the court buzzed again. 'I don't remember any of it.'

'But would you accept the account that the two witnesses gave of the incident? Considering they were there and, I believe, sober?'

'I suppose so,' said Gareth.

'You suppose so? Can't you do better than that?'

'Yes,' he replied. 'I accept their account of it.'

'I see,' said Harkman. 'Can you tell me, Mr Bentley, whether in your own words you would consider yourself incapable of hurting someone in that way?'

'I don't think I could, no.'

'But you've admitted that you did.'

'When I was a boy, perhaps.'

'A drunken boy. And it wasn't so very long ago, was it?'

'It's . . . I never meant to hurt him.'

'Mr Bentley, I presume you were sent down from Harrow after the incident?'

Gareth shook his head. 'No,' he said. 'No, I stayed on.'

'Really? How extraordinary! And after such a violent fracas? How on earth did you manage that?'

Gareth looked up and in the distance he could make out the figures of his mother and father at the side of a row, Roderick with head bowed and body crumpled in pain, Jane staring at him, her lips moving to guide his answer. He had a sudden memory of how she used to mime the words of songs he performed at school concerts when he was a child; how she had focused her eyes directly on him, knowing the words he had to say almost as well as he did himself. This was like a macabre echo of those youthful, simpler days.

'I believe my father made a contribution to the school and—'

'He bought them off, am I right?' asked Harkman.

'I suppose so.'

'In order to protect his son, he bought them off. Well that's entirely reasonable. Perhaps in the same situation any of us would have done the same thing. But there's no one to buy you out of trouble this time, Mr Bentley, is there? Your violent ways have caught up with you at last, haven't they?'

'Objection, Your Honour!' cried Sir Quentin, climbing to his feet.

'Did you kill Raymond Davis?' shouted Harkman over him. 'Did you brutally murder him that night in Bedford Place?'

'No, I didn't,' said Gareth, flustered now, trying to

appeal to his parents for help. 'It's all such a mess . . . I don't know what happened . . . I woke up and—'

'You were the only one there, Mr Bentley! You must have killed him. In a drunken violent rage, you attacked him.'

'I don't see how I—'

'Objection! Counsel is—'

'Mr Davis arrived at the door to see Mr Montignac, and you – because you had not enough of a sense of responsibility about yourself to keep sober and your wits about you – set about him in a drunken rage and brutally attacked him.

'I don't remember it,' shouted Gareth. 'How can I answer your questions when I don't remember it?'

'But you don't remember attacking Aidan Higgins either. And you admit now that you did. Isn't it perfectly conceivable that you attacked Raymond Davis and have forgotten that too?'

'It's conceivable,' he said, his hands on either side of his head. 'I suppose it's—'

'It's more than conceivable, isn't it, Mr Bentley? There's no other logical explanation. You woke up covered in the man's blood. You killed him, didn't you?'

Gareth looked up as the court went silent. He scanned the faces, looking for someone.

'Didn't you, Mr Bentley?' he roared.

Gareth looked from left to right, over the figures of the court reporters, past his parents, ignoring the strangers who were revelling in his discomfort.

'Didn't you kill Raymond Davis, Mr Bentley?' shouted Harkman, gripping the stand before him. 'You're guilty of this crime, are you not?'

Gareth found who he was looking for, the white shock of hair in the back row directed him to the face of Owen Montignac, his friend and employer, the man who'd given him a chance when he needed one, and he found that Montignac's eyes were locked directly upon his own, as if he had been guiding him to find him, and his head was moving very slowly up and down, up and down, so that after a moment Gareth's head found itself doing the same thing. Very slowly he broke away eye contact and looked back at Mr Justice Harkman and, like a drowning man finally giving up his hold of the small piece of wood that has kept him afloat for so long, he slipped under the waters and allowed the suffocation to follow.

'I don't know,' he cried, his body sinking in the chair. 'I don't know what to think any more. I can't remember any of it . . . any of Aidan . . . or Raymond . . . or . . .' He started to shake his head sadly and the words became lost in an explosion of tears and heaving shoulders. 'It's all . . . I don't know what I did . . . I thought it was . . .'

From his seat at the front of the court, Roderick Bentley had heard enough. He leaned across to his wife and said gruffly, 'I have to go.'

'Go?' she asked, turning to stare at him, barely understanding his words, so wrapped up was she in her son's pain. 'Go where?'

'I have to take care of something,' he said. 'I have to fix this.'

'But Roderick, you can't just—'

He stood up and made his way quickly and noisily along the row and out on to the aisle, practically breaking into a run as he made his way to the door and the corridor beyond, completely oblivious to the fact that every set of eyes in the courtroom except for his son's had been watching him. Particularly the eyes of Owen Montignac, who allowed himself a small smile as he checked his watch.

Pushing his way through the door Roderick stood against the cold stone wall for a few moments, trying to catch his breath, knowing that he had no choice now, whatever happened their old way of life had just come to an end. Finally he knew just how little his integrity was worth.

5

Lord Samuel Keaton's office was located on the second floor of the Palace of Westminster with a view over the Thames and Tower Bridge. Roderick climbed the stone stairs with a heavy heart. From the moment he had first been called to the Bar, and again when he had taken silk, he had sworn to uphold the law and had never once allowed his personal feelings to interfere with his professional duty. He had defended clients for whom he had no respect and had got them off serious charges on technicalities because the police had failed to uphold their part of the legal bargain. He had upheld the Golden Thread of Justice throughout his time in the courts and had never knowingly erred. And as a judge in sentencing he had never discriminated between convicted criminals on any grounds save the nature of the offence. And now, at the age of fifty-two, he was about to destroy his integrity and sacrifice his king in order to save the life of his son.

He knocked on the door and waited for a response but none was forthcoming so he tried the handle and the heavy oak door swung open. Poking his head into the room he saw Lord Keaton sitting behind his desk on the telephone, leaning back in his chair as if he didn't have a care in the world. Keaton noticed him and beckoned him to enter.

'I have to go,' he said to the caller, winking at Roderick as he said, 'important visitor.' There was a pause while something was said to him in reply. 'I believe I'll be able to call you back within an hour with that information,' he continued. 'I'll know the answer very shortly.' He hung up the phone and smiled at Roderick. 'I wondered how long it would take you to get here,' he said.

'Did you indeed,' said Roderick grimly, sitting down in the chair opposite the desk. 'Well I hope I didn't disappoint you.'

'Not at all. I wasn't sure, of course. One can try to read another man's actions but we're all unpredictable souls.

But after your son's performance on the stand today—'

'You heard what happened then?'

'Heard it? My dear fellow, I was there.'

'You were in court?'

'I was in the gallery looking down on you. You wouldn't have seen me. I wanted to make sure that the whole thing hadn't been a tremendous waste of time. I did feel sorry for Jane, though; she looked absolutely devastated.'

'*Don't* talk about Jane,' said Roderick sharply, causing Keaton to hesitate before continuing.

'No,' he said quietly. 'Although there's no need for us to be unpleasant about things. How's your boy doing anyway? Did you speak to him afterwards?'

'Do you really care?' asked Roderick.

'Well believe it or not, Roderick, I wouldn't wish any harm on the lad,' said Keaton. 'Particularly as I'm about to save his life. You know you could give me a little credit for that,' he added.

Roderick shook his head. Credit, or thanks, or any kind of appreciation were beyond him now.

'Sorry about the office,' said Keaton after a few silent moments had passed.

'Sorry?'

'That it's so dingy. All the best ones are on the top floor. I've had to put up with this pit for years.'

Roderick looked around in surprise; the room was both spacious and luxurious with a splendid view. But he had been in the Lord Chancellor's suite many times and it was palatial in comparison. He could only imagine the egos that worried about such things in a place like this.

'Well I don't suppose you'll have to put up with it for too much longer,' said Roderick.

'You think not?'

'No.'

'You've come to a decision then?' he asked.

Roderick nodded. 'It hasn't been easy,' he said. 'I feel like the worst kind of traitor.'

'Yes, but your name won't live through the ages as one,' said Keaton. 'You'll be forgotten, as will I, but the event will always be remembered. And it will have come about through our good offices. Precious few men get the opportunity to influence history like this.'

'Is that supposed to make me feel better?'

'It's supposed to make you realize that you're a part of something bigger than all of us now, whether you get the recognition for it or not. Isn't that something to be proud of in itself?'

'Nothing about this makes me proud,' said Roderick. 'But before I commit myself to anything, how do I know that I can trust you?'

'I'm sorry?' asked Lord Keaton.

'If I change my vote, how do I know that you can influence the judge to spare Gareth's life?'

Keaton shrugged. 'Well I can't give you any guarantees,' he said. 'You'll just have to trust me, I suppose. But you can, you know. You have nothing to worry about on that score.'

'Is that supposed to be good enough for me?' he asked with an embittered laugh.

'My dear fellow, if I let you down you can always go to the newspapers, can't you, and tell them the whole thing? Of course you'll destroy your own career along with mine because you'll have to admit that your opinion was for sale. And all the cases you've presided over throughout your whole career will be mercilessly raked over and the prisoners released, for who knows how many bribes you've accepted over the years?'

'I've never accepted a bribe,' said Roderick angrily, leaning forwards in his chair. 'Not once. Not ever. I have never done anything to be ashamed of—'

'My dear fellow, there's no point trying to convince me,' said Keaton cheerfully. 'I'm the one man in the world who knows exactly what your price is. Perhaps your so-called integrity was just never challenged before. Now you'll have to trust me but for what it's worth, that was Lord Sharpwell I was talking to on the phone when you came in. He does favour the death penalty, of course. Thinks a crime like this can't go unpunished.'

Roderick sighed. 'And what's in it for him?' he asked. 'What are you blackmailing him with?'

Keaton burst out laughing. 'I don't have to blackmail him,' he said. 'He's a solid man, Sharpwell. Knows what we're up against. He sees what will happen to the country if the king isn't set aside. No, he's a Baldwin man through and through.'

'And does he know about the little promotion you have in mind for yourself when this business is over?'

'Well that's neither here nor there, is it?' he replied. 'I'll look after Sharpwell when the time comes. He knows that. Men of our calibre have to stick together. You're one too, Roderick, you know. I have a lot of respect for you, believe it or not. You're a young man still. You have another fifteen or twenty years on the bench before you. And believe me, I won't forget what you've done for me when I'm sitting on the woolsack. You may find that your future is a golden one. There are so many ways that we could help each other in the future.'

Roderick nodded. 'I thought you might say that,' he said, removing an envelope from his inner pocket and laying it on the desk. It was addressed to the Lord Chancellor of England. 'You'd better not open that until you have the job,' he said. 'Or you may get done for opening another man's mail.'

Keaton frowned and picked it up. 'What is it?' he asked.

'It's my resignation,' said Roderick. 'You don't seriously think I could continue to try cases after what I'm about to do, do you?'

'That's a little melodramatic, don't you think?'

'I do not. I'm leaving this office today with the equivalent of thirty pieces of silver in my pocket. I couldn't look at myself in the mirror if I continued to think I had the right to judge others. My legitimacy has been stolen from me.'

Keaton sighed and shook his head. 'You're such a drama queen,' he said with a smile, making Roderick want to stand up and punch him on the nose. 'But I'll hold on to your letter for now. And I won't read it, as you say, until this business is over. And even then I'd rather not accept it.'

'You won't have any choice. You may consider me officially retired as from today. When the Christmas recess is over, I will be gone.'

Keaton shrugged. 'If that's what you want,' he said. 'But I think you're making a terrible mistake.'

'I've made many,' he said. 'But never while I've been wearing a judge's robes. And I don't intend to sully them now.'

Keaton nodded and reached into a desk drawer to remove a piece of paper and pass it across the desk.

'What's this?' asked Roderick.

'It's your vote,' said Keaton. 'I've told Hailsham that you won't be attending the final meeting due to your family problems but that you're determined to have your say. He knows we've spoken about things and when you sign that piece of paper you'll be stating that I have the authority to speak and vote on your behalf.'

Roderick sighed and read the document through. It was brief and to the point and did exactly as Keaton had said. When he looked up again, a hand was reaching across the desk and offering him a pen.

'It's for your son, Roderick,' said Keaton quietly. 'And

you may not appreciate it now, but it's for your country too.'

He took the pen without a word and signed his name in the appropriate place, the nib cutting into the paper as he did so, and stood up without a word. Turning his back on Keaton, he walked towards the door but hesitated for a moment before looking back. 'What happens now?' he asked. 'What should I expect?'

'You don't have to worry any more. Your boy will be found guilty, I imagine, tomorrow morning or afternoon at the latest. We'll be in session in the morning before Hailsham speaks to the PM and I believe he's planning on speaking to the king sometime after lunch. And your son will get a light sentence, a couple of months, perhaps a year, no more than that. And after that? Well the future is in the hands of the gods really, isn't it?'

'He may surprise you, you know,' said Roderick.

'Who?'

'The king. He may be made of sterner stuff.'

Keaton laughed and shook his head. 'You don't know him.'

'No, but you never know. What if he sets her aside?'

'Then I lose,' said Keaton with a shrug. 'And there will be absolutely nothing I can do about it. The last laugh, as they say, will be on me. But you needn't worry, once you've voted my way in the morning I'll tell Sharpwell and your boy will be safe. I'm an honourable man, Roderick. I always keep my side of bargains.'

Roderick nodded and made for the door.

'He should have just followed in your footsteps,' said Keaton as he walked away. 'Your son, I mean. If he'd just done what—'

Roderick wasn't listening any more. The former judge closed the door behind him and made his way slowly downstairs and into the early December evening, where a light drizzle was starting to fall and the shadow of the Houses of Parliament along the Thames made him wish that he was anywhere else in the world other than there.

6

He decided not to go to court the following morning. Instead he sat in his study, staring at the volumes of legal books that made up the majority of his library, wondering whether it was time to place them in boxes and take them off his shelves. He could barely stand to look at them without feeling like a traitor to his entire life. He turned away and his eye caught the photograph of his son, Gareth, that sat on his desk, taken when he was younger and more carefree, a wide smile plastered across his face, his future before him.

'Roderick, aren't you ready yet?' asked Jane, stepping inside quickly, adjusting an earring and looking around her as if she had lost something.

'Ready for what?'

'For *court*, of course,' she said. 'What do you think?'

He shook his head but couldn't look directly at her. 'I'm not going,' he said. 'Not today.'

'Not going?' she asked, stopping quickly to stare at him. 'But you have to.'

'I don't *have* to do anything,' he snapped. 'I can't take another day of it, if you want to know the truth.'

Jane laughed bitterly. 'And you think I can? Just get ready, please. We have to leave in about ten minutes.'

'I said I'm not going,' he shouted, standing up from his chair and walking around to face her. 'Why can't you listen to me when I speak? If I say I'm not going to court then that's exactly what I mean. I couldn't care less if I never see the inside of a courtroom again.'

'You actually mean it?' she asked in an astonished voice.

'Yes, I mean it.'

'And what about Gareth?' she asked. 'The judge might send the jury out today. Don't you think he'll want to know that we're there for him?'

'He knows that already.'

Jane stared at her husband in exasperation; she couldn't believe he would let her down at this crucial moment. She opened her mouth to remonstrate with him some more but then hesitated, a thought occurring to her. 'You did it, didn't you?' she asked.

'What's that?'

'You're not coming to court because you know that Gareth's going to be all right. You changed your vote.'

Roderick sighed and looked away. Very slowly, almost

imperceptibly, he nodded his head and Jane let out a deep sigh.

'I knew it,' she said. 'I knew you wouldn't let me down.'

'And you think I haven't?' he asked.

'You did what you had to do. For our son. You have nothing to feel ashamed of.'

'Then how is it that I do?'

'Roderick—'

'Listen to me, Jane, there's nothing to be so happy about really. Yes, I changed my vote. Yes, Keaton will influence the judge and Gareth won't receive the death sentence. But what does it change really? He's still going to be found guilty. He's still going to jail.'

'You don't know that,' she cried.

'I don't? How many years was I a barrister, Jane? How many years have I sat on the bench? I can read a jury, I can hear evidence and decide on it. Unless Quentin pulls something out of the bag then there's a horrible inevitability to all of this. Do you really think that Gareth will survive in jail? Look at him, for pity's sake. He's already a shadow of his former self. A couple of years will be the end of him. All I did was prolong his misery.

Jane shook her head; she didn't want to hear defeatist talk such as this. 'I have to go,' she said. 'You stay if you want but I'm going to court. I won't let him hear the verdict without me being there to support him.'

'Then I'll see you tonight.'

She hesitated, wondering whether she should make him change his mind, but decided against it. He had done what she wanted. He had made sure that their son's life – *her* son's life – was not in jeopardy. That was all that mattered. What happened after that was for another day's worrying. She said nothing more to him now, simply left the room, collected her bag and coat, and slipped outside and into the car without another word.

Roderick moved to the window as she made her way through the journalists, a sudden urge overcoming him to go outside and fight them, get them off his property once and for all. But there was no fight left in him any more, he realized. There was nothing more to be done. He sat down on the sofa instead and looked around, wondering how he would fill his days from now on.

Jane arrived at the courtroom later than she had hoped; a traffic jam along the way had delayed her and the seat she normally sat in at the front was already taken. She sighed in frustration, craning her neck for a view of Gareth in the dock but all she could see was the back of his head and she was unable to make out if his breakdown on the stand the previous day had had any bad effect on him.

'You'll have to take a seat, ma'am,' whispered a policeman to her and she nodded quickly and moved to a row near the back, finding a place at the end of it where she settled herself quickly and tried to take in what was happening. Sir Quentin was on his feet questioning a witness, one she didn't recognize, and she frowned as she tried to decide who it might be.

'Don't worry,' whispered the young man sitting directly to her left. 'He's only just taken to the stand.'

'Mr Montignac,' she replied quietly, turning to look at him, her face flushing a little in embarrassment as she recalled their last encounter in the gallery. 'I didn't notice you there.'

'I saw you the moment you came in.'

She gave a small smile, unsure whether he meant that as a compliment or not, and nodded in the direction of the witness box. 'Who's that?' she asked.

'The coroner,' said Montignac.

A hand stretched forwards between them, resting on her shoulder for a moment; it belonged to the policeman who put a finger to his lips to silence them and she nodded before turning her attention to the front of the court.

'Now, Dr Cawley,' Sir Quentin was saying, 'you were the coroner who performed the postmortem on the body of Raymond Davis, is that correct?'

'Yes, sir, that's correct,' said Cawley, a middle-aged man who spoke in confident tones and appeared to be accustomed to giving evidence in court.

'And can you tell us what you found to be the cause of death?'

'The cause of death was a blow to the cranium which smashed the frontal lobe of the skull. My examination revealed that there were three such blows inflicted but it is likely that death was instantaneous with the second blow.'

'I see,' said Sir Quentin. 'And you've examined the candlestick which has already been offered into evidence by the prosecution?'

'I have, sir.'

'And can you tell us whether you consider this implement to be the same one that killed Raymond Davis.'

'With complete certainty, yes,' said Cawley, nodding his head. He glanced in the direction of the judge for a moment as he continued with his evidence. 'There were flakes of paint consistent with the candlestick still lodged in Mr Davis's wounds,' he explained. 'Added to this there were blood and hairs and various skull matter on the base of the candlestick. I don't believe there can be any question as to this being the murder weapon.'

'Thank you, Dr Cawley,' said Sir Quentin, who was strolling around the top of the court in a very casual way – a little too casually for Jane's liking – as if he knew something that no one else did. 'And you were also able to fix the time of death of the deceased, were you not?'

'Yes, sir. My examination revealed that the time of death was somewhere between two and three o'clock on the morning of August the nineteenth.'

'Some five to six hours before the police discovered the body at Bedford Place?'

'As I understand it, yes.'

'Thank you, Dr Cawley, no more questions just now.'

The judge raised an eyebrow at the last part of Sir Quentin's sentence but then looked in the direction of Mr Justice Harkman, who rose for the prosecution. He stood there for a moment, looking slightly baffled.

'I don't have very many questions for you, Dr Cawley,' he said, looking across at the defence counsel suspiciously. 'It seems to me that Sir Quentin has asked much of what I wanted to ask you. But just let me clarify. Mr Davis was definitely killed between the hours of two and three a.m. in the flat on Bedford Place, a flat whose only occupant at the time was the defendant, Mr Bentley?'

'I can answer yes to your first two statements,' said Dr Cawley carefully. 'As for the occupancy of the flat, I'm afraid that's outside of my jurisdiction.'

'Indeed, indeed,' said Harkman thoughtfully. He licked his lips, knowing full well that there was something he was missing. Sir Quentin was clearly leading him up a blind alley and until he knew what lay at the end of it the sensible thing to do was to sit down.

'Thank you, Dr Cawley,' said Judge Sharpwell. 'You may—'

'Actually, Your Honour,' said Sir Quentin, rising again. 'If I may, just one or two more questions.'

'Go ahead,' said the judge with a sigh.

'Dr Cawley, when you examined the body of the deceased, did you restrict your examination to the wounds at the front of the skull, the wounds which had apparently caused the death of Mr Davis?'

'No, sir,' said Cawley. 'I did not.'

'I see. And in your examination, did you find anything noteworthy on the body of the deceased?'

Cawley reached down for a notebook and flicked through it until he found the page he was looking for. 'Yes, sir,' he said finally. 'There was another injury to Mr Davis which became evident during the course of the postmortem. An earlier injury.'

A low murmur broke out around the courtroom and the judge reached for his gavel to silence the spectators.

'What did he say?' asked Jane, looking towards Owen Montignac for clarification. 'Did he say an earlier injury?'

'He did,' said Montignac, narrowing his eyes and listening carefully.

'Dr Cawley,' continued Sir Quentin, enjoying the tension of the moment. 'Can you please tell the court what the nature of the injury was?'

'Yes, sir,' said Cawley. 'At the back of the head, just above Mr Davis's neck, there was a second injury, a blow struck, I would conjecture, by a heavy instrument, perhaps a poker or a steel rod.

'I see. And would this injury have been enough to kill Mr Davis?'

'No. It was aimed far enough below the skull to render the victim unconscious but would certainly not have caused death.'

'And were you able to determine by the wound when exactly it took place? Would it have been a few moments before the fatal blows to the front of the head, for example?'

'Definitely not,' said Cawley. 'The level of bruising was quite advanced in relation to Mr Davis's other wounds. I placed the time of the earlier injuries some eight to ten hours before, or between the hours of four and five thirty p.m. on the evening of the eighteenth.'

'Up to ten hours before the fatal blows were delivered,' repeated Sir Quentin for added effect.

'Yes.'

Once again the courtroom broke out in noise and on this occasion the judge let out a roar, ordering that everyone be silent. Jane arched her neck, desperate to get a better view of the front of the court. Montignac checked his watch anxiously.

'Dr Cawley,' continued Sir Quentin, 'you're telling the court that Mr Davis was struck unconscious ten hours before he was murdered. How long would such a blow have rendered him unconscious?'

'From the swelling and the manner in which the blood had clotted below the wound, anywhere from six to twelve hours I would imagine.'

'And there is nothing to tell us that the initial blow took place at the Bedford Place flat?'

'I don't believe it was. There was nothing in the flat which might have delivered a blow like that.'

'So it would be reasonable to assume that the blow was struck elsewhere?'

'I would think so, yes.'

Mr Harkman rose to his feet and objected loudly. 'Is defence counsel actually implying that Mr Davis was knocked unconscious in one place and brought to another for the purposes of murdering him?' He sounded outraged, as if this was a slight on the principles of logic.

'Well, Sir Quentin?' asked Sharpwell. 'Are you implying that?'

'No, Your Honour, I'm stating it,' said Sir Quentin. 'I am stating that Mr Davis suffered two attacks that night and that the perpetrator of the first waited up for nine hours before finishing the job. Your Honour, if you please, I would like to recall Gareth Bentley to the stand.'

Sharpwell looked at the prosecution counsel, who shrugged his shoulders reluctantly, and Gareth, looking more and more dazed, emerged from the dock, barely glancing at Dr Cawley as he resumed his place in the witness box.

'He was with us,' stated Jane under her breath, as she considered the matter. 'Mr Montignac, I know what he's going to be asked and he was with us.'

Montignac raised an eyebrow and offered her a brief smile.

'You realize you're still under oath, Mr Bentley, don't you?' said Sir Quentin.

'Yes, sir,' said Gareth nervously.

'Then I have just one question for you. On the evening of August the eighteenth, nineteen thirty-six, where were you between the hours of four p.m. and five thirty.'

'The evening before Mr Davis was killed?'

'Just so, Mr Bentley. Where were you?'

Gareth thought about it and cast his mind back. He glanced around the courtroom and looked for his parents in their usual seats but they were missing. Jane followed the trajectory of his eyes and wanted to stand up and shout to him, to offer him her support, but she knew this was too important a moment. He had to answer the question. He had to remember.

'Where were you, Mr Bentley?' asked Sir Quentin.

'Well I was at home,' said Gareth.

'And were you alone?'

'No, my mother was there. And my father.'

'Both your parents were with you at home. Including your father, Sir Roderick Bentley KC. The well-known high court judge?' he added, looking to the jury to make sure they were all clear on Roderick's status.

'Yes, sir.'

'And was anyone else there at the time, do you recall?'

Gareth thought about it. 'Yes, I remember Sophie and Nell were there too. Our cook and maid. They always come back around four o'clock to start preparing the evening meal.'

'I see,' said Sir Quentin, delighted with Gareth for getting it right at last. 'So there were four witnesses to your being at home, is that what you're telling me?'

'Yes, sir.'

'And what time did you leave for the Threadbare Gallery?'

'Around twenty to seven.'

There was a gasp throughout the courtroom and Jane put a hand to her breast; she felt as if she needed to keep breathing. The room was swaying slightly.

'What does that mean?' she asked Montignac. 'What does all that mean? Does that mean they've proved he didn't do it?'

'What it means is that you need to let me out,' he said quietly.

'Pardon?'

'I'm about to be called to the stand,' said Montignac, as if he had been expecting this all along.

'You are?' asked Jane. 'But—'

'Your Honour, I would like to call Owen Montignac back to the witness box if I may,' said Sir Quentin, his voice booming now as if he had just got to the end of a long but triumphant speech on the stage of the Old Vic.

The judge nodded and Montignac was already on his way up there, being watched in fascination by Jane Bentley. He passed Gareth on the way and the younger man was sure that his former employer offered him a slight wink as one made his way to the witness box and the other back to the dock.

'Mr Montignac, you too realize you're still under oath?' asked Sir Quentin.

'I do,' said Montignac.

'Mr Montignac, I have a number of serious and

delicate questions to put to you. And I must insist that you are frank in your answers even if they are embarrassing.'

'I understand entirely,' said Montignac.

'How long have you lived in the flat at Bedford Place?'

'Almost four years.'

'And during that time, have you ever allowed another gentleman to sleep there?'

'Never,' said Montignac. 'I only allowed Gareth – Mr Bentley, that is – to sleep there to prevent him the embarrassment of returning home to his parents intoxicated.'

'Mr Montignac, can you tell us if you are a gambling man.'

There was a long silence while he did his best to look repentant. 'To my shame,' he replied, 'I must answer yes.'

'I see. And do you have any outstanding debts at the moment?'

'A number of them.'

'For a large amount of money?'

'Yes, sir.'

Harkman rose to his feet. 'Your Honour, I fail to see what Mr Montignac's financial position has to do with anything.'

'I'm trying to establish a motive for the crime, Your Honour. I believe that it's been clearly proven that Mr Bentley did not inflict the initial blow and therefore it would seem highly unlikely that he delivered the fatal one. And I would simply like to establish a motive for the murder before asking for the case to be dismissed.'

'You may carry on,' said Judge Sharpwell, who had received instructions from Keaton that morning that Roderick had changed his vote and so there was no further need to cause unnecessary difficulty for his son.

'Mr Montignac, I assume that it is not a bank to whom you are in debt?' asked Sir Quentin.

'No, sir. I am in debt to some people who generally seek recompense through more violent means.'

'Mr Montignac, had Mr Bentley not got drunk that night, you would presumably have ended up asleep in your flat alone, yes?'

'Yes.'

'And woken the following morning with a dead body there?'

'Indeed.'

'The dead body of a man whose proposed marriage to your cousin you were well known to be opposed to, covered in his blood. In fact, we most likely would still have been here today, only it would have been you standing in the dock, accused of a crime you did not commit, rather than Mr Bentley. Wouldn't you say so?'

The court held its breath and waited for Montignac to answer. Finally he looked up and nodded.

'I think that seems very likely,' he said. 'I think that whoever killed Raymond Davis framed the wrong man. They assumed that Gareth was me.'

'But you weren't there,' said Sir Quentin.

'No.'

'And Mr Bentley would not have been present when the first blow to Mr Davis was delivered.'

'Apparently not.'

'Thank you, Mr Montignac. Unless Mr Harkman has any questions for you?'

He looked towards his opponent who hesitated before shaking his head. It was all over; he'd been in the game long enough to know that.

'Then you may return to your seat with the court's thanks. And at this point, Your Honour,' continued Sir Quentin, 'perhaps I could petition the court to dismiss this case out of hand before any more time is stolen from my client or any more injury is done to his character?'

7

Lord Keaton shook his head. 'If you'd told me in advance, I can't say I would have been as confident as you. I would have made you think twice about it.'

'Which is why I didn't tell you,' said Montignac.

'It was a risky thing to do,' insisted Keaton. 'You're not worried that the police haven't closed the file on Raymond Davis then?'

'Not particularly. I have an alibi which you so generously purchased for me. To catch me would be one thing but it would by default, lead you to the dock as well. After everything I've learned about you I can't imagine that happening. Your friends would never allow it.'

'No, you're right,' said Keaton with a shrug. 'But still. What's this Gareth Bentley to you anyway?'

'Nothing at all,' said Montignac. 'But I didn't want to see him hanged if I could prevent it. I'm not totally heartless, you know. You got what you wanted, I've got what I wanted. There was no reason for Gareth's life to be destroyed. He's enough of a loser as it is without my adding to it.' He glanced in the direction of the wireless. 'Is it time?' he asked.

'It will be soon,' said Keaton, looking at the clock and tuning into the station which was playing some music at the moment. 'Did I tell you I had a visitor last night?'

'No, who?'

'Roderick Bentley. Came charging over here immediately after the case collapsed, wanting to take back his proxy. Well it was too late by then, of course. The poor fool didn't realize that he and his wife were their son's alibi all along. They didn't need to go through any of this. Slightly ironic, isn't it?'

Montignac tapped the desk nervously. The sound was coming through quite clearly and he couldn't help but glance out the window in the direction of the palace and wonder what amount of chaos must be going on there. The two of them would make quite a picture, he thought, if anyone looked in. The ageing judge and the youthful art gallery manager, sitting around a desk listening to music on the wireless. They didn't say anything to each other for the moment; for both, it was the climax of their year and everything they had done during it came down to this moment.

The music died away and a voice broke in, the posh received pronunciation of the BBC announcer.

'We interrupt this programme to bring you an announcement direct from Buckingham Palace, where His Majesty King Edward VIII is to make a special address.'

'Here we go,' said Keaton in a chirpy voice, clapping his hands together in delight. 'Hold on to your hats.'

A crackling sound came through the wireless and they held their breath as the thin, sorrowful voice began to speak.

'At long last I am able to say a few words of my own. I have never wanted to withhold anything, but until now it has not been constitutionally possible for me to speak.'

'Could have if he'd wanted to,' grunted Keaton. 'Don't know who could have stopped him if he'd had a mind to it.'

'A few hours ago I discharged my last duty as king and emperor, and now that I have been succeeded by my brother, the Duke of York, my first words must be to declare my allegiance to him. This I do with all my heart.'

Keaton's face lit up and he grinned across the table, raising his eyebrows in delight. He made a triumphant fist.

'You all know the reasons which have impelled me to renounce my throne. But I want you to understand that in making up my mind I did not forget the country or empire

which, as Prince of Wales and lately as king, I have for twenty-five years tried to serve.'

'Bloody hypocrite,' said Keaton. 'Freeloader! Wastrel! Thief!'

'But you must believe me when I tell you that I have found it impossible to carry the heavy burden of responsibility and to discharge my duties as king as I would wish to do without the help and support of the woman I love.'

Keaton was shaking his head now, as if the whole thing was beyond ridiculous. 'Can you believe it?' he asked Montignac. 'For a woman? Absolutely extraordinary.' Montignac frowned. He wished Keaton would stop editorializing; he didn't want to miss a word.

'And I want you to know that the decision I have made has been mine and mine alone. This was a thing I had to judge entirely for myself. The other person most nearly concerned has tried up to the last to persuade me to take a different course. I have made this, the most serious decision of my life, only upon the single thought of what would, in the end, be best for all.'

'Best for you, you mean,' said Keaton.

Montignac found it hard to relate the desperately unhappy voice emanating from the wireless to the happy, jovial character he had recently met in the Unicorn Ballrooms, but of course it was one and the same. Even now, listening to the speech, he found it hard to believe that he had been part of such an ambitious plan.

'The decision has been made less difficult to me by the sure

knowledge that my brother, with his long training in the public affairs of this country and with his fine qualities, will be able to take my place forthwith without interruption or injury to the life and progress of the empire. And he has one matchless blessing, enjoyed by so many of you, and not bestowed on me – a happy home with his wife and children.'

'They'll try for a son now,' said Keaton quickly. 'You mark my words. A queen's not the same.'

'During these hard days I have been comforted by her majesty, my mother, and by my family. The ministers of the Crown, and in particular Mr Baldwin, the prime minister, have always treated me with full consideration. There has never been any constitutional difference between me and them, and between me and parliament. Bred in the constitutional tradition by my father, I should never have allowed any such issue to arise.'

'Oh please,' said Keaton. 'He behaved like a petulant child throughout, throwing his playthings out of the pram whenever he got a chance.'

'Ever since I was Prince of Wales, and later on when I occupied the throne, I have been treated with the greatest kindness by all classes of the people wherever I have lived or journeyed throughout the empire. For that I am very grateful.'

'It's goodbye to all that now,' said Keaton.

'I now quit altogether public affairs and I lay down my burden. It may be some time before I return to my native land, but I shall always follow the fortunes of the British race and empire with profound interest, and if at any time in the

future, I can be found of service to His Majesty in a private station, I shall not fail.'

'Not one to just wander off into the sunset then,' said Keaton. 'Knew it was too good to be true.'

'And now we all have a new king. I wish him and you, his people, happiness and prosperity with all my heart. God bless you all! God save the king!'

'God save the king,' echoed Keaton.

'Don't be such a bloody hypocrite,' said Montignac, as the wireless was switched off again. 'Now, where's my money?'

8

The party took place a few nights later at the Bentley home on Tavistock Square. Montignac had been surprised to receive the invitation but, on a whim, he decided to accept it but showed up late, just after ten o'clock at night. Jane had invited quite a few friends, as much a display to the world that there would be no more scandal attached to their name as a show of support for their son, who had been released and had returned home a few hours after Dr Cawley, the coroner, had delivered his crucial evidence.

The front door was open and there were a few people drinking wine and chatting loudly to each other in the hallway when he arrived. He stepped inside and looked around for someone he recognized but the hosts were lost within their phalanx of friends. Before setting forth into the mass of party guests he turned to his left and ascended the stairs in search of a bathroom. Emerging a few minutes later he caught sight of Gareth Bentley through a half-open door, walking around his room slowly before stopping and sitting on the bed. He watched for a few moments before crossing the corridor and tapping gently on the door. It opened a little more as he did so, revealing a young man of exhausted and desolate appearance.

'Owen,' said Gareth, looking up in surprise.

'Hello, Gareth. How are you?'

He shrugged and stood up, stepping over to close the door behind him to stop anyone else coming in. 'I didn't know you'd be here,' he said.

'Your mother invited me. I was a little surprised myself, to be honest, but I thought I'd drop in and say hello. Relieved it's all over?'

Gareth stared at him and Montignac was sure that he could see the beginnings of tears in his eyes. He opened his mouth to reply but then simply shook his head and sat down on the edge of the bed instead; Montignac pulled over a chair and sat opposite him.

'The whole thing,' began Gareth, 'has been a nightmare from start to finish. I still can't believe it's all over.'

'Well it is,' said Montignac. 'You don't have to worry any more. You can put it behind you.'

'I don't know that I can,' he replied. 'You have no idea

what it was like in there. And every night, thinking about what might happen to me—'

'There's nothing to be gained by that. Just get on with your life, that's all.'

He nodded but seemed unconvinced. 'I feel I owe you an enormous apology, Owen,' he said in a quiet voice after a few moments. Montignac raised an eyebrow in surprise.

'An apology? For what?'

'Well for dragging you into this business. If I hadn't got so drunk that night—'

'Then it might have been me fighting for my life in court. And I mightn't have been so lucky. Let's just say all's well that ends well.'

Gareth shook his head, wanting to say more. His hands were trembling slightly and Montignac could see how much weight he had lost over the previous couple of months. His hair had flecks of grey in it too; his entire youthful carefree appearance had been sapped by his experience.

'You've been a very good friend to me, Owen,' said Gareth. 'Standing up there and admitting all about your debts. It must have been humiliating.'

'It wasn't the proudest moment of my life,' he admitted.

'And you did that for me. I can't tell you how much it means to me.'

'Then don't. I think it's best we both move on from this, don't you?'

'I wondered about my job,' said Gareth in a nervous voice, looking up at Montignac hopefully.

'What, you mean at the gallery?'

'Yes.'

'To be honest, Gareth, I'm thinking about getting out of the gallery business. I've been there too long as it is. I'm a young man still, I feel there might be other ways to make a living. More profitable ways.'

'Oh,' said Gareth, a little downcast. 'Mother says I have to settle down. I'm not to go into the law, Father's turned against that for some reason. But apparently they've talked to Jasper Conway's father and I'm to take a position at the bank.'

'Sounds very sensible,' said Montignac cheerfully.

'You don't think . . . well, whatever it is you decide to do next, that is . . . you don't think I could perhaps—'

The door opened suddenly and they both looked up to see Jane Bentley standing there; she froze, her face a mixture of astonishment and unhappiness at seeing them together.

'Mr Montignac,' she said. 'You made it then.'

'Yes,' he said, standing up and shaking her hand. 'I thought I'd call in to see how Gareth was getting along.'

Her jaw seemed to go rigid slightly as she glared at him and then turned to look at her son. 'He's doing fine,' she said. 'And he will get better in time just as soon as we can put all this wretched business behind us.'

Montignac nodded; there was an uncomfortable

atmosphere in the air. Gareth was barely able to look up from his position on the bed.

'I wonder if I might have a word with you, Mr Montignac,' said Jane. 'In private? Downstairs in the study?'

'Of course,' said Montignac.

They stared at each other for another few moments. 'You'll follow me down then?' said Jane.

'Yes,' he replied. 'Let me just say goodbye to your son.'

She seemed unwilling to make a scene so nodded and turned to Gareth. 'You need to go downstairs and mingle with people, Gareth,' she said. 'They're all here to wish you well.'

'*I* didn't invite them,' he said petulantly.

'No, but I did. So please go and say hello to them.' She turned and made her way through the door. 'Mr Montignac,' she added before walking away. 'I'll see you in a few moments.'

When she was gone, Gareth looked up and narrowed his eyes. The tears were definitely there now, Montignac could see the glazed expression and how hard the boy was trying to hold them back.

'I didn't want a party,' he muttered. 'I can't believe she invited all these people. I didn't want anyone around me.'

'I better go downstairs,' said Montignac, anxious to be gone now. 'I'm glad to see you're well anyway, Gareth. I hope things work out for you.'

'So that's a no then?' he blurted out quickly, before he could stop himself.

'I'm sorry?'

'I said, it's a no? You won't . . . take me with you. To whatever you do next.'

Montignac stared at him and allowed himself a small smile. 'I'm sorry, Gareth,' he said. 'I think it's best we part company here, don't you?' He hesitated and looked around to make sure that no one else was listening. 'You might think I'm something special, you know,' he said quietly, feeling a little sad even as he uttered the words. 'But I'm not really. I'm nothing really, Gareth. You're probably ten times the man than I am.'

Gareth stared at him. 'A few months ago I was talking to Alexander Keys,' he said. 'Just before I came to ask you for a job. And I told him that the thing I most dreaded in the world, the thing that kept me awake at night, was the idea that five years from now I'd be doing something I didn't want to do, be with someone I didn't want to be with, just because I was too frightened to actually be the man I really am. I told him that if that happened, well then I'd rather be dead.'

Montignac looked at him and for a moment an image of his cousin, Andrew, came into his head on the morning that he was killed. He shook it away and turned around, walking back out on to the landing.

'Take care, Gareth,' he said, walking away without looking back.

'Mr Montignac,' said Jane as he entered the study. 'Finally.'

'Yes,' said Montignac. 'Thank you for inviting me by the way.'

She shrugged her shoulders and turned to the other man in the room. 'You know Sir Quentin Lawrence, don't you?' she asked.

'Of course,' said Montignac, surprised and unsettled to see him there, but shaking his hand nonetheless. 'How are you?'

'Very well,' said Sir Quentin. 'We won and that's what counts.'

'You must be very relieved,' said Montignac, accepting the glass of wine that Jane offered him. 'But I can't stay very long, I'm afraid. I thought I'd just put in an appearance and then leave.'

'Of course,' said Jane. 'But before you go, I wanted to thank you.'

'There's really no need.'

'Oh I think there is. Don't you, Sir Quentin?'

'If you hadn't said what you said on the stand it would have been more difficult, certainly,' he replied.

Montignac nodded. For two people who were apparently showing their appreciation, there was a distinctly chilly atmosphere in the room. Jane, particularly, was looking at him with contempt.

'I'm just happy to have been of help,' replied Montignac with a polite nod of his head.

'But there's just one other thing I need you to do for me,' she said. 'If we haven't asked too much already. It's about Gareth. Has he spoken to you about coming back to work?'

'I've told him it's a nonstarter.'

'Good. Because I couldn't allow that.'

Montignac opened his mouth in surprise, not sure he wanted to be insulted by a woman who had made it clear she would sell herself to him for the cost of a perjury. 'Really,' he said. 'And might I ask why not?'

'I don't think you really need to, do you?'

'What Lady Bentley is saying,' said Sir Quentin, stepping in now, 'is that we would prefer it if you stayed as far away from Gareth as possible from now on. Do you know how many years I've been a barrister, Mr Montignac?'

'Quite a few, I would imagine.'

'Quite a few, indeed,' he said, with a silent laugh. 'That's one way of putting it. But do you know what the most important thing I've learned over that time is?'

'No.'

'How to spot a guilty man. That's what. I had no hesitation defending Gareth Bentley, Mr Montignac. It was clear to me that he had made many mistakes but that he hadn't killed anyone. When I put him on the stand, I could tell he wasn't a murderer. Not that I could say that about everyone I put on the stand. Not in this case,' he added.

Montignac breathed heavily through his nose and placed his glass down on the desk. 'I think I better be going,' he said.

'I'll find a way to prove it,' said Jane, stepping close to him. 'Do you understand me? If I ever hear that you've even so much glanced in my son's direction again, I'll find a way to prove it. If you're seen walking down the same street as him, I'll find a way to prove it. You stay away from him from now on, you understand me? You have nothing more to do with him.'

'That was always my intention anyway,' said Montignac.

'Then this is the last time we'll meet,' she said. 'You leave us alone and we'll leave you alone.'

Montignac considered challenging her – it wasn't often that someone faced up to him like this – but the sensible thing to do was to nod his head graciously and turn around and leave, closing the door quietly behind him.

Jane left the study herself a few minutes later and was surprised to see the figure of her husband, standing alone in the kitchen. She sighed, wishing her entire family could just gather in one place, where the guests could see them. They had done nothing wrong, she insisted to herself, nothing at all. It was time for life to get back to normal, as if none of this had ever happened. Why did they all have to behave like the villains of the piece?

'Roderick,' she said, stepping inside. 'Why aren't you at the party?'

'I don't feel particularly festive,' he said.

'You should. People will start to wonder.' She came towards him and took his hand. 'He's safe, Roderick. That's all that matters, isn't it?'

'I've sentenced three young men to death during my time on the bench, Jane,' he said quietly. 'Three sons of mothers and fathers like you and me. And I never thought twice about it. Even when pressure was put on me to commute it I stood my ground and protected my integrity. And look how easily it was for sale.'

'Easily? Your son might have been killed!'

'I should tell you that I've resigned as a judge.'

Jane's eyes opened wide. 'Resigned?' she asked. 'But why?'

'You think I could continue to serve now?'

'Well of course! Why not?'

Roderick smiled sadly and shook his head. 'I've always had a particular image of myself,' he said. 'As an honest man. A true man. But look what I've done. A couple of days ago I found myself running into Keaton's office begging for my proxy vote back, trying to buy back my pride, but it was already gone. Even if he'd let me, it wouldn't have mattered. We both would have known what my price was.'

'But this is ridiculous, Roderick. You're throwing your career away for nothing.'

He stood up and looked out the window. 'I think we should get away,' he said. 'Move away from London altogether. Sell up and go somewhere more peaceful. What do you think?'

'But the garden parties,' she said, protesting. 'And they say the coronation will go ahead as planned next summer.'

'That life is over now,' he explained to her. 'It doesn't matter that he got off in the end. He did nothing wrong, but I did. And so that life is over. You need to realize that.'

Jane stood in the centre of the room, looking from left to right. To one side she could hear the sounds of her friends all drinking and laughing in the next rooms, the celebrations for the return of their son. To the other, there was Roderick, telling her that it was all pointless, that they could celebrate all they wanted but the life they had known was just a distant memory now.

She looked in both directions and, for the life of her, didn't know in which direction to walk.

9

The house seemed utterly deserted. Compared to the Christmases of his childhood there was something unforgiving about Leyville now. Montignac's aunt, Ann, had always made the house seem incredibly festive, with an enormous Christmas tree in the downstairs hallway that stretched halfway up the house, past the staircase, in the direction of the first-floor bedrooms. The mantelpieces were always covered with holly and cards; stockings were pinned by the fireplace. Wrapping paper and presents were to be found in every nook and cranny. There was nothing like that now, just the stark emptiness of the rest of the year and the echoing silence of generations that had passed through the house and died.

Montignac went from room to room without sight of anyone. Even the small parlour that for years had served as Margaret Richmond's private retreat, where she would go with a book when the children were getting too boisterous for her, was deserted. He checked the kitchen and the fridge was stocked with food for the following day but nothing festive, no turkeys or Christmas puddings, just a stuffed chicken and a small ham. He assumed she had gone into town; he had declined the invitation for Christmas and had only changed his mind earlier that morning and taken the lunchtime train.

The morning had been spent tying up some loose ends. He had got enormous satisfaction out of going to the Unicorn Ballrooms and handing Nicholas Delfy his forty thousand pounds.

'You know,' Nicholas said, 'this really has accrued more interest payments over the last few months.'

Montignac stared at him and didn't know whether he should laugh or cry.

'But since you've done such a magnificent job collecting the money in time, I've decided to let you off them and call us quits.'

'Very big of you, Nicholas,' said Montignac, relieved. 'It wasn't easy, that's for sure. But I got there in the end.'

'I never doubted you for a moment. And forgive me if I implied that you would come to any harm should you have failed. You know I only say such things to protect my business concerns.'

'Of course,' said Montignac with a smile.

'And, since it's Christmas, I have a little present for you,' said Nicholas.

'Really?' he asked, surprised. 'What is it?'

'I've reinstated your credit here. You are welcome to play at my tables again. Shall we say a ten-thousand-pound credit limit to begin with? No point in learning to run before you can walk.'

Montignac laughed and shook his head. 'No thanks,' he said. 'It's a very generous offer but my gambling days are behind me. From now on, whatever I have, I keep.'

Delfy nodded. 'Fair enough,' he said. 'But if you ever change your mind, you know where to come. Although I have to say, Owen – and I only say this because I'm curiously fond of you – I think you're right to quit while you're ahead.'

'Not that I am very far ahead,' he admitted. 'I just gave it all to you. Don't suppose there's any chance of a rebate for getting it here in time, is there?'

'No chance whatsoever,' said Delfy cheerfully. 'But always worth asking. What will you do now anyway?'

Montignac shrugged. 'Try to start the new year off better than the last,' he said. 'I'm flat broke, have no prospects, very little income and no chance of a decent inheritance any more. But there again, if I can make forty thousand pounds for you in under six months, just imagine what I could make for myself in twelve.'

'Indeed,' said Delfy, reaching across and shaking his hand. 'Shall I trust that I won't see you here again then?'

Montignac nodded and left for good, waving a cheeky goodbye to Henderson and Dempsey as he went, happy that Delfy had never allowed them to get to grips with him.

It was in this spirit of cheerfulness that his legs had guided him towards Liverpool Street and he had taken the train to Leyville. Twelve months earlier he had been there while his uncle Peter was still alive; now there was just him and Stella left, and even she was due to leave shortly. Although there was still the matter of persuading her to stay; that or find out whether Margaret had been sincere in her threats. But perhaps, after all, she was right. Perhaps they could make it work between them.

Margaret Richmond had complained that Leyville was too big for just one person when she was worrying about being left there alone. But as he wandered from room to room Montignac felt himself disagreeing with her. Had it come to him – like it rightly should have – he would have revelled in its opulence and grandeur. He would have ruled his estates with discipline, like the Montignacs of old. He wouldn't have just handed the place over – lock, stock and barrel – to the National Trust.

He went upstairs to his bedroom but there was very

little left there belonging to him. The bed wasn't made up and he frowned; he would have to ask Margaret to do that later and she would grumble about being treated like a servant again. Stepping outside he glanced down the corridor towards Andrew's room, the door of which was rarely opened any more, and then further along towards the door of Stella's room. He stepped along to it quietly and stood there, pushing the door open slightly, and looked inside. Of course his eye was drawn automatically to the bed. He felt a shiver run down his spine. It was here that Andrew must have stood on the morning of his death when he had discovered them. Here he had watched them before turning on his heel and leaving the house, gun in hand. Montignac had never been sure why he had done that; perhaps in his confusion and fury he had decided to shoot rabbits rather than shoot his cousin, Owen. For that, his life had probably been spared. Stella hadn't seen him, of course. It was up to him to get up and claim a missed appointment and run off into the woods after him.

He shook his head quickly; he knew there was nothing to be gained from these memories. They were too bad, just like most of the memories of those years. But if Leyville had come to him, if the stolen property had been returned to its rightful master, then things would have been fine. Everything that had happened would have been for a reason.

He stood there for a few moments and remembered

what Margaret Richmond had said to him the last time they had met, in the tea shop just beside the Old Bailey. She had begged him to get Stella to stay. There was nothing to stop them any more, she said, and the more she thought about it the more he realized that she was right. All those years of dreaming about her, the countless missed opportunities, the inability of any woman to enter his soul like she had done. Perhaps things could be different now.

Perhaps – and it was almost too much for him to hope – but perhaps he could live a happy, decent life.

A thought occurred to him and he bounded up the stairs two at a time to the top floor, then took the side stairs to the small door leading to the roof. He knew, even as he reached for the handle, that it would be unlocked and sure enough it was. There was a light breeze blowing outside, the sun was starting to set, and taken together it felt like a beautiful evening, the beginnings of a new world. He looked to his right, past the picnic table, and there she was.

'Stella.'

She spun around in fright and put a hand to her breast as she laughed.

'Owen' she said. 'You have to stop doing that to me.'

'Sorry,' he replied with a laugh. 'I didn't think anyone was here.'

'They're not. Margaret's gone into town. She won't be back for a while. You've come for Christmas after all?'

she asked, and he was unsure whether she had betrayed a note of hope in her voice.

'If I'm welcome,' he said.

'Of course you are. It's your home too. I've always told you that.'

He nodded and looked out at the grounds, standing beside her on the parapet. 'It's beautiful this time of night, isn't it?' he asked. 'Very clear for December too. You can see right across the estates. It's no wonder our ancestors loved this place so much.'

'Yes,' she said. 'It's quite something. I was just thinking how this would be my last Christmas here.'

'Your last one?'

She turned to him and nodded. 'I was going to tell you when I came to London next week. I've booked my passage. I'm sailing on the Queen Mary on the third of January.'

He nodded and sighed. 'You're sure then?' he asked.

'I'm sure.'

Montignac bit his lip. It was so difficult to find the words to express himself correctly. There were so many years of repressed feelings, so much anger and pain that had, as their strange and bewildering foundations, love.

'Do you think . . .' he began, before shaking his head. 'Do you ever think that if things had gone differently, we could have been happy here?'

She looked at him, lost for words, that old expression on her face that meant they weren't to talk about such things. But it was too late for that, he felt, and it was time to tell her.

'There's no one here, Stella,' he said gently. 'It's just you and me. And soon you won't even be here any more. Just tell me what you think.'

Years of silence on her part crumbled too and she found herself exhaling deeply and shrugging her shoulders. 'Nothing could have been different, Owen,' she said sadly. 'It was so long ago anyway that it's hard to remember now.'

'I remember everything,' he said. 'Every word. Every gesture. Every moment we shared together.'

'You can't,' she replied with an insensitive laugh and he didn't know whether she was being honest or not.

'I do,' he said.

She looked at him quizzically. 'But why?' she asked.

He turned and looked directly ahead. There are moments in life, he decided, when one must speak or lose the opportunity for ever. This was such a moment and it was time to speak.

'I don't think you should go,' he said, unable to look at her. 'I think you should stay at Leyville. I think we should stay here together.'

'How do you mean?' she asked hesitantly.

'I mean we should do what we promised we would do all those years ago. We should be together for ever.'

'Owen, we were just children then . . .'

'Yes, but we're not children any more. We could do this. You've always wanted to, I know you have.'

She laughed nervously and looked away. 'Have you been drinking?' she asked, a poor joke to lighten the moment.

'No, I haven't been drinking,' he said irritably. 'I'm not Gareth Bentley.'

'Don't mention his name,' said Stella, looking away.

'Well he's a part of this, isn't he? You wanted to stay at Leyville, you can't tell me that you didn't. And now you actually can. You can stay here with the man you love.'

She stared at him as if he had lost his reason.

'Owen,' she said slowly. 'You're not serious.'

'I am.'

'But . . .' She looked away and hesitated before continuing. 'Owen, I'm not in love with you.'

'Of course you are,' he said, as if it was the most obvious thing in the world. 'You told me you were.'

'I told you I was ten years ago. And I was then. But I'm not now. Times have changed.'

'But they don't change,' he said, shrugging his shoulders, confused by her; he had always believed she still loved him. He had built his life around this illusion. 'You've just forgotten, that's all. You've forgotten how we felt about each other. We can fix things now. I can forgive you, you know, and you could—'

'Forgive me?' she cried. 'Forgive me for what?'

'For what you did, of course,' he said with a laugh. 'For leaving me like you did when you went to Geneva. For costing us our child. I can forgive you for everything if we start afresh. Heaven knows I need forgiveness too.

We're neither of us perfect. But look at how I took care of you then, how I looked after you. You think it was easy getting rid of Andrew like that? It wasn't. It was horrible. But I did it for you. For us. So we could be together. And now all I ask is that you remember your feelings and bring them back to life. Here. This is our birthright. It's my birthright,' he said forcibly.

She took a step backwards, away from him, and wrapped her shawl further around her shoulders; the night was growing chillier now.

'What do you mean by getting rid of Andrew?' she asked. 'Getting rid of him how?'

'That day,' he explained. 'He saw us, you see. He saw us in bed together.'

'Andrew—?' she asked, appalled.

'So of course I went after him. You knew this. He'd gone with his gun. If your father had been in the house he might have gone directly to him. Perhaps he took the gun to prevent Uncle Peter from killing me, I don't know. But I went after him and confronted him. You knew this,' he repeated.

'No,' she said, shaking her head. 'No, it never happened.'

'Of course it did. You didn't really think it was an accident, did you?'

'You said his gun was faulty, that it misfired on him.'

'I had to say that, don't you see? He told me he was going to expose us. He said that he would tell his father and that I would be turned out of Leyville. He said that I never had any business being here in the first place when, of course, let's be honest with each other, I had more right to be here than any of you thieves who stole it from me.' The spittle was bouncing from his lips as he moved closer towards her. 'But what could I do, Stella, you tell me that? What could I do? What would you have done in my place? He would have told, we would both have been ruined and I would have lost my birthright just like my father did. They killed him, you know. If they had left him alone he would have been here with my mother, not in France. They killed him by disowning him.'

'Owen, your father died in the war—'

'Did you think I could let him do that to me?' he continued, ignoring her. 'To you? Do you think I could let anyone do that to you, Stella? You were for me, don't you understand that? You were part of my birthright too. You belong to me.'

She was shaking her head slowly, tears starting to fall down her cheeks.

'No,' she whispered, beseeching him. 'No, none of it's true.'

'You knew it, Stella,' said Montignac, crinkling his brow in confusion. 'At the back of your mind you always knew it was true.'

'He was my brother!' she screamed, so loud that the birds lifted in unison from the surrounding trees, a screeching cry emanating from them as they scattered into the sky above. 'He was my brother. You killed him for . . . for . . .'

'For you! And I'd do it again. I'd kill anyone who tried to hurt you. Anyone who laid a finger on you.'

Stella stood at the parapet, resting her hand on it, trying to steady herself. The tears stopped. A million thoughts ran through her mind, each one more outlandish than the last. Finally they dispersed and clarified and the fragments settled into one perfectly distilled thought. She stared at her cousin and spoke quietly to him.

'You killed Raymond, didn't you?' she asked. 'It was you.'

Montignac looked away for a moment and laughed, as if the idea was totally absurd, but then looked directly at her, fixing his gaze on her eyes. She was all he could see now. A decade's pain seared through him, and his mother's pain, and his father's pain, their pointless deaths. Caused by her family.

'He was no good for you,' said Montignac. 'You needed me, not him.'

She gasped and her face grew pale. She felt she would be sick. Her legs seemed to buckle beneath her.

'It was you,' she said. 'It was you all along. And you framed Gareth Bentley for it. I should have guessed.'

'I saved him in the end, didn't I? And, Stella, it's over now,' he beseeched her, although he knew this would fall on deaf ears. In a few minutes the work of a lifetime had been undone. There would be no piecing it back together now. He had no choice. He offered her a final chance. 'We can be together, like we always said we wanted to be. It's up to you.'

She stared at him and shook her head. 'After I went to Geneva,' she said in a clear voice, 'I cried over you for a few months. And after six months, I met someone else, just someone who passed through my life. No one special, just someone who made me forget about you entirely. And in all the time from then until now, I've never given you more than a second thought. You meant nothing to me. Nothing at all.'

He inclined his head a little to the left. *You meant nothing to me.* He wondered whether a day had gone by over the previous ten years when he hadn't woken up with her face in his head, whether he'd ever once fallen asleep without imagining her lying there beside him. Whether an hour had gone by when he hadn't wondered where she was, and what she was doing or who she was with. The hundreds of letters he had written her, the tens of thousands of words, all crumpled up and thrown in the wastepaper basket rather than sent. The well of emotion.

'Nothing?' he asked, unable to conceive that she could be telling the truth. 'Nothing at all?'

'Not so much as this,' she said, clicking her fingers together in the air.

He nodded his head slowly in acceptance of a life wasted, a decade thrown away, and then – as he had done so many times when he was a child – lunged towards her, right foot stamping the ground like a bull ready to charge, left foot rooted to the stone beneath him. The sudden movement achieved its desired result.

She gave a brief scream and sprang backwards as her feet caught in the hosepipe that was lying beneath her and she lost her balance, falling over the parapet and crashing suddenly – one moment before him, one moment gone – to the ground below, where she lay broken, her arms and legs stretched out at irregular angles from her body, the last of Peter Montignac's heirs, dead in the grounds of Leyville, the Montignac estate.

His estate.

10

It was a few days later – after Margaret Richmond had discovered Stella's body on the stones near the west wing of the house, after the frantic phone calls to London to summon her cousin Owen Montignac back home, and after the police had completed their initial investigation – that the note written in Stella's handwriting was discovered in the top drawer of Peter Montignac's desk:

Living without
Raymond
is too painful

Margaret had broken down in tears when she saw it but acknowledged that it was Stella's handwriting. No one, however, had seemed more surprised by it than Montignac who had to be helped to a chair when it was first shown to him and started to shake so hard in his grief that for a moment the officers thought that he was laughing.

The funeral was a much quieter affair than that which had been held for Peter Montignac earlier in the year. There were no crowds of old family friends, no dozens of wreaths and cards to dispose of later, and certainly no invitations for anyone to return to Leyville afterwards for tea and sandwiches.

Those guests who did attend took note of Montignac's polite eulogy but felt it wasn't in the same league as the poetic tribute he had paid to his uncle earlier in the year; but then that was only natural. He could hardly be expected to out-perform himself at every funeral he attended and this was a little too soon since the last one, and there had been so much death and unhappiness visited on the family during 1936 that no one could blame him for wanting to keep the function as quiet, quick and private as possible.

'We discussed a will,' said Sir Denis Tandy when he met with Montignac in the study a week or so later, 'but Stella wanted to wait until the paperwork had been completed for the handover of the house to the National Trust before tackling it.'

'You've informed them of everything, as I asked you to?' inquired Montignac.

'Yes, I went to see them yesterday. They were bitterly disappointed, of course.'

'I have no doubt of it.'

'It was your cousin's wish, you know. She was very specific about it.'

Montignac shook his head as if the whole thing was neither here nor there. 'Oh I don't think she would have gone through with it in the end,' he said. 'Leyville is the Montignac family home, you know. It represents something. It's our birthright.'

'Yes, but she made it clear to me—'

'Let's move on, Sir Denis. I have the London managers coming to see me in an hour or so. You were saying about the will?'

'Yes, well she had intended writing one but unfortunately hadn't got around to it yet. So as she died intestate, naturally the estate goes to her heir.'

'Me?'

'Just so. As she had no children, you are her closest relative.'

'And when you say the estate, you mean—'

'The house, the land, all the land around London that's part of the Montignac portfolio, the bank accounts, the investments, sundry business holdings. I will prepare a more detailed analysis for you over the next few days.'

'Yes, I'd like to see that. And I'm not bound by the terms of Uncle Peter's will, am I?'

Sir Denis shook his head. 'No,' he said. 'The rules

regarding sale of property were there purely for Stella's benefit. I daresay he hoped that she would have a son and then he would inherit—'

'Well she didn't have a son,' said Montignac, curling his lip slightly. 'So there we are. Thank you, Sir Denis. I'll look forward to receiving your report shortly.'

The lawyer nodded and stood up, packing his belongings in his briefcase.

'You're not thinking of selling Leyville, are you?' he asked.

Montignac shook his head. 'Not in a thousand years,' he said. 'It was built by my ancestors, passed down by them. It belonged to my father, you know, although he never had a chance to bring his family up here. But it belonged to him by rights. No, I'll never sell Leyville. It stays in the family.'

Sir Denis nodded; he was glad to hear it. 'I'll speak to you next week,' he said, closing the door behind him and leaving Montignac alone.

He had never slept in the master bedroom before but he did so that night. The room was a little chilly but he didn't mind; he made a mental note to tell Margaret to light the fires around the house the next day before she began interviewing staff. (He was in need of a full-time cook, a butler, a few serving-girls and a valet. Plus someone to take care of the apartment in Kensington for when he visited London.)

He stepped across to the enormous bay windows to

pull the curtains and looked out at the grounds below. There was a full moon in the sky and it lent a silvery sheen to the tops of the trees and the lawns which, he had realized earlier, really could do with some landscaping. He would hire someone for that too; someone from the Royal Horticultural Society perhaps. He was sure they would do an excellent job.

The bed was enormous but comfortable; the new sheets smelled clean and fresh, like a life had just begun. For the first time since he had been brought to Leyville as a five-year-old child, he felt that he truly belonged there. He could close his eyes and sleep as the master of an estate and fortune that were rightfully his and that he had come to reclaim. *I've done nothing wrong,* he thought to himself. *I've taken nothing that didn't belong to me.* He lay there, determined that he had nothing to feel guilty about.

But still, sleep wouldn't come.

The Congress of Rough Riders

John Boyne

William Cody grows up surrounded by his father's tales of Buffalo Bill, to whom he is distantly related, and his fantasies of the Wild West.

Though he escapes his heritage by fleeing abroad and starting a new life for himself, he finds that he is always drawn back to England and to his ancestry.

When his father proposes that together they should recreate Buffalo Bill's stage show, 'The Congress of Rough Riders of the World' for a contemporary audience, William refuses to have any part of it. When tragedy strikes, however, it is to his father that he must eventually return.

'The charm of history in this book lies in imagining how exciting it would have been to live there'
Observer

'Boyne is an engaging writer who succeeds in making his readers care'
Daily Telegraph

Crippen

John Boyne

July 1910: The grisly remains of Cora Crippen, music hall singer and wife of Dr Hawley Crippen, are discovered in the cellar of 39 Hilldrop Crescent, Camden. But the Doctor and his mistress, Ethel Le Neve, have vanished, much to the frustration of Scotland Yard and the outrage of a horrified London.

Across the Channel in Antwerp, the SS *Montrose* sets sail on its two week voyage to Canada. Amongst its passengers are the overbearing Antonia Drake and her daughter Victoria, who is hell-bent on romance, the enigmatic Matthieu Zela and the modest Martha Hayes. Also on board are the unassuming Mr John Robinson and his seventeen-year-old son Edmund. But all is not as it seems . . .

'Engaging'
THE IRISH TIMES

'Compelling'
PHILADELPHIA INQUIRER

'Addictive'
PEOPLE MAGAZINE

The Heart's Invisible Furies
John Boyne

Cast out from her West Cork village, sixteen years old and pregnant, Catherine Goggin makes her way to Dublin to start afresh. She has no choice but to believe that the nun to whom she entrusts her child will find him a better life.

The baby is named Cyril by his adoptive parents, Charles and Maude Avery, a well-to-do but deeply eccentric couple who treat him more like a curiosity than a son. You're not a proper Avery, they tell him. And perhaps he isn't. But through them he meets Julian Woodbead who, even from childhood, seems destined for an infinitely more glamorous and dangerous life.

And so begins one man's funny and moving search to find his place in a world that seems to delight in gently tormenting him at every turn. Buffeted by circumstance and, at times, the consequences of his own questionable judgement, Cyril must navigate his emotions and desires in a search for that most elemental human need . . . happiness.

'A substantial achievement'
GUARDIAN

'A bold, funny epic'
OBSERVER

'Written with verve, humour and heart . . . at its core,
The Heart's Invisible Furies *aspires to be not just the tale of Cyril Avery, a man buffeted by coincidence and circumstance, but the story of Ireland itself'*
IRISH TIMES

A Ladder to the Sky
John Boyne

You've heard the old proverb about ambition, that it's like setting a ladder to the sky. It can lead to a long and painful fall.

If you look hard enough, you will find stories pretty much anywhere. They don't even have to be your own. Or so would-be-novelist Maurice Swift decides very early on in his career.

A chance encounter in a Berlin hotel with celebrated author Erich Ackerman gives Maurice an opportunity. For Erich is lonely, and he has a story to tell; whether or not he should is another matter.

Once Maurice has made his name, he finds himself in need of a fresh idea. He doesn't care where he finds it, as long as it helps him rise to the top. Stories will make him famous, but they will also make him beg, borrow and steal. They may even make him do worse.

'A deliciously dark tale of ambition, seduction and literary theft . . . compelling and terrifying, powerful and intensely unsettling. In Maurice Swift, Boyne has given us an unforgettable protagonist, dangerous and irresistible in equal measure. The result is an ingeniously conceived novel that confirms Boyne as one of the most assured writers of his generation'
OBSERVER

'Maurice Swift, the novelist protagonist of John Boyne's A Ladder to the Sky, *is a bookish version of Patricia Highsmith's psychopathic antihero Tom Ripley'*
THE TIMES